Shadow

of a Soul on Fire

by

Shirley Meier

To My riding partner !

Feb. 17, 2019

HENCHMAN
H
PRESS

A **HENCHMAN PRESS** book

Shadow of a Soul on Fire

©2018 Shirley Meier. All Rights Reserved.

ISBN-13: 978-1-941620-37-3

Cover by Shirley Meier
Edited by Wayne Borean
Design by Travis Adkins

This is a work of fiction. All the characters and events portrayed in this book are fictional, and any resemblance to real people or incidents is purely coincidental.

Printed in the United States of America.

To Tristan and Raphael,
my paladin and my angel.

BREAKING NEWS!!!

An Official Miracle of the Divine Pair Has Been Inflicted Upon The Country Of Inne
Official Announcement from the House of the Hand of Inne, Acting Hand Wennifar Kenacyen
—by Teel James, Raconteur, Scribe and Editor

To all Broadsheets, Papers, Pamphlets, News Criers and to the Nomads of Cylak, the Palace and Country of Yhom; to the Independent City States of Riga; and the independent City of Imaryu

The Coalition of these Civilized Lands is affected and must be informed.

Inne has lost its beloved Hand of the People, though not to death. He is as lost to us as if he were.

The priests and priestesses, the truth-sayers and hearers; the Apphoreitos—the best empaths of the Government and the Coalition are agreed that our Hand, our Beloved Ahrimaz, was snatched out of his bed in the middle of the night and replaced by another man, all without the First Wife, Yolend and the First Husband, Pelahir, being disturbed.

The man who woke in the marital bed was also named Ahrimaz, and identical to the eye, save that the Sacred

Brand upon his chest is not our Hand and Leaves but a raised and Flaming Sword.

The best our Divines can make out is that this man is from another world. He believes himself to be an Emperor, brutal, vicious, and in the assessment of the Imaryan Healer of the Kenacyen family, utterly mad.

The family of Kenacyen are calling for an immediate election for a new Hand, while the Hand Emeritus, Wennifar Kenacyen, steps in to ensure the country and the Coalition are minimally disturbed.

This Emperor Ahrimaz has been incarcerated for his own safety and the safety of all around him. Our Beloved's father postulates that the Coalition not kill this man. Would the Divine who perpetuated this miracle upon us all give us our own man back if we did? It is in the Hands of the Divine Pair. We shall not murder out of fear, and for fear of losing our own Ahrimaz forever.

1   I Write From Hell

I, AHRIMAZ KENAÇYEN, EMPEROR OF THE OWNED LANDS OF INNÉ, Wielder of the Flamen, the wonderful sword that burns the world, the destroyer of the wild nomadic reindeer riders—the Cylak, Subjugator of the Singing City of Yhom, killer of the Heretical City of Imaryu, Master of Innéthel, Creator of the House of Gold, now abject prisoner of the Kenaçyen family, my own family, though not mine at all, do set my pen to paper and record my memories and my life, to assist the healer Limyé Ianmen, an Imaryan, in his understanding of mental illness and how monsters are made as well as born.

I submit my horrors and failings and gory history, the history of one of the bloodiest monsters of Empire, capable of beating and abusing his wife and his children, to the pitiless judgment of my Imaryan healer.

* * * * *

I watch the funeral flames wreath around what was left, the skull bursting with a steamy pop that signals the old monster is finally gone. He's gone. My crazy brothers are gone. Mother droops artistically under her widow's weeds, all ostentatious Dowager Empress in mourning for her beloved husband. He beat and abused her as he did us.

The feckless, indulged, drunken young sot who is my idiot and only surviving brother stands, blinking at the flames as if he cannot believe that he's free. The old man is dead, Arnziel.

I am not free. Even with the old man dead, he lives in my mind. He lives behind my eyes. I will never be free of him. In the years that he tortured me, he gouged out a space, gathered all my evil together as a most comfortable nest for himself. I gave up my soul to him and his whip and his pain and his rape years ago and he made me a pimp for Scorching to the deepest pits of hell.

The fire hisses as I turn away, releasing everyone to scuttle into their gilt apartments in what is now my court. At least after the official period of mourning. Vipers. Scum in high, red heels and silk and brocade. I'll make them remember the old man. Oh, yes. They'll compare our reigns, they'd pick apart every moment, every breath. They are all dogs that roll onto their backs and piddle in fear to power.

I will be in mourning on the battlefield. The enemies of my Empire will see me take my mourning for my father out on them. So funny. I killed the old man and I will pretend to have loved him all these years. Behind my eyes I can feel his glee, my glee, at the lie. Who am I trying to fool? My glee. I am become the old monster.

* * * * *

I wake in the cool darkness of this dungeon where my captors have me incarcerated. The nightmare of the funeral fades slowly. It was better than the never ending nightmares of searching for my mother, searching for safety, hearing someone weeping for me. I thought I'd buried those dreams under the scars in my mind years ago.

In this cool damp basement I am alone, abandoned even by my God and cannot call so much as a candle-flame to my fingertips, where once I could call the Fire of God to crown me, however much it harmed me, burned my guts, charred my wits. I could still do it. But not here.

These people. These vile, petty people who don't have the guts the God gave a woman, they locked me up here in the lamplight in the basement where I can't see any natural thing, any true light, not a ray of the God's own divine Sun. I am dying here. These stones press into me, closer and darker, hammering spikes of despair and the Demon's darkness into my spirit.

Help me, Burning One, Tiger Master save me from these Demon-eaten, Drowned horrors who keep me here in silence and lamplight.

Out of my depths of despondency and desolation I cry to the divine, and thus break my vow to my father, to never pray in truth to the God, or the Demon, since Gods and Demons were only fictions to control the mob.

In anguish greater than any inflicted on me before, I am reduced to pleading with the Deity of my innocent childhood, before pain made me a man and I knew that there was no Divine ear listening for any prayers from me, or mine.

Of course I taught what I learned from the old man. There is no God. There is no Demon. There is no loving Father, Tigermaster Aeono. No. No. No. Over the years I passed on my father's wisdom. As any child who screams in uncontrolled rage and stamps its feet, ultimately acknowledges the astuteness of the parent's acumen, I acknowledged father's understanding and passed on that wisdom and strength to my own children. There is no kind Father God for us. There is no Aeono.

At least my captors are not cruel enough to leave me in the dark. But I might as well be in my grave here even though I breathe.

I drive the nib of the pen into one finger so that the prick of pain and my own tiny red reflection in the drop of blood reassures—or horrifies me—that I still live.

My cell. It is four steps across one direction and ten in the other. A bed with a peasant's rope mattress, and feather bedding upon it. A feather quilt for a coverlet. Two feather pillows. A peasant's bed. The bed might as well be made of nails for all the comfort it gives me. A table with turned legs and no sharp edges. A chair, also with round legs.

The table is fastened tightly to the bars of the cell since the light from the lamp falls upon this page only from the shelf in the hallway, well out of my reach. Even if I were to be answered by the Most Holy God, he would not have been able to burn me out of here. The flame of the lamp never wavers, much less answers me. It sits, locked behind its cage of glass and does not come to me.

To the left there had been a cellar window, now bricked up as far as I can see. To the right was the second door, just as locked as my cell door. There is a pass-through in my door so that a tray can be rotated through in such a way that I never touched the guard.

Outside that hall door, that second locked door, is always a guard. They'd told me my guards were deaf and mute. Whether they'd told the truth I could not tell. They are disciplined enough not to flinch if I make a sudden noise so perhaps they've told the truth. They... them... *his* wife, *his* Yolend, that muscle-bound warrior with female parts and that dirty Cylak *Pelahir*, who explained everything to me.

Cylak, with their furs and their stinking, fetid refusal to settle, following their herds of reindeer over good land that should be better used for appropriate agriculture. Feh. Cylaks. Scorching wild animals, better tortured into the speechlessness of beasts to spend one's seed in, no matter that they have human shape. Beautiful in form, animal by nature.

And Yolend. Here I never pulled Yhom down, never silenced the infernal, demon-driven racket of their city. Here their castle in the crags sings in the wind, still. And their princess Yolend came to wed their beloved Ahrimaz instead of what happened to me. I seized her from the battlefield, gravely injured and honoured her by wedding her before she died… but she didn't die. She lived and gave me children. I tamed her, broke her spirit so she is safe for me to have.

In this world no one has broken her. And the Cylak isn't in that feckless man's dungeons but in his bed, with her. Vile equals. Dangerous. Free.

Cowards. They knew what a warrior I might be. They knew enough not to try and fight me. If the milk-sop, sucking on his momma's teat, diaper swaddled, beloved, oh-so-perfect leader of their civilized world was anything like me they were correct to be so very careful. Their Ahrimaz. Their 'Hand of the People'. My fetch. Or am I his?

If he were anything like me. That's enough to make me laugh. Who is to hear? I write that and lay my pen down and laugh and laugh until I roll off my chair and onto the floor, holding myself together with my arms. I laugh until I am tired, then I lie on the floor, limp. Do I even care what the low-born peasant guard thinks?

Master of Lightning, what nightmare must I have done for this to happen to me! I suspect that the much reviled God and the hell-Demon might exist since I am where I am. I have no other explanation for this. My tutor, dried up old stick, quick with a rod, always insisted that the simplest explanation was the most likely.

How else could I have come to this twisted, evil, benighted and Demon eaten world where my Empire does not even exist?

2   Face of the Enemy

THE CLICK OF A KEY IN THE HALL DOOR BROUGHT AHRIMAZ KENAÇYEN, one-time Fire Lord, Emperor of the Dominions and Possessions of Inné, to his feet. It wasn't a meal. The putative mid-day meal had just been cleared away.

The guard let the robed man in, closed the door behind him without a sound except for the click of the lock. He wore the distinctive multicoloured, predominantly green robe of an Imaryan healer. His brown hair, kept back off his face in one of their patterned braids, fell to his waist.

Ahrimaz lunged for him, stretching his arm through the bars as fast as a striking cobra, his narrow features twisted in rage. "You stinking anal-smear! You dare show your smug and oh-so-superior pacifist, I-don't-even-kill-the-plants-I-eat pride to me? You supercilious, arrogant, condescending, patronizing, toffee-nosed, fit for nothing but spending my seed into every hole you have and every new one I can cut, haughty, full of yourself, self-righteous sack of Scorching shit! I'll kill you. You and every one of your people. I did it in my world and I'll do it here!

"I invaded your oh-so-sacred city and slaughtered every single soul there, many with my own hands! I raped until I could not any more and then used my weapons and not one of them did anything but kneel and accept. They didn't even scream! Only the babies who had not yet been inculcated into your foul, weak-willed, spineless grass eating cult screamed in protest before they died."

The calm face of the Imaryan didn't change as he stood quietly just beyond Ahrimaz's reaching fingertips as he listened to the vileness pouring out of the man in the cage.

Ahrimaz raged and swore and turned to strain one arm the extra bit that might give him grip on the healer, but all he could touch was the heat of his cheek with the tip of his longest finger and he could not even dig a scratch onto that hateful face. When, at last, he'd gone hoarse and then silent and finally clinging to the bars to stand, glaring, the healer spoke softly.

"My name is Limyé Ianmen. I am the physician of the family of the Hand of the People of Inné. As well as my posting here, I have a life-long calling attempting to discern the roots of illnesses of consciousness. If you will speak to me, I will be able to compare you to your double, our Ahrimaz, whose care I have had this past ten years."

Ahrimaz's voice was reduced to a harsh rasp. "No. Find someone who cares to help you, you turd under my horse's hooves."

"It may be," the Imaryan continued. "That I might be the only company that can bear being anywhere near you. None of the family, on my recommendation, will speak to you."

"Unless you can find a way to put me back in the world I belong, piss on you. Piss on your demon-fucked 'Hand of the Lunatic Mob' even if he is me in this world."

"Very well." Limyé passed a hand through the barred window in the locked door and waved to get one of his guard's attention and they let him out.

3 ⎯⎯⎯⎯⎯⎯⎯⎯⎯⎯⎯⎯⎯⎯⎯⎯
The Day Ahrimaz Woke Up

THEY GAVE ME BOOKS. Two actually. Blasphemous books that show the Demon as God's Wife. Equal. Also a God. It makes me sick and I would destroy that trash but I cannot tear out the hideous pages of praise to *her* without damaging the holy words of God. I open them to read the *Tiger Master's* words of war with clenched teeth that I lay hands on blasphemy. But I have nothing else to read unless I unbend enough to ask for other books. This world has more books than it has fleas, more presses and more printers than an Imaryan has remedies.

There is no Empire in this world. THERE IS NO EMPIRE. NO OLD MONSTER. NO CAPTIVE NATIONS. They are all working together with the Republic of Inné in a so-called Coalition.

At home… my world. I cannot forget that. This is not my world, even if the man I replaced was identical in almost every way. I have more scars than he… and the brand on my chest. The Hand of the People, beloved, Ahrimaz Kenaçyen. My name. But I was feared by most. My soldiers were in awe of me and fawned like the lesser dogs they were. They were still better by far than any other warriors of the puling, slavish countries around Inné.

How did this other Ahrimaz get such love? How is he so beloved that he saves even my life? They preserve me in the hopes that they might get him back. Killing me would kill their hope of his being returned to them, though how they can be so sure of that I don't know.

I hate him. I hate him with a passion for having all the love that I deserved. He got love. Beloved even by my greatest enemy, that stinking Cylak. Loved by the warriors, loved by the stinking masses, loved by the Imaryans. Loved by the war cats and war hounds and even the stinking mousers in this plaster and timber termite-eaten pile of a palace that was MY HOUSE OF GOLD. Even the scorching horses loved him, I'm sure, though I never got near his stinking war horse.

I was feared. Not loved. Feared. The old monster taught me how to be feared. Even Kinourae learned to fear me, though he was the most stubborn when it came to loving me. Father broke that love away from me despite the old man's recalcitrance. I have seen no sign of his existence here in this world.

I am here, with paper, with pen, with ink. I should write what happened.

I, Ahrimaz Kenaçyen went to bed, alone, in my own bed. Alone. I, the Master of the Known World, the most feared warrior of his generation, had a full bath to cool off in the summer heat and once Kinourae dried me off I slid into gold silk sheets and spread my arms out in the lovely, solitary coolness. In my bed I had only my nightmares to disturb me, without the stinking press of a wife or a concubine male or female, no one to sweat on me, no one to snore or fart, no one to suddenly touch me in the middle of the night and wake me, already killing them, or about to. Not even the dogs or cats would sleep with me because I kept being jerked awake strangling some hairy beast that had touched me wrong.

In solitude I am safe. So in a strange way these soft, overly sensitive dung-eaters have given me what I always said I wanted. Solitude. Silence. Safety.

No chattering sycophantic court stinking of perfume, with the bad breath that rich food and wine and beer gives one. No pissant Sen-Grand with his five little villages shoving yet another powdered daughter under my nose in the hopes I'll want to plow her, give her little silver blond Kenaçyen bastards and shower her family with gifts.

They don't realize that my wife… my elegant princess captured from the Yhom right off the battlefield holds my attention for women. And as for boys… well yes. They are like kerchiefs to spend my seed in and throw out next day to become pages or starve in the street, it's all the same to me. They have as much influence on me as the fat blue flies I catch and smash. Less actually because the flies annoy me. I *hate* flies.

And the Cylak… Pelahir, in my dungeon at home. I am wandering in my writing.

I went to sleep gloriously cool and alone, letting my eyes wander over the splendid gold ceiling depicting my victories… and after a nightmare that had me paralyzed, again nothing new for me, I woke up. Here. My nose in what I thought was my wife's hair, my arm around a concubine, though he was heavily muscled for a boy, a massive, purring weight on my feet.

I was buried in bodies and couldn't breathe, fought my way out of the sheets and clutch of hands and the startled screech of a war cat that had me flailing for my swords or the Flamen but nothing was where it was supposed to be and I ended up standing in the middle of the room, hands clenching, empty, staring at the bed.

It wasn't my bed. It wasn't my bedroom. It was cotton sheets and my wife, Yolend, sitting up, pregnant and huge and naked, hand reaching out to me in a way she no longer dared, because I'd taught her better. And… my breath howled up in my throat and I lunged for the Cylak. He was the one most likely to kill me. He was the deadliest enemy I had, but he sat there, also naked, bare except for sheets, looking *concerned*. I fell over a war cat that got between my feet and ended up on my knees at the foot of that hellish bed.

"Ahri," he said, softly. "It's all right. It's just a nightmare. I'm not the Cylak who hurt you. It's Pelahir."

"It's all right," Yolend said.

And that's when I knew I must be going mad because even as I tried to work some spit into my mouth and call my guards… how dare they be so slow? My guards burst in and the one wearing something like Captain's insignia, was my dead brother Ahriminash.

My brother who was dead because I killed him with his own court sword when he tried to kill me. My brother who was the only warrior I feared because he could perhaps be as good as I and I would one day have a 'training accident' and then he would be prepared to step into my place. I felt him bleed out over my hand, saw the life go out of his eyes.

I laid him on his pyre with my own hands, lit the pile with the Flamen, the burning sword that is our family's most precious treasure, because I was supposedly so grief stricken that he'd had the very 'accident' I was going to have.

Their words had given me an out till I could figure out what happened. "A… nightmare. A scorching nightmare…"

My guard captain dead brother put up his sword, clapped me on the shoulder in a way that had me flinch. "S'all right, brother mine." He turned to the Cylak and said, "We knew if it was serious the three of you would have taken care of it. Stand down, lads and lasses." *Women in my guard?*

Really?

They left me there, on my knees, staring after these chatting soldiers whose discipline was so lax they may as well have been unarmed and wearing bed-robes. Left me alone, on my knees before my wife and a free man who I, in my own place, was going to break. Here… he *loved* me? "I… I'm not feeling myself."

I wrapped my hands, that so wanted to rip his head off, beat her into submission, around my middle. Where they working together? How had they even met? I had one in seclusion in the women's quarters… yes, still hugely pregnant… and the other in the dungeon, recovering from having one of his fingers removed. Here… that hand… was still whole.

"I'm… dizzy…"

"I'll fetch Limyé," she said.

"No need, First Lady," a hateful Imaryan voice said behind me and I tensed and shivered. I was going mad. There *were* none of the supercilious, sneaky Imaryans left. I'd killed them all and banned their foul healing, put proper physicians in their place. "I am here. Let me see you, Ahri."

Shock on shock on shock. So familiar with me. And Pelahir and Yolend… in the same bed, holding hands! Both *naked,* and a damned, vile Imaryan laying comforting hands on me. I shook all over with the need to be still until I could make them all go away, including the damned cat which hadn't quit snarling at me.

I was naked as well, but one of my hands was up over my brand of office, the mark of the Royal House, lucky for me because they didn't just instantly see that I wasn't their beloved Ahrimaz. *His* brand was the square of flames with the hand in the centre. *My* brand had the same box of flames, but with the sacred sword upright. In my world the hand was the symbol for the vilest sorcery. I was shaking and speechless.

"It's all right, Ahri," she says. "You don't have Coalition sessions till next week, you can skip training. If you feel sick you can take a day to recover. Come back to bed."

"No…" I managed to make my tongue work a little. They obviously don't see me as a threat… I needed to fool them into thinking I'm who they think I am. Whoever that was.

* * * * *

Ahrimaz flung his pen across the page, spattering ink everywhere, slammed his hands down on the table, making the journal, the pages, the ink pot and sand pot dance. His chair hit the floor and he ran the three steps to the back wall, slamming both his hands flat against the stones of the wall, back to the bars as if he could burst his way out with energy alone.

Back and forth, back and forth like a tiger raging in his cage. He flung off his coat and did push ups, press ups, caught the bars at the front of his cage over his head and pulled himself up vertically a hundred times, five hundred times. Then back to slapping the walls.

He dropped to the floor and did press ups until sweat poured off the tip of his nose, he found himself with his hands clawed into the feather quilt, threatening to tear it apart, but stopped himself. It was damp and cold in this basement and he didn't know if they'd give him another if he ruined this one. He flung it hard against the wall.

He ended up sitting in the middle of the room, finally worked out enough so he could be calm, exercised hard enough that his head was reeling, even in the confined space. He'd managed to bend the bars slightly, pulling on them and one of the guards was examining them, then staring at him through them.

"Not trying to get out. Need to work... need to move!" He shook his hands out. Who cared if the guard heard him or not? His words echoed off the stone as if no one had.

He rose, put his sweaty clothing in the box they'd built for that... the outside door would not open until the inner door was closed and latched. That door was a sheet of iron so he couldn't break the latch off and leave it in its slot to reach through... there was a towel... then he shied sideways, startled when the guard came back with a bottle and a bowl and another towel and... oh scorching heavens... soap! He was startled into a smile and there was a flicker of response from the guard, but only a flicker of a return smile then nothing else.

4

The Silence

I REMEMBER. I remember when my mother was allowed to love me. That was when I could bear to be touched. I hadn't yet been tortured into unbearable, dangerous sensitivity. The whip Father used on me was wide so it would not mark me. It turned my back into a reddened, swollen fire of 'don't touch me'. It was to toughen me up. I was too soft. I loved. Until I broke and hardened into the image Father wanted. When I could torture my own brothers, when I could torture Kinourae, without leaving marks, except on their souls. When I could remember... her... without tears.

Kinourae loved me even after. Even after that hideous day. He loved me. He still loves me, but he is my body servant. His family fell into debt and they sold themselves into servitude at the House of Gold, generations ago. Three generations? Four? He is by nature loving and caring. Why should I laud him for expressing his nature despite all that my father and I could do to him? He's...like a healer that way. Like Imaryans. I could have killed him, but I couldn't make him hate me.

I miss him.

Ahrimaz snapped awake, naked on the bed, rolled onto the stone and began pounding his fists against the floor. "No, no, no! Scorching God, KILL ME! Just KILL ME! Don't torture me like this! Hell and flaming damnation! Don't do this to me! KILL ME! It would be a mercy!" He shouted. Then he screamed until his throat was raw and his voice a whisper, his hands raw and bloody. He pulled his clothing off and lay naked on the floor in the smears of his own blood. "I can't. I am too weak. I am not strong any longer. I'm broken. Just kill me."

There was no servant to come fetch his clothing. The guard was just opening the door. Ahrimaz rolled onto his back, watching. Any contact was suddenly precious. The woman… a woman as a guard, though she looked tough as his old combat instructor, with seamed and grim face. Moving quietly despite the armour, she pointed at him, then at the water in the basin, then at the pass-through. Clear enough. He made a kissing noise and thrust a rude finger in the air at her, the blood on his hands already drying and crackling.

She turned without acknowledgement and left again. Also clear. It was a meal time. He could smell the food, outside. A Cylak curry. His stomach rumbled. He had to clean up after himself or they wouldn't feed him. Fuck them.

He threw his arm over his face and tried to go back to sleep.

* * * * *

They didn't stint him water. Every time they came in they pointed at the mess he'd made, then at him and then at the pass through. He stared at them until they left him alone. It was a nightmare of his father, starving him into submission that had him finally sighing, getting up and using the blasted chamber pot. Did they not have plumbing in this benighted world?

He wiped the nightmare sweat off himself with the old towel, bundled everything into the shirt and set it all dirty water, flask, bowl, laundry, in the pass through. Put the lid on the stinking chamber pot and put it in its own pass through… you'd think with so many holes in a cage he'd be able to wiggle some way out of it. But every door between him and out, had a lock and a guard. And every guard had that stinking Imaryan knock out drug on a cloth ready to clamp over his nose and mouth should he get that far.

He could kill a dozen but someone would clamp it over his face while he was busy breaking someone else's neck. Why were they so careful of his life and his health? They'd interrogated him, making it clear they knew he wasn't their beloved. But they'd explained nothing, really.

The guard actually looked surprised when she came in. Took out the mess, Came back, took out the chamber pot and then, to his amazement, brought breakfast. He would have punished any prisoner he kept with another day's fast. They were all soft. Not an Empire at all.

He folded the journal closed where it had sat open since he'd stopped writing, set the tray down and folded open his napkin. There was a pitcher of malik, the rare and precious hot drink imported at such enormous expense through the Riga City States, until Great Grandfather had stolen seedlings and established plantations.

Malik, or malak, depending on the Rigan dialect, was something that anyone with enough coin could buy in the Empire. Who knew how precious it was here? Malik and cream, steaming hot and invigorating. A gigantic egg like he'd never seen before, even as Emperor, fried, with green onions and peasant rye toast to dip into the orangey soft yolk. He found he loved it. The glass of berry juice tasted like sunlight and he closed his eyes as he forced himself to eat slowly, rather than wolfing down the food.

5 How They Caught Me

I DON'T WANT TO WRITE ABOUT HOW THEY CAUGHT ME. It was her. And the damned animals. The dogs snarling at me, the cats fleeing me. I only lasted a day.

I thought I was smarter than that. I pled illness and they finally let me alone in the room half the size of my real bedroom.

The chapel door was still where it was in my room. But nothing else was the same. The windows had horrid ripple glass in tiny leaded windows. The city outside was a tiny town compared to the Innéthel I knew. I could recognize the Hunter's Cathedral though it had far too much blue and green on it… Demon's Drowning colours. But this so called palace of theirs didn't even have walls to keep the stinking masses away. The gardens came right up to the palace walls and were open to the streets. Madness.

The clothing in the cupboards, bright and gaudy, every waistcoat a riot of colour and metal thread embroidery. I had several such waistcoats but not in those colour combinations. The worn scabbard of the sword hung on the hook by the door was almost identical to my second best sword. Nothing like the Flamen. The books in the headboard of the peasant's bed I'd woken up in finally told me what I had to know.

I was no longer in my own world.

I was in a Coalition… a group of countries that actually made up my Empire at home. This was a world where the Demon was worshiped alongside the Tiger Master as his equal, as his wife. Such a twisted world. I found their image of my brand and realized what a fortuitous escape I'd had.

I found a night shirt with long sleeves that covered up the damning brand and the self-inflicted bite calluses on my arms, thank the God. I couldn't make myself open the chapel door realizing I'd see their hideous female deity and her creatures and plants all as if they were sacred, painted on the walls with my God.

My much maligned, and I thought fictional, God.

A child's history book, pulled from a shelf of nothing but books for children—did he read to his children in his own place, that other me? Hold them as if they were anything but sickening little grubs that would one day replace him?

These people printed books specifically for children. Hundreds of them. But. It was one of those that told me what happened.

Two hundred years ago, what I know as the Mob Rebellion, or the Peasant Rebellion, take your pick, here was the Brother and Sister War, or the War of the Vote. My esteemed ancestor, Ahrimiar the First, apparently never had a child. The leader of the country was his sister. A voted in Hand of the People. Her child was the one, in my world, who became Emperor after Ahrimiar, as his son.

Was that man the boy's uncle rather than his father? Did he kill his sister and make the Empire?

Here, he never succeeded. She and her mob beat him and he is reviled in their histories as an evil man who would have stolen the vote.

I broke into a cold sweat. How had I come here? I woke up here! I had to hide from them, until I could get away, find allies, found my Empire here in this peasant world.

But it was the blasted war-cat and a pack of dogs that made Yolend suspicious. I never knew she had truth-teller in her family. Scorching hell who knew that the Yhom had that skill at all? That means she probably does in my world and I am in a fire of agony just thinking that she kept that secret from me, all those years. The stinking duplicitous bitch deserves another beating just because she can see my secrets and never told me, never gave me access to that talent?!

Ahrimaz put the pen down, pushed the heels of his hands over his eyes. They burned as though he could weep, though he hadn't done so in years. His head felt heavy and the burning lump in his chest, that always lived there, blazed up hotter and his throat constricted. He took his hands down from his eyes, sank his teeth into the pad of raw and ragged callus on his right forearm, then bit into the one on his left arm as well before forcing his palms flat upon the table and compelled himself to breathe calm onto himself. Control. When his hands no longer shook he took up the pen once more.

In this world, she and Pelahir came back in, with a tray of food, lay down with me as though we were married… in this world we are married. I had double rings on my hands, same as them. They fed me with their fingers and I forced myself to be soft and feed them, relax in their arms as if they were helping me. But I didn't see the look she gave him and the next thing I knew I was trapped between them, them lying on my arms, he clamped the cloth over my face and everything went dark before I could kill them both.

6

Calming the Vicious Beast

WEEKS, I THINK. Silence. No human contact but the occasional dumb show when they want me to thrust my hands through the bars so they can shackle me and clean my cage. I don't fight them. Not yet. I'm still studying. I will find a weakness. I will get out.

Silence is become oppressive. I sing to myself. I recite every passage out of the Holy Book of God... that I remember. My memory is being blurred by this blasphemy I read. I even went so far as to memorize Goddess passages to bellow at the mute, indifferent walls.

Nothing. The lamp is lit in the morning, I assume. I study it, every day. Then it is put out in the evening. Their schedule. The woman, and three men. No boys. They've all fought. I can see it. A dirty blond, two brunette and a mahogany red-head. The woman is one of the brunettes. They are now refusing eye contact as I get louder. They're good. Not mute, not deaf, I think. They're good. They hate me for not being *him*.

I bow under silence. I held up the Holy Book they gave me and signed 'please' for more. They don't know that I would get on my knees to my captors for more books at this point. If I stare at the walls during the day I can make them swim in my sight as if I tried a bit harder I'd make them go transparent. I'm going mad. They bring no more books for me. Who may I grovel to, for books?

It must be fall by now. The air is getting colder and there is no sign of a stove down here. I couldn't burn anything down. It is clammy. I think they have a brazier outside the corridor here. A puff of dry warmth sometimes blows through the barred window.

I sing every hymn I know. Every drinking song my soldiers taught me.

Every child's nursery song, dredged up from my memory before I forgot innocent things. My throat goes raw and I am reduced to a hoarse whisper but I cannot fill the silence. The silence encases me in stone. I spent my life driving people away from me, not realizing I was clinging to them like a howling toddler unable to bear being alone.

No wonder I craved the war trail. I am… I was…not only feared by my soldiers but adored because I protected their lives fiercely. They didn't know that I couldn't bear losing them; being with them, mingling with peasant or middle-class soldiers around their campfires. Not having to say anything, just be there and listen. They seemed so alien to me with their talk of sweethearts and mothers and fathers who loved them, who they loved. But I could be with them, gladly, and didn't have to defend myself from them or their dreams.

I sit and stare at the page before me. Please. God.

God cannot help me. I can help me.

* * * * *

Ahrimaz tore a scrap of paper out of his book and scribbled a single line on it, folded it shut and wrote 'Limyé Ianmen' on it, laid it on his tray. When the guard came to get the dishes, Ahrimaz, carefully standing in the middle of his cell, waved to get his attention. He pointed at the note and put his hands together, palm to palm. Please.

The guard stared at him suspiciously, tucked the note into his belt, took the tray and secured the pass through.

Scorching hell, please let him deliver it. Please don't let him just toss it in the nearest flame.

* * * * *

He had no pocket watch, left in another world for another him to wear and consult and slide into his watch pocket.

The outer door clicked and Ahrimaz was on his feet, like a sight hound confronted with a distant hare, tense and quivering.

The guard let the Imaryan in, set a folding chair under the shelf with the light. He set a stack of books on the floor next to the healer and locked him in.

Feeling as though his voice had rusted shut, Ahrimaz coughed, cleared his throat and somehow managed to force the pleasantry out. "Thank you for coming."

"You are welcome. It was a very politely worded request."

"You made it clear last time that rudeness wouldn't be tolerated." It felt so good to speak and be answered.

"I will come and listen to you, speak with you, Ahrimaz. If we can have good conversation then I will stay, of course. If you slip and revile me, I will allow two such mishaps. If you accept me as your healer you may say what you wish and I will not leave you to rot alone in this place, whatever you call me." He didn't mention the books, nor look at them.

Aha! Of course he wants me in this thrall… he wants to catch me as his patient. Vile manipulator.

"For the moment I think we are at the good conversation stage, Ser Ianmen."

"If I may call you Ahrimaz then you may call me Limyé."

"Limyé. Certainly." *I know how to hide what I truly feel from those in power. I could hide under my father's eye for long enough to kill him. Though when I was a little boy I always had my heart out and open for him to stamp on.* "Please, tell me, what is the weather?"

7

Clinging to Pain

"IT IS CLEAR AND COOL THOUGH WE HAVEN'T YET HAD ANY FROST. We are hoping for more rain after the last harvest, and perhaps it will rain after the Goddess Night." *Of course. They have a Demon festival after last harvest. I heard whispers that female witches soaked the ground with blood around that time, to spread disease and death to assist the winter in killing us off.*

"Why do you care for rain then?"

"To fill the rivers and lakes before the deep cold comes. You know very well that the water is necessary here at the navigation head." The Imaryan settled down on the chair, folding his hands open in his lap. *He's right, the bastard.*

I don't understand him. He's not afraid of me. He knows I'd kill him in a second. Torture him and kill him if I had time. But he's completely calm and just... just there. He is giving me his careful and specific attention despite my intention.

"How can you be like this?" Ahrimaz finally asked him, straight out.

"Like what?" Limyé raised an eyebrow. In the light of one candle it was hard to see his expression; dark lips against milk-and-malak coloured skin, even the whites of his black eyes were ivory. "We have an agreement."

"And you believe me?"

"Yes. Why should I not?"

Ahrimaz sank down to the chair he'd brought over to the bars. "Why should you not?" He repeated the question incredulously. "Imaryan, I'm a self-admitted monster who killed your entire race in my world. I threatened your life the last time you were in here with me. You have absolutely no reason to trust me in the slightest."

"I am not foolish, Ahrimaz. You'll note that I am staying carefully out of your reach."

"As well you should."

"Why do you hate Imaryans?" He asked.

"Well, they're despicable," Ahrimaz answered. "No one alive can be that forgiving and that generous in spirit. They're hiding something. They're hypocrites, I'm sure of it. They're dangerous."

"We are devoted to life and health. This makes us dangerous?" He made a note in his book.

"Yes. No one is that honest. Everyone has evil in them. My father taught me that. Everyone. Even those who say they love you. Perhaps most in those who profess to love you." Ahrimaz paused, looking at his hands clenched on the bars hard enough to make his knuckles white. He was panting in terror. *Why did I say that?*

"I'm glad you are safe from me, then," Limyé said, gently.

"GODS SCORCH YOU!" Ahrimaz clung to the bars, pressing his forehead against them hard enough to pain him.

Limyé rose, bowed, *the bastard…* and said, "That's once. Good evening, Ahrimaz. I will come back tomorrow."

"Come eat with me." *Why did I ask him? I can't command him. Help me God, I'm going mad.*

"Perhaps later. Sleep well."

Dammit dammit dammit scorch it Tiger Master Lion Master Demon eat him he has the power over me. Power to control my words. I'll not be his patient. I won't. I won't. I don't need healing. I'm already a good man. I don't need him to make me better.

* * * * *

I'm standing in a clearing that has knee-high sear grass in it, surrounded by a sky high wall of rose brambles. One side of this clearing has a swamp thick with sunflowers, blighted by the look of them. No wonder since they are growing in an alcohol swamp that occasionally shoots a blast of blue-white flame up to incinerate another flower.

There is a thatched cottage in the middle of the clearing, though the roses are grown up over half of it. A gigantic spider has woven a web over the door and a serpent that is green as grass and thick as my forearm lies upon the steps like an artificer's toy but not small. Not the length of a hand or forearm. Metres and metres of length lay across the steps, enough to swallow a man.

They are guards, I know, somehow, and in my dream a man comes staggering through the alcohol swamp, his hair singed and bright, his clothing slashed to ribbons by the leaves of the flowers, skin blistering from the thickets of nettles. His ruined sleeves are up over his face and I startle when he lowers his arms, falling onto solid ground, almost at my feet. Arnziel. He doesn't see me. I am a ghost to him.

He is weeping, shivering. "God, Oh Heavenly Master, help me!"

A voice answers "He cannot hear you."

Arnziel wraps his arms around his torso and looks longingly at the swamp. He even turns to cup a palm full of the alcohol up almost to his lips and freezes, until the liquid is slopped away because of his tremors. "I could stand a drink," he says and laughs as though his throat is full of broken glass. "But not today." He scrubs his palm dry in the grass and gets up like a very old man.

"I need to go in," he says to the snake. It raises its head to stare at him and then hisses something. The spider jerks side to side at the door, snapping its pincers. "Please," he says. "He's dying."

Who is dying? Surely no one in this Demon guarded hovel? It cannot be someone we know.

The spider pulls its own web down and the snake slithers aside. Arn climbs the steps as tired as if he carried the earth upon his back. His scarred back. The scars I put there. Father was careful to use the wide whip on me, to not mark his heir. He wasn't so careful which whip he rammed into my hand, to use on the most useless of my brothers.

The door creaks open and inside, a squalid mess tumbles out. Incense burners with holes burnt through and broken Tiger Masks and charred sacred flames, a veritable mountain of rotting religious paraphernalia packs the hovel. Deeper within, I can see a giant of a man. A golden man, but with hair and beard that grows over him and the bed he lies upon, and out into the broken regalia of God.

I see Arnziel stoop and begin to clean away the mess with his own, bleeding, blistered hands. I throw my hands up over my eyes, somehow my chest is twisting filled with pain, loneliness and despair.

I am weeping. How dare I weep? How could I weep for an old and dying man that I don't know? That my brother is caring for? I must not weep. I clamp my breath tight and stop the tears by stopping my breath.

A big pair of arms folds around me, drawing me gently to a soft breast. "It is all right. You may weep now. You are allowed."

That undoes me and I bawl like a baby in a mother's arms. "No one heard me!" I scream like an infant. "I cried and screamed for help and there was no one to hear, no one to save me! No one heard me, even God was deaf."

"I heard you. It took some time for me to come, for me to save you. The God was dying. He will hear you again one day. But until then, I hear you."

* * * * *

I woke from that nightmare shaking, soaked with sweat, my face and hair and neck and even my shoulder soaked with tears. I stagger over to the table and write down my dream. It seems as though I should, but I don't understand why.

I write it all down and then take my shirt off, kneel down on the stone floor and snap the cotton into a twisted strand that I can flog myself with. I'm going soft. I must punish myself for tears. It is part of my training. The shirt is nowhere nearly as effective as a flogger and I miss the one in my study at home. My knees are already aching from cold and from the stone and I've only been here a short time. Soft.

Like this world. They're going to break me. They are going to re-make me in the image of that Ahrimaz and I will cease to exist. I strike harder, trying to raise a sting against my back, filled with horror.

8   Attempting a Breakout

THE HEALER STOPPED, JUST INSIDE THE FIRST DOOR. Emperor in exile Ahrimaz lay on the cold stone floor in the middle of his cell, wearing only his trousers, shirtless, flesh pressed against the rock.

He turned to wave at the guard, young Oriké, who came in and startled, grabbed for his keys. The Imaryan put a staying hand on his, mimed with a hand over his nose and mouth. The guard nodded and fetched Pleta who was also on duty.

They locked the outer door, then the two of them waited while Pleta, with rope and kerchief, carefully went in to check. He went to one knee, pressed fingers to Ahrimaz's neck, looked up at the Imaryan and nodded. The instant he took his attention away from the body on the floor he exploded up, snatched Pleta's wrists and with a single move had him immobilized, arms straining, nearly pulled out of their sockets, armour creaking under the stain. Ahrimaz stared out at them over Pleta's body, leaning to press the boy's head forward against his own gorget. His breathing began to rasp. "Let me go, or I'll kill him." As the other guard moved, Ahrimaz twitched. "Show me the damned knock-out cloth!"—"Slowly." Limyé's fingers moved and Oriké, moving carefully, used two gauntleted fingers to pull the cloth free.

"Wait," the healer said, as the cloth came free. He reached out, pushed the barred door open and walked into the cell. Calmly he stopped in front of Ahrimaz and said. "Let him go. It's me you want to kill."

Ahrimaz shoved the choking guard away from himself, lunging toward the Imaryan healer, whose only move was to bring up the stole around his neck and as Ahrimaz's hands closed on his throat, pressed it to his attacker's face.

* * * * *

How many times in this world am I suddenly weakened, wrapped in blackness? My hands fall away from the damned Imaryan's neck, leaving only the barest red imprints of my fingers. I was startled by him just walking into my reach like that. He's got more guts than any Imaryan I ever saw. It didn't work. I should have stuck to the plan to get me out of here, rather than being side tracked by a deliciously offered bit of side murder.

The guard I would have been less likely to kill. He's a soldier and even if he's not mine, and deaf and mute to boot, I cherish soldiers. Damn you, Imaryan, for distracting me. Damn you.

* * * * *

Ahrimaz's eyes blinked open and a thunderous headache crashed around in his head. He was in the cell. Lying on the bed. *Damn you it is NOT my bed. The bed.* He closed his eyes as he heard the rustle of cloth from outside.

"The soporific will give you a headache, I'm sorry to say. Water with a bit of juice in it will help." Limyé said, from his place safely outside the bars.

"Why did you come into my reach, Imaryan? You were right."

"It would distract you enough for me to apply my nostrum," Limyé said quietly.

"How could you do that so calmly? Imaryans don't fight."

"But we do defend ourselves from our patients. I was an orderly in the Hospital for the Violently Deranged before I became the Hand's personal physician."

"I'M NOT YOUR PATIENT!" Ahrimaz coughed, wheezing up onto his side.

"Indeed. And you have reminded me." Limyé rose and brushed off his robe, turning to go. "That's three times. The two I warned you of and a third attack on me. Goodbye, Ahrimaz. I will continue my research in a less dangerous place."

You don't have the guts to walk away from... wait. Wait! "Wait!" He cried and the Imaryan turned back at the outside door but didn't say anything.

"Would we be back in the conversation stage if I apologised?" He coughed again.

Limyé stood still, looking at him for a long moment and the candle lamp flickered and hissed, just for an instant, flaring up. Then he sighed. "That would depend entirely on if you meant it or not. Good day, Ahrimaz,

I will think about hearing an apology from you for a short time."

The guard opening the door was Pleta who glared at him before pointedly locking the door behind the Imaryan.

9

I Cannot Heal

AND NOW I AM BACK TO SILENCE. The guards are not happy with me and have shortened my day, I think. It brings me back to the horror of when the old monster broke any hope of us being a family.

He hauled us boys down to the dungeons and locked us in. Then he brought the girls. And mother. She had just had another miscarriage and was not well. She'd born us, all seven of us, and had four lost children.

I can't remember that. I won't remember that madness. It was madness and horror and every one of us broke that night, howling for our mother though we all knew. Every one of us cried and screamed and he left us there. Fail him and he'd kill us. Until he brought mother back and made her release us. She felt different. Wrong. She was never the same, after, cold as ice.

The court was told that we were ill and in seclusion. True enough. And he didn't leave us a light.

After that incident was when we all went truly mad, I believe. That was when Arnziel started drinking. Ahrimiar began buying slave girls. Ahriminash became a fanatic at fighting. I started hunting, killing things. But I could ride outside and there was my valley, the Royal Preserve. The only place I would never kill anything. I don't know why, to this day, why I wouldn't. Outside where there were no walls, no bars, no blood on the floor, no shit or piss or semen. There were flies but not masses of them covering... no. Only the occasional flying bug, outside.

There was a peace that I could get by letting father see me torment some animal. It was better than have him make me torture people.

The valley was the one place I could find some kind of sanity... it must be here in this world. I hold that close to my withered and rotten heart.

My hunting party knew what I required and would go racketing around the hunting preserves all around. They… covered for me, bringing back meat for the court's table while I would sit at the waterfall.

The waterfall and the tree. Though this tree was on the royal preserve somehow people would manage to sneak in and there would be ribbons tied onto the branches, cages with open doors though I used to laugh at the song birds sitting inside still. I would take those home and give them to my sisters and little Alama would actually train them to be free.

I'd be waiting at the tree at the end of the day, step out of its cool shade and meet my 'hunting party', get blood all over me and ride my lathered horse home. Oh, not all the time. Once or twice I would run from the racket of slaughter but most of the time I was in it up to my elbows. Wild boar were the best. They'd be the most likely to kill you and I admit I almost longed for it at the time. I could see I was lost and would become the beast, the ravening monster. I was so like the doomed boar. Destined to either kill everyone around him or bleed his life onto the ground. I could see it and couldn't stop it, couldn't turn aside any more than the pig could, helpless in the face of horror.

How long will the Imaryan make me wait? An orderly in a House of Violently Deranged. Well. You can certainly say I am that.

I have no appetite. The food on the plate looks and smells disgusting. I drink the malak because I think I would faint from lack of energy if I didn't. I put the lid back on the tray and shove it out the slot.

The valley. The waterfall. The tree. I have not allowed myself to miss them. As an adult I put aside childish fancies, like naiads in the water and sylphs in the tree. I stopped going out there. But I did not forbid my children to go. My young Ahrimiar. He looks nothing like the hardened old bastards the Kenaçyen line are. His smile is still sweet.

The silence. I blink. There is nothing in the hallway. I stare at the candle light and try to imagine the night sky. I want out so badly I can taste it.

* * * * *

Days of silence. I managed to eat this morning. A handful of berries. A piece of toast. I am burning off any fat I might have built up not being able to exercise more than I have been. Limyé is so conscientious that he even shaved me after he knocked me out. After I tried to kill him, force them to let me out.

Between my beard growth and them clocking my days and nights by lighting and dousing the lamp, I guess that I have been punished with silence for approximately two weeks.

Then when he comes back he doesn't speak to me but sets a box down, ties his trailing sleeves back at the small of his back, girds up his robe exposing skinny black legs and bare feet and begins painting on the wall. "Limyé… Sir. Sir Ianmen?" He doesn't answer me at first. I sit down at the bars, out of reach. "I'm sorry."

"I accept your apology," he says, carefully tracing a line onto the rough whitewashed stone. "You have no more chances. Should you attack me again I will not come back."

"I understand."

The painting takes slow shape under his brushes and his fingers. He sometimes plunges his hands into the paint and draws with great sweeping smudges of his hands, wrists, even the edges of fingers that resolve, in the flickering light, into leaves, twigs, flowers.

"Why are you doing this?"

"Because I wish to," he says.

I nod. *Bullshit. He is still trying to get me to become his patient.* "Limyé, you do realize that I can never become your patient?"

"Why is that?" He isn't even looking at me.

"I… can't… I just can't."

He's silent a long time standing, looking at his work, one paint covered finger leaving a green splotch on his lip. "It seems to me and you just cannot bear the idea of being healed."

10   I Will Try

THE HEALER WIPED HIS HANDS AND BEGAN PACKING UP HIS BRUSHES AS Ahrimaz stared at him. He, the fallen Emperor sat on the floor, open hands on his knees. "But... no that... well..." He lapsed into silence.

The paint box closed with a click. "I think I shall leave this for today," Limyé said as he turned and sat down on the floor as well, eye to eye with Ahrimaz. "Something I have understood, finally," he said. "You see being a patient to anyone—especially an Imaryan—as being in thrall to them, being vulnerable and open. You have been taught that to be vulnerable is to open yourself up to abuse and harm. It is quite insidious that you were taught to hate the very process that might have saved you."

"Saved me? What on earth do you mean?"

"Bear with me, please, since I must present Imaryan thinking. As an adult, you made yourself safe, in control, in power, with the life and death of everyone around you in the palm of your hand. No one could hurt you. But inside it seems to me that you are in pain, and lonely, disconnected from all these people you control. When I say 'saved' I mean that all beings are safest when they are not in pain, either internal or external."

"So you would save me from myself?"

"If I could, yes. I am dismayed by seeing anyone in that state. Most Imaryans would be. I suspect that you killed those you despised... in other words all of them... because they had the temerity to pity you for the pain you were in."

Ahrimaz opened his mouth. Then closed it. That was hardly cowardice. The images of Imaryans dying—even as he killed them they had been blessing him. He shuddered and lunged to his feet, turned his back on

Limyé. "I… must not regret." He managed to scrape the words out of his dry throat.

"I understand that. May I ask that you try to eat tonight?"

"I'll eat," Ahrimaz said. "Whether I want to or not."

* * * * *

The bastard sent me soup. He's treating me like his patient. But I've pushed him to his limits. I have left myself no wiggle room. If I am his patient I may revile him. If not then I am constrained to absolute politeness.

The soup was chicken and some other fowl. Possibly the enormous eggs are laid by that unknown creature. Thumb-sized dumplings and greens. It is soup that would make a dead man sit up and demand a bowl.

Why? Why on earth is he so good to me? Is it because they love 'him' so much that they perforce love me too? Not likely. Some part of me wants to damage myself just to make us more physically different. Cut holes in my cheeks perhaps. I have nothing to cut with, but perhaps just the beard will be enough to make us different in their eyes. The beloved is a smooth-shaven, cultured man, not the bearded ragged maniac I have become. There are no rain-closets here, I am not allowed a bath. I don't think I can bear to cease washing.

So… why am I fighting being his patient? What harm would it do, other than to my self defence? Am I not already captured? The silence alone will break me. Flame knows I used that tactic myself. I have been broken before, and re-made in my paternal monster's image. Why should I not let this Imaryan break me and re-make me in the shadow of the beloved?

Would it kill me, to be liked? I hold out no hope for love. That is *his* prize, *his* great reward. Mine was Empire. It was power. But I was and am empty.

If I become his patient will I be able to weep for my mother? Will I be allowed to rage that the old man made me watch when—no. I won't think of that. Will I be able to scream with the pain that he inflicted on me and then made me inflict on my brothers to escape that same torture?

* * * * *

It was late, and the guard had replaced the candle when Ahrimaz had waved his pen at him, put his hands together and begged, rather than putting it out. Pleta shook his head at him, but fetched a short, night candle.

The door clicked and Ahrimaz was on his feet. It was no guard. It wasn't Limyé. It was Yolend.

He retreated to the absolute back of the cell. "Leave me alone," he snapped at her, even as he stared longingly at her face, her creamy chocolate skin smooth in the candle-light can standing out against the white wall and her white robe. "Truth-teller, get out of my head."

"I'm not," she said, and sat down on Limyé's chair. "A truth-teller, I mean. I couldn't sleep and realized that I'm sensing when you cannot sleep either."

"That's invading my privacy, woman!" His hands shook. He swallowed hard, once, twice, turned his back on her because he couldn't help loving her, even though she was *his* wife, the wife of that Hand, not his own wife. And because his love was rotten. He could feel it decaying inside of himself and knew that one day he'd become the old monster to his bones and likely kill her in front of his children... This... this incarceration was a blessing then. It would save her, in the world of Empire, because that Hand was there... and he was here unable to affect this world in any way. He was free of that gnawing knowledge. He didn't have to fight to keep his hands off her neck, the ugly fascination of her death no longer riding his every feeling.

"I wished to see how you were doing," she said. "I'm missing my husband and the man I see in his place... well, his soul isn't the same. It burns."

"I burn. But, Yolend, you wouldn't be here if you were a truth teller. You MUST hate me. You couldn't bear being near me."

"It comes and goes with me." She made no distinction between statements that she was replying to. Perhaps she meant all of them.

"I see." He studied the cracks in the wall where a window had once been. His nails had made no marks on the mortar at all. He wanted her to keep talking. He missed her voice.

"In this world, how are the children?"

"Ahrimiar is recovered from his cold." He half turned to see her put her hands on her belly. "The baby sits well." He turned away again. "Shashe will be coming back from Imarya soon, since her latest round of lessons will be done. She will not be coming to see you, for she could not bear it."

He sat down, facing away from her, forehead against the wall. "She's a full Teller then."

"Yes." *I destroyed that in my Shashe. I beat it out of her, made her child-like and forever innocent. I damaged her.* A tear forced its way out of his eyes and he held his breath until the urge to weep went away. Inside he could feel the raging fire tiger that clawed him up and clung with gnawing jaws on his heart. He dared not love. He dared not grieve. He dared not be sorry. He had to drive her away.

"You leave me alone, you bitch queen of a mewling coward. You are not my wife. I am not your beloved. Go away and forget this shadow of *him* in your basement. Go sleep with that Cylak bastard who was my greatest enemy—"

"And, along with me, one of Ahrimaz's great loves," she broke in.

He ground his teeth and began to beat his head upon the stone. "Go. Away. Go. Away." He broke the skin on his forehead and felt the warm trickle that took the place of tears. "Please."

He could hear her rise, the rustle of cloth and could track the three steps to the door. He imagined her slender, strong hand waving through the bars. Heard the click of keys. "Yolend!", he called. She stopped. "Tell Limyé I will be his patient. I will never be *him*, but I will try to… to…"

"I will tell him. I'm glad you ate tonight. I made the soup."

The keys rattled again and Ahrimaz began to laugh. A tearing, screaming laugh, howling like an animal released from torture.

11

A Bath

HE SLEPT ON THE FLOOR, too exhausted to crawl over to the bed. When the guard came in with breakfast, Limyé was with him. "Yolend tells me that you agreed to be my patient."

Ahrimaz stared at him. "Yes," he managed to croak out of knotted tight throat.

"Will you swear to do your best to heal?"

"I swear, on my hope of God and my fear of the Demon. I swear on my head and my testicles."

"I suppose that will have to do," Limyé said. "Do you want to go outside? Or would you rather have a bath?"

Ahrimaz shook his head hard. "Did you just say 'outside' or 'bath'? He started trembling. "Or am I dreaming?"

"No. You will sicken if you are not clean. Even your astonishing constitution needs support."

"You're basing your understanding of my constitution on *him.*"

"Indeed I am."

"Bath…" Ahrimaz stammered and staggered to his feet, hands stretched through the bars. "Tie me. I don't trust myself."

"Very well. I would rather not have to knock you unconscious again, especially since you seem to be trying to hurt yourself in various ways."

"The pain focusses me," Ahrimaz said. "It's how I learned to fight. It's how I learned to plan. Always in pain and having to rise above it."

"That's very hard on your body," Limyé said, but wrapped the fastest knot Ahrimaz had ever seen, with a wide band around his hands, placed a rubber ball between then and then lashed them together.

"Interesting," Ahrimaz said, as he backed away from the door. "I've never seen this way of tying someone before. It's almost gentle."

"We don't want you to cut into your flesh if you try and wrench free. By the way, I am going to have to lash you to the bars, and tie your ankles as well." He smiled. "You've sworn, but I am not inclined to just trust you right off."

"Very wise."

Ahrimaz stood while they secured him to the wall bars and then opened the door. Limyé tugged his boots off and his trousers, though Ahrimaz tensed when the air hit his bare skin. He draped a towel around his hips that tied in place, and then removed his shirt somehow without untying his wrists. "Hey! How did you do that?"

Limyé shrugged. "Magic trick."

"Ha." Ahrimaz was suppressing shivers and when they led him down the hall, hobbling in half-steps that the soft bindings allowed, past braziers, he raised his head, sniffing. "You use a lot of salt in your baths."

"They have it naturally. We try and pull most of the sulphur out."

"Naturally? A hot spring? We don't have such a thing at home." He could see the guards' faces as they kept sneaking looks at the brand on his chest.

"It's always been here. Brace yourself, the paintings are what you would consider Demonic."

"I'd kiss Herself's arse right under her barbed tail for a bath, Imaryan." He paused after a few more hobbling steps. "Thank you for warning me."

"You're welcome."

"You know, I have nothing to fight you for. You're going to break me and re-make me."

"That's not how I would put it. Here we are."

The bath was a tiny room really, and it was hot enough to make his hair go flat in an instant. The ties on his ankles allowed him to step down each stair and he looked down rather than see the the blasphemous paintings on the walls. A guard held his leash as he sank down chin deep in the steaming water and leaned his head back on the headrest.

A gentle touch on his head and his eyes flashed open, to see Limyé leaning over him, cloth in hand. "Let me clean the grit out of this scrape." *Why bother? It's only a bruise. I didn't come near cracking my own head open, except the skin a little.*

"Do whatever you want, Limyé." Looking up at the brown eyes that had a hint of smile in them let him ignore other things in the room. He closed his eyes again and was surprised how little it hurt. "An orderly in the

Hospital for the Violently Insane," he said. "It seems rather a change to becoming a personal physician to a head of state."

"Well, it was after the Cylak war, when Pelahir and Ahrimaz were both captured by his Stag Lord and in the process of escaping found that they were on the same side. Yolend got them both out of the tower they were imprisoned in and Ahrimaz wouldn't leave Pel. They got Ahrimaz, grievously injured, to Imarya."

"Well, that's different. In my world Pelahir was the loyal warrior to the Cylak, fighting Inné, and I captured him on the field. He nearly killed me, that man."

"He and Ahrimaz were so close as warriors, they found mutual attraction."

"Not for me." *I refuse to remember the absolute joy when I found that I had him in my grasp, knowing that he was mine.*

"Hmm."

"Were you serious about letting me get outside?" Ahrimaz struggled to keep the eagerness out of his voice.

"Quite serious, though it will be in the evening,"

"Still keeping it quiet that I'm not their beloved?"

"Of course."

"You realize that's the first step toward tyranny. Hiding things from your people. I know."

"Of course you do."

12

In the Face of That Eternity

I WILL KILL YOU ALL. You'll never hurt me again. Why did he *get love and I get torture?*
I'm alive and I will outlive you. You will all serve me and grovel to me and give me the
respect and fear. Fear hurts me. But it is better than being vulnerable, like a child. Children
are to be beaten to make them respect authority.

"So children deserve to be beaten because they are vulnerable?"

"Who are you who dares ask me such a question?"

"A mother. A mother who does not think you deserved to be abused."

"Mothers die. Mothers are murdered. You cannot save them. They cannot save you."

"Your mother is safe with me where no one can harm her. I am concerned for you and
distressed that you were wrested from me."

"YOU AREN'T MY MOTHER AND YOU NEVER WERE."

"How do you know?"

"You don't sound like my mother."

I am surrounded by loving arms and rocked, even as I rage and squall and call her
names. I can feel how strong she is and how she loves me. I scream myself hoarse and then
into silence and her loving never wavers.

I am loved? As horrible as I am? She loves a monster? I raped and killed and destroyed
and burned. I tortured. I beat my own children. I beat my own wife. Yolend. She's close to
giving birth. She is safe from me, with me in this cell. I cannot beat her to miscarriage and
her soft, gentle, loving Ahrimaz would never lay a finger on her, even to pretend to be me.

There is the Imperial birthing chamber and she's there... she's surrounded by courtiers
all in cloth of gold with their long walking sticks and truth-tellers, in their surgically precise
robes and hoods, their genderless faces blank as they prepare to announce the birth and
whose child this is.

This is my Yolend. I can tell. But she looks happy and determined. I see there are no bruises on her face, or her wrists, despite her skin being bare of paint and powder. She looks as strong as this Yolend, and yes, she is singing the child into the world, the way her people did, before I demanded that they stop. He's letting her sing. He's letting the Yhom sing again. Oh, Gods, that hellish noise!

"Your mother sang to you. Out of her pain, she sang to you. You tried to save her. That was why it happened. You nearly got her away from him and he couldn't have that."

"I failed her. He made her say it to me…"

"Under duress. Not true. She loved you."

"She still died. I don't know who you are, but I'll tell you. He left her with us. I don't know how the flies found their way underground, but they did."

"I know. I was there with you, though all I could do was witness."

"Scorch YOU! Scorch you all to the fiery hells!"

"Your mother is still alive in this world."

"She's still alive in the other world! No. No no no no no nononono—ahhhhhhhhhh—"

I floundered off the floor, screaming, throat hurting me, chest hurting me, arms wrapped around my chest as if to keep my heart from beating out of it. And then, of course, soaked with sweat, my nightclothes wrinkled and uncomfortable, I wrote it down. Limyé will want to read my crazed dreams.

I run a hand over my chin and decide that I will definitely continue with the beard. It makes me different from *him*.

* * * * *

Limyé, washed my hair though I refused the offered shave, took me out to the valley. All the way outside the city. It was quite late at night and I'm so surprised that they even have the streets lighted at all, they are so backward. He put me in a litter and my two on-duty guards carried me out to where I could imagine I was alive. I've been buried so long that I did weep, though I didn't snivel so they wouldn't see or hear.

The tree… was the same… though there were thousands more empty cages hung on the branches, candle glasses to not harm the tree. Ribbons. I could see the ribbons floating in the breeze and beyond the highest branches… stars.

"This is the Goddess's Veil," Limyé told me.

Of course it is. I am outraged that this is a Goddess Shrine, open to everyone. This was MY place. MY safe space. This is the Royal Preserve! How dare all these people rub their souls all over the only place I could cry? How could they? But I cannot hold onto my rage. The water drags it off me, the sound of the wind, the flocks of tame songbirds. The raked gravel paths, so peaceful. The moss covered carved seats these people have put in. Glass candle lanterns set here and there, flickering light in the darkness. The lanterns are green and blue and gold and have little tiger faces on them so that the light shines through their eyes. In the depths of darkness the God is here. How...odd.

There are rivulets all along the ridge, some larger than others but the last three sometimes become one if there is enough rain, or snow melt.

That waterfall is usually a crescent perhaps four paces across, and the water is about ankle deep at the lip, above. Below is a carved out space behind the water. Even at the highest water one can walk behind the veil of it and hear nothing but the rush. It is barely thick enough, when it plunges into the pool, to hide behind at low water. The pool it falls into is deep enough to swim all year round so I used to dive through the waterfall, just to feel the splash and the roar, the pounding on my back, the soothing of my oft-bruised skin with cool water. It didn't hurt like a flogging at all. It helped me bear the beatings.

I was still only wrapped in towels, and my wet bonds. I pulled on them experimentally and found to my disappointment they were not about to stretch, or give way. Limyé you know I have to keep trying this, so don't take it personally when you read this.

He helped me out of the litter, once they'd taken me past the tree and down the narrow, raked path to the Veil. Then got into the pool with me, robe and all, and let me float, my head on his hand, looking at the stars. They are the same as in my world.

Perhaps, in the face of that eternity, I am not so bad.

13
No One Owns Them

LIMYÉ GRABBED A HANDFUL OF LEAVES AND GRASSES, with a single night lily before Ahrimaz went back to his cell and placed them in a tiny bowl of water, under the shelf with the light.

Ahrimaz sat, pulling his hair forward to smell the lingering greenish scent of the valley's water, eyes closed. "You're trying to re-make me into *him* and you aren't going to succeed."

"No, actually, I'm taking mental notes on the similarities and differences I see between the two of you," Limyé answered.

"I shouldn't imagine we are truly that similar," Ahrimaz answered, sweeping his hair back off his face. "And aren't you sitting with me rather longer than you should? You've not been inflicting your questions on anyone else?"

"No, the family is healthy. I should inform you that this world's Épouse de Le Main, Yolend, has birthed a healthy baby boy."

"A boy." Ahrimaz smiled. "If this and that world are still so similar then I have another son. Legitimate. I have half a dozen bastards. Does your 'Hand' have them too? I shouldn't think that Yolend… or even Pelahir… would tolerate him sleeping around on them."

"Such restrictive and strange customs you have," Limyé said, sitting down.

"Restrictive? How the *scorch* do you know which are your children? Your Heirs? Your seed?"

"Why does it matter? They all know who their mothers are."

Ahrimaz found his mouth hanging open at the implications of that. "They know… that's right… you worship the Demon equally with God. As His other half… as far as sex goes for beings that don't *have* sex as far as I've been taught. And women have this Divinity they can pray to who won't scorch their tits off every time He gets passionate."

"Yes. The Inneans say that Her rain cools His flame but just as His fire doesn't dry Her up, She does not douse Him."

Ahrimaz snorted. "So balanced. They get steam between Them then."

"It's all power, motive energy. We Imaryans think that life is embodied in Her, because we are so wet, but somehow the flame that burns everything somehow lives in us as well."

"That makes sense in a strange way. So you don't own women in this world."

"No and neither do they own us. We own ourselves."

"How do you manage to raise children if children own themselves?"

"Adults own themselves, if they are competent to own anything. Various countries in the Coalition have different ideas of what constitutes an adult. Parents have the responsibility for their children until their particular culture's adult signpost."

"That's just so messy and so sloppy."

"It seems to work well enough."

"Except that you people are all backwards barbarians. You don't have indoor plumbing. You don't have tile stoves and are probably worried about denuding the countryside of trees to keep warm in the winter or if you are burning coal then you're digging into your hills all around here, just to keep Demon Ice from freezing your testicles off. You have people who are deafened by the sickness we call the Swelling."

"What's your mortality rate in the Empire? Mothers and children?" Limyé made another note. He was scribbling pretty constantly.

"I don't know."

"Ah. Women and children aren't important enough?"

"No."

"I see. Well, how is your disease control?"

"The Empire has eradicated the scourge of the Swelling. The summer sweats kill off the lower classes every year. Oh, not all of them, but quite a few." Ahrimaz paused to think. "And there are a dozen winter killers that usually carry off the oldest, the youngest, and the weakest… though, since we've started making everyone keep the water clean… and make the cheapest stoves free… those illnesses have dropped dramatically in the last generation." He paused. "The free stoves were an idea of mine since there were a horrific number of fires across all classes. I made open fires in tenements illegal and then made the stoves available. Fires are cut down across the land and people hail me as a hero. I needed more people, more workers, to support my army." Ahrimaz shrugged. "I'm a user. I need to have people to use."

"I see." Another note. "That sounds very 'power of the masses' to me, though phrased like an Emperor instead of a Hand."

"I'm NOTHING... like him." Ahrimaz subsided.

"Of course," Limyé said. "Might you be able to speak about how your mother died?"

"No." Ahrimaz flung himself onto the bed, face to the wall. "She's not dead. Go away, Limyé..." he paused and forced out a razor edged, "Please leave me alone."

"Very well. It is quite late. I will see you tomorrow."

14

Her

I NO LONGER KNOW WHO I AM. I dream of my brother. He has the tiny cabin in the clearing scoured clean of trash and the dying? Man? God? Is now clean. He no longer lies buried in human sacred filth. Arnziel is cleaning himself up and the rain that falls on him falls out of a clear blue sky. He prays to the Tiger Master and his face is ecstatic, sun falling on his face.

Where is he? I can see his bruises and bleeding scars all over his soul softening and beginning to wash away in the water. Is he a witch to command water? Scorching shit I don't understand.

I stand in the pool of the Goddess Veil, Demon Bitch that She is, and feel the water pour over me, dragging my carefully cherished agony away.

I feel Her hand on my head, slicking back the water that hides my tears. It is cool, not hot, not flaming. "Is this how you seduce the women to be witches?"

"And the men. If there is no water, no coolth, there is no life. It was killing the male half of Me. Your priests, burning women, burning and hanging witches, are… or were… killing the God you hold so high. He burns with fever and there is no water to quench His thirst, no wet cloth to cool his brow."

"But… but… You're evil!"

"Yes. But you see I am also Good. Nothing is just one thing."

"Just as the God drives a human heart beat, and warms a body in the winter, warms a house, gives you motive power for your engines… He is also the fire that burns the forest to the ground, that bakes the soil into a hard salt pan that grows nothing. And He needs water to create the steam that drives your engines, of civility and of war. Both."

"But…"

"I am the water in your blood, the moisture in your eyes and mouth. I am only as evil as you are."

I start laughing. "Then you're lost because I am ALL evil."

"I reserve judgment on that, my son."

"I am not your son. I am the Great God's. SCORCH YOU!"

"Thank you for your heat. My husband's passion is enchanting. And because of you, and your other self, He will live. Your brother will be his new priest. A priest who truly believes."

"Arnziel?"

"Yes."

*   *   *   *   *

For once he woke in the cool darkness of the cell in peace instead of shrieking, flailing nightmare. The bed under his back was soft. The pillow cradled his head and he could feel the difference between the warmth his body made and the cool, damp air he breathed in. It was a balance. He reached out from under the covers, shivered at the reaction as his arm chilled, took up the glass on the floor to drink. Well water.

We were once in the Cylak desert waste and we baked under the hellish sun, praying aloud to the Scorching God to look away from us. It was a dream I had that told me to wait until dark, and then to turn our shields to the sky.

Every man exclaimed as they watched beads of water form on the hot metal, and eventually pool, enough to keep them alive, though not enough to quench their thirst. I offered the Tiger Master sacrifice, though I wonder now if we were all saved by the Tigress of Water.

That's what they called Her, here. He'd read all the blasphemous chapters. Memorized them because there was nothing else to do. All of those chapters about water and ice and snow and trees... apple trees mostly... and—though it made him sick—birthing blood and fluids and even life's blood that he had shed so freely as a warrior. All those Goddess chapters and he became aware of his heartbeat.

The Fire of God drove it, but it needed the body's blood or nothing would move, nothing would live.

All those chapters called for balance between forces. In the Empire they'd killed every woman they could get their hands on who practised water medicine, like the Imaryans. Water magic. Ways to keep water clean and to cleanse fouled water. His grandfather had had an awful outbreak of disease in his Empire that coincided with witch burnings.

15

That Cylak Bastard

I SHOULD HAVE KNOWN THAT IF YOLEND CAME DOWN TO ME THEN THAT bastard Cylak would as well. He's there, all in his deeply tanned, black-haired, green-eyed glory. Chiseled chin. Muscled like a junior God. He actually almost looks like the Cylakian ideal of their God, but without the Stag's antlers.

When they let him in, he stands in the hallway as quietly as the Imaryan, though his gaze is more intense. A warrior's gaze.

I stood in the middle of the cell, wanting to touch him, break him, smash his fingers, break his arms, make him service me… I wrapped my arms around myself. That was the monster. Limyé had already pointed out to me a number of times that it was the only way I was allowed to touch, as a child and that I was starved for touch of any kind. I harmed people because it was the only way I could fulfill my craving for contact. I could run my fingers along that cheekbone only if I were being a sadistic bastard.

How funny is that? I have a desperate skin hunger and the only way I could touch anyone at home was violently. He said nothing at first, letting me control myself. I bit my right forearm, struggling with it. If I could touch no one else then I could set my teeth in that callus and make myself feel real and in control.

"Ahrimaz, you don't need to punish yourself," Pelahir said, his voice like velvet and acid on my heart. I must must must hate him. I don't have to here. I don't have to deny that I'm attracted to men as well as women, here. I'm safer hating him.

I turn my back on him. "Pelahir," I say, addressing the wall. "How nice of you to visit."

"I'm sorry we couldn't just let you go," says he.

"Why can't you?"

"Well, when you were coming out of the soporific the first time you raved about how you'd rebuild a decent Empire and kill us all for having foiled you in the first place. And Ahrimaz, and therefore you, must be a good enough warrior that you'd be able to kill more people than we would like if we left you unfettered."

"I see." I knelt down, still facing away from him. "How did you go from being his enemy on the battlefield to loving him so much?"

"The war was an immoral one, and my Stag Lord insane, even though physically perfect. He ordered me to slaughter innocents to get at Ahrimaz, and then when I refused, Ahrimaz and I fought together to protect the children."

"How paladin-like of you both."

"The guards tell me that you're as strong as my Ahri. If it were him in there, he'd be going mad from inactivity."

"Yes. So you've come to see the physical and emotional wreck I've become confined in this tiny space? Come to mock my deterioration?"

He gasped. "No!"

"Why else would you come? I am not your beloved paladin, your ass-boy, spreading his cheeks for you to spill your seed in and upon."

"You're very angry, embittered, and hurting."

"So speaks the Master of Truth!" I manage to turn around. He's such a beautiful man. Why should I deny myself looking at him? In my dungeon I could look at him all I wanted. Now I was in his and there was no reason to deny myself anything.

He grinned and bowed as if I'd made a joke. "Yes, yes. Always speaking the truths right under everyone's nose, the speaker of the obvious!"

"How is he so lovable?" I finally managed to get that question out. "I'm hateful and know it. I don't know how to be loved, at all."

He sat down, cross-legged on the floor opposite me. "Ahri…"

"Don't call me that! I'm not HIM!"

"So what should I call you?"

"How about Shit-Head? Or Rapist? Or Murderer? Oh, I have it! Call me Raving, Violent Lunatic!"

He stared at me for a moment, then his lips twitched. "Such a plethora of names to choose from." He shrugged. "As you wish. You see, Shit-Head, my Ahri earns love by being loving. The Shit-Head Kenaçyen I see before me knows how to earn hatred, by being hateful."

As he went on, calling me Shit-Head with a straight face I felt my face crack. I couldn't stop the silly, stupid smile twisting my lips into an unaccustomed spread. "... as far as I know, Shit-Head, the reason that you are so different from my Ahrimaz—"I fell over, laughing hysterically. Wildly. Idiotically. He stopped and just watched me, grinning like a fool.

When I finally ran out of air, I managed to push myself back up to kneeling and glared him in the face with my best 'I'm going to kill you glare' before letting my dumb grin come back. "Good choice of name."

16 He's Not the Hero

"So, AHRIMAZ," he says after he quits laughing. "I suggested to Limyé that you need to exercise and the only people who can really work you out are me, Yolend, Rutaçyenne, and perhaps a couple of the Maison du Loup students."

I, who am usually more articulate than most, was stunned speechless. "How on earth do you expect to keep me from trying to kill you all?"

"Well, first of all there's your oath to Limyé, to be his patient. In his defence, he is horrified by everything about it, except the exercise. And my beloved, as far as I know, never broke an oath except one given under extreme duress."

"I keep telling you, I'm not him."

"So are you a liar then?"

"How dare you doubt—"bit my tongue. "You're good."

"So I'm told." Again that grin. I found myself watching his lips.

"If the best warriors of three Coalition countries, the war-master of the Maison, and an Imaryan healer with soporific can't discourage you from trying to either kill us or break out—against your own sworn word, I again remind you—I'll have to say that we couldn't restrain you at all, as we demonstrably have. Also, there aren't many places in this world where you could either hide, or try to do the empire building thing. Apparently that opportunity came and went hundreds of years ago."

He's right. The bastard is right. "So why are you here in Inné instead of licking your Stag Lord's boots?"

"I am the Stag Lord in this world and the Herd is most effectively ruled by the Does. Sagari had me give her a child and then told me to get myself scarce, unless a war cropped up. So I came to be with my beloved."

"What?" Again, I'm poleaxed. "You're the Cylak Stag Lord?"

He held up both hands in that expansive, enormous shrug of theirs. "I was the warrior who caught the King Stag and rode him home."

In this world, Ahrimaz and his loves are... all three... Kings in their own lands rather than being slaves to me. This is so wrong. I'll think of that later.

"I give my word that I will not try to break away from training, though I swear I will do my best to hurt all of you." An imp of the perverse poked me. "By your King Stag's antlers, I so swear."

He nodded. "I accept in the name of the Doe and her First Fawn."

I got up and thrust my hand through the bars. Would he trust me to take it? Would I trust myself to keep my own word? He looked at the hand, then at me. Then he rose, removed his gauntlet and took my hand, skin to skin.

I wanted to howl. I wanted to crush his fingers with mine. All that happened was that I shook hard enough to rap my forearm against the iron bars of my cage. There was this awful whine coming out of my throat and I fought to turn it into a snarl. I managed a cough. He held my hand as though I was his beloved. Warm. Supportive. Loving. Like velvet over iron because I could feel how strong he was in this world, where I hadn't... confined him, the way they were confining me. Tiger Master—and Tigress, I suppose—this is ironic.

I snatched my hand back and tucked it into the opposite armpit. "We'll come and get you tomorrow morning," he said. "And the war master intends to whip you into shape again quickly, for your mental health, and ours."

I managed a nod. The war master's name I didn't recognize. Not one of my eerie ghosts from another world.

*   *   *   *   *

Sleep well, my child. Sleep sound. You are approaching a breaking point and will need your strength.

"*Who are you?*"

"*You know. Deep in your blood you know me and have from before the moment you first drew breath.*"

"*But I really want a name.*"

"*Of course you do. Humans. Namers. You have to clip the infinite into pieces so that you can comprehend them. But you can actually comprehend the whole if you let go of yourself.*"

"*That makes no sense. I have to protect myself.*"

"*It is ego speaking. And the wail of the infant below that. It becomes the ultimate safety. Your father used pain to lock you in ego and id, tie your intelligence, your passion and your compassion to agony.*"

"*Tell me something I don't know, Darkness.*"

"*That's a good name for me. If you've been in the desert under the God's Brutal Eye, I come as a blessing.*"

"No. I'm not a witch. I'm not I'm not. I call Fire, not Water."

"I am only allowed to protect you from Fire so much, my child. Your brother drags the flames away from you, in both worlds."

"You know about both worlds? How?"

"I am focused on these two as the source of contagion."

"Who is ill?"

"God." I am rocked even though I long to rend these loving arms, long to bury myself in them and be safe from pain, both at the same time.

"He's dying, you said."

"No longer. Your family's prayers are powerful... and your other self is healing the other world."

"NO NO NO! He's not better than I! He's not the hero! I am. I have to be!"

"You are the hero, my child. Everyone is."

17

Daddy, Aren't You Proud?

I CANNOT SLEEP. I'm so concupiscent, strung out, desperate for sex that I tried to pound myself off, but the training from my father held true and I couldn't climax until I bit myself bloody. Monster. I can only peak when there's pain. Since I made the old man strangle on his own tongue it's been other people's pain that let me ease myself. Scorch it, I came on the old man's pillow when he died. I'd been aiming for his face but the paroxysm made me miss. He still smiled. He'd taught me that, linked my sex with pain and death.

Limyé, I'm sure you will have to vomit at what I am about to write. You do not understand how twisted I am. I'm your patient, at your insistence, so here is what set me off. Pel. Pelahir. I am not allowed to love. Yolend. I am not allowed to do anything but use and rape.

I had Pelahir in my dungeons for months and trained him to beg for pain, just as I had been, though my father was careful not to maim me physically. In my world I had truly just begun to maim him. I would go down and have sex with his restrained body, even as he raged at me and cursed me and then would begin screaming as his body would respond. I could bring him to the point of coming and hold him there, wouldn't let him climax, until he was crazy and, as I was taught, only allowed to peak while in pain.

I had just gotten him to the point where I was buried in him as deep as I could, holding my favourite knife to the smallest joint of his left hand and he'd been screaming for release, alternating with begging me not to maim him, until he begged me to take the joint.

So I did.

That cleaned bone lies in my world, in a jewel case made specifically for it, with space for every bone in that hand down to the wrist. Cylak have a terrified horror of physical deformity. In my world he will never be accepted as Stag Lord, even if that devil Hand, shadow of me has saved him.

Just writing this has allowed me to climax three times, even though I have had to bite on both my forearms to trigger the last two. My penis feels raw inside, scorched clean of sex. I stink of semen and I imagine telling this to oh-so perfect Pelahir in this world, that innocent man who loves Ahrimaz enough that he's willing to train with his likeness.

I imagine hurling those words at him, scarring that perfect face with the understanding that I broke his other self in my world. That man, that magnificent warrior, that astonishing body, I could use and he would beg me to hurt him, enough so that I could love him.

I broke him and I could love him to death.

* * * * *

The pen nib snapped under the pressure of Ahrimaz's writing, stabbing metal splinters into the index finger, splashing blood and ink across the page. His hands clenched in the mess as he remembered that sweet climax, that scream that tore through his orgasm like love, like kindness, like power.

He lifted his bloody hand to the candle flame and prayed, his guts twisting as he felt the power of God roar through him. The candle flame finally, finally answered his prayer and jumped from the wick to his bleeding fingertip and he set the flame on the tip of his own erect penis, either as reward or punishment, he could no longer tell.

His scream doused the flame as water puddled from the air to snuff the fire dancing over his hands and his lap. He sat, staring into the darkness, at the water that had soothed his burns and somehow soothed his ink-filled wounds that he'd so brutally cauterized.

His face twisted tight to hold back tears and he just knew that outside, it had begun to rain; a gentle hand of rain blowing over the Royal Preserve… the Vale in this world… and the trees there, filling the waterfall to a silvery sheet, blessing the river below. The waterfall… Goddess Veil? No, he couldn't think of it as that. Not yet.

He raised his arms to his face, left and right, bit his calluses, struggling to climax yet again even as he knew he wouldn't be able to. Then he sagged in the chair, covered in sweat and a bead or two of blood still, feeling the harsh edge of the wooden chair bite into the backs of his legs. *Unburned*, he thought fleetingly.

"I was become the monster who eats pain," he whispered to himself in the darkness. "I devoured everyone's agony and it tasted so sweet.

"Daddy, aren't you proud of me?"

18

Just Strike!

PELAHIR STARED THROUGH THE BARS AT THE MESS IN THE CAGE. It looked like nothing so much as a savage beast's den, with the ruins of the bed scattered all over it, soaked with water, full of scorch marks, spattered with brown flecks.

The body lying wrapped in the shredded feather quilt was alive, and just visible under the edge of the mounded up, sodden and scattered feathers, naked.

The table was untouched, save for the ink and blood splashed book.

"Hey," he said. "I thought we were going to train today, Shit-Head." He turned to the guard who stood with the breakfast tray and motioned with his head and hands. *Limyé. In the salle.* He set the tray down, nodding.

There was a harsh whisper from Ahrimaz, on the floor. "Read the book. Just read the scorching book you Cylak boy-toy."

Pelahir pulled the journal towards him, looking at the mess it was, pulled it through the bars and then opened it, began reading. He turned back a page, read through to the end. He folded the book shut, softly, staring at the wreckage in the cage, set it back through the bars onto the desk.

"You tried to set yourself and us on fire," he said. He pulled off his deerskin gloves and looked at his hands, palms and then backs. "But you're naturally a Goddess priest. Working with the Flame makes you ill." He looked around at the soaked bedding.

No answer, not even a reflexive "I'm not *him*."

He shook himself and put his gloves back on, unlocked the cell door. "What are you doing, Cylak?"

He came in, knelt down next to the lump and put his hand on it.

Ahrimaz reacted as if he'd drawn a sword, rolling out from under his touch, managed to stagger to his feet, launched a kick at the Cylak warrior's head.

Pelahir ducked under and pushed the heel of Ahrimaz's foot, setting him spinning, nearly staggering. "Scorch and Burn you!" he shrieked and tried to strike, a flurry of punches and kicks that would have been lethal had they been a hair faster, or if Ahrimaz had been less frail. "Strike! Strike me! Strike back you cripple! Strike me!"

Pelahir ducked or blocked, only one strike came anywhere near, skimming past his cheek. "Good shot," was all he said.

Ahrimaz tried to pin Pelahir against the bars, trap him between the desk and the ruins of the bed but the Cylak slid away from every blow as though he were made of water. "Hit, me, you bastard! Hit me!" Ahrimaz was panting, flagging now. "Avenge your other self! Just scorching, flaming… hit me!"

He was nearly out of breath, staggering. "Burn me," he panted at last, falling to his knees. The dry feathers had been kicked up like a blizzard as he'd chased Pelahir around the tiny cell. "Why? Why won't you hit me?" His hands fell and he leaned forward on his knuckles, all but crouched on the floor. "Why?"

Pelahir reached out to touch his shoulder and all that happened is Ahrimaz shuddered but didn't move. The Cylak knelt down and put his hand under Ahrimaz's chin and raised his head to look him in the eye. Ahrimaz tried to glare but had to squeeze his eyes shut against Pelahir's open and trusting face. "Because you want punishment so badly," Pelahir said, finally. "I won't be the lash to flog you, you Shit-Head. You never hurt me. You maimed a ghost of me. A nightmare in this world. And my Ahri is there, in your Empire to save him, now. Is that not punishment enough for you? You want me to add physical pain to it all as well?"

Ahrimaz, eyes still clenched shut, nodded spasmodically, against Pel's hold. "It's what I deserve isn't it?"

"No." Pelahir gathered Ahrimaz against his shoulder and helped him up, one arm flung around his waist. "Let's get you into the bath, Shit-Head. You've lost a lot of training locked up here." He helped Ahrimaz stagger out into the hall and past the outer door that was unlocked by Limyé who stood by and nodded, following on.

"I don't understand," Ahrimaz said dazedly. "I don't understand how you can be so forgiving. I don't understand why you won't beat me. I gave you every incentive."

"I know. Your father was the *real* shit-head to do this to you."

Ahrimaz didn't have the strength left to shout. "Don't soil my father's character with your Cylak tongue."

"Why not? He'd have had me suck him off if he could, soil his dick with my tongue."

"True."

Limyé took over supporting Ahri into the bathing pool, and Ahrimaz stared in shock as Pelahir stripped his armour and padding off to slide in on the other side. "We're going to get you back in shape fast if you're going this hard, Ahrimaz," he said.

His mouth closed, then he just shook his head. "I just don't understand."

19 ──────────────────

The Vastness

I AM A STRANGER IN A WORLD where everyone is both the same and totally foreign at the same time. It is as though some foolish artist has rebuilt the world around me with mechanisms that look identical to my family and my people. But not one of them reacts properly.

Ahrimaz sat in the tub with the almost searing hot water bubbling around him, Pelahir naked sitting across, and Limyé... thankfully not one of his ghostly mechanisms because he did not recognize him... he shied away from the memory of the Imaryan genoicide... The Imaryan sat in the pool as well, in a tunic that was girded up and shone blinding white against his dark skin.

He had no energy to rage at them, to scream at them to leave him alone. If they weren't going to beat or torture him why were they there? *I am the rotting corpse of their friend, their love, their leader, however much I seem to be healing.*

Limyé took one of his arms out of the water, dried it, dripped one of his medicines on the thick pad of callus there and the new, raw teeth marks. Like most Imaryan medicines it didn't burn or sting or do anything more than sooth. He caught his breath as the pain in that arm went away. That brought tears up to his eyes in a way that the worst agony would not.

"No, please..." *I am reduced to begging him not to ease my pain.*

"It is all right, Dark Ahrimaz," he said. "It will only take a moment for me to do the other arm."

"That's not what I meant... oh, scorch and burn it, you're taking more pain away from me!" It was the most energy he could muster. The Imaryan paused then continued patting the arm dry.

"I understand. You are clinging to any kind of pain because we are starting to show you that life can be different, that you don't have to nest that pain inside yourself so that you can use it as a shield."

"A shield?" Ahrimaz paused, then said, "Yes. It is the thing that made me real." He clenched his eyes shut as the pain in his left arm, and that tightness there, eased and flowed away like this water on skin. "When I was a child I used to cut myself. My father caught me at it and forbade me... saying I'd maim myself and not be a good warrior."

"In his inimitable way, no doubt," Pelahir chimed in. "I'll bet that's when you started biting yourself. You could blame that on an animal or a victim if your father noticed it."

"My youngest brother was the first one to bite me... and gave me an excuse for father. So, yes."

"Let me guess," the Cylak went on, just talking to the ceiling, not to me so Ahrimaz could actually bear it. "You needed 'toughening up'."

"I wasn't 'manly' enough for my father, ever," he said to the insides of his eyelids.

"Such a dreadful outcome of your first Emperor, a man who wanted all power to himself and destroyed his sister to get it," Limyé said. "He must have started this insane 'Emperor training', when he forced his nephew to forget his mother."

Ahrimaz thrashed up and out of the pool and stood, shivering in the cool air against exposed flanks. "I... don't know why... I can't... I... I...!"

There was nowhere to run. There was nowhere to go away. He tried to fling himself into the pool to break his own neck and drown, just to make it stop. Just to make it stop. *But I should have known that the bastard would catch me and haul me up to his chest, even as I thrashed and howled and then I did manage to find some kind of darkness though I could not say I was completely unconscious.*

Somewhere in the soft and warm darkness wrapped around him he heard, distantly, Pelahir's voice. "You're right, Limyé. He's getting worse."

* * * * *

"You are not alone, my son. Even as you descend into what feels like death, I have you. You are not going to manage to throw yourself into the Lava Pit for eternity. Your suffering is mine. Give it to me."

"No. My prayers are to my fictional God. Not to his fictional Wife."

"We are not fictional. We are here."

I feel a drop on my tongue in the world and fall deeper into darkness.

"How are You not fictional? And how can You still call me Yours when, in my world we've burned and slaughtered and raped the women who prayed to You?"

"Their pain was short compared to what their spirits received."

I am looking out over a vista of mountains and forest, like the land around Innéthel. There is no city, only the river, forest growing to the edges of the water and the rock. Then there is an overlay, a village, then one where the land is the same but it is a desert, a city, a volcano, a battlefield, a blizzard scoured waste, hundreds then thousands flip past my eyes and I understand that this is the same place but each one is very different, lying one next the other, like pages in a book.

Then it is my Innéthel and my House of Gold. And we fly up and up and up till the world is a ball of green and the Sun is a cold and tiny marble then there are tens of worlds in a line, then hundreds, then they become a block and then the block becomes a cube and then… it fills my sight and understanding and I scream as there is too much to take in.

I fold myself shut tight as a seed and it all goes away, the vastness of worlds and the vastness of darkness and the vastness of time can all hammer on the outside of me for a while.

20

Hand Émérite

AHRIMAZ COULD FEEL WHEN THEY DRIED HIM OFF, hair and all, wrapped him in a robe or a sheet, and he knew it was Pelahir who carried him. He knew.

They spoke to each other in Imaryan, guessing that he would not know the language and for some reason Ahrimaz was completely unsurprised that Pel knew it. Every name he called the Cylak he knew was a lie. Trying to make the muck he was throwing at him, at them, at their whole world, stick. Trying to make it reality. Trying to make it evil and wrong, for if they were evil then he could safely revile them. The other way around, if they were good, was damnation for him.

Pel eased him through another doorway and set him down on what felt like a stack of mats, but more resilient than any training mats Ahri knew. It echoed like a big space. *The salle.* But it was different, noisy with the roar of water. It would be hard to command anything here with that racket bouncing off the walls. Ahri made his heavy eyelids rise and he stared around at the oddest training facility he'd ever seen.

It looked as though the river actually ran through one end of the hall and the water foamed and rushed along its channel, with ropes suspended above. On the other side was a cliff wall with thousands of hand and footholds and ledges. Limyé was just descending from a rope to one of the ledges, where he would be safer, should Ahrimaz attempt to harm him. He had to laugh, to himself. He felt weak as a baby bird and would find it difficult to even sit up, much less threaten anyone's life.

One of his guards drew a gate across the end wall where the river entered and reduced the flow till it was quiet... still tricky to cross, but no longer foaming over the stones they had set in its bed.

He managed to sit up, finally, prying himself up with his arms shaking. Father would have beaten him for showing such weakness. One reason that he always drove anyone away when he was sick. *I smashed so many vases and cups and hand mirrors, flinging them at Kinourae.*

He was unrestrained, save for the winding sheet that he finally saw was wrapped around him. He shrugged at its resemblance to a shroud. After all, hadn't he just tried to snap his own neck? Had he not just tried to drown himself?

Drowning would be the perfect way to go. Like a witch. And these people just kept saying things like 'God Flame makes you sick' and 'you naturally call water'. He supposed he recognized somewhere deep inside that he was by nature a witch, called to the Demon Wife... the Goddess they most often called Lyrian instead of to the God Aeono. Probably why the most honourable monster father had punished him so hard.

Pel stood, in cotton trousers, shirtless, speaking to a ma...wo... person in a cream coloured robe, girded up, who leaned on a staff, listening intently. It was as hard to tell the person's gender as it was to tell which sex a truth-teller, an *Aporrheitos*, was because they had either shaved or lost all their hair.

The guard at the door, Oriké, opened the door and let two older people in, their hair both in gold and white braids falling down their backs. The woman had two braids looped over her wrist while the man had his in a single elaborate eight-strand confection falling down his back. They spoke to Oriké and then turned to Pel.

Ahrimaz couldn't stop staring at these people. The Innéans were letting other people know that he was not their Hand of the People? His heart thundered in his chest and he couldn't breathe. He knew... he knew those two. But he didn't. He couldn't. Of course he hadn't asked. He'd just assumed.

They, with Pel, turned toward him and Ahrimaz froze. *If my brother isn't dead. If my brothers are not dead. If Pel is whole and unmaimed and loved instead of hated... why did I assume? Why did I not think?* He couldn't breathe, he couldn't, he didn't dare. He managed to straighten as far as his knees and kowtow to the older man approaching him. His muscles were turning to water, he barely managed to keep from voiding his bladder, feeling a heated drop or two on his thigh.

"Émérite," he whispered. "Father of the other man."

21

Ahrimiar II, Wenhiffar and Rutaçyen

AHRIMAZ COULD FEEL THEM LOOKING AT HIM, staring down at him, aware over every thumb length of his skin where he was. There was a rustle and Ahrimaz couldn't look, couldn't force his eyes open. *The old monster is dead, he can't hurt me any longer. I heard his skull pop. I saw the life go out of his eyes. I killed him. I did. This isn't him. This isn't him. This isn't him.*

His body didn't believe it and shook and sweated in terror. "I understand that you are not my son, though you look like him." His voice was the same, though there wasn't the dangerous edge in it. Different. "I assure you that you need not bow to me, young man. I have no will, nor inclination to hurt you."

"Even having usurped your son's rightful place?" He managed to squeeze the question out of thickened and harsh vocal cords.

"You have not. The people are currently debating who should lead Inné, since you are indisposed."

"Who is in the running?" Ahrimaz managed to open his eyes but even as he eased back away from the man, he couldn't raise them. The man, Ahrimiar the Second, had knelt down before the stack of mats where Ahrimaz sat, the woman a vague blur in white and blue off to one side.

"You are concerned? This is not your world, so Pel and Limyé tell me."

"Yes, I care. It is still Inné even if it is not my beautiful Empire... my father's beautiful Empire, and his before him."

"I see." He sat quite still. "Your brother Ahriminash is most likely to take over, or Arlinaz. Arnziel has recused himself as High Flame of Crowned Tiger."

"Really? Arnziel in this world found his vocation?"

"Oh, yes, he was nine when the God woke in him."

"Nine." *Scorch and burn and scar me. Father made me kill that in him then. Not this man. Father.*

"And he's a warrior priest?"

"Just as Arlinaz is a healer priest of the Veil."

A witch priest. Like me. Every muscle in his back was cramping. "With your permission, Ser, I would like to rise."

"Oh, yes, please do. You don't require my permission. I repeat, I am not your father Emperor."

Ahrimaz sat back further, raised his head, carefully, dared glance out of the corner of his eye. This man looked like his father's brother. His face was as open as Pel's, or Limyé's and the bulk of his wrinkles were smile lines around his eyes. His mouth lines all turned up. Father's face had been compressed and dark as if the scorching devils sat behind the centre and pulled it into a mask of rage and despite. In fact the only time Ahrimaz had seen his father's face at peace was a moment after he died as his soul drained out of the meat.

"Ser?"

"Yes, Ahrimaz?"

"Is it allowed to rage? Am I allowed to bellow 'why him and not me?' Is it possible for me to express how angry I am that he was born here and I was not?"

"Indeed. The God in Flame is an excellent way to express rage, though not if it makes you ill."

The woman, who Ahrimaz had not been able to even look at, while focused on the father spoke up for the first time. "Yes, Ahrimaz. The Goddess allows all. Scream your rage to Her."

Ahrimaz sat, frozen once more, tongue locked in his jaw as if it would never move again. He wrapped his arms around himself and managed to squeak out "Mama?" before things began to shatter in his mind. The person who looked like an *Apporheitos,* who had spoken to Pel, stepped up next to his mother... the other Ahrimaz's mother... and put her hand on her shoulder. They had the same face. Twins. "But... but..."

A shattering memory. His mother, strangled before him by his father. Her body lying on the dungeon floor for days until it no longer resembled anything human, a mass of fly maggots. Another mother being brought in by his father, who looked identical to what had been Wenhiffar, a seethe of maggots, a squirm of maggots on the stone floor, was never the same as 'Mama'. Cold, calculating. Distant. Safe. Maggots make a pattering noise on stone.

Ahrimaz fell over, his hands flung over his face, locked into rigour. Distantly he could hear Limyé, and feel their hands on his limbs. He could not move. He could not speak. He could not die. "Too much at once," his pseudo father said. "Let him alone for a while. He needs to recover."

"If he recovers," Pelahir said. "We have to make sure he's all right if we have any hope of getting our own beloved back."

"We might not. This Ahrimaz might be all we ever have again. We are dedicated to saving him, because he is our son," Wenhiffar said. "Rutaçyen… can you help him?" The other woman… her sister. Her twin sister… *Mama's twin sister* was close by.

"I will try," she said. "But his pain might be too great. That dark old man obviously twisted him and he may not be able to grow straight again."

22   Can't Fling Off the Vermin

THEN AHRIMIAR AND WENHIFFAR AND PEL MOVED OFF TO TRAIN. Rutaçyen sat next to his rictus self, the rigid and staring statue of a man in ruins. She was close enough for him to feel the heat of her body in the cool salle. Outside it began to rain. He could tell from a spatter of droplets on the tiny port-hole windows above.

Their training was odd. It wasn't a lot of screaming and repetitive motion. Not like whipping juniors on to the point where they could really learn. They traded a song as they sparred against one another. Every note, every word seemed to have a dozen possible strikes associated with it. Singing. Sparring.

Rutaçyen laid a hand on his shoulder and occasionally sang out, apparently some kind of instruction because three on the floor changed their songs and their wooden swords rang and clacked differently, more intensely somehow. "You are free to lie there, lad. No one is asking anything of you," she said and called two of the Innéan war dogs over to guard him. Or just to keep him warm. They were both gold and white and short-coated, just big enough that an armoured man would find it hard to pick them up and throw them. Block headed. Both of these had lolling tongues and goofy faces. "Stay," she said to the dogs. "These are Sure and Teh," she said to him.

Ahrimaz wasn't sure where he was, wasn't sure he was even in his own head. He could feel his heart beat and his lungs expand and contract but it was as though the inside of his own head was broken into a thousand thousand pieces of glass and he didn't dare do more than breathe or it would all come shattering down and cut him into chunks of darkness and blood.

The dogs lay down on either side of him, panting, pressed up close. One put its nose under his ear and he could hear it begin to snore. They didn't hate him. Even the animals touch differently in this world.

A huge snuffle in one ear nearly broke him out of his stasis, whiskers tickling in his beard. Wait. Both dogs were still there on either side of him. What animal was this? He couldn't make himself move. A heavy weight settled over him and the dogs, like a blanket, and a tongue as rough as emery paper began scraping through his hair and beard. Purring. One of the war cats. It was as big as the two dogs put together. He couldn't be bothered even to twitch, much less fling the vermin off.

The warriors' song had changed again and they now sat, bare handed, moving slow-speed, in a box, knee to knee, Their song eventually became a unified hum. That sound, that meditation, sent him tumbling slowly, mixed with the purr, out of broken stasis into true sleep. *The animals even smell good. Like cinnamon and malak.*

*   *   *   *   *

The dungeon. The mass on the floor. Servants gathering it up and taking it away. The look on Father's face as he directs 'Mother' to get us upstairs and presentable. I never knew that my mother had a twin. In the Empire she was forced to abandon herself and become her sister, Wenhiffar. My aunt, Rutacyen.

In this world. Nothing so twisted. Ahrimiar... the old man... and his wife Wenhiffar are still alive and still married. Rutacyen is a war teacher of some kind. She looks like an Apphoreitos. But she is clearly not hiding her gender. Why am I terrified of them all?

In my world they conspired to hurt me, to torture me. Well, the old man made it so. In that world we were all helpless in the face of his violence. In this world... from what I saw... Ahrimiar the Second in this world is a warrior who would put my father onto the mat in moments. Father was too rigid, too fixated on winning. He always had to dominate. He beat me down until I could beat him. My other teachers taught technique, so I could escape that rigidity and become a better warrior. Father taught brutality.

In this world they spar to teach not to win, not to prove the teacher's superiority. Oh Tiger... Ma... Mast... Scorch and Drown. Tiger Mistress... am I truly yours? Am I? Can You help me? Can You save me? I'm lost and drowning in all these loving touches. I cannot bear to be touched. It hurts. But these people... I hear the purr in my ears even as I... I'm in the bed.

The repaired bed. I sink into the feather mattress. They fixed it. It's warm, it's safe. This isn't a dungeon any longer. It's a place where I can lock them all out if I need to. Except the dogs and the cat. They can all squeeze through the bars. All three of them have come and are helping me stay warm. The blasted cat I don't even know the name of lies on me and purrs almost constantly and I have to move sometimes or he... she? He for now. He'd rasp my cheek raw. I am apparently a hurt kitten with a filthy coat.

I *am shaking all over and a hand slips behind my head, offers me water, offers me Imaryan remedies. The fungus that soothes the raw edges of my life and my pain and lets me into the safe dark of Lyrian. I'm a witch, a lover of both women and men, no one will torture me here or make me rape and torture my brothers. Nor my sisters. That the old man kept to himself.*

I *am a witch? Lyrian. Mama. I am in darkness, gathered into someone's arms, against someone's chest. Safe.*

23

What Would Your Teachers Think?!

THE SNORING AND PURRING OF THE ANIMALS BECAME ALMOST CONSTANT in his dreams and the sense of being held. Pel, Yolen and he knew that the baby was there, though not close, Ahrimiar and Wenhiffar and Rutaçyen. They were treating him as if he were their own injured boy.

The tears running, unchecked down his face were also all but ubiquitous. Then another hand on his shoulder. He couldn't bear to see who it was, who they had told. He felt so ashamed and exhausted and overwhelmed.

"I can feel that you are not my daddy," the young girl's voice said. "But that's all right. You're starting to heal."

"Shashe," he said, and choked on her name. "You should not be near me." His throat hurt because he hadn't spoken in so long.

"You aren't going to hurt me, Uncle."

"Uncle. Yes. That's a good phrase for me. I am as close to your father as a brother." He couldn't open his eyes, couldn't lift a hand. The cat on him was a big old tortoiseshell with a missing ear and one fang. She butted her head under his chin until he had to turn away, found himself with one cheek on top of Teh's bony head, looking at his 'niece'. "I..." he coughed and coughed again, found himself swallowing his rage at himself. How could he have damaged his own girl so? He hadn't been able to bear having her anywhere near him after she'd healed speechless, gradually growing more and more withdrawn.

Shashe was nearly as dark skinned as her mother, with long wavy brown hair with his gold highlights in it, same as his own girl, with the piercing Kenaçyen blue eyes. Her hair was caught into an Imaryan healer's braid, with the blue apprentice beads clicking gently off the bottom fringe. Aware eyes, not vague, not wandering, not brain-injured. She wore an Imaryan robe and the Innéan sunburst with a Lion's face together and she sat, still. Astonishing for a child of her age. The gemstone below the sunburst was a star sapphire teardrop. The Apporheitos 'Eye of Truth'.

Ahrimaz's voice froze but he managed to choke out an 'I'm sorry.' Before he fell back into the hell that was his mind. But Shashe's hand was on his shoulder.

"You don't need to run away into the madness, Uncle," she said quietly. "There is no shame here."

"There... is... shame enough... in my world. The blame is all mine." She nodded. "I destroyed my little girl's mind in my world. The Shashe I know plays with her fingers and drools instead of sits and consults with my healer." *Why am I confessing this? Because it is truth. She will hear it. Yolend will hear truth. And my terror. I give up. I cannot defend myself against truth. I am a monster and deserve this pain.*

He repeated his thought out loud and her young brow furrowed. "I understand why you feel that way. But I hear a lie buried in it."

"Oh?"

"You did those things. You learned not only to bear and enjoy hurting people and animals, killing and frightening everyone around you, all those monstrous things because there was nothing else for you. The little boy inside you hasn't ceased screaming. Not for all these years. So part of your armour is to be a monster. That part is true. But not to all of you. That is one lie. The other lie is that you deserve punishment for it."

Limyé's voice came from near the door. "Thank you for your analysis, Apprentice. I thought so, but you've just confirmed it."

Ahrimaz struggled to sit up, struggled to get out from under the blanket of animals. All three groaned and moved, though reluctantly whining or hissing or grunting. "I'm glad you didn't let her in here by herself!" His anger rose. "How could you do that to her? Feeling me? She's family and she's no more than fourteen! How could you treat her like that!" He could see her smiling slightly, out of the corner of his eye.

"Spoken like a concerned father, or uncle," Limyé said. "Yolend sent you more soup, because you need to eat something."

"I'm not hungry."

"That's a lie, Uncle." Shashe said. "You're suppressing your body's needs because you don't think you deserve care."

That was true. He was desperately hungry and he was weakened and shaking.

Ahrimaz's head snapped from glaring at Limyé to glaring at Shashe. "I am Limyé's patient, young lady, not yours. I'll thank you to get out of my feelings! What would your teachers think?! If they are anything like my Apporheitos, discretion is their first learning!"

"I'm sorry, Uncle." She rose. "I'll come down and see you some days, all right?"

"I can't stop you," he snapped. "But I insist you respect my privacy!"

"Yes, daddy."

He just froze as she passed Limyé sitting at the desk and opened the cage door. He watched her as she stood to be let out.

"I'm not him," he whispered, but that was long after the door had closed behind her.

24   What A Thought

HE TURNED, STARING AT LIMYÉ. "I will eat. But you have to discourage that child from trying to be my healer."

Limyé set a bowl of soup and a fresh loaf of bread on the desk, poured a cup of malak, strong enough to make Ahrimaz's head come up to sniff the aroma. Pats of butter each on its own bit of paper, perfect for a piece of bread. No knives, not even butter knives, Ahrimaz noted. Instead the bread was baked to be torn apart. He had no doubt that everything was fresh, even though he could have sneered at it as peasant food.

The Imaryan turned and opened his paint box to begin adding more birds to his tree painting on the wall and Ahrimaz looked at the door of his cell. He hadn't seen Shashe or Limyé lock it. "I will discourage her," Limyé said. "But only because I discourage children from seeing their relatives in distress."

The scrape of the chair legs was harsh and Ahrimaz half fell into it. He took up the loaf and tore it in half, suddenly aware of Sure sitting attentively on his right side and Teh on his left. The cat was luxuriously sprawled, taking the whole bed for itself.

"Limyé..." he stopped, dropped the bread and sat staring down at his hands. "I can't do this. I should never have become your patient." He pushed himself away from the desk, tried to get up. Put his face in his hands. "I ... shouldn't have."

"Why is that?"

"Because I wish to live."

"Oh? It doesn't seem like it if you are not eating."

"That will pass. My appetite will come back or I will force it. To put it bluntly, I wish to live and… once I became I began to grow a conscience."

"And this will kill you, how?"

"If I grow a conscience… or let it out of its cage… I will be forced to recognize exactly how much evil I have done, how truly monstrous a man I've been and realize what horrors I have inflicted on the innocent. I will have to kill myself."

Limyé didn't stop, but turned to mix another colour of paint. "I think that I can help you get through that dangerous time. It is part of recovery from that mental illness wrought by violence."

Ahrimaz lowered his hands and just stared at him for a long moment, shook his head and slowly dragged the chair back to sit at the desk, forearms braced. He stared at the food not able to eat at first, cursing himself for letting it grow cold. But as it became less palatable he was able to force himself.

One bite of dry bread. One spoon of soup. Spread the butter. Another single bite, though your body is screaming that you feed it, feed it NOW! Pour the cream into the malak, watch the dark brown liquid roil around till it is the exact colour of Yolend's skin. Limyé is darker than un-creamed malak.

"Good. So, who have the mob chosen to usurp me?"

"Not usurp. Take up the burden of government to give you time to heal." The door clicked again, unlocked.

"This is a busy place for an isolation dungeon," Ahrimaz said, staring down into the clear broth with what looked like salat leaves gently floating with onions and bright bright green cubes of kohlrabi. "Take up the burden, yes, that is one thing that is the same."

It was Ahrimiar, who immediately waved him to sit as he jolted upright, away from the food. "Sit, eat something, you're getting skinny, boy." He settled himself cross-legged on the stone floor and waited quietly until Ahrimaz, wary, sank down into the chair again. His father would never have allowed anyone to sit with his head higher than the crown. "I heard what you were asking. It will be Ahriminash, though he argues that he's a better guard captain than any kind of head of state."

"That sounds like him." In the Empire Ahriminash, though he was second in line for the throne and a constant threat until he overstepped and got killed, had always preferred training on the field to training in the salon.

"Limyé tells me that we might be at a turning point for you," the older man said quietly. "We've been locking you up and treating you like a wild animal for too long already."

"What? You're going to tell people I'm not their beloved Ahrimaz and let me go?" Ahrimaz laughed. Then he stopped laughing as he realized Ahrimiar was nodding.

"If you will continue to be Limyé's patient. He is offering the family his services in exchange for his research with you so you needn't worry about payment— *I hadn't even thought of that. What is it costing them to keep me here?* "— and not kill anyone or break any laws, we are not right to keep you isolated. It was a panicky move on our part. We were so shocked at what happened and you presented as a horrific danger to all of us."

"Just… let me go…" Ahrimaz tapped the spoon against the empty bowl, poured himself another out of the tureen. "I, personally, think you'd be mad to do so."

"I don't. The worst problem you'd have would be being badgered by the writers for the Broadsheets, the novelists who want to make a romance out of your predicament, and so forth. They can be quite persistent."

"Writers." Ahrimaz's lips quirked. "And I'm not allowed to injure any of them?" It was only a half-question, teasing.

"Exactly."

"You obviously think that I, alone, am not a danger to your Republic, or your Coalition."

"Not if you continue with Limyé, and Rutaçyen, along with both Pel and Yolend."

"Where… would I go?"

"Where you wanted."

Ahrimaz was silent for a long time, spooning soup steadily into his mouth, dusting the crumbs of bread off his hands. "It seems too open, too trusting, just to blurt out this disaster to the country, destabilizing for one thing."

"It's not a disaster for the country. It is not even a disaster for the family. We will publicly apologize for having confined you and we will compensate you for that. It won't be a fortune but you'll be able to find a place to live in Innéthel—"

"Compensation! Set me loose with no skills other than warrior or tyrant? I'd get mobbed in the street and starve before spring!" Ahrimaz had to laugh again. The fear he was familiar with settled under his breastbone and he looked around at the cell.

"Our people, the Innéans are not inclined to mob, and I'm sure we could find something you could bear to do to support yourself. Your notoriety alone would sell books."

"A 'Tell All' in my own words, printed in their hundreds or thousands, given the number of presses you people have. What an obscene thought, baring my soul to every pest-ridden peasant from here to the Riga City states and beyond."

"Far beyond. Riga ships trade with a countries across the sea that they discovered... One of them, they call Tuinos."

"What a thought." The terror of being uncovered, ripped open, laid bare before the world's eyes rose up to choke him and he clutched the edge of the desk as if to keep himself from flying off the face of the earth. "Could I... may I... would it be you I have to beg to stay here?"

25   Books and Discretion

LIMYÉ TURNED AWAY FROM THE PAINTING, put a hand on the door of the cell. "You aren't being forced out, Ahrimaz. If you feel safe here, you needn't go out."

Ahrimiar had waved at the guard beyond the outer hall door and they unlocked it, left it open. Ahrimaz collapsed onto the floor, staring over Ahrimiar's white hair.

Pleta, Oriké and Katishenne came in. Each had a heavy stack of books in their hands. Ahrimiar had one in his hand as well, held out to Ahrimaz. "Here's the one that has the laws against confinement that I talked about. I thought you would be interested. Had you taken us to court with this one, and could prove to an Apporheitos arbiter that you weren't a danger to anyone who didn't attack you, it would have forced us to let you go."

"But... why... but... you aren't fighting me on this? You're just handing me the laws? You kept me in ignorance and now you hand me, the starving man, a banquet?" Ahrimaz clambered to his feet and reach out toward Limyé who still stood at the closed cell door, fingers laced through the bars.

He didn't flinch as Ahrimaz closed his hand on his fingers. Ahri squeezed, staring into Limyé's eyes and then eased back, flung his other arm up and set his teeth in the callus on that side, eyes clenched shut. "You didn't hurt me, Ahrimaz. You pressed hard but stopped at the point of hurting me."

Ahri was sobbing through his teeth, through his flesh, forced his eyes open and looked at the books now neatly lined up on the shelves of a folding bookshelf that Pleta had brought in. He took a deep breath, looked at Limyé and then over at Ahrimiar.

He left his eyes on the older man, teeth still clenched in the flesh of his forearm, as he reached out again, carefully, and slowly touched the iron latch—raised it with a click that rang through him like an earthquake because it moved. It wasn't locked.

From where he'd staggered back, a step or two, nearly falling over one of the dogs, he stared at them all. Limyé, who hadn't moved, Ahrimiar who was just sliding the law tome into the shelf from where he sat, long arm stretched out, to Oriké who had just brought another few books in.

"You're all mad. Madder than I am. You're treating me as if I deserve to be treated well, treated like I'm injured or ill instead of scorched in the wits. You're all open and giving and so trusting and and I... can't... stand... it!" He flung his hands over his face.

The big old cat hit him softly behind the knees so he went down onto the floor and the three animals clambered onto him, pinning him down. Not licking, not nosing him, just... keeping him still and warm.

"I'll see you again," Ahrimiar said. "Once you are composed perhaps you and Pel might go to one of the libraries to pick out something that interests you, instead of my guesses, here." He waved at the shelf. "And you should probably rest after this upheaval and eat more. When you're up to opening that door by yourself, you should come and start training with us. Or just watching the new classes. Rutaçyen has given her permission for you to come and go at the salle, at your discretion."

"Discretion??? DISCRETION?" But he didn't have the strength to start screaming. These people, these animals were all mad.

Limyé turned and began painting a Red Breast onto a branch of his tree, humming.

"You're not going away too?" Ahrimaz cast a glance to see that the outer hall door was now open. There was no guard sitting on the stool there. Insanity. These people were giving insane.

"No. I would not abandon my patient in crisis," he said. "I will just be here for if and when you need me."

"Aaaawwww, awwwhhh, awwwwhhhhnnngh!" The sound forcing its way out of Ahrimaz's terror-constricted throat was almost a bray. Not a laugh, not a scream but a bit of both as he writhed on the floor under the dogs and the cat who kept him from biting himself. They had his arms pinned down. "You... you... you're all mad... fire-fucking insane... drowning crazy! I'm drowning in all this emotion! You've ripped the lid off it and it's so deep and so wide I'll drown in it. It's endless, bottomless..."

"You feel it is unending," Limyé said, then put his tongue out the corner of his lip as he concentrated on a line of paint, glancing over to see if the animals still had him cuddled. "It's not."

Ahri had enough strength, just from having eaten, to weep. "I'm going... going... going to melt into a puddle of tears if you have your way!"

"No. You just have a few years of tears to get caught up on, even if they are currently dry sobs."

26

Dragons in the Underbrush

I DO NOT TRUST THEM. I do not test the doors to see if they are open. The guards are still there. At least one… someone brings me food. Good food, not slop. And pots of malak and cream and there are the books.

My life becomes nothing but the bed and piles of books. And when I am too stiff and too filthy in mind and body I ask Limyé to go with me to the bath. I do press ups, pull ups, squats but I am a shadow of myself. I do war routines, empty hand smashing them against the walls to toughen them up.

I clean myself. Then retreat back into the cell to read. They have broadsheets, every two days. There are three papers, named Inné Times, All The News, and Did You Know? And they alternate so that there is a paper out every two days or so. Granted the Did You Know Broadsheet is mostly pap. Gossip.

They are speculating on my disappearance. They criticize the Kenaçyen line for having so many foreigners from the Coalition close. They chat about the royal families and extended families. Did You Know has an Innovator's page where people with science papers publish. It is fascinating to find that they are only speculating on building double shot-pistols and have not set about making them one of the armies hand to hand weapons.

There are no wars to report, apparently.

I have the animals lying across my legs and outside… because there is a weather column and a weather forecast column… and a weather history column I know that it is the heaviest snow in thirty years.

I read.

Limyé comes to paint. There is a whole jungle of trees now, in the hall outside my cell, crammed full of birds and he's starting to paint flashes of stripes here… predator eyes there. It's not a peaceful, safe jungle he's painting.

Most of it is fantasy. Riga and the Imaryan city are hot temperate but even they do not have dragons. Their weather is pounding rain for a double handful of minutes every afternoon… then steaming dry under a sun that bites into tender Innéan skin. I cannot tell if an Imaryan even can tan, they are so dark. Yolend comes and reads to me. Shashe has gone back to school, safely away from me. And Yolend insists on showing me the new larva as if I care about the child before it can speak and be orderly. He has my eyes. And her smile.

I think Limyé is painting dragons in the deep dark patches. My illness. My evil. My monstrosity. All buried under normal green trees and flowers and birds.

The war-cat's name is Heylia. "Of the Sun" Appropriate with her solar eyes and patches of rusty bleach against dark. She kills things. Then she drags them in to give them to me. I find the corpses of snakes in my bed every morning. I praise her as a mighty killer and a ferocious monster and she brings me baby crocodiles. Limyé says that she used to hunt birds but Ahrimaz my brother didn't like it and everyone trained their war-cats that what they wanted were rodents and crocodilians out of the river.

I curse Limyé when he comes in the morning but he tells me that my words no longer have force and passion behind them. Pelahir comes and I snarl at him and he snarls back until he gets me to laugh. I want to go out… I don't want to go out. I am safe here.

Ahrimiar comes and speaks to me. I might be able to speak more freely to him soon, after the 'freeing me' conversation I have been reduced to 'yesser' 'noser'.

My mother… Wenhiffar comes and speaks to me. She even sings with me. The old folk songs are very similar and she and I sing. "Star-Flower Morning" and "Bright-Eagle Eyes" and even nasty old silly songs like 'Fart Under the Eaves' and ones I didn't know… 'Maiden's Vindication' 'Feather of Truth'… all these songs about girls shown to be honourable and warriors and mothers and free and…

Father would have stared at these wild women and they would have taken him down like the rabid dog he was.

No wonder the First Emperor slaughtered his sister. If he wished men to rule he had to make the women evil.

Evil.

A man's sex is supposedly all there is. Women are not to have wants or needs, except as passive receptacles for seed and being the skin envelope to grow children.

Because women wanting sex terrified the Old Emperor. Women terrified him. Where did you grow so small and scared, Old Man that you had to slaughter anyone who spoke back to you, called you on your bull shit, fought back?

How could you be so petty as to force obedience with the closed fist and the bruised cheek?

Old Man… Goddess? How did you let this first monster take over and start killing your priestesses? Why did You allow this atrocity that led to my brutalization? Yes, yes, free will and all that… I read those passages and I snarl because people should be made to obey… and then I realize. That is the fearful impulse that drove *him*.

We men are animals. Predators. Dragons in the underbrush. Why? It hurts to be that. It is the most painful thing, to sit with my mother, and know that she loves me and that in the Empire my father killed her in front of us because I, at the tender age of twelve, nearly got her free of him.

27

You Traitorous Cur

As YOLEND AND PELAHIR NEARED THE DOOR OF THE CELL they heard slow, monotonous cursing. "Scorch and damn and burn you, mutt! Why don't you bite me? Drown you! Scorch you! Come back here you traitorous cur!" Sure trotted out of the door to the hallway and down toward the stairs, but stopped half way down the hall and lay down, whining, staring back at the cell.

Pel looked at Yolend and she grimaced. When they entered the hall, now filled with Limyé's paintings, they found Ahrimaz kneeling naked in the middle of his cell, teeth set into his own arm, eyes clenched shut as he shuddered but could not manage to climax, though the two could tell he was in agony, trembling on the edge of it.

Yolend nodded at Pel who whispered, barely audible, "Come. Taste that delicious pain. You are lonely."

It was enough. Groaning Ahrimaz fell forward, blood on his arm, blood on his teeth, curled protectively around his genitals as he climaxed.

Yolend eased out and a moment later "Hello, Sure! Who's a good dog then?" echoed outside. Ahrimaz jerked as if he'd been shot, scrambled forward into the bed covered to the eyebrows as Yolend came in, bringing Sure with her. "Good evening, Ahrimaz! Are you ill?" She and Pel sat down on the chairs under the lamp.

"Go away, both of you."

"Oh?" Pel crossed his arms across his chest. "You'd have to get out of bed naked to make us leave you realize."

"Curse you, I shit in your heart, drown you, burn you, I'll fuck the front row at your funeral, scorch you, flay you, I eat your heart—"

"After you've shit in it?" Yolend said, raising her eyebrows. "I think that would taste bad."

"Damn you, woman you interrupted a perfectly good tongue lashing of this one-eye'd, split-tongued Cylak!"

"Ahrimaz, were you trying to get the dog to bite you just now?" Sure hadn't squeezed through the bars but sat, with her head pressed against Pel's thigh. Ahrimaz lowered the edge of the feather quilt. The two were both wearing light cotton clothing, as if for bed, if he didn't know that they slept naked.

"What if I did?" He sat up, dropping the bedclothes to his waist. "She's just a cur."

"Why?" Yolend rose and stood just outside the door.

"None of your business, you cunt-mothering witch!" Ahrimaz's hands curled into fists as she opened the latch with a click that echoed in his head, the terror roaring through him. He choked silent as she stepped in and pulled the desk chair over next to his bed.

He sat, rigid as a statue as she took his arm and turned it over to look at the crusted and bleeding wound on his forearm. "It's only the one arm, now," he gritted. "The other one's healed up." He thrust the other arm out violently to show the darkened scar tissue next to the wound.

"Ahrimaz," Pel had followed Yolend into the cell. For the first time both of them were inside, with him. "You don't need to hurt yourself or anything else to get sexual release."

Ahrimaz wrenched his arm out of Yolend's too tender grip and flung his back to them both. "Go away, just go away. Let me rot here, you don't want to like me, shadow-copy of your lover, smeared with blood and shit and injury. You don't want this breathing corpse to get anywhere near you."

"It's not your responsibility, really," she said quietly and laid her hand on the back of his head, while Pel took hold of his calf through the featherbed. "We will like who we like and…"

"I don't want your pity!" Ahrimaz shouted at them but his face was buried in a pillow and though he twitched with the force of his shout, he didn't try and throw off their hands.

"You need to listen to Limyé when he says that the next step in your healing is learning to be gentle with yourself." She pulled the bedclothes down and touched an old scar on Ahrimaz's back. He bit the pillow and choked as Pel reached under and laid a hand on his bare skin. They sat for a long moment before Ahrimaz began shaking.

"You don't want to do this," he said, finally. "I want to tear you two to shreds."

"Then try," she said. "We can look after ourselves. It's not for you to say."

Ahrimaz lunged out of bed, striking for her face quick as a viper. She moved to match his speed, easing her face out of the way and Ahrimaz snapped his fist back just in time for Pel to bundle him in the bedding and the two of them rolled him onto the floor. By the time he'd untangled himself, roaring with rage, they were already out in the hallway, and Yolend spun the chairs into his way as she dashed out the door after Pel, Sure scrabbling all four sets of claws on the stone to run ahead.

Ahrimaz scrambled after them, screaming, but his long sedentary hours had cut into his phenomenal speed, and they made it to the stairs up to the salle with him half way down the hallway. On the stairs he somehow found his wind and rhythm, ceased raging and chased them silently. Yolend darted through the salle door first and Ahrimaz was within arm's reach of Pel's back when the Cylak ducked under that reaching arm, flung an arm around the him and spun them both into and across the room, straight into the roaring stream.

It devolved into a splashing, ducking, swinging, struggle because kicks were too slow and Yolend would disappear into the foam and suddenly her hands would find his ankles and yank him under. Pel would haul him up, duck or block a strike and then dump them both under. Neither tried to strike back, but in the tumble Ahrimaz lost his balance and smacked up against a boulder and breathed in a lung full of water.

A hand grabbed his hair, another his beard under his chin and hauled him up to blessed air where he vomited and then fought to just stand on his own two feet and breathe. Sure danced on the artificial bank and barked.

When he'd coughed up what felt like half the river he found himself clinging to the two, standing in the circle of their arms. He stared down into her face and for a fleeting moment considered biting her, found himself kissing her. *Bile and river and her sweet, sweet mouth.*

He tore his head up, looked around wildly. "I must not. I must…"

"Come on, Shit-Head," Pel said kindly. "Let's get you dry and talk."

28

Pray

AHRIMAZ FOUND HIMSELF ONCE MORE ON THE STACK OF MATS, wrapped in towels and all but immobilized between Yolend and Pelahir. Sure came scrambling over and onto the mat thudding her blockhead into his middle with a grunt. He grunted as well and then subsided and let her be. *Stupid dog.*

"Why are you doing this?" he said, finally. "Why are you treating me like *him?*"

He could feel Yolend shake her head. "We aren't. You're getting away with horrible behaviour that we wouldn't tolerate in our Ahrimaz."

"What?" He was confused. "But..."

"We'd have hauled him out to the valley and ducked him under the Veil for behaving like you."

"I... see."

"But because I'm insane you let me scream and injure myself." Ahrimaz just closed his eyes, let them hold him. "I've never let myself be held down like this." He was too tired to fight them, too sore, his lungs hurt. He could do nothing but lie and accept comfort.

"Basically, yes."

"That's crazy."

"No," Pel's voice rumbled in his ear. "It's like training. Tire them out until they can't get it wrong."

"I... see, I think." Ahrimaz could feel the fear biting at him because of their closeness, but it was small and distant and far away. The sensation of being held close in their arms when they weren't going to hurt him was foremost. And the sensation of kissing Yolend lingered on his lips.

He had managed to climax and still felt sore from it, even though the damned dog wouldn't bite him. That would have made things so much easier.

"We're thinking that we need to unhook your pleasure from pain."

"Is that even possible?" Ahrimaz clenched his eyes shut. "It took him long enough to train it into me. I might never be able to…"

Sure raised her big head and wagged her tail, thumping against his leg. "Hello," Limyé said. "Do you mind telling me what happened?"

"These two came down and nearly interrupted me while whacking off; then wouldn't quit touching me. So I chased them out here and we did some sparring."

"That's basically it, in a quail's eggshell," Yolend said. "Though with his spin on it."

"Negative, of course."

Ahrimaz sighed, gritted his teeth. "Would you two *please* let me up?"

"Certainly – —of course," They said and even helped him sit up on the mats, pushing the dog off to one side and somehow still managing to keep hold of him.

"How are you bearing all this touching, then?" Limyé looked interested rather than prurient.

"I'm too tired to fight them." Ahrimaz found that his arms and legs were trembling with fatigue and drew a deep breath to try and seize control of himself. "They were just telling me they thought I could have my sex drive uncoupled from pain."

"They're right." Limyé nodded. "There is a protocol that often works."

"Don't tell me," Ahrimaz could feel his lips trying to curl. "Imaryan."

"Naturally. One reason I think you were driven to kill us all in your Empire. It was too dangerous to have anyone around who might actually be able to heal you."

"How can you just talk about it like that?" Ahrimaz hitched himself up and away from Pel and Yolend. "It's the most brutal of genocides and it was proof of my evil. Just as my beating my Shashi into imbecility."

"And your Yolend into docility." This Yolend said, quietly. She was cross-legged now, the cottons dry enough that they mercifully fell away from her body. Even though Ahrimaz had taken the worst of his lust away, he wasn't dead.

"None of which are forgivable. Torture, murder. Just because I was Emperor and could do all of it with impunity, didn't get me off the butcher's hook!"

"Your father put you there," Limyé said. "Does that make it your fault?"

"No! Just my responsibility!"

"Heya, Shit-head." Ahrimaz's head snapped around to stare at Pelahir as he continued. "It seems to me that you've already got the conscience you're afraid of."

Ahrimaz started, then stared around at them, sitting with him in the middle of the training salle, even the dog. He was constrained in towels and sheets and none of them apparently hated or feared him. He fisted his hands over his eyes and bent forward as if someone had stabbed him in the gut.

"As a first step, Ahri," Yolend said. "We'll be with you while you pray."

"Scorch you! Char you to drowning!"

"But," Limyé said. "Our Ahrimaz is made quite ill by praying to Aeono and being answered. He is naturally more able to pray to Lyrian."

"You've said," Ahrimaz gritted. He straightened abruptly, raised his hands and began the prayer to call on God to cleanse foulness.

His hands flared into blue-white flames and he was crowned with it dancing over his head. "...burn all that is dross, Aeono!" The flames reflected in all their eyes and they watched, peacefully, until Yolend raised her slender fingers into the air, palm to palm.

"Father Tiger, bless me, bless all children, save us from the fires of rage that possess us and flay our souls." The flames jumped to her hands, wrapping around her head and shoulders like a shawl.

"No! Oh, God. Oh God!" Ahrimaz dry heaved into the bowl that Limyé had produced. "Tiger Master!" He vomited bile and blood.

"You are burning, Ahri. You need water."

He shoved the bowl away, staring at the softly flickering light that crowned Yolend. Pel held out his hands, cupped like a bowl under Ahrimaz's chin. "Will you pray with me?"

"I don't know how to pray to that bitch."

"Well, first you have to stop calling a divine being names, though She's bigger than that and doesn't much care. She won't answer if you do, though."

"Lyrian." Ahrimaz husked and as he spoke, a drop of water appeared in Pel's hands. "M...m...other..." a blue white fountain danced over Pel's hands, overflowed over their knees. "Sooth me? May I pray to You? I've hated you so long. I don't know how. I..."

Pel tipped his hands forward and Ahrimaz put his own up automatically to catch the waterfall. He stared down at the fountain rising out of his hands, the feelings welling up in him, splashing on his skin like tears running down his face, dripping off his chin. "Mother, help me." And put his hands to his lips and drank until his raging thirst and pain were gone.

29 — I Disgust Myself

THAT WAS ANOTHER TURNING POINT. The first one that I acknowledge was the moment I agreed to be Limyé's patient. It was only the first of many.

That agreement was grudging and hard fought, with the silence and the loneliness, the realization that there was no other course for me.

When I agreed to pray to Her – I still find it hard to refer to Her as Goddess, Mistress, Exalted, or by Her name or call her Mother—I began to actively participate in my own healing. I went from snarling animal, to dull acceptance and then to seeking out the things that caused me the most sweating terror; to seize the roots of them, rip them out of my soul and see if they were truly mine. Or to see if they were the alien, vile seeds of horror planted in me, poisoning me, growing into and through me. The illness is like a parasitic weed, wending about my soul, deceiving me into thinking it is my own, even as it battens on me, draining me dry, withering me.

It is more than merely parasitic. It changed me. It shifted my mind and my heart, my thoughts and the way my body reacted to any kind of stimulation.

Every prayer now eases that. Every mindful draught of water, every mouthful of food, every drop of water that cleanses me. The jagged, ragged edges of my life, that once cut me with every breath, are slowly being eased out of the flesh of my mind and the depths of my soul. Limyé gives me remedies that leave me floating peacefully, for the first time it feels like, in the state half-way between waking and sleeping. The cat comes to lie upon me then and Heylia's thunderous purr seems to deepen the effect of any remedy that Limyé gives me.

And the talking. Day after day after day. Limyé is gaining a copious wad of notes for his study of how the difference of nature and nurture of the same man, in effect, affect him. I never believed I would say this to an Imaryan. I'm sorry.

I'm dreaming of all those innocent souls I killed, watching my former self, blood on my face and hands, white bared smile blinding against the red, killing and killing, dashing children against walls.

And I cannot stop him.

I wake screaming.

Even the ink in the lamplight seems to fade before my gut-wrenching horror of myself. I eat and then sit rocking, holding my gut because some part of me does not want it, does not feel I deserve it.

I do not deserve food, sleep, peace. And if I do not deserve peace then I may not kill myself to escape this wretched agony. I deserve this anguish, this woe and torment of myself. It fits right in to my pattern of self-punishment. I am not *allowed* to commit suicide.

In my dreams I fling myself in my own way, screaming "Kill me, not them! Kill ME!" But I am invisible, inaudible and the monster steps through my ineffectual ghost to commit another atrocity, set another fire in Aeono's name, stick another mortal blade into the God's heart.

No wonder the God is dying. No wonder miracles are become tawdry sideshow tricks and flashy, false executions. The Empire is killing Him. WHY is the Empire being allowed to affect Him so? Isn't He above all that? Perhaps that is the reason. He and She have given us free will, but still care for us enough to remain enmeshed in our worlds, obeying the rules under which They created us. We come ever closer to destroying ourselves and the Gods who made us. With every witch accused and flamed. With every horror done in His name. Our prayers have power because They created us so and are helpless in the face of our evil, I suppose. But They love us too much to abandon us, cut us off. Father, Mother, you are enduring the pain of our free will. I'm sorry.

I'm sorry, I'm sorry, I'm sorry, I'm sorry

What can I do to make it right? I cannot touch the Empire's villainy, much less my own. I cannot even fix what I did. Helpless to do anything that might atone for the dreadfulness I've personally wreaked upon my world. I am repulsed by myself. Ahrimaz, my other self, save them, heal them. Hold strong in the face of my evil and save my people from me.

The gifts I've commanded, the science I've fostered to make people's lives easier, longer, more productive do not compensate for the violence and heartbreak I have personally meted out. Sen-Lum's families wiped out if they crossed me, Sen-Grand's stripped down to nothing... if I didn't kill them. Sen-Regal set at each other's throats for my regard. I used people with no regard for their humanity. My children and my wife abhor and fear me.

I disgust myself. I'm sorry, I'm sorry, I'm sorry... please do not forgive me. I don't deserve forgiveness. I do not deserve such grace. I'm sorry, I'm sorry...

I'm sorry I'm begging for forgiveness. I know it isn't possible. How can anyone forgive me if I cannot fix it, make it right, atone? How can anyone else truly forgive me if I cannot and will not forgive myself?

I'm sorry.

30

Will I Call You Teacher?

THE DOORS WERE NO LONGER BEING LOCKED. There were no guards. Ahrimaz just couldn't make himself leave the cell by himself. Any time someone called him out, he would go. Not willingly but he would step outside as he was asked.

He looked up from the remains of his breakfast, peasant oat cakes in the winter and found Rutaçyen standing on the other side of the bars. He startled back then set his hands flat on the table. "Don't DO that," he snapped.

She tilted her head to one side. She was wearing the plain cottons most of them wore indoors. "Do what? Walk? Stand?"

"Sneak UP on me like that," he snarled.

"I see." But she didn't apologize. "Finished breakfast?"

"Just," he snapped and drained the dregs of his malak. "Now I'm done."

"Good. We need to get you working out regularly instead of all these wild attempts at killing followed by your exhausted collapse. It's not good for you."

"You who were my mother's fetch are truly a war teacher here?"

"Yes." She turned and walked out of the hall. "Come along. You're lucky," she said over her shoulder as he stood up, fuming that she was just strolling away from him. "I don't take many students anymore."

He snatched the cell door open, trotting after her. "New student? I'm Limyé's patient not your student!" He reached out to grab her shoulder and found he had hold of nothing, stumbling forward as she turned and put one finger under his elbow and somehow he was falling. He rolled to his feet and found himself with her flat hand resting gently against his nose even before he could get his hands up.

"Let us continue this in the salle, shall we?" She turned, waving her hand to indicate they should continue walking just as if he had never tried to grab her. He set his teeth and clenched his hands together at the small of his back, walking beside her as if they strolled in a garden.

"I suggest we do some work and then you decide if you wish to accept me as teacher," she said mildly. "I am busy and do not really need another private student, but if you decide then I will grant you that." She looked at him sideways. "How damaged is my other self?"

He snorted. "Like a burnt out building. Nothing in her life but embroidery and power games that were going to get her executed one day."

"Attempting suicide by Emperor?"

He stopped and stared at her.

"Exactly. I never thought of that. Father ruined any chance of her doing anything but replacing m... m...mother."

"I'm astonished how close our two worlds are, even as they are so wildly different. I didn't find out I had a vocation for warrior priestess until our Ahrimaz was captured by the mad old Cylak."

"When was that?" He found himself curious. He held the door for her without thinking and she smiled and bowed herself in. He followed, bowing himself in, formally.

"About fifteen, maybe sixteen years ago."

Ahrimaz stopped. "That was when... that was when..."

"When your father killed my sister in that world and forced my other self to take her place. No wonder she's broken."

The river wasn't running through the salle today, shut off completely, leaving a dry stream bed in the middle of the room. She led him to a low table with cushions and a stack of paper. "Sit down, hmm? What shall I call you? I can just use your name but find I want to address you as student, or lad, but those are not appropriate and I refuse to call you Shit-Head."

Ahrimaz had a laugh startled out of him. "Um... Ahri? You and I are closer than almost anyone here."

"Ahri it is. Please sit." He settled. "I'd like you to mix the ink please."

"You don't have fountain—ah. It is the old brush."

"Indeed. Ink stone, brush. Paper."

He took up the stone, chipped a fragment off and ground it to powder. Tipped it into the ink well, and did it again as it was not enough. "Tedious."

She sat opposite him, hands open in her lap, watching. "Interesting that you know how much is enough, when you have pre-made ink for you at home."

He shrugged, added a bit of gum to the grind and then fluid from the eyedropper bottle. "I had a calligraphy teacher when I was a little boy." She nodded.

"Draw me a line," she said.

Ahrimaz stared at her, shrugged, dipped the brush and then realized he'd not laid out the paper. He set the brush down, grabbed the top sheet, and the brush rolled to spatter on the floor. He cursed under his breath. "Scorch."

"Breathe," she said.

He snapped his gaze up at her, suddenly enraged, drew breath harsh through his nose. He laid out the page, picked up the brush, smashed it into the ink pot and slashed a line across it. "There!"

"Good," she said. "Again."

"Why? This is stupid!" He laid down another ragged, splattered and blotched line. Then a third when she nodded. "I've never had a fight teacher have me do something so asinine!"

Ink spots spattered the page and his hands, made dark circles and smears on his pants and shirt. He was suddenly aware that he must have ink on his face.

"In your world do you have the book 'Sword of Ink'?" She asked.

"No. It sounds like witchcrafty stuff and was likely burnt or hidden in the forbidden archives."

"I see," she said and held out her hand for his damaged, mangled brush. She drew it softly through a cloth and laid out a sheet of paper on the floor by her knee. She dipped the brush and drew three graceful lines on the page. "Like so. Each line is a sword stroke." As she finished the last line the brush was empty of ink and she placed the poor battered thing in its rest. "Come run with me."

He rose to run the circuit around the salle with her, fuming at his own ink-spattered state and whining inside that her hands and clothes were clean. "Sword of Ink?" he asked, drawing up beside her.

"It's a good book," she said. "A little faster. I'm going to be careful today. Limyé advised me how much you could do."

"I can do it," he snarled, and stepped up his pace to match hers, hands clenched. "I can do more."

"Of course."

31

Am I Already Broken?

Damn and Scorch and Burn that woman! I'm so tired I can hardly pen this, my hand would be shaking with rage except I'm so... oh.

* * * * *

Ahrimaz set the pen down and looked down at his hands, turned them over, stared at the backs of them. They were still. Not shaking with fear or rage, or anything else, though he could have sworn he was enraged enough to be quivering.

Rutaçyen had asked him, merely, to keep up with her. She'd even hummed to herself, like one of the Yhom, as she took him through the dry boulder field, up the wall, down the wall, at speed, another circuit of the salle though this time she climbed the ladder wall and walked along the top of the framework that held the pells. Walked? Scorch, she danced along the beam—it was only as wide as her foot. His feet were wider and hung over the beam on either side and he found himself tensing as he stepped out to follow her. "Breathe," she'd said. "Relax. If you fall the floor is padded and you know how to fall without hurting yourself."

The rage had come on him then, red falling down over his eyes and when he came to himself found that in their running around, somehow, the cold winter river had been let into the room and she was on the other side of it. He'd apparently plunged in after her because the icy shock of water had brought him to himself and he was soaked through. How had she gotten across completely dry?

He picked up his pen once more.

* * * * *

There's some of that. Again. 'Sword of Ink' stuff. Too tired to wield a pen badly. I stopped and stood there like a fool, dripping and she'd risen and— jumped? Floated? Bounced? Walked on Scorching water?—and crossed to stand next to me.

"Drive the water out of your clothes," she'd said and I'd tried to steam myself dry by calling fire but she cut me off. "No. You've been trained that way. It hurts you. Be calm, sit," she folded down in front of me as if she had not a care in the world that I should attack her. By all evidence she DIDN'T care if I attacked her... so I sat down too.

"Like the fountain you accepted from Pelahir," she said.

"He TOLD you that?" I snapped at her, feeling sick in my guts that more people knew I was by nature a witch.

"Of course he did. I'm his teacher too."

"And Yolend."

"Of course. I wouldn't let three of the best dozen warriors in Inné go slack now, would I?"

"I don't know. I don't know you except as my horrid ghost mother."

"Indeed. Yes, Pel and Yolend and your other self were three of the best. There's another eight or nine in my classes that might one day reach their potential. Things have changed quite a bit since Ahrimaz insisted that we all learn Imaryan techniques."

I just snarled at her, set my cupped hands in my lap and... stared. I didn't know how to do this. "How do I ask HER to move the water?"

She smiled at me, the bitch. "The answer lies in your question. You don't command or demand. You ask."

The idea made me ill. I sat, for too long in wet clothes fighting with myself. I'm used to demanding, to commanding. But it makes sense, I suppose, that one really shouldn't try and command a God. Scorching hells, one doesn't even try and command a demon. One petitions. Hmmm. "I'd have to approach Her like a child approaches their parent and I'm not comfortable with that."

"Yes. How about this? Imagine you have a butterfly upon your hand and wish for more to come to you, do you flail your hands around, jump and yell?"

I snorted. "Of course not."

"So... call butterflies into your hands and ask that they take the form of the water in your clothes."

"That's just stupid."

"You can stay wet. Your choice."

I snorted at her and closed my eyes and pretended I was a little boy in the valley. Butterflies had once come to me, before the taste of blood on my hands drove all away except the carnivorous ones. I held my breath then breathed out over my hands and called the drops of water to me. A sheen of water glistened for a moment, as I cracked my eyelids to see, I was marginally drier. I clenched my hands and cursed myself.

Rutaçyen caught my clenched hands and shook them, and me. "Stop that. You are stopping yourself. Give yourself praise for having succeeded as much as you did."

"But I didn't do it all, or well! I should be beaten for such a bad attempt!"

"No. You should not. It's why you failed."

I just don't understand these people.

She drew her hand along my face, just as mama used to do when I was too young to be trained for war, patted my cheek and said. "Open up your heart, Ahri. It's all right. You're safe here in my salle."

I must have stared at her like a lunatic. Her face was open her eyes clear and calm, not twisted in terrifying rage. I don't remember having had a teacher or a tutor who didn't hate me. "Breathe."

She cupped her hands under mine and they… went soft somehow. Gentle. And the water in my clothes and hair ran to her and my hands like they were scurrying to safety. "There," she said. "Like that." She didn't drop my hands. When she let go it was as though she still held me, held me firm against the shrieking rage beating in the back of my head.

"I'd… like to be your student," I stammered, flinched back and waited for her to drop her support of me, waited for the laughter, the betrayal. I was such a dupe, to actually ask…

"I'd be happy to be your teacher. I will talk with Limyé about how I can help, as well."

She rose, as graceful and as silent, bowed to me and left me alone in the salle, the room where I had spent so much of my childhood, being broken and remade into a warrior. This salle… might not break me. Or I am already broken. I don't know.

32

Do You Want It Back?

IN ONE CORNER OF THE ROOM WITH THE HOT POOL there was a glass door to outside. It was strange enough that Ahrimaz didn't even see it, to begin with, taking it as a sealed window, made up of the tiny, hand sized pieces of glass that this Inné thought was the height of technology. One couldn't see out of it really and this House of Gold was actually part of Innéthel itself instead of being isolated from the mob.

Heylia had padded into the cell this morning, bunted the door open and then waited for Ahrimaz to follow her as if she somehow knew that he couldn't make himself go outside.

"Yes, yes, I'm coming, cat," he grumbled. She led him to that door and bunted at it with her head, meowing. "You want out? Why me? Why here? You could just have had someone else let you out."

He had to hunt for a moment to find the latch and it opened with a click, popping open to let a billow of steam rush out into the snow beyond as Heylia shoved her nose and head and the rest of her enormous self outside. He couldn't see anything but steam for the longest moment as he stepped after her, the threshold mercifully blurred, not even noticing that he was barefoot.

The slate under his feet just felt cool and barely damp to him and he left a slow trail of black footprints as he went. Heylia bounded off into the trees and Ahrimaz paused, looking around.

The door had sighed shut behind him but there was still steam, or fog, or snow in the air, he wasn't sure. Everything was either white or stark black, the trees swimming out of the fog like iron bars, but so spread apart that it seemed as though they were holding the white sky away from the white ground.

He sat down in the snow for a moment and just revelled in the silence. It was calm. The overheated rage that poured on him his whole life just seemingly went away, evaporated into still and white and cool. His hands opened softly and water ran from all around him into his cupped palms. His skin was almost shockingly hot when he drank.

He found himself looking into the eyes of a little girl sitting across from him as his hands came down and startled backwards into the snow, his equanimity shattered and he realized how wet and cold he was, lying in the snow. "Who the scorch are YOU!" he snapped, scrambling up into stance, finding that his feet slipped on the ice under the snow.

She had long, long black hair and white skin that glowed almost as white as the snow around them. Her eyes were black and her lips were the only bright red splotch all around them, like blood on snow and he found himself terrified, gasping, his hands up, shaking.

"You don't need to be so scared," she said. "I'm just the horrid darkness that's lived inside you since your father killed your mother."

"W...w...w.." he couldn't speak.

She held up a double handful of snow and it disintegrated into a pool of blood in her hands. "It was the only way you could survive."

"You're evil!" He snapped and scrambled further away from her.

"How did you survive after you tortured Kinourae?"

"B... bbb....by enjoying it!" She nodded. In her hands, the pool of blood began to coalesce and move, a regular motion like a heart beating.

"Father required... father required..."

"He made you do it. He tried to prove to you that you had no heart."

"Exactly!" He straightened, brushed his hands down over his clothes as if to wipe the memory off himself along with clots of snow and twigs and dirt.

"And what did Kinourae say to you, even as you harmed him?" She held a beating heart in her hands.

Ahrimaz flung his hands up over his face. "No. You cannot make me remember."

"You're right, I cannot. But you might. Should you choose to." He sank to his knees, the wind whipping around him where he knelt, hiding everything but the girl, snow and cold, an unfeeling ache in his chest where the ice had formed that let him live, even as he broke his own heart.

Ahrimaz gulped and felt how hot his tears were. "He... said... I love you still."

She held out the beating heart to him. "Do you want it back? He's kept it for you, all these years."

He stared at her, horrified. "That..."

"... is your heart, yes. I've helped him keep it for you."

As she spoke she grew from a tiny girl into a grown woman and then became a white tiger, with the beating heart held suspended between its fangs.

"I... can't." His hands crossed over his aching chest and his head bowed until he was wound into a crouched knot in the snow.

"Brother?" A hand touched his shoulder and he snapped up to stare into Arnziel's concerned eyes.

He flung his head back and screamed in agony. "Why will you people not understand that I am not him? Why do you insist on loving me as though I'm HIM!"

He found himself helplessly gathered up into his youngest brother's arms and onto his lap, surrounded by Aeono's heavenly fire in answer to the urgently sung prayer. "Father Aeono, help us, give us surcease from the Lady's winter."

33

Dry Weeping

SCORCHING, FLAMING, BLAMING, CHARRED UP THE ASS, ASH HOLE. Everything just went grey and when I came to myself once more I found that I was in the bed, naked, buried in feathers, hands wrapped in warm towels and someone massaging my feet.

I thought it was a dream at first and just groaned with pleasure. "Ah, you're awake," my little brother... no, HIS little brother said. He was the one working on my feet with beeswax that was almost hot. "You really shouldn't do that, Ahri, before you know how to petition the Goddess. You could lose fingers and toes that way."

"Arnziel." I tugged at my foot in his hand and he didn't let go immediately.

"Wait. I'll wrap your feet up or you'll get wax all over the bed." He whipped a Rigan hard cotton towel around my foot and then a fuzzy one, so, as I struggled up onto my elbows I realized all four of my limbs were similarly swaddled.

I stared down at the wads of white at the ends of my limbs. "I was outside. Heylia took me outside."

"Ah." He nodded as if that made any kind of sense. "Then she came and got me, so that you wouldn't hurt yourself. Harsh teacher that cat. But she doesn't hurt any of her kittens."

He looked like Arnziel. He sounded like Arnziel, but here he wasn't the twitching little fop who would scream in shock if you suggested he wear shoes without satin stockings or puce with chartreuse. He wasn't a habitual drunk either; you could see it. His eyes were clear, not yellowed. His skin was clear, he didn't stink like a drunk sweating the noisome mess out of his skin every day. He wore Aeono's yellow robe, with the flames embroidered all over it, as if he was comfortable wearing it. *My* little brother always wore religious robes like they were about to set him on fire, itching at him.

He just sat, watching me, calm as Rutaçyen. I voiced my horrid suspicion. "You train with HER too, don't you?"

Arnziel just laughed. "No, shadow brother. I fence well enough to honour Aeono. I'm not a hot spur, or a hot shot like you and your shadow."

"You have carbines, here?" I addressed his 'hot-shot' comment. "I've only seen archaic swords and bare-handed. Do you have cannon? Do you even NEED cannon?"

"Yes," he said. "Aeono provides. Ahrimaz only used cannon once in the Unification war and that was to bring down the Cylak's passes, to force the man to fight or surrender. Mostly the Riga… from Riga Feren… mount two pounders on their deep sea ships to protect them from ravening packs of Tauzahn (I translated that in my head, 'Thousand Teeth' or 'Teeth Teeth Teeth'.)

"How very enlightened of you." I started prying at the edges of the cooling wax towels, wanting my hands free. "I used my cannon to bring down the Yhom's Singing Palace."

He blinked and looked sad.

"I'm sorry to hear that."

"It still sings when the wind blows," I said shortly. "Which is always up there. Only now it sings grief. You can't make it shut up, even when it's in pieces."

"I'm hoping that my brother will be able to help or save your brother in that world," he said quietly. "I've been having prophetic dreams about him."

"Yes and what's this about you being a priest? I mean a REAL priest?" He took hold of the wax on my hands and the towels, peeled them off in a single, smooth block. I rubbed my fingers together, feeling the slick waxiness that I wiped on the cloth he gave me before moving back down to free my feet. He shrugged. "I am a priest. Aeono spoke to me—"

I cut him off.

"Let me guess, when you were around nine?"

"Yes, in fact. I was hearing God so loudly around that time I was setting things on fire."

"Oh Scorch." A corner of his mouth quirked.

"Scorch indeed." He bundled the hardened towels into a basket before settling down cross legged on the floor next to me and I suddenly felt like we were illicitly sharing a late night snack on my bed, like two little boys. "Limyé was saying that you think you are weeping all the time."

"I have been," I snapped. "My face is always wet here. I'm surprised my skin isn't raw." The internal ocean storm of my tears threw waves at my barricades, hissing, breaking, driven high by all these people poking at me.

"That's interesting," he said and unfolded one of his long, lanky arms up, reaching to snag the tea pot to pour. "From our perspective you've been dry weeping. We haven't seen you shed a single tear."

34

Not a Rotting Man

I PAUSED IN THE ACT OF HOLDING OUT MY TEA CUP FOR HIM TO FILL, but it wasn't long enough to show. I sipped the horrible fruity grassy tisane and raised an eyebrow at him. "I've been saying that you're all mad this whole time. But I would never accuse you of being blind."

He nodded. "How are the scars?" He nodded at my forearms, hidden safely under my sleeves. "Fine!" I snapped at him, switched hands and thrust out the arm for him to see. "SEE?" It was a dark patch of skin, roughened and raised, a thick callus.

"And the other one?" He sipped at his own tea, not looking at me.

"You in this world are right drowning bastards, did you know that?" I finished my tea and he filled it again.

"Yes, so I understand." He looked into my face in a way that Arn hadn't, for years. It was like part of me began filling up again, after being burned dry. "Did you want to hear about what I've been dreaming about your brother?"

"Of course I do!"

He laughed but didn't explain what was so funny. "He's going to be doing a spirit journey in your world… he's fighting the Goddess to try and get to the God."

I was startled. I wasn't used to priests just talking about the Divine without unctuousness, or carelessness. He just… meant it. They were real to him. I couldn't get the image of a white tiger, holding my beating heart in – her – its fangs. That little girl. That was the voice I dreamed speaking to me. Lyrian.

"That doesn't sound very sensible," I said and put the cup upside down on the desk so he wouldn't refill it.

"He's actually fighting his own fear. She's there, but truly She's not the one he's fighting."

"And why would he have to fight through to Aeono, anyway?"

"Because He's dying."

"What? No. No. No. Gods don't exist anyway. How can a God die?"

He sipped his tea. "Out of your own mouth, Ahri." He shook his head. "We still believe, but when the whole other world that you are from questions His existence because everyone knows that priests are all false anyway..."

"But the God we attacked was Her not Him! His worship is spread all over the same area as your Coalition!"

"Yes. And anyone who dares whisper a prayer to Her in the dark believes far more strongly than your Highest Priest."

I bolted up to my feet, hissed as my newly tender skin scraped on the rough floor. "How do you know all this? How can you know all this? This is all scorching horse shit!"

"You are here and our Ahrimaz is not," he said gently. "There was a path ripped into our worlds and it seems that when you were exchanged there was created a conduit where prayers can travel back and forth. And dreams." His smile was so like mother's that my breath just froze in my throat. "I'm very glad that my other self isn't dying of slow alcohol poisoning any longer."

Not a loose-lipped stinking, horridly rotting from the inside man anymore? He wasn't drinking? Aeono bless me. "Its about time that that scorching dipshit did something right!"

Had I said that out loud? I put my hands up to my eyes. "Scorching hells, Arn. You're wrong about tears, see?" I hold my wet fingers out to him.

He nods, looking solemn and holds up a silvered hand mirror so that I can see the bloody tracks down my cheeks. I'm not weeping. I'm bleeding where tears should be.

35
You'll Not Exsanguinate

"NO. NO. NO. That's not possible. It's a phantasm of an overheated brain." Ahrimaz stared down at his reddened fingertips. "I was weeping. I am weeping. As a man does."

Arnziel reached up and gently pressed a cloth to Ahrimaz's face and it came away imprinted with a bloody image.

"You're sweating blood too. From my perspective it is your reaction to developing an empathic understanding that your monster father stamped on in you. It will be all right. You aren't bleeding enough to exsanguinate."

"That's reassuring," Ahrimaz snapped, staring in horror at the cloth. "It looks like the imprint after Summer Solstice."

"Imprint?"

"You don't do that? After the fight through the fires I take off my helmet as they carry the endarkened foe away... a few years ago it was Arnziel who played that part. I nearly lost it and almost took his head off with those antique great swords... anyway. Once the helmet comes off I drink the 'Cup of the Sun' and speak prophecy and burst into a bloody sweat. Highest Priest takes my bloody face image just as you just did. The priesthood keeps them."

"Cup of the Sun? Is that a full wine glass? Enough to make you bleed like this? Warm and Blessed Aeono how in Heaven's name have you not killed yourself? How long does it take for you to recover from that?"

Ahrimaz shrugged. "If I pray and take on the Sun sickness I can burn it out of me in a few days... sometimes a week... then I have to recover from feeling I've scorched my insides."

"You have. Dear and Blessed Aeono. May I tell Limyé?"

Ahrimaz shrugged and roughly scrubbed his face dry, not looking at the smears of read on the white cloth. "Don't see why not. I AM his patient."

Arnziel tilted his head to one side, the fire-beads woven into his hair clicking. Ahrimaz hadn't noticed them before and stared. *It can't be.* "I expect that you and he and several other of his helpers will have an intense session with his dreaming remedies."

"Probably." Ahrimaz didn't know if he wanted more of those sessions where Limyé's nostrums blurred the line between reality and dreaming and were astonishingly effective at uprooting pain and rage in his head and heart that he had thought would never shift. "Everyone said you were an Aeono priest but no one ever said that you were second Highest!"

"Really? I thought someone did. Probably when you were ranting about how much of a... hmmm..." he laid a finger thoughtfully against his lips before quoting, "...gutless, spineless, pathetic, listless, apathetic, lazy, gormless, dim, stinking, drunken, asinine, vile, scorchless, lack-witted, moronic, cretinous, drool-lipped, loose-tongued—"

Ahrimaz cut him off. "Yes, yes, you can repeat from memory perfectly everything I believed about my brother, thus proving that you are none of those things. You needn't defend yourself to *me*."

"You killed your younger brothers, did you not?" He didn't look as though he was accusing at all. "and the old man, all to protect yourself."

"Yes," Ahrimaz snapped, shortly.

"And your Arnziel is still alive by being the hopeless ass that no one will confide in if they are plotting against you?"

"Y...essss." Ahri sat up straighter and dropped the bloody rag upon the floor. "I'm starting to see."

"How hard did he have to work to make you believe he was that stupid?"

"Not... that hard. Very smart, Arnziel. If I get home I'll just have to kill him because I can't trust him anymore."

"Not what I had in mind. It seems to me that he's willing to be left alone. Probably without trying to disgust you into pushing him further away."

"I... have to think about this. Thank you for the books, by the way." There were a new stack upon the desk.

"You're welcome."

"Not bloody scorching likely," Ahrimaz snapped but it was half-hearted. He picked up his tea cup and held it out to Arnziel. "Why don't you pour and we can talk about what that idiot Arouet d'Rig-Un wrote in 'Separation of Church and State'.

Arnziel poured and set the pot down. "Not an idiot, certainly. But..."

36

The Clockworks and Explosives Set

THE RUMBLE OF THE BALES OF PAPER BEING LOADED INTO THEIR STORAGE bay was a barely audible thunder in the Coalition News's main office, but the smell of ink and hot lead and fixatives and colours all wafted up from below as if it were a chimney.

Teel James leaned back on his spring chair, wheels squeaking as he propped his heels on the desk. He was a very tall man with a mass of curly salt and pepper hair that cascaded almost to the floor as he leaned back. His waistcoat was an astonishing blue Rigan silk, for all that it was a decade out of fashion, and stained with years of ink. His stockings appeared to be cream coloured though he knew that they'd begun their lives as pristine white, and his red-heeled shoes were only slightly down at the heel. His great coat hung sloppily tossed over the coat rack over his small sword. He flipped the next page in his notebook and addressed his colleagues, Marcedi and Dauf.

"Something stinks up at the House of the Hand," he said. "The whole family has been very tight lipped on Ahrimaz's 'illness' and the House has all but unanimously voted in Ahriminash."

"I received a note from Yolend, saying that Ahrimaz has become violent and needed to be restrained to keep from hurting people," Marcedi said. She was originally from Yhom and had come with the First Wife when she'd married Ahrimaz. Her black hair was kinked and knotted into a headscarf to keep out of her way as she tracked down stories.

"Violent," Dauf said. He was the most average of the three main rédacteurs of the News. His hair was brown and cut short, he had a bit of a paunch and his waistcoat was a burgundy brocade over brown shirt and pantaloons, though his stockings were brown and white striped. "That's not like him."

"The last shift of staff said it was true." Teel said, running a hand through his hair. "They did lock him in a basement in the fall. But nothing really since then."

"I heard a rumour that THE warmaster was teaching him, though how that could be if he were violent, I don't get," Marcedi sniffed.

A tap on the door brought their heads around, all three to see one of the younger writers for the broadsheet standing with papers in his hands, his quill thrust into his hair. "Um Mr. James, sir?"

"What?"

"We just got a note addressed to the Writers and Inventors about a new kind of pen that doesn't need to be dipped, sir."

Teel waved. "And you figure you need to interrupt us, you pup?"

It's from Ahrimaz Kenaçyen, sir."

Marcedi lips pursed in a soundless whistle as the boy went on. "There's a plan for a stove that burns fifty times more efficiently than our fireplaces, a commentary on a breech-loading fire-arm instead of a muzzle-loader, a 'speculation' on improving cannon…" He held a stack of pages in his hands. Teel held out his hand and gestured imperiously with his fingertips.

"You did right. Give me that!" The boy handed his wad of papers over and fled. Teel began flipping through the stack and then broke it into three parts, handing them off to the other two. There was a silence as they flipped through and read here and there as their eyes were caught by diagrams or by turns of phrase.

"Huh," Dauf said at last, staring at his section of papers. "If Ahrimaz has gone crazy then he's gone crazy like a fox. These are brilliant! These are going to change our world!"

"Well then!" Teel let his heels thump to the floor. "I'm obviously going to have to pay him a visit!"

"Not just you," Marcedi said archly. "I'm going along…"

"Me too!" Dauf said. "We all three need to find out what's going on here. I was just going to say that I needed to send a junior over to Aeono's temple and speak to the Second Most High about his brother. So I'll do that. When are we going to speak to our madman in the cellar?"

"Tomorrow," Teel said. "That will give us time to have copies of these made and to read through them ourselves. The Inventors pages will have a field day with these!" He yanked open the door, calling down the hall to his science editor.

"Mal! Get your adorable ass in here! We've got an exclusive for the Clockwork and Explosives Set! Breaking news even!"

37

Go Away. Leave Me Alone to Quietly Starve to Death.

LIMYÉ LOOKED AT THE BREAKFAST TRAY, untouched on the desk, and the lunch tray in his hands. Then he looked over at the lump under the featherbed.

Heylia lay mostly sprawled over the body in the bed, and his hand hung out from underneath to rest on Sure's head. When the dog raised her head to look at the Imaryan, Ahrimaz's hand slid off to hang behind where the dog lay.

"Ahrimaz." Limyé called. There was no answer, no response. The Imaryan nudged the cell door open with his foot, set the second tray next to the first and went over to check. Sure scrambled up to greet the healer and Heylia raised her head, her purr heavy and echoing. Ahrimaz's pulse beat strong and sure under his fingertips and Limyé tucked it back under the edge of the feather quilt.

"Leave me alone." Ahrimaz's voice rustled out from under the quilt and fell on the floor as if it were too heavy. "Just. Just go away."

"It is all right that you have no energy," Limyé said, quietly. He pushed his hands under Heylia and began slowly massaging Ahrimaz's shoulders where he lay face down. "You have no demands on you."

Again the words dragged out. "That's the problem. I used my pain and my rage to keep going. I was necessary for the Empire to continue. Now my 'oh so beloved half' has his stinking, ash hands on it and is 'SAVING' it." "Ahriminash has been voted in. I am not useful here. No one would care if I ceased drawing breath. I'm a useless waste of skin and I'm taking up everyone's time and energy looking after me. I just want to stop. I just want it to stop hurting." But he didn't throw off Limyé's gentle hands.

"In the other world you would have run to the end of your rage and your strength and died young to get away from the pain," the healer said. "Here you can re-learn how to live without burning hot or burning out. You are allowed to live without the fire that has been harrowing you your entire life."

"There's nothing but ashes left anyway. I've got no fuel left."

Limyé nodded and didn't answer, letting his hands work down Ahrimaz's ribs and up along his shoulder blades. "Your 'stabbed in the back' spots aren't so tight anymore," he said.

"Eh?" It was just an inquiring grunt.

"Right between your shoulder blades, where your spine is not protected by anything but muscle. When warriors train or fight, they tighten up there. Not just warriors, though. Most people. Whenever they are in a conflict of any kind. Between partners, between parents and children, between working partners... everyone tightens up there, raises the shoulders, harden all around the torso as if preparing for a physical assault. Stabbed in the back spots."

"Ah."

Heylia stretched up to her paws, arched her back and kneaded all down Ahrimaz's back, below where Limyé's hands worked, stomped down Ahri's legs before hopping off onto the floor, nose raised toward the congealed bacon on the breakfast tray. "No, cat, that is Ahrimaz's food to give or eat as he chooses," the healer chided.

"She can have it. I don't want it." But Ahrimaz finally stirred away from lying on his belly and Limyé let him up. He rolled around and sat, curled into the hollow he'd worked into the feather mattress, rope supports creaking. "Give her and Sure the bacon. Sure will want the egg too since it is cold."

"You still care for things," Limyé said as he shared out the ruins of breakfast. When he came back there was a steaming cup of malak in his hand and he held it out. Ahrimaz hesitated but took it almost more automatically than with any forethought.

"No. I don't. I'm a monster, remember?"

"We disagree with you." Limyé said mildly and settled onto the chair by the bed.

Ahrimaz drained the cup, shuddered and set it down with a sharp 'crack'. "There. I've consumed something. Are you happy?" He put his head down on his knees.

"I'm glad that you have consumed something. There was a bit of cream in that. And it is a stimulant so you might find a bit of energy there. Maybe enough to disagree with me, when I tell you that you have been taught to be a monster and no longer need to be one."

Ahrimaz turned his head sideways to stare at Limyé. "Why don't you just leave me alone to starve to death quietly?"

"Because I'm your healer and you are my patient. And I'm getting an amazing amount of information for my book… perhaps multiple books on the difference between nature and nurture in nearly identical subjects."

Ahri snorted a laugh and turned his head back down so his forehead was on his knees. "Of course, it's all self interest. Not concern or care for me at all!" The sarcasm was thick enough to cut. This time it was Sure who bounced up on the bed and flung herself into Ahrimaz's knees. "Go away, dog," he said, but there was no heat behind it at all. "Just all of you, go away."

There was a tap at the door and one of the house pages peeked in. "Limyé? Sir?" Since the guards had gone away, the pages had taken over serving Ahrimaz but they only called him by the honorific, since they couldn't apparently make themselves call him Ahrimaz.

"Yes, Daryl?" Limyé answered him.

"There's a bunch of raconteurs to see the sir, Limyé. The three owners of the Coalition News."

Limyé nodded and Ahrimaz just melted back down under the feather bed, moaning. "Oh, Aeono, scorch no. No. No!"

"I take it you sent your wad of papers down to the newspapers?" Limyé wasn't so crass as to smile at Ahrimaz but there was some amusement in his voice.

"I did. Just tell them all to go away!" Ahrimaz groaned.

"Sir, they say they can wait until you're ready to speak to them. And your honourable almost father said he would come to be with you when you speak to them."

"Almost father. Almost mother. And raconteurs. Scorch me up the anus with a red-hot, hooked climbing pole." He rolled over and Sure rode the wave of his motion, grunting, then wiggled up to where he wrapped his arms around the dog, clutching her to his chest. His eyes looked lost and tired. "Limyé… please. Please."

"I will speak to them. We can arrange for their visit another day, when you are stronger."

38

As Peculiar as Ahrimaz

THE THREE RACONTEURS SAT QUIETLY IN THE FORMER HAND'S OFFICE, notebooks filled with scribbled words, confusion on their faces.

Ahrimiar the Elder sat quietly, toying with the handle of his cup as they sat. Limyé was cross-legged upon the carpet, his braid coiling down behind him, sturdy brown fingers folded peacefully in his lap.

The fire in the fireplace crackled and then puffed a faint cloud of smoke up to hang against the painted ceiling, the candle lanterns fighting to bring more light to the room on this dim, grey day.

The world outside seemed faint and very far away, the distant sounds of the House market muffled in the winter snow, the High Temple bells chiming softly in the distance as their carillons spoke the evening song to each other across the river.

M'ser James," Ahrimiar said quietly. "I understand that it is incredible and fantastic and utterly impossible. This is why we have all our Celebrants researching if anything has happened like this in all our recorded and oral history, back to when we were a wandering tribe. So far, nothing. But the Two Gods have a history of speaking to us, showing us what we can only call miracles."

"But. But he's not Ahrimaz? Our Ahrimaz? Please Eminence repeat this. You are known for having some Aporrheitos skill and can tell the absolute truth from lies." "His name is Ahrimaz, he looks and sounds like your son, he has many similar scars, except for the brand that marks him as the Hand of the people though different, yet he is not the same man?"

"This is the best explanation we have been able to surmise, pieced together from all the family's observations and from Ahrimaz's own mouth.

This Ahrimaz woke up in the bed where our boy went to sleep the night before. He is not the same man. He was, what many Innéans would call insane, because he was and still is Emperor of the Owned Lands of Inné, down to his bones."

"That's... incredible," Marcedi said. "And you admit to locking him up, in a panic, and he then threatened to kill you all?"

"Exactly. To the best of our understanding, we think that our Ahrimaz is in the other world... where he is playing the part of Emperor. All we have to go on is the word of this Ahrimaz, and the dreams of our Seers and Celebrants, including Ahrimaz's brother. The family healer," he nodded at Limyé, "has taken him on as a patient, even though he has been violent more than once. Our war master is assisting, since it seems to us, that he might be brought to sanity."

"Will he sue you for unlawful restraint?" Dauf asked. "Why are you coming out with this now?"

"And is that why he just sent our inventors a stack of machine designs and technological miracles? They are from this invisible, untouchable Empire?" Teel leaned forward as he asked, scribbling in his notebook. He licked the pencil, paused and looked at it. "I mean even something so simple as a pen with a reservoir of ink in it?"

"He may, though it has not occurred to him yet that he might sue the family, but we are supporting him, because, for all intents and purposes he IS our son. We accept him as such." Ahrimaz sighed. "At first we were careful of him because we hoped that this... this... switch... might be undone, though that has not happened as yet. One could say that we are forced to consider that this circumstance is permanent and that *this* Ahrimaz is our boy for good; thus our current honesty to the people of Inné."

"When can we speak to him?"

Limyé spoke up. "He is currently in a very vulnerable state in his healing. His rages are mostly under his control at the moment and we shall let you interview him, when he deems himself able to bear your questions, at his own recognizance."

"So he's of sound mind?"

"Yes, if you consider that he believes he owns everyone around him."

Dauf whistled slightly then looked chagrined. "Excuse me, Eminence."

"I am not offended, M'ser."

"Have any of the other countries of the Coalition been notified?"

"No. They only know that Ahrimaz has been ill and that his brother Ahriminash has been established as the Indefinite Ancillar Hand."

Teel leaned back and raised an eyebrow at Marcedi. She had an in with the First Lady. She nodded slightly. "Our inventors are gibbering and foaming at some of the things he's diagramed. Does he intend to continue releasing such things? Inné would certainly vote him a stipend just for this contribution to the society."

"I will make sure he understands that. He doesn't realize how valuable these ideas are. Lyrian bless, he nearly gave himself frostbite in the snow the other day, because he cannot pray to Her for help."

"He can't?" That was a startled exclamation from Marcedi. "Ahrimaz was known for how the Lady answered his prayers. Why can this Ahrimaz not pray to Her?"

"In his world there is no Goddess. They have made her a Demon and water-burn all who cleave to Her as witches."

"Lyrian bless!" The words burst out of Teel's mouth and he placed his fingers over his lips, chagrined at his own outburst. "That is truly hideous."

"And it is the world that this Ahrimaz is from. He was forced to manifest Aeono's fire, and only that, from a very young age and it hurt him terribly."

"Eminence, how are you and the family feeling about all this?" Ahrimiar the Elder raised a gently inquisitive eyebrow at Marcedi and her cheeks darkened as she blushed.

"I'm not sure, M'ser," he said to her. "We've never had a peculiar child before. At least not anyone more peculiar than my Ahrimaz."

39 Even Without Elephants

SCORCHING SON OF A BITCH BASTARD found me standing on the threshold of the cell. Unable to make myself go outside. By myself.

Pelahir set his shoulder against the hall doorframe and crossed his arms but didn't say anything. Ahrimaz felt as though he chewed and swallowed live coals but wasn't going to let *him* see his weakness. He turned away from the door as if he'd just been thinking of what to write next, set his pen down, pulled up a smile on his face and stepped out. "Let's spar, shall we?"

"Certainly," he said and smiled back. "You know that you *can* leave if you want to?" *Scorch him.*

"Of course. Wenhiffar told me so. She also mentioned that there are hordes of raconteurs waiting in the outer rooms of the House, eating our food, writing their stories here rather than in the Broadsheets' offices. How many broadsheets' and newspapers and book printers do you *have?"*

"The Innéans have the five big presses... three Broadsheet and two Universities'. Wealthy people who have almost unlimited credit might have a personal printing machine that most of their street or district use. There is a childrens' press. Each Riga City has one. The Yhom have two." He grinned. "Someone is trying to come up with one that can be packed on a reindeer."

Ahrimaz just shook his head and fell in beside Pelahir and they strolled up to the salle as though they were the best of friends. Ahrimaz's hands itched with the need to lay them on the man, clutch him, hold him, hurt him, love him. He wasn't quite sure which was the strongest impulse and to hide his twitchy fingers knotted them tight in the small of his back, as if he sauntered along a folly walk.

Out of the corner of his eye he caught Pel's glance and squeezed his eyes shut for a moment. "You're attracted to me and Yolend both," the Cylak said quietly. "It's all right. Neither of us is going to jump on you, hold you down and ravish you."

"You mean like I did your counterparts in my world?" Ahrimaz asked harshly. "The week before I woke up here I'd just started torturing you and had given Yolend a black eye. Shashi, poor blighted thing, would run screaming from me if I came into the room and startled her."

"Just as you say 'I am not him,'" we can say 'we are not them,'" Pel responded and held the door of the salle, the disrobing antechamber, open for Ahrimaz with a courtly wave of his hand. "Yolend would kick your ass if you tried to lay a wrong hand on her."

"And you as well." Ahrimaz said. "And Shashi would say something that would likely throw me on the ground wailing." He smiled, more than a little grimly. "That is surprisingly reassuring. However I got here, I got put in a place where not only am I not allowed to harm anyone else, I'm not *able* to harm anyone else."

Pelahir hung his brocade coat and waistcoat on a hook by the door. It was the first time Ahrimaz had actually seen him in full Innéan court garb rather than his own country's leathers and feathers. "What's the occasion?"

"You've forgotten, haven't you?"

"Forgotten what? And why is the salle so ashing dark?" He stepped from the disrobing room into the dim salle and just had time to gasp before a flint struck in the dark and a candle flared. Then a dozen candles.

"A small surprise, you Shithead," Pel said from behind him as he gaped at brothers, wife, lover, father, mother, healer, teacher... he wrapped his hands around his head and sank to his knees in silence... his children all held candles illuminating their faces. "You've forgotten your own hoofless birthday."

Limyé handed off his candle to be placed in the great candelabra with the others and Arnziel cranked it up, creaking, swaying and flickering to light the room from above. The healer wrapped his arm around Ahrimaz's back where he crouched. His hands came down off his head and grabbed onto the floor as if his fingers were claws and his head swivelled back and forth like a bewildered war cat, as he took in the feast spread on low tables in the middle of the salle and the training river set as a trickle of gentle noise behind it all. "Breathe," Limyé said softly, holding a censer under Ahrimaz's nose. "Breathe in calm and peace. Everyone here is of good will toward you. No one blames you for anything."

"They can't love me. That's not allowed," Ahrimaz rasped but the sweet smoke fuddled his senses, and everything was taking on a rosy tint. Edges were softening. "I'm not him."

Limyé offered him a sugar chip and he took it, automatically.

"We know that. But we are allowed to like you." Ahrimaz was vaguely aware that Pel had taken hold of his elbow and he and Limyé were steering him like an errant paper balloon to tether him to a cushion at the main table.

Everything seemed so... nice. So calm. The children, giggling, didn't enrage him. It was funny and he began to giggle himself. "You've drugged me!" It was so funny. He wouldn't be able to bear it if he weren't floating on the fuzziness of the drug. The little girl he'd met in the snow danced around the outside of the room, all black and white and red, carrying his beating heart in her hands, but she was smiling and she was being careful with it. He couldn't help smiling. It was so beautiful.

He could feel the pain he lived with, every day, the jagged wounds and pus-filled bags of filth in his head and in his heart, but it no longer seemed so immediate. Someone handed him a plate of food that he stared at for what seemed like forever. "My favourites!"

"And there will be petit-fours for after the meal," Wenhiffar said. "You're not my son but you have his tastes, it seems."

"I'm not supposed to indulge myself like that... like this... this is for babies." But he gathered up a butter-crust meat pie and bit into it, finding that it had venison and red wine gravy. He couldn't keep talking with his mouth full so she... and everyone else just kept on talking. It was so... pleasant.

"Babies generally get it right. It's grownups that mess up their heads," Rutaçyen said, waving a blue-painted rattle toy over the baby's head. She had the new baby in her lap.

Ahrimaz just gazed at her, sitting next to her twin, with the child and he couldn't howl, he didn't want to weep. It was beautiful. The memories of the maggot-ridden dungeon faded then faded again like a painting hit by flood and dried in Aeono's sun. This just felt good.

People had the new broadsheets out and were reading bits to each other, Ahrimiar the younger, the Heir, his alternate's boy, finger tracking along the line bravely read out ".. the family says that this man is their son, for as long as he is in our world."

"And so it is," Ahrimiar the Elder said. "Happy birthday, Ahrimaz, my other son." And that didn't hurt either. He wasn't even afraid of the old man, when he was in this state.

"I should be angry that you drugged me," he said dreamily to Limyé, "but this is helping. It's letting me remember how to feel good again."

The girl with his heart in her hands smiled and held her hands up over her head. Ahrimaz suddenly realized that no one else, save Arnziel, could see her. He caught Arnziel gazing at her with astonishment.

The blood in her hands poured down over her and flowed away in the river, while his heart hovered there, under one of the little waterfalls, being cleansed and purified. He took a deep breath and saw it begin to glow, just slightly, while in his chest he felt an easement as if a whip lesion had kindly, tenderly given way to whole flesh and unmarked skin.

He took another bite of his pie, licked the gravy running down his hand and smiled at Arnziel's slightly stunned look. "I think this is going to be the best birthday party I've ever had, even without elephants."

40

An Alien Creature Far From Home

"WHAT'S AN ELEPHANT?" That was Ahrizael, crown prince, a bit younger than Ahrimiar. He had a huge glass of blueberry juice in one hand and a deep fried cebolla, dropping crumbs, in the other.

"A tribe of creatures... not human... from so far west you couldn't see their lands if you stood on a promontory and stared through a seeing glass..." Ahrimaz turned aside to Yolend who was closest. "Do you *have* seeing glasses?" Upon her shrug he turned back to the little boy. "... and stared as hard as you could, you'd not see it. Elephants have a hand in the middle of their faces, on the end of a long, long grey nose, and two long, long teeth on either side of their mouths, pointing up, not down, like war cats. Two of their ruler's youngsters came with a Rigan ship to visit our lands and I really, really wanted to keep them."

"Why didn't you?"

"Well, they were young, right? And their ruler wanted them back. The Rigan captain assured me that these two were small. They grow big enough to reach the chandelier up there without trying hard. I didn't want to start a war with creatures that big." Ahrizael's eyes grew very round, trying to imagine a creature that big wanting to fight. "So one of them... his name was Jagunjagun, gave me a ride on his neck, around Innéthel. It was..." he paused, then shrugged. "...amazing." He bit into his pie, finishing it up in three bites.

"He still writes to me, or did, now and then. Not in Innéan, but in picture inks that they press onto a dried-leaf paper."

Pel was staring at him suspiciously. "Elephants."

"I *swear*, it's as I said. Though it could have been the monkey-man—

named Ologbon—who came with them who spoke ten languages who might have been translating for them, who—in truth might be the intelligence behind them—writing. Personally I thought they were about as smart as Sure here." Ahrimaz offered his gravy-sticky hand to the dog to be licked clean. "Their 'translator' was so dark that he makes Yhom and Imaryans look sickly pale."

"It sounds terribly un-aggressive for you," Yolend said and leaned on one elbow to sip her wine. "Especially if they couldn't get word back to their people."

"I thought of it. I considered keeping them and sending word that they'd died."

"Why didn't you?"

"I... don't recall." Ahrimaz stared down into his juice. The older of the two elephants had been injured by some crazy hill people bowing to neither Cylak or Inné, and even his physician hadn't been able to help. "I sat with Jagunjagun's friend while they were in Inné... actually heading for Riga-Dham to take ship and go home." Didara had been bigger than Jagunjagun and had laid down in the emptied stable, on the straw, with a groan and a rumble that had shaken him to his hands and knees. He'd known, somehow, that she was grateful for the place to rest and he'd sat, ignoring politics, ignoring everything but sitting in the crook of her foot, just under her chin, staring into her enormous eye with eyelashes as long as his fingers as she'd wept in relief, and then later in pain.

"My physician, Etienne, assisted Didara, while they were in Inné," *For all the good it did. There had been one bullet missed and that ultimately killed her. Jagunjagun wept on me when she died.* He sipped his juice, breathed in more of the smoke from the censer though it didn't seem to be able to touch real grief. "Then I wished them well and waved them home."

"Interesting. We should send expeditions to the Elephant's Countries."

"You'd find a lot of interesting things," Ahrimaz said, thinking of Didara's gilded skeleton standing in the central hall of the House of Gold, and was surprised he felt warmth welling from his eyes. "I don't want to bleed—" and saw a single clear tear on his hand. He set his cup down with a click and threw his hands over his eyes.

At last. True tears. For an alien creature lost and dead far from home. "It's all right, Ahrimaz. We will think no less of you." That was the old man speaking and that undid him completely.

41

Yes, Please

ONLY LIMYÉ TOUCHED HIM AS HE WEPT UNTIL HE HAD NOTHING LEFT, no tears, no energy. He looked up, in time to see the black-haired girl blow a kiss across the heart in her hands and droplets, butterflies, scarlet and black butterflies made of blood and ache fluttered out and to his out-flung hand.

He was lying on the pillows and the children were distantly playing, in the stream, everyone all around just there. No one was quivering in fear of what he might do. No one was crying with him. No one looming over him shouting for him to stop. "It is not all about you in this world," Limyé said quietly.

Everything was edged in a rosy pink colour now and Ahrimaz felt like he floated just above the pillows. *There he was, below, looking like a skinny, ragged, bearded, version of himself. "I would like to show you something,"* the black haired girl said.

"All right."

She didn't touch him but they floated up through the ceiling of the salle and up through the rest of the building. So small compared to his own House of Gold. Then below them was all of this Inné. Also small. Fewer streets were paved and they ran hither and thither as though someone had let a cow wander the hill and declared every meander a street.

Then he realized that all the lights he saw were people. Not their physical selves but the light that Aeono saw. And, he supposed, the light that Lyrian saw. Some people were dim and small, others flared like burn-metal blazing white. It was a song of light, it was a tapestry that twinkled. "There needs to be dark," he said, "or you couldn't see them."

"Yes," she said. *"And living hurts, until you grow up enough to realize that it needn't."*

"Really?"

"Really."

He could see his world, a shadow to this one, both darker and brighter, higher contrast, like a backdrop to this quieter, bigger world. Bigger? How? There was a sense of vast distance all around as though he could not comprehend it all. More worlds? More lives? As the gemstone of a planet turned beneath him he could see in this world a fiery conflagration across the sea, and groups of sparks of souls in the sea itself. "But..."

The world was wrenched sideways again as it expanded into the past and the future and all the lives and deaths, all the prayers and songs and screams, all love and compassion and gratitude. Gratitude. For life. For death. Gratitude. Love. Compassion.

It was as though all of creation was trying to climb into his chest, into his heart, into all the narrow, pinched off, burnt and scarred places and as they ripped open, as they split asunder he opened his mouth and rather than a scream a single word emerged, whispered into the vastness. "Please."

He tumbled and fell toward the globe, toward the country, toward the House of the Hand, limbs loose, chest open, hair and lungs ripped at by the wind of life, rising, floating up to the Divine, down to the Divine, out to the Divine. There was no word for that direction. It just was.

His whole body jolted as he opened his eyes, feeling Limyé's hand on his shoulder

"Do you think he could bear being touched?" he heard Yolend say with his living ears. He lunged to catch her proffered hand, and clamped down on Limyé's, curled around them, hugging, cherishing their solid touch.

Yes, please," he managed to say, even as he'd said to... oh. The black-haired girl was his image of Her. Even as he'd said to the Goddess with him. "Please."

42

Drown Me. I'm Terrified.

"SO YOU ARE THE OTHER AHRIMAZ? I'm Teel James, one Editor/Raconteur of the premier Broadsheet of Inné, the Coalition News."

James is a tall man. His stockings are cream silk, and his brocade vest is white and gold and has tiny cherries upon it. His great coat is dark blue brocade and his salt and pepper hair is curly and down to the centre of his back. He's got a walking stick almost as tall as his chin, with a quill gracing the top of it. Aside from the middling quality of the silks he'd fit right into my court, but his eyes are blue and open and honest, unlike my courtiers. He gives me the shivers. My M. James is my best friend in the world, in the Empire, and the head of the Aporrheitos, Master of all Spies in the known world.

"Why yes. M. James, I understand that you wished to interview me. What can I possibly tell you that you cannot get from the family?"

"The personal view, ser. You must feel very lost here."

"Indeed, yes. It is an understatement."

I don't trust him.

"M. James… perhaps we might interview another day? I am not feeling well."

"Oh, certainly!" *His look says 'you're full of scorching shit', but he's polite. I pull the feather quilt up and lie down again as he leaves.*

* * * * *

Well that party was all well and good. Healing and all that. And my mind has just gone to the scorching hell again and won't come out.

I'm sitting in the bed after James's abortive visit. I can't even make it to the desk. I'm too tired. I'm too overwhelmed. I can't think straight.

I'm scribbling this with a smudge stick because I don't want to fight with ink pot and quill in the bed. Limyé says this is normal. I had so much good that my mind got frightened and retreated into this horror once more, but it's only temporary.

I'm tired. I'm sick. I'm tired of being sick. I'm sick of being tired.

The only time I feel I can breathe is when one of the scorching animals is lying on me. Heylia keeps trying to get me to follow her. I have the stinking suspicion that if I do I'll find that black haired girl again and I cannot bear it. It is too good for me. I'm realizing that I'm a witch. And that that Goddess is no Demon. Arnziel comes every night now, to read to me or with me, or just sit.

Dammit why did he actually turn out to be such a good priest?

And the Goddess's books. How on the drowning green earth did my maligned ancestor manage to vilify Her? I have found darkness in Her books but it is darkness that brings relief from too much light. When we were in the desert I found it very hard not to see evil in the Sun coming up. The cold brought us water, and the starker the difference the more water. I began to pray for the cold dark nights, though I prayed to Aeono, not knowing any better.

Like my mother, She is there for her children and I'm starting to wonder about the timing of my... transposition? My relocation? My swap? Arnziel says that it might have taken so long to happen because his brother might not have been able to withstand the pressures of Empire as well as the blandishments thereof, until now. Really? He took thirty years to become a good enough man to not become me, leaving me and my world and my family and all of us screaming for assistance? Goddess, you are cruel.

Well, we men are cruel. And we're slow. I understand that. The father tells me that I am not so vile as I make myself out to be. As I was forced to pretend, by the other father. He broke me, as a boy. Broke me down so thoroughly that I was re-formed as a hidden child. Limyé wonders if I am one of many inside my skull. The Girl who is the image of love and pain. The Monster who can do all the evil things not only with relish, but honest glee. There's the Politician. He does the work. There's the Baby who weeps and screams... but can laugh. The Sufferer, who holds our sexuality.

It seems too easy. I am not these others. They are their own people and I only know the Monster intimately. I've only met the others fleetingly and seen them as dreams or nightmares. I am a shattered mirror upon the floor and the other father broke me, took up the pieces and fit them back into my frame, leaving out the bits he didn't want. Those pieces I have in the hands of my mind; bleeding fingers clutched tight to precious glass shards that are the rest of me.

I cannot bear to look at them yet. I might find a Lover. A Singer. A Priest of the Goddess. A Paladin. All these things that these people tell me are possible. The other Ahrimaz is facing all the parts of me that were shambling along, driving the world before it. I am facing the parts of me... of him that I've not been allowed to bear. Goddess. Drown me. I'm terrified.

43

Shake On It!

THE VERY NEXT DAY AHRIMAZ STARED THROUGH THE BARS AT TEEL. "You aren't going to go away until you get your interview, aren't you?" he snarled.

"Ser, I just want to let people know the truth. People need to know what is going on in their government, in their House of the Hand. People deserve to know what is going on!"

At least he showed his difference from the James he knew. He wore the same outfit. The spymaster in the Empire wouldn't be caught dead in the same coat two days running. "In that, at least, you are like the man I know in the Empire. Truth is his God."

"Truly? Might I quote you on that?"

Ahrimaz sighed and waved towards himself. "Come in, sit down, talk to me. I will, however, not trust you. In my world the man who wears your face and your voice is the Aporrheitos, the Head of the Truth-tellers school, my best friend and spymaster."

James didn't even check or hesitate at all as he pulled the cell door open and settled on the chair by the bed, notebook already out, even as his cane settled against his knee. *You know.* Ahrimaz thought. *That is a very heavy cane for something supposedly so light.* "How heavy a sword do you have in there?" He leaned back against the wall, eased the coverlet out from under his thigh in case he should have to use it as a shield.

Teel's face fell. *I'd know in a heartbeat that this man isn't my spymaster. His face is wide open and shows everything.* "You could tell? Drown it, I've been practicing!" He offered the cane to Ahrimaz without a second thought.

"No, actually, *my* spymaster has a small sword in his cane and has saved my life with it, more than once." He twisted and the cane popped open to reveal the court sword inside. He drew it with a hiss and then sheathed it with a smooth motion, shutting it in place with a click. "Very nice."

"Spymaster?" James prompted, taking his cane back, pencil and notebook poised.

"Yes. Well. The Aporrheitos school draws from the whole Empire and trains truth-tellers specifically. I haven't seen a single one here."

"They are like an order then?"

"Very much. I understand that most people in both worlds have a trace of it. The School concentrates it."

"How interesting. Did you set up this school?"

"No, it was my great grandfather. He decided that no one should be able to discern the sexes of the Truth Tellers. They wear red robes from head to toe, red gloves, and shave all facial hair, including eyebrows, though our physicians dissuaded us from having them pull their eyelashes."

"Huh. It sounds… extreme."

"Oh it is, but it is a system where no one will question your class or your sex. You are there to tell the truth and a Truth Teller has personal servants, their own horses, but not their own houses since they stay in the Temples while on duty."

"So, promotion by ability and merit then." James scribbled. Ahrimaz found himself looking at him, struggling to see the differences. The most obvious was an unbroken nose. A duelling scar through an eyebrow was also missing. He looked up, catching him looking. "How are you managing this 'different world' business?"

Ahrimaz caught his breath. There was the same sharpness that he knew. "Badly. Lousily," he said softly. "I'm actually considering trying to kill myself just out of sheer misery, but the Kenaçyen family don't want me to do that. They're worried that any possibility of getting their own man back would be harmed." He grinned slightly. "I've also thought that might be a way of getting my own back. A bit of revenge for all this healing they've thrust upon me."

"I… see." James leaned back. "Your healing was forced, then? Why don't you just kill yourself then?"

"I… don't know. I feel as though I somehow have this will to live nailed to my breastbone in place of my heart."

"You've just proved that you're not a monster."

Ahrimaz raised an eyebrow but didn't say anything. The two dogs came trit-trotting in, sniffed around James and then Teh sat down between the chair and the bed and Sure jumped up to pin Ahrimaz's legs down.

"Yes. You see a monster would have found out what the family was afraid of and then cut his own throat in front of them, laughing." James put the notebook down and leaned forward, elbows on knees, one dangling hand petting the protective Teh. "You realize as well that you need someone to talk to who doesn't have a stake in your healing?"

"Yes, but I hadn't thought there would be anyone in this world who didn't have a stake in keeping me healthy in the hopes of getting their Beloved back." Ahrimaz shifted the dog up to his lap and she sprawled, belly up, legs waving and he scrubbed her belly absently with both hands. "And if you think that you can offer yourself up to be that unbiased ear, then you're wrong. If you have as much strength to read people emotionally as my friend, they you must know that. You are committed to telling people the truth and you'd be encouraging me out of any self-delusions I have both for that reason and the fact that you'd be more comfortable if I were not lying to myself. My friend in the other world actually breaks out in rashes in the presence of lies. He's terribly uncomfortable in my court because it's a sea of lies that he's swimming in, constantly."

"You can see that I am not scratching. You're telling me the truth as best you know it. And with me there's not any kind of sexual tension, or political tension or even tension of expectation."

"And you just want to write things about me. Tell people about me."

"I could come and talk to you every day, I think, without running out of interesting stories. I'm actually thinking of beginning a column just to let people know about you and the other world."

Ahrimaz snorted and fell over sideways into his pillows. "So I get hours of talk from Limyé, hours of talk from the other fellow's parents and lovers, several hours of training from Rutaçyen, an hour of philosophy with Arnziel and you think I'll have time left for you, much less time to scratch?"

"We could make it part of your training... or while you go out to walk or run. I'd keep up with you."

"Would you now?" Ahrimaz's grin emerged from the pillows, covered by tousled hair. He raked it out of his face. "And if you can't keep up, you'll go away?"

"It's a bet!" James thrust his hand out. "Shake on it!"

44

Your Intrepid Correspondent

The Man Named Ahrimaz

—By Teel James, Raconteur for the Coalition News, Chronicles of Inné and Innéthel and their environs, Late Winter

I am sitting in my study, with my cravat undone, a warming stone in my chair for my back and my feet in a pan of hot water and salt. I am so fatigued that I am shaking and my head aches abominably, but I kept up with the current incarnation of Ahrimaz Kençyen during his training session with the great sword master Rutaçyen, and then on a run up to the Veil. This means that I shall be able to continue interviewing the man and writing his story for my readers.

He looks like our Ahrimaz, except that he is bearded with faint strands of silver in his pale gold hair. He is thinner than our Ahrimaz and his eyes are more haunted, with deeper care lines. He looks like our Ahrimaz, just after his rescue from imprisonment and torture by the old Cylak King.

But he is not our Beloved. He is more akin to him than a brother but he clearly is a harder man. He is learning that concern and compassion are not weaknesses and in all his life he's known only a mother's love, and had that untimely ripped away from him.

He has been trained for war, just as our Ahrimaz was, but in a school far more brutal than ours, and he pushes himself and everyone around him unmercifully. Rutaçyen had the two of us sit and do ink sword practice... she watched me, great percheron that I am, huff around with her student who is more like a greyhound, and had mercy on me and had me as her student as well, as long as our bet holds.

You see, dear readers, as long as I can keep up with this man named Ahrimaz, I can interview him and if that is through wheezing gasps of words as I labour to breathe, as he lightly bounds ahead, so be it. The things I do for a story.

The sword of ink, for any of my readers who have not had any martial training whatsoever is a technique developed hundreds of years ago, when we turned from a wandering people to a settled one, and our Innéan warmasters became fascinated with how a brush pen stroke flowed like a sword stroke. Our sword masters teach ink, to teach the sword. A swift and decisive slashing stroke with enormous control so that ink does not spatter. A comfortable circle floated onto the page. Wings and eyes and motion and life, all portrayed with a single stroke.

So there we were in the training salle of the House of the Hand, kneeling, grinding ink. In my case struggling to haul my sadly neglected wind out of the basement of my torso.

When I studied small sword, and great sword, my own teacher had me learn a fine hand. I was secretly delighted to find that this astonishing warrior's hand is frozen when presented with a blank page.

And then I found myself confounded. He fought so hard, fear and terror ground into his smallest muscle, that sweat stood on his brow as he ruined or broke a dozen brushes. He looked up at me, despair in his eyes and snarled "I don't need your pity!"

"Indeed, ser. I do not pity you," I responded. "I'm merely glad to find that after having run me into the ground like a spavined horse, you have perhaps one thing that gives you a bit of trouble."

He stared at me and then started laughing. He laughed hard, waving his finger at me and sputtering 'spavined horse' sufficient to begin to be annoying, but as he subsided, Rutaçyen placed a new brush in his hand, a new page before him and with his attention still on me, he shrugged, still chuckling, and drew a single perfect line.

The brush fell from his hand and he threw his hands over his face. I rose and bowed to the sword master, who bowed back. "I shall see you tomorrow, then, ser," said I, and limped out to write this piece.

He is not our Beloved. It is as though someone took our Beloved away from us and brutalized him, his whole life, till he believes that he deserves that brutality. Our Beloved, twisted. Only time will tell if the man that Rutaçyen and Limyé Ianmen, the Kenaçyen's healer, is even in there. Only time will tell if the shattered pieces of a man are knit back together to some kind of integrity.

Until that time, I am Teel James, your intrepid correspondent recounting from the House of the Hand.

45   Language Unworthy of the Veil

THE WINTER HAD BEEN A GODDESS'S BLESSING, though the snow was heavy. It had stayed warm enough to snow, and snow a great deal, and there had only been two or three storms this season. Only one of those had been what anyone would call a blizzard and that had been early on before there was enough snow to drift up high.

It had fallen, steady, thick and deep, burying and protecting the earth and the plants, insulating from killing cold. If it melted slowly in spring, the deep water aquifers would be replenished instead of tearing flash floods ripping grass, trees and mud away. Fortunately Innéthel was only in high hills, or howes, at the navigation head of the river, rather than sitting under a mountain that would shed avalanches, though the Yhom had their sound cannon to shake anything loose before it got too deep or too deadly.

The path to the Veil Falls led up and around the hill, rising slightly as it went and James's boots squeaked on the hard-packed snow path, shovelled drifts as high as his waist in places as he walked. The Goddess tree loomed stark and leafless now, but the lower branches and up as high as youngsters could climb, empty cages hung, symbolic of freedom, doors clicking in the wind. Ribbons fluttered, some washed pale by long exposure, some bright, depending on the prayers people had to give. This time of year there were no flowers but people made up fir cones with fat and seed so it was full of birds, endlessly cheeping. It gave him a kind of satisfaction that the birds flittering about would often land on the empty cages since everyone knew that was how they'd originally arrived.

Grey birds, brown birds with white flashes, birds with their top half slate grey with white bellies. Even some big bright blue bullies with flashy black and white slashings and regal blue topknots. Chickadees. All the winter birds. Crows muttering the very top of the tree as well as their larger Raven relatives. Only in the spring and summer would there be the brighter birds, enough jewel bright humming birds to rival the drone of bees everywhere, the indigos and yellow blacks, the orange and black fruit eaters. For a moment he felt a slight touch of vertigo as if he could see both images one superimposed on the other. He shook his head and it settled back down to reality. For now it was winter birds, mostly dressed in grey and white and black.

He tucked the broadsheet, warm off the press, tighter under his arm, heedless of the ink. His greatcoat was black wool and wouldn't show it. His cane swung out almost jauntily but dug into the snow with purpose to give him a boost up the slippery hill.

An acolyte in their white winter robes and wool stockings paused in her grooming of the path and he touched the rim of his high fur felted hat to her. She set the tamper and broom down and set her mittened hands together and bowed him over the lip of the hill and down into the valley itself.

From the top of the path he could see the vague movements of a half dozen priestesses or priests of Lyrian, hard to see in the snow when they were all wearing their winter vestments. He paused a moment just to see them working on the winter garden of the Veil. It was immensely soothing and he found himself heartily glad that he had this and Aeono's enclosed temple both together as this other world, this Empire, did not.

He couldn't see Rutaçyen, Pelahir, or Ahrimaz but he wasn't expecting it, since they were likely down next the pool. He adjusted his folded up broadsheet once more and began his descent to where the largest waterfall ran.

The cliff edge to his left, in the summer, was a wall of mint that hundreds of tiny trickles of water flowed through before joining together to make the beginnings of the river. This time of year it was a fantasy of icicles of a rainbow of colours. Clear, blue, green, brown, a silvery one, one that seemed to be crystal clear with flecks of gold.

He could hear the rushing of the waterfall even now because unless the cold got bad enough to freeze the river solid, water ran out from underneath the skin of ice and over the crescent edge. In the icy grotto that the waterfall pool became he could see the three he was looking for.

As he came up to them, Pelahir rose and offered him the peculiar Cylak hello, an upward jerk of chin. "Greetings, gentlemen." Ahrimaz and Rutaçyen stayed cross-legged and Pel settled back down into the hollow in the snow that he seemed to have melted. In fact he could feel the heat pouring off the three of them from where he stood. "Hello, Warmaster." He acknowledged her with a hat tip and she nodded back.

"Hello, student. You come in good time."

"Hello, Teel," Ahrimaz said quietly. "I hope you're ready to continue our bet in a moment."

"Indeed I am. But I brought the new broadsheet along new-printed to show you my piece about you." He settled down in the snow, pulling his wool greatcoat under himself as he sat, and proffered the paper.

Ahrimaz looked at it as though it might bite him but reached out a bare hand and took it. "I have it folded correctly so you might…" Teel trailed off as Ahrimaz was obviously already reading it.

Then he froze as Ahrimaz's face flushed bright red, he convulsively crumpled the pages in his hands as his fingers clenched shut. He glared at Teel with murder in his eyes.

"You powder burning, misfiring, scorching, villainous, burnt soul, flaming charcoal dicked, ash headed INSTIGATING scribbler! Aeono's flaming acid anal beads! Every piss-ant peasant and burgher, slave and merchant paunch all over Inné KNOWS ME THIS INTIMATELY?!"

46

I'd Like It If You Could

WITH HIS EYES STILL LOCKED ON AHRIMAZ'S FACE, Teel smoothly reached into his great coat, pulled out his notebook and licked the tip of his pencil. "May I quote you on that?" He said.

Ahrimaz made to lunge forward but both Rutaçyen and Pelahir had him by the wrists. Teel looked down, scribbling. "Was that 'ash-dick or charcoal dick'?" he asked.

Rutaçyen shook her head at him. But Ahrimaz subsided, staring at him. "What?"

The warmaster shook him slightly. "Was he untruthful in what he wrote?" Her touch on his wrist actually was a light hand, not physically holding him back, but he reacted as if her touch chained him to the ground. "Did he insult you?"

"No! But. No!"

Pelahir tugged at the crumpled paper in Ahrimaz's hands and he let go of it, and Pel's eyes skimmed down the mangled sheet. "It seems very... gentle."

"Yes! No! But..." Ahrimaz subsided back onto his heels, where he'd knelt before, and shook his head, bewildered.

"What do you need to fear that you are so angry about?" Rutaçyen asked quietly. There was a long silence as Ahrimaz thought it through, the rushing of the waterfall behind it all. Teel could feel the spray beginning to soak into his coat, but didn't move from where he sat, pencil poised over his page.

A raven swooped down from the Goddess tree above, settled on a branch right over the lip of the waterfall, bobbing up and down as it swayed and then when it opened its beak an amazing liquid trill of notes poured out, instead of a harsh croak. It sang and as it sang Ahrimaz's head tipped back as if he looked at it, though his eyes were closed.

"I'm... sorry, Teel," he said at last and Rutaçyen and Pel both let him go. "I am afraid of people. I have always been hurt by people. Soldiers I understand, and subjects can be commanded. I am terrified of what free people will think and do."

"Would you be hurt if I told people that?" James wrote it down, even as he asked. Ahrimaz lowered his head and opened his eyes. A breeze blew a swirl of snow down on them and the raven flapped away as if called to urgent business elsewhere.

"I... suppose not." Ahrimaz looked at Pel first, measuring his reaction. Pel shrugged.

"It's a generous piece," he said. "And doesn't make you look like anything but what you are, at least from Monsieur James's point of view."

James bowed from the waist where he sat.

Ahrimaz leapt up then. "Since you are here and neither of us is welching on this bet," he said sharply, "I'm going to warm up before the war master teaches me anything. Keep up, if you can, James."

Even as Ahrimaz moved Teel was on his own feet, peeling off his greatcoat and dropping his notebook upon it next to his cane. Ahrimaz wheeled to his right and took off next to the river, Teel on his heels. The riverbank was treacherous with rocks and slippery so he could not run as fast, he turned up the bank to the groomed path and they hurtled past the priestess there, neck and neck. Teel took as much advantage of his longer legs as he could but even the path, though smoother than the riverside, was uneven enough to slow them both down.

"You aren't wearing a waistcoat today?" Ahrimaz said, panting.

"Nor a cravat!" Teel huffed back. "The... back... of your... pants are wet."

"Get... in... front... if you... don't want... to... look!"

Then they saved their breath for running, Ahrimaz putting his head down and settling into a steady, ground-eating pace.

Rutaçyen and Pel stood watching them disappear around the path, away down the long loop out of the valley completely, before turning back and then toward the bridges that would bring them back around the other side. Once they came back from their long run, that path would have them scrambling up the opposite side of the waterfall and hopping the slick stepping stones across before bringing them back to where they'd started.

"In case you're wondering," Rutaçyen smiled at Pel who was beginning his own slow set of poses as his warm-up.

"No, Ru," he smiled back at her. "Not wondering at all why you aren't running along with those two idiots."

Rutaçyen and Pel had done their forms and sparred and actually settled back down to meditate before they distantly heard the thunder of footsteps on a wooden bridge.

She nodded from where she'd stood up and settled back down to her cross-legged pose in the snow. After a time they could hear Ahrimaz and Teel puffing up the path.

"Moron," Ahrimaz puffed.

"Who's... the... moron?" Then just gasping breaths for a bit. "I'm getting training from the best AND... I... get... a... story..."

No answer as the two men scrambled up the cliff path on the other side of the waterfall, throwing up puffs of snow. At the top Teel gathered a handful of snow off the edge and tossed it sideways onto Ahrimaz's head. His head snapped around and he flung out a hand to catch Teel's ankle.

He slipped the grab but responded by scrambling backward and managing to put together another snowball. He threw it, hit Ahrimaz in the face with a light 'pumpf' as it exploded. "Cheater!" Ahrimaz managed to shout. Teel slowed down and looked back over his shoulder just in time to get a slush ball in the side of his head and both men stopped running to begin hurling snow at one another.

Rutaçyen watched them, smiling.

Pel stood up and watched them as Ahrimaz lunged for Teel and managed to knock him over and they rolled in the snow.

"Hey!"

"Peace! This isn't sparring OR our bet!" Teel had both of Ahrimaz's wrists in his hands and he was a taller and heavier enough man that he had him solidly, at least for a moment. Ahrimaz rolled right over his head, snatching his wrists out of Teel's hands but didn't get up. He stayed, sprawling, head to head with James.

"You're right," he said quietly. Pel, standing below could barely hear them over the sound of the water.

Teel rose, beating snow out of his clothing, put a hand down to offer if Ahrimaz wanted his help getting up. "The other Ahrimaz and I were friends," Teel said. "I'd like it if we could be."

Ahrimaz stared at the proffered hand and actually made a motion to take it before snatching it back to his chest, rolling over to lie face first in the snow.

"Drowning hell, Ahri," Teel snapped and grabbed him by the collar.

"Quit that."

And Pel closed his eyes, waiting for Ahrimaz to explode and actually punch James. Nothing. He opened his eyes to see Ahrimaz standing in the snow, covered in it, visibly shivering, in front of Teel. "Come on. You need to get back down to the House to get into the tub." He looked over at Rutaçyen who nodded. "And I don't give a rainy fuck if you don't want to." He took Ahrimaz's arm over his shoulder, bending down to do so, and began steering him over the stepping stones and to the path back down to the House.

"I think they will be fine," Rutaçyen said quietly.

"I didn't know James was that good," Pel said.

"Most people who are good warriors don't tend to boast about it a great deal," Rutaçyen said. "Draw please and give me a good attack, Pelahir."

47

Always Groomed

PELAHIR FOUND JAMES IN DEEP CONVERSATION WITH LIMYÉ outside the tub room. The rush of water effectively masked their voices and he cast a quick glance down the hall to the cell. "He's asleep," James said in his deep voice. Limyé nodded.

"The intense exercise is helping break down the memory of torture in his body and mind both," the healer said.

Pel grinned. "And I didn't even need to get beat on to tire him out, thank you Monsieur James."

Teel grinned back. "Just Teel, please. It's odd but I find I like him. The other Ahrimaz often seemed... cool toward me. Not that it was a problem but..."

"He was nervous of you," Pel said. "He said you could see to the heart of things and then draw it out bleeding on the page."

Teel blinked. "Really?"

Pel's grin went away. He set his teeth and turned away from the other two men, set one hand against the smooth polished stone and his forehead against his hand. "I miss him," he said through clenched teeth. "I miss him every day as though someone ripped a hole in my heart and Yolend and I... thank the Twin Gods we have each other."

"I'm sorry." James said quietly. Limyé put his hand on his shoulder.

"You need to come speak to me soon," the healer said. "This is such a strange happening, and such a..." he shrugged, hands spreading expansively. "... such an unusual thing. I am here to hear you. And I am starting to wonder how many things are being healed by this... exchange. I have no information about the other world except what I get from this

Ahrimaz and he does not think his Inné is crumbling."

James leaned on the wall next to Pelahir, took the offered shoulder, silently. "So you think this might be a way of 'fixing' this Empire, you think? I'd like to hear your theories."

Limyé smiled. "So you may write them up? Of course. The basic thought I had is that both our men reflect the country. As Hand of the People Ahrimaz has no choice in a sense and if the civilization is healthy, if the people are healthy and the Gods then he, at one point, I would have said was the healthiest man in the Coalition."

"And the Empire?" Pel straightened to turn and put his back against the wall, rejoining the conversation.

"Was sick. The court is corrupt. The nobles are suffering the illnesses of overindulgence. The Emperor is forced to channel all of the Divine through Aeono alone, though it makes him ill. People who worship the Goddess are murdered publicly." He paused, and gulped. "All of Imaryu was slaughtered and Ahrimaz tells me that physicians are now people's only recourse when they are ill, and are often charged more than their lives for their services."

"And just as our Ahrimaz reflects the health of the nation... or nations, so does—"

Pelahir cut James off. "The Emperor."

The three men were silent for a time before Pelahir said quietly. "I am no priest, but this might be the salvation of that Empire, if our Ahrimaz can resist becoming sick with it."

"And you have to be strong and healthy for when it all unravels, if it ever does," Limyé said quietly. "The Empire might kill our Ahrimaz. It might take his sacrifice to... to..."

"Pull the peace out of the war," Pel said quietly. "It's what he swore to do." He straightened. "And we may never get him back. I'll come down to talk to you day after tomorrow, Limyé. Tomorrow I have all day with Rutaçyen and Ahrimaz."

The healer nodded.

"May I talk to you a bit longer?" James asked, pulling out his notebook. "If you have time, of course?"

"Certainly."

* * * * *

Their voices faded off down the hall and Ahrimaz clung to the bars. He hadn't been asleep, though he had been drowsy. Clinging to the bars, through some trick of acoustics, he'd been able to hear every word.

* * * * *

Of course. How gently they rip out my guts and trample them into the muck. This isn't about me at all. He is being driven like a donkey, probably by a God—dess, to save MY country. MY people. Ahrimaz, my brother I begin to feel sorry for you. I begin to feel that this is hardly fair. You did everything right and were the hero, the Beloved.

I rubbed my forehead slowly back and forth against the bars. I want to whine like a child and cry 'What about ME?' I grit my teeth and straighten like the warrior I am. I've never been groomed to be the hero.

I've always been groomed to be the monster of the piece.

48

If You Won't, He Will

HE STOOD AT THE DOOR OF THE CELL. The door itself was wide open. The lamp in front of the painted mural hissed to itself then was silent. His toes touched the line of the threshold as if pressed against a rock wall.

Ahrimaz held to the door posts not sure if he was holding himself up, holding himself back, or bracing to try and lunge through the opening, breath shuddering in and out of his lungs.

He could cross that threshold if asked, by anyone else, even the animals. When Rutaçyen had asked him to step in and out of the cell a dozen times he could do it without a thought. When he tried to leave the cell through his own volition, every muscle locked solid and he could go nowhere.

One finger at a time he pried his grip off the door posts, took a deep breath and tried to overbalance out the door and he lashed out and grabbed rather than take that step. He could hear Limyé and the dogs coming, at least he assumed that Limyé was with the multi-scramble claw-clicking rush of dog nails on stone. He closed his eyes and stepped back from the dangerous threshold, went down on one knee to be swarmingly greeted by slobbering dogs's wet noses and tongues. How he had changed. Before he would never have tolerated it.

But when he looked, Limyé was not there. "Yes, yes, it's all right, you're good dogs yes, yes, what the scorch?"

He flinched back as the dogs each took a sleeve and began tugging him toward the door. "Have you beasts gone mad?" He had to stagger to his feet, at least part way, or fall on his face, though the blocky dogs weren't quite tall enough to let him stand straight with his cuffs clenched in their bull-baiting jaws.

They dragged him along, play growling, huffing, his hair over his face and when they had him at a door he didn't recognize they let him go, sitting down so smartly that it looked as though he had commanded them. Ahrimaz didn't recognize the hall or the door, save that it was an outside door, heavy only against the weather. A rack of woollen cape/coats hung by the door. He stood looking at the dogs, then shrugged and took a coat, before opening the door to see where they'd brought him.

He nearly stopped dead in his tracks but Sure seized his sleeve again and Teh ran ahead along the dark breezeway to tug on the rope obviously put there so that the animal could open and close the door.

Sure dragged him into the building and Ahrimaz did sit down in the sand as Teh closed the door behind them. It was the oddest riding arena that he had ever seen and was different enough that he could seize control of his fear and the knotting in his stomach and just sit.

"Father, those are already being trained as warhorses, even if they're just foals." The old monster had looked at him and started to smile.

"You'll have to try harder than that, son. You go down there and choose your horse. That's why I gave you a rope. If they bite you, if they kick you, fight back. Punch them. Grab a stick… there's lots in the paddock."

The foals… really they were nearly yearlings… had already learned that their job was to be killers. They'd had slaves sent in before, unarmed, and the men knew that if they got out of the field alive they were free. At this point in their training none of the slaves ever got out.

The herd had their own hierarchy. He could see that. He focused on the one that would be lead, and picked up the rope. Then he went in like a maniac, screaming, running for 'his' horse making them get in each other's way. They'd knocked him over once but he'd slid into a gap between two trees, wheezing. It turned out later that sometime in the scrum they'd broken his ribs. When the lead horse reached to bite him Ahrimaz reached back and, lightning fast, pinched his top lip, whipped a twitch around it.

He staggered out of the paddock, leading his killer by the nose, the rest of the herd milling behind them, confused.

The wind picked up in this early morning hour and the light gradually got stronger, filtering in through the translucent panels all around the top of the walls. The stables were all apparently arranged around the arena. The warm smell of clean horses helped ease his gut as he sat, even as the rest of him tried to panic.

I'm not hurting, learning to ride.

There was an interested equine head poking out over every stall door, long noses bobbing as they turned their heads this way and that to catch his scent. Every stall had a line of shapes along the front wall where the horses could reach and when the light grew a little stronger half a dozen of them started tugging on the green circles.

One started kicking his door and trying to bull his way out, making nasty, aggressive whistles, yanking at his green flag hard enough to rip it loose. He chewed on it, still screaming, though muffled until he dropped the mangled remains.

"Scorch and Drown you lot!" Ahrimaz cried. "Do even the horses in this world get votes? I don't know what that means! But I know you! You're a killer."

But the dogs apparently did understand and trotted to several of the horses—though not the one making the most fuss—to casually pull their stall doors open and Ahrimaz lurched to his feet, ready to run. "You all can't be killer warhorses now, can you?" He began backing up slowly arms spread, eyes fixed on the first horse out of his… her stall. She was a two-colour patched mare with a white splash on one side of her face and a bay on the other. She paced out deliberately, a few steps ahead of a black and white filly and a dapple grey.

His attention fixed on the horses, he forgot to yell at the dogs who had put him in such danger. Teh had vanished from his immediate vision and he backed up a bit faster, only to fall backwards over the dog who knocked his knees out from behind.

He rolled to try and get to his feet and run but found the coat pinned him and knocked him flat once more and he lay on the sand with three of the horses around him, and the damned and scorched dogs, all looking down at him, standing or in the case of the dogs, sitting on his clothing to immobilize him. He lay, panting, wondering idly if the dogs had finally picked up on his desire to die and brought him to this pass. *I've killed enough war-horses, in war and out of it. Surely they can smell that on me.*

He tried to summon the indifference he'd learned but failed utterly and found his body giving in to the panic and the pain he felt around horses. It cut through the pink haze of the drug that Limyé had him on completely.

He look up at the flaring nostrils, lips loose, showing the enormous flat teeth that could bite so painfully, heard the scream of a horse still confined and him kicking and banging on the closed stall door. "If *you* aren't going to stomp me to death," he said mildly, "… just let him out. He'll do it for you."

49

"You're Schooling Me!"

THE STALLION TOOK A BREATH AND SHUT UP, finally, and Ahrimaz wondered why they were all taking so long to savage him. The mare's long, wet, gooey lips suddenly slapped all over his face and she snorted green goo on him and then danced away, tossing her head in the air, whinnying, for all the world *giggling* at him.

He surged up and out of the sleeves of the coat and found himself on his feet, facing her, hands and sleeves scraping the mess off his face. "Not funny!" He spat at her, bent down to scoop a double handful of clean sand to scrub his face and someone *goosed* him so he staggered forward, found himself draped over her neck rather than sprawled on his face.

A muffled thump beside him and Heylia appeared to levitate onto the horse's rump. Just… appeared. And the mare didn't jump either, though her ears flicked back and then forward. One of the others whinnied again, snorting as though he were the funniest thing she'd ever seen.

"You are all in this together, obviously," he snarled and made to step back from the mare but found he was boxed in by the dapple, pressed up against the bicolour, but very gently for animals this size. He managed to turn so he faced the same direction as they at least and the horses began slowly walking him around the arena, pinned between them, Heylia purring in his ear.

His head swivelled around to see the dog lying in the coat on the sand, watching, the other mare gone back to her own stall. They wouldn't let him run or squeeze out from between them. When he tried to stop they just flicked their inside ears at him and walked on. When he tried sliding down they both stopped and sank on their hocks until they were all crouched on the sand.

He started laughing around then. "You... you... bitches!" He gasped as they slowly rose up and walked on. "You're *schooling* me!"

Both of the mares whickered, Heylia meowed and the dogs were dancing around their little cortège, youping. "The animals..." he gasped for breath and the mares eased up on the pressure a little, and he found himself with an arm over both necks. "In this world seem vastly more aware than in mine. Please don't tell me they've all been made more stupid by us!"

The voice from the door was reassuring. "No, they're probably keeping it more secret from you so you can't use them as effectively. After all... the animals here, now, are mostly Goddess animals."

It was Wenhiffar and Ahrimaz went weak at the knees, holding himself up on the mare's necks. They all faced the door and the dapple stepped away to go press her forehead against his... mother's... chest. The duo-coloured mare stood rock steady and Heylia had her nose pressed into his ear, one paw draped firmly over his shoulder.

"Really?" I mean... I thought only cats were Aeono's... I mean Tiger Master, Master of Lions and so forth."

"Big cats. War cats and smaller are Lyrian's." Her hands rubbed up over the dapple's poll and down to scratch behind the jaws, slow, slow circuits of rubbing. Ahrimaz was almost mesmerized just watching.

"Come on, C'est Belle," she said finally. "Son, stay where you are for a moment if you will." She whistled and the dogs stopped zooming and wiggling about, settling at heel as though cast out of stone. She and the dapple—Ahrimaz could put no other word other than 'marched'—over to the stallion's stall.

She stared into the dimness arms crossed and there wasn't any sound from within. "He's a killer, Wenhiffar," Ahrimaz couldn't help saying. "He's—
"There was a scream from inside the stall at his voice and as the snaking head of the stallion flashed out, ears flattened, skull-like, Wenhiffar slapped his nose, the mare bit him and both dogs jumped and nipped his neck. He suddenly stood, torn between 'I am a killer' and 'don't hurt me, I'm a foal, see?'

"You great fool you've pissed on your hay, shat all over the place and trodden your straw foul, you've ripped splinters off everywhere and broke your signals AGAIN." The dapple mare emphasized each word, pawing at the sand. "WIND HEART OUT OF FAIR WIND, YOU ASSHOLE!"

Ahrimaz put his forehead against the bi-coloured mare and listened in awe, very glad that he'd never heard his mother's voice angry enough to use every name he had, turned on him. That would have hurt more than almost any of the monster's tortures.

50

Wanna Bet?

"HEYA, TEEL!" Dauf stuck his head into the office, leaning on the doorframe. James looked up from where he was writing, carefully, with the new pen based on the ideas from the House of the Hand. He had a board balanced on his lap and his heels up on his desk, to get maximum light from the lamp behind him. The new pens tended to blot and often leak onto one's fingers but this batch was an early attempt. The innovators had a set now with much better seals. It was astonishing just to have the ink flow for so long and as smoothly as it did.

The only problem was that he had the habit of licking his pencil so now he had a number of blue streaks on his tongue and the ink just tasted nasty.

"Yes, Dauf!"

"Just opened the courier bag from the Rigas…"

Teel rolled his eyes. "And they found true sea monsters on one of their expeditions?"

"No! It's a couple of monster ambassadors from across the sea!"

Teel's heels hit the ground and a splash of ink sprayed across his page as he put his board down, thankfully not obscuring his story, or very little of it. "From Riga-Dhaum?" He asked. "Large grey ambassadors with a hand in the middle of their faces?"

Dauf blinked, surprised. "Yes! How did you know? That hand has two fingers…"

"Special edition!" Teel cried. "These two are from a country we've never heard from before! Aliens! Monsters! The edition will gain the offices triple credit from everyone!" He stepped up and plucked the missive out of Dauf's hands, eyes scanning down the page. "You have enough for your story?

Good, I'm heading up to the House." He was shrugging into his great coat, settling his hat upon his head, seizing his cane, even as he spoke. "Oh, Dauf?"

"Yes, Teel?"

"Wanna bet me a week's credit at the public house that one of the ambassadors is named Jagunjagun?"

"No, James. Not takin' it."

"Dang."

"Maybe Marcedi will take you up on it."

"We have elephants too, Dauf! Wait till I tell Ahrimaz!"

51

No Saddle, No Bridle

HE FOUND HIMSELF CLOSE TO THE BI-COLOUR, warming himself against her, his breath puffing out white as he watched Wenhiffar and the other mares drive the young stallion out of his box. "We're just going to put him in with his mama and the aunties," Wenhiffar said over her shoulder as she pulled the big door wider. "That'll straighten him out quick enough. If you can why don't you clamber up on Yustiç there?" The other mares drove the stallion out with swift and authoritative nips to his hindquarters, one wheeling to cow-kick him as he tried to break away from them back into the arena.

He noticed that while the young male squealed and hollered and lipped and hunkered down as he ran, the mares didn't let up on him. Neither did they break skin.

The door slid shut, cutting off the fascinating lessoning. Ahrimaz found himself still pressed up tight against the mare. "Yustiç?" He said quietly and she turned her head, nosing him in the face hard enough to set him back. "I don't have a saddle, I don't have a bridle… just… bareback?"

She stopped, solid, except for her quivering lips that she slobbered at him. Heylia jumped down and flopped between her front hooves. He stood, forehead against her shoulder. She was larger than he'd first taken her for, her hooves clean of feathers but still big. She radiated heat like a furnace through her thick winter coat.

He shuddered and jumped, flinging himself into his fear of the animals, suddenly in the middle of the war horse herd trying to kill him, his father laughing. He found himself astride, adjusting himself so he didn't smash his delicate bits against her spine. No bridle to control her. No curb bit, no heavy war saddle. Yet his legs settled against her sides quite naturally and he shifted his weight forward.

As she began to walk forward, on the off lead, he tensed up, dizzy and terrified once more, clenching his hands under his armpits because he didn't know what to do with them. She stopped, just short of his coat in the sand, bobbing her head up and down until he relaxed a trifle.

He found he could bear a few steps forward before his gut panicked and he and perforce the horse, froze. She was being very good. Then after a half dozen stops and starts, including him leaning and finding himself requesting a turn in the corner, she shook her head and plunged forward into four or five spine jamming trotting steps before she stretched into a happy canter.

It was like sitting a cloud he thought, finding his hands loose on his thighs as she coursed the big circle, the dogs skipping happily around her heels. Heylia sat on the high carriage seat of a buggy tucking into the corner, tail wrapped around her feet. He could just ask, and didn't have to force her head down. Or rip at the soft corners of her mouth with a heavy curb bit to make her obey. "If I'd done that to you," he said to her ears which twitched back to hear him, "you'd have bucked me off right into the river from here."

Without stirrups or bridle he found himself hair-trigger to her every motion, a stumble had him sitting back and she dropped to a walk. Without thinking he signalled for a parade walk and she snorted and nearly bounced him straight up to the roof but when she settled it was into the high-stepping 'fancy'.

"A little harsh on that change," Wenhiffar said where she leaned against the doorpost. Teel James loomed behind her, another horse, a dark bay, beside him, though this one had a light bridle and a riding pad upon it.

She walked in and retrieved his coat from the sand, brushing the dirt and dog hair from it, slinging it over her arm. "She likes you. The tack room is behind that door, to the right. M'ser James, if you would, since you requested, please begin by showing me your riding skills."

"Yes, Ma'am!"

52

You Speak! You Hear!

IN RIGA-FEREN THE CROWD WAS CONSIDERABLE AS THE SIDE OF THE ship was lowered to the pounding of a large drum, the enormous noise generated by a tiny dark man on the deck of the long-distance ship.

The Feren Doge and her entourage waited at the end of the dock, in raised chairs, gleaming in the best silks imported from Tuin, glittering like a flock of peacocks and secretary birds. They'd had frantic messages from the other Rigan cities, starting with Dham, and were the best prepared. The ambassadors from Rummummalo had seemed more amused than affronted by peoples' reaction to them and the name of their country was the best translation that could be made of the peculiar low rumble.

The Doge leaned over to her closest advisor, who straightened an already immaculate shawl of office, points not daring to be anything but perfect. "They are herbivores, truly?"

The advisor nodded. "Leaves, grass, fruit. So my people tell me. Though they were tremendously surprised at wine and seem to adore the sweetest. We are almost certainly assured of an enormous trade. They're willing to trade their ancestor's teeth, or parts of them, for our goods."

"Excellent. See if they like fruit brandy, from Inné, hmmm? Should we try and discourage them from going on? Let them trade only through us?"

"The Doge of Dham has already attempted that. They learned of all of the peoples here and wish to do at least a survey of everyone they can easily reach."

"Drown it," the Doge said mildly, smiling and waving her gilded and bejewelled fan. "And they're too big to restrain."

"I wouldn't want to offend their Queen, my Doge..."

"Of course. Here they c... oh, my."

The side of the ship had been dogged down, forming an enormous gang plank, and from the dark of the interior a shape loomed.

The first elephant that Feren saw raised a wave of astonished oooh's and one or two frightened screeches from children. He paced out of the hold, holding a staff in his trunk. It was ivory and as tall as a man, carved and painted and decorated every thumb length from pointed tip to gold band at the other end. His ears were elaborately painted in gold filigree and his own tusks had gold sequins embedded in them that flashed every step he took. On his forehead a round mirror shone and he wore a white and gold and grey cloth drape that ended in silver tassels around his... knees? Yes, his knees. A net of silver lay over his back, with each junction adorned with enamel plaques.

"Oh my," the Doge whispered. "He's five times the size of the Cylak King Stag."

The elephant paced deliberately down the dock, then somehow managed to spin in the tight space and bend his front knees as the second elephant emerged and drew a shocked silence from the crowd at its size. The drummer on the deck of the ship ceased his drumming and the elephant raised its trunk to pick him up, swinging him down to sit upon its neck, in a space on its neck scarf where people were apparently allowed to sit.

Where the first elephant had silver paint, this one had gold and instead of gold sequins, diamond chips glittered. The tusks this one had emerging from its mouth were carved much more intricately than the first and this one had no net upon its back. This one had gold bells set in a series of rows all down the gently flapping ears and the glittery chimes flowed out into the silence.

The elephant stepped off the gangway and its eye caught the Doge, whose chair was its own eye level. It nodded once, raised its trunk and the second elephant joined in the thunderous sound of trumpeting. It was so loud, and so unexpected that people fell right over here and there, to be caught or picked up.

The Doge stood, and as she did, the elephants trumpeted once more. "Welcome, heralds of your Queen, Ambassadors of Rummummalos!" As she did her best to repeat the low-rumbling name, the fellow on the second Ambassador's neck nearly fell off in shock.

"Grand, Grand Doge!" He said, his voice very low for someone his size. "That..." and here he made a sound like a deep rumble that carried up through people's feet. "Grand One speaks, hears like Earth Movings!"

The advisor hissed into the Doge's ear. "Apparently only a few people can hear the elephants true speech. I'd heard the rumour from Dham…"

"Welcome to our home," she said, not turning away from the Ambassadors, but clearly taking in her advisor's words. "Good to know."

53

"THESE FOREIGN iti-igi can hear and speak more than our own," Didara rumbled to Jagunjagun.

"And they like the shinies that our iti-igi make," he answered quietly. He was very calm for a young male. *"Perhaps we should cease our explorations with these cities for now? The iti-Queen/Doge of Mak did warn us that there are musthe iti in the hills who may attack us for our shinies."*

"And because they fear us as monsters." She added swaying from foot to foot as her iti continued to speak to the Feren Queen/Doge. Against her gold coat Ologbon was a dark figure that waved his iti-igi like arms, his smile very bright. He was a good friend and she felt very safe with him. They'd grown up together and he'd not hesitated a moment when she said she wanted to explore across the great strange sea when the Riga had appeared in their magical sailing ships that could carry all the Rigan Iti AND more than one of the People and their iti partners.

"The branch-head iti-igi Queen has promised us escort. She says her stag is in this Innean place Innetheloooom."

Didara, the Truly Curious, of the Research Curious, laid her trunk over Jagunjagun's head and watched Ologbon speak with the Riga-Feren Queen/Doge. A child iti-igi broke away from his mother in the crowd, ducked under the reaching hands of the iti-minders and sat down between Didara's feet. *"These strange calves are so trusting,"* she rumbled. *"They are not our Iti-igi who know us and grow with us."* She patted the child on the head and lifted it, squealing with delight, over the heads of the minders to offer it back to its parent.

Ologbon looked over his shoulder and boomed at them. **"Come come come please. Speech."**

"Let us go and be diplomats instead of the Curious." Jagunjagun said severely.

She shook her ears at him, making her bells clash. **"You do the talking. I shall take notes."**

* * * * *

Teel had his booted foot up, crossed over the saddle, stretching. He leaned his elbow on his knee and watched thoughtfully as Ahrimaz, whooping, landed the jump, on a strange horse, no bridle. Then a second and a third in quick succession.

Wenhiffar watched them do another round and then said. "Enough for today! Here!" She tossed his coat up at him as he thundered past, a wide grin on his face. He did another round of the arena, finishing with a triple jump before he and the bicolour mare reared to a playful stop in front of their instructor. "Nicely done," she said. "The two of you should ride them cool on the woods path. She waved. "M'ser James, you've had very good teachers, but they've let you get away with a lot of things. I am not about to put up with that. Should you choose me as a teacher while I'm working with my fetch-son here, be aware of that."

"Yes, Maitre!" he said and swept her an elegant bow, even from his awkward position.

"Go on." She sniffed and left them to walk their horses cool, the stable children… for some reason addressed as 'Tiger'… waiting to rub them down and put their blankets on, once they came back.

Teel straightened up and led the way outside, calling 'Door!' as he ducked under the lintel, Ahrimaz, with a bemused look on his face, following. In the woods, the trail through the thick winter trees barely wide enough for one horse, Ahrimaz let the mare take her own pace, both hands on her withers, just soaking up the heat she radiated.

In the steam rising off the horses images swirled up and broke apart and he blinked, wondering, thinking he was seeing things. Faces. Mostly women, hair floating up around them. Horses running. He shook his head. Why was he seeing Didara, alive? Her gold belled ears flapped silently as the image broke apart. "Teel?" He could finally focus on why the raconteur had insisted on joining him in what seemed to be an entirely unnecessary riding lesson. "You have some kind of question that's set your trousers on fire with urgency?"

Teel half turned in the saddle as his horse turned a near hair-pin corner on the trail to head back to the barn and it let him look back at Ahrimaz.

He grinned. "You might say so. You're a prophet now, you know?"

"What in Aeono's great and grand world are you babbling about?"

Teel raised his voice so that it carried as he turned his head forward, but the trail widened so that Ahrimaz could urge his mare up beside. "Why don't we let the children take the ladies in and I'll tell you inside, over a cup of hot wine? I'm very chilled."

"Son of a scorching leopard. You have some kind of news that you've been twitching with for the whole lesson! I know you... or at least your equivalent on the other side." Ahrimaz shrugged and dismounted. "Here, child, she's nearly cool."

"Thank you, M'ser Ahrimaz," she said and he nearly stopped again. Where had he learned to just speak to the lowly like that? And where had she gained permission to just answer? These people. No propriety at all.

"Why don't we go upstairs to speak for a change?" Teel raised an eyebrow at him "You've been hiding in the basement for moons now."

"I... suppose. I'm not sure..."

"Use the Green Parlour," Wenhiffar said from where she sat mending a piece of tack. "M'ser James, you know where it is."

"Yes, Madam." Ahrimaz bit his lip as they went inside, wanting desperately to go down and hide from everyone once more. Sure and Teh were at his heels and blocked him turning to the stairs.

They finally sat down in a small room painted like a Yhom forest, dark green spike-needle trees, with cups in their hands. The brand new stove based on Ahrimaz's designs brought from the Empire burned pine and was tiled in white and dark green.

Ahrimaz gulped down the hot brandy laced wine set the cup on the rustic table. "So?" He sat on the edge of the cushioned chair. "What's the news you want to startle and surprise me with?"

Teel sipped and grinned at him over the rim of the cup. "Your elephants are here, just as they were in your Empire. We have them in this world too." He grinned over at Ahrimaz. "Two of them have landed in Riga."

Ahrimaz froze, hands clenched together. "You... they... ELEPHANTS? Didara and Jagunjagun? HERE? ALIVE?"

54 Lyrian's Carbine Horse Guards

"AHRIMINASH! *Ahriminash! AHRIMINAAAAAAAASH!*" The fading crash of smashing tea cup and plate fading behind him and Teel's laggard boot heels were drowned by Ahrimaz's shouts as he sprinted up to the dimly remembered office that he'd first tried to pretend to be *him* in.

He bounced off the door jamb of the partly open door and found Ahriminash already up from behind the desk and his father with him, already responding. He nearly stumbled making the turn into the room. "I need a squad of carbiners! Right now! You have a village down toward Cylak... name of Mudredyr? I have to leave the Ambassadors are in danger and in this world I'll be able to do something! Save Didara! I need a physician surgeon and Limye and a squad. I can do it with a squad! This time those villains won't kill her!—"

"Whoa! Whoa! Son, please slow down." Ahrimiar caught him by the shoulders, turned him around and sat him down at the stove. "You need to tell us what you need and a squad takes a bit of time to get together."

Ahriminash sat down next to him. "I'm not saying I won't give you a squad but you have to be a bit more coherent than that."

Teel arrived at the door and at Ahriminash's nod joined them. "I just told Ahrimaz that there are elephants in this world as well as his world."

Ahrimiar turned to look at Ahrimaz's desperate face. "In your world they were attacked? And didn't you say that one of them died in your world."

"They were on the way to Inné... got waylaid..."

"What's this town you're talking about? At a place called Mudredyr if I managed to pick that out of the flood of words you just poured on us?"

Ahriminash turned to ring a bell on his desk and a page came trotting down the hall. "Would you fetch the Stag Lord, please?"

"Mudredyr… it was on the Cylak route-lands… the war kind of washed over it and it was half-rebuilt as an Innéan town… um… Innéan settlers."

"What happened?"

"The elephants were waylaid by bandits who were drawn from all over this area by the gems and gold they wear as normal clothing. The Rigans in my world didn't successfully warn them that they'd be drawing riff-raff like flies and only gave them infantry escort… their horses wouldn't go on with elephants and we had to teach our horses that Jagunjagun wasn't a horse-eating monster… Didara… their version of a scientist I thought… had an injury, a wound. It was a bullet that their medic couldn't get out and they pushed on here to Innéthel to get physicians help but it was too late for her."

A door slammed down the hall and Pelahir and the page sent to summon him came panting in. At least the page was out of breath though Pel wasn't.

"A problem in Cylak? The herds don't even come down toward Inné till spring," he said. "I've had no letters."

Ahriminash laid out what Ahrimaz had blurted out in such a rush and Pel got to his feet. "I'll have my *coronshion, - That's the Cylak military escort for their King Stag* - at your military dock in less than three hours." He pulled his pocket watch out of his vest, chain dangling. "Make that three and a half hours. That village Mudredyr… we can reach faster by the river and then taking the White Road across. From my recollection of our Routes."

"There's a road from White?" Ahrimaz asked and Ahriminash cleared a swath of papers off his table. An Innéan and Cylak and Yhom map, with the Rigan cities on the edges, had been painted as a new top. "Here," he said, pointing. "Dah if you would…"

"I'll get the Lyrian Carbine Horse Guard. They should be up to this. Ahrimaz, you'll need to arm up with my son's things… I'll lend you a sword since we won't hand you the country's sword for this. We can save your friend and perhaps arrange better contact with these people."

"In this world that's a Cylak ford and yes they've had bandits in the hills for years."

Ahrimaz leaned over the map, hiding his shaking hands by tracing all the strange roads the connections between three separate countries, listening to them just accept his crack-brained demand and start putting together a military force that they were apparently just going to hand him. "Um… not your Ahrimaz? You're going to just let me ride away with Innéan soldiers?"

Ahrimiar raised an eyebrow at him and Ahrimaz froze, cringing inside, waiting for a wrath that never came. "What would you do with them? They all know you aren't our boy but that I'm accepting you as my son. They think I'm crazy or that you've gone crazy and if you give them insane orders they will not obey. If you give them sane orders, and Pelahir and his escort are with you, they'll do as they're told."

"Pelahir and his *coronshion*."

"His *coronshion*, yes and all our horses will run with Cylak stags. Particularly this Horse Guard," Ahriminash said. "We can't slight the Cylak Stag Lord our protection. All are excellent shots with both carbines and bows. We don't have as many guns as your Empire seems to have. Inné has had bowmen for years. Now we have our different shooters."

"I... yes... how can I help get us on the road faster. Teel, where did you have word of the Elephant Ambassadors? The **Rummummalo**?" The familiar rumble shook its way out of his chest and all the other men in the room jumped.

"That's their tongue?" Teel asked, then nodded sharply. "They were at Riga-Feren, last I heard."

"And Mudredyr is ten days away by fast horse from there," Ahrimaz said. "About the same as from here. They were ambushed a half day closer... in the broken hills there." He pointed on the map. "If we leave today, we can make it."

"Especially if you go by river."

"May I come with?" Teel leaned over to lay his finger on White. "I grew up there."

"Get your kit together raconteur," Ahrimaz said idly, mind already racing, already thinking of how to arrange his men for river and then road. "If you fall behind, I'm not coming back for you."

55 ——————————————————
A Harsh Place

OLOGBON, SO COMFORTABLE ON DIDARA'S NECK THAT HE SAT CROSS legged, dropped the last mirror chip he'd just embroidered around back into the basket.

"**Aren't you going to put those on my hat too?**" Didara rumbled at him as they walked the narrow, wet road.

"**There's already not much room to put any more mirrors, Di!**" But he smiled and stretched his fingers. "**The Queen stag's people say there's a storm coming and they hope to open one of their herd shelters.**"

"**What kind of storm, Olo?**" She asked. "**This rain is starting to turn white and the road is getting slippery as if it were mud instead of good stone! This is a crazy country where rain is white and doesn't go away. And I'm cold! Water moves from a liquid state to a solid state in many more forms than I thought. This will make a wonderful science song to match my theory of water becoming invisible and part of air under pressure of heat!**

"**I'll transcribe notes for you once we reach the herd shelter,**" he said, grinning, but she interrupted him.

"**I can transcribe my own notes, thank you, Olo! I'd rather you embroidered more mirrors on my hat! Or on Jagunjagun's muff I suppose.**"

"**I'm not so vain, Didara,**" he said from his place just behind the Queen stag's Antlers… They were armed and acting like they were in imminent danger, from more than just the oncoming storm. "**I like the fur lining but can do without the shinies. You can have my share.**"

They turned a sharp corner and entered a clearing where they turned off the road and followed edge of an abrupt drop off around to what looked like a bitten-off chunk of hill. The road they followed now was a path beaten by centuries of hooves it looked like, though the top layer was muddy and slick. It took them a good while to make it around and down to the floor of the byte, and Didara and Jagunjagun moved into the centre of the area.

"This is their shelter? Jagunjagun swayed back and forth, his ears waving in distress. **"The head antler said this storm could drop enough snow on us to bury us to the armpits! Even if this is out of the storm wind's path!"**

"No, Jag," Ologbon said. **"See? They can cover enough of this space for a herd of a thousand apparently."**

"That seems a bit over optimis…ah." Didara interrupted herself as their Cylak escort fanned out and looped ropes around what looked like great hoops arching across the ground. The High Antler came and bowed to them, the high, fast gabble almost too much for either Didara or Jagunjagun to follow.

"They want us to pull, if we would be so kind?" Jagunjagun trumpeted laughter. **"Olo, hook us up!"**

He laughed and slid down Didara's shoulder to squeak at the High Antler, who laughed back and the ropes were quickly passed to Olo, as Didara and Jagunjagun turned around at his direction.

The two elephants both wore neck swags under their newly designed winter coats and there were hooks that snapped open at their shoulders where the ropes were quickly looped in and then, in unison, they stepped forward. One step pulled the ropes up out of the mud and squeezed water out of the fibres. The second step brought the ponderous hoop up out of the trench it had been buried in and the ends were locked against the cliff wall so as the elephants walked it rose up and out, followed by a slightly smaller hoop, then a third and a fourth and a fifth.

"How on earth do they lift this without us?" Didara asked and Olo, at her ear, walking forward with her, shrugged.

"Probably a lot of deer and a lot of people," he looked back at the Cylak escort and they waved them on.

"He said he needs a six hoop roof… ah." The sixth hoop locked in place at an angle that would let Ologbon duck under it, as the first hoop touched the cliff face, the elephants facing the rock wall with the ropes pulled back by Cylak deer and men. People scrambled up to lock the hoops tight to the wall and then the cords came loose.

"Look at that!" Didara turned and raised her trunk, delighted, as people drew bales of leaves? If they were leaves they were double the height of these tall people and whistling to speed themselves up they began spiking them to the hoops with nails made of what looked like huge thorns, lashing rawhide ropes between the hoops to reinforce them.

The wind was already howling through the trees above the cliff, and gusts would hit the needle trees outside their byte. Snow in tiny ice pellets swirled above, even as the roof and walls closed out the darkening sky.

"The Cylak say that it will be safe to light fires inside, once they finish. Only a little snow will get in right at the start. And there will be enough leather leaves to make a dry floor."

"Ingenious. These leaves grow here each year? They must or they wouldn't be able to gather them in such quantities but those trees we saw are all needle trees. Where do they grow? How on earth do those trees gather enough energy to make such sized leaves?"

"I'll go help with the floor, Di, so I can do more embroidery and then you can take notes of all your questions!"

"Get one of the antlers to talk to me later, would you?"

"Of course, Di, we just need to get everyone under cover first."

The wind note dropped even then and the snow swirls became whips that began hissing over the newly sealed shelter, every Cylak running to get the leaves tied down tight. They'd have to cut a door after but solid shelter was more important.

Two fireplaces at the cliff face, with natural chimneys, already had fires laid and candle lanterns were being lit as they closed themselves into darkness, oppressive even when it was taller than Didara. Jagunjagun found himself with his trunk tucked carefully into the fur muff under his chin, standing near one of the fireplaces, across from where the horses and the riding deer were, gently swaying almost hypnotically to the hiss of the now vicious wind outside.

"This is such a harsh place," he rumbled below even where Olo could hear him. **"Didara, these are very tough people."**

56

Spousal Abuse?

TEEL WATCHED AHRIMAZ PACE UP AND DOWN THE ROAD by the military dock, fuming and thunderous, as the young priest did his best to pray that the barges be released from the ice.

They'd made good time the first two days, the river still flowing slush and chunks of ice and then, when they'd tied up at Mantes-la-Jolie the temperature had dropped overnight and they'd been frozen in hard.

The young Hunter priest sat, cross-legged at the bow altar, with both hands out of their mittens and clutched around the copper line spanned around the boat at the waterline... or in this case the thin film of water and ice line. His head was bent and he was struggling to pray, again, for the God to warm the boats free.

The riding mare that Ahrimaz had been training on trailed at his heels like the two dogs, the war cat draped over the mare's blanketed back. Every time he turned, boot heel grinding his frustration into the snow, the animals turned with him. He didn't notice, fists swinging to raise puffs of snow from his sleeves as he shivered and tried to beat some heat into himself. The Captain had already stopped him from screaming at the young priest twice and sent him off to pace the bank until he calmed down.

"Like a raging tiger, pacing the bars of a cage." Teel wrote in his notebook and looked up as Ahrimaz slowed by the gangway and stopped, digging his toes into the filthy snow. "Here," he said finally, looking around at the entourage of animals around him. "You lot get back on board."

The mare's ears twitched forward, then back, then she bobbed her head and carefully tripped up the wide gangway, to her tent-stall onboard. Heylia swiped at Ahrimaz as they went by, stealing his scarf right off his neck. He grinned and caught it long enough to make her bite it in a fury before letting her have it and turned up the wool twist collar of his great coat against the biting cold wind.

"The snow, you say, is probably going to pass south of us?" He asked the barge master as he trudged up onto the barge, scowling down at the ice. The hull squealed and groaned as the pressure changed and Ahrimaz winced.

"Looks like," he said and spat over the side to leave a brown splot against the enemy. Teel followed along, ducking under the tent flap and welcoming the heat the horses generated. Ahrimaz cleared his throat at the Horse Guard's desk. Really it was a postage stamp sized board hung on a strap around her neck to make a shelf over her lap when she sat. She looked up at him, frowning.

"Captain," Ahrimaz said quietly. "I have an idea. Let me take my Imaryan and speak to our priest? I promise not to discommode him."

Captain Jeanne rubbed a hand over the power-burn scar on one cheek. "And you were going to grab him and shake him like a pup not two minutes ago?" She shook her head. "The Hand made me swear not to let you channel the God as it would harm you, even if you could break us out."

"I also swear not to channel the God, Captain. I have an idea that turns my guts and makes me weak in the knees but it might open the river and give a lesson in being a priest to your Hunter boy over there." He nodded at the tent wall where the priest knelt.

"Then go ahead, Ser!" She snapped. "If you make him unhappy and cut him off from Aeono I'll scorching warm your hide personally!"

He smiled at her, as if she were a puppy savaging one of his slippers, Teel thought. "Thank you, Captain."

"Eh! Limyé! Would you be so kind?" The Imaryan looked up from where he and the young chirurgeon, Etienne were consulting one of the medical books.

"Ahrimaz?" He rose and they became a little entourage heading up to the bow.

"Limyé I need you to make sure I don't slip and get angry or frustrated. The Innéans think that the God and Goddess are a couple, correct?"

"That is correct, Ahrimaz."

"And I come from a world where there's a lot of spousal abuse happening."

"I don't understand where you're going with this, Ahrimaz."

"I think I see a little of it here. I recognize someone trying to force something out of fear, am I correct?" They'd stopped just back from the altar and Ahrimaz faced the stern, the wind practically ripping his quiet words out of his mouth.

"You could be right," Limyé said. "Are you going to try and explain it to him?"

"In my best and most priestly and healerly manner."

Teel stared at him in shock. "Priestly? Healerly?"

Ahrimaz grinned at him. "Just like your oh-so-precious Ahrimaz Hand of the People, beloved blah blah blah…" He turned and stepped up onto the altar step and knelt beside the young Hunter priest and turned his mittens and his uncovered face up to the icy grey sky.

57

We Can Only Ask

DIDARA THE CURIOUS, IS IT YOU? Is it just a phantom of my friend? I don't know I don't know I can't chance it I HAVE to get us over to that ambush site in my world, on the edge of the Boundless Grimy Fen.

I can't tell that young medic that in my world he's my personal physician that I am poisoning, needing me to give him an antidote every morning so that he not die...

Limyé I need to keep talking to you. I need to keep taking those remedies of yours... But right now, the thing I need most of all is to be moving or I will go foaming at the mouth mad. Ahrimaz ground his teeth in rage, felt the priest sense it and try and ease a fraction of a finger-width further away, without making it obvious. *He thinks he's being unobtrusive and is frightened of setting me off.*

Lyrian Mother of Tigers, Demon Witch Nurse, may I sacrifice my rage to You? May I give it to You? Or will that just... even as he thought this he could feel a wave of relaxation wash over him, his stomach unknot, his hammering heart cool. The tight band around his forehead and the cables attaching his head to his neck suddenly clicked and loosened. He could see or feel or somehow hear the fire in his blood pouring into his centre and there somehow being removed from the flow. He removed his mittens and stuck them in his belt. *Thank You.*

"My Father, in the other world, spent years of his life trying to beat me open to take the God in," he said conversationally, still looking up at the sky. The priest realized he didn't necessarily want a response and sat silent. "It never worked. Oh, I forced myself open and they made me drink the Fire Cup every year, as Hunter, as the Fiery Killer." He paused remembering the nauseating pain of it, like swallowing a live scorpion. "What they've all forgotten in that world is that people cannot demand if they have no power. It's like a toddler having a nasty tantrum until the Divinity gives them what they're whining for with an exasperated 'HERE!'"

The priest was startled into laughing. "I've been doing a lot of learning, here," Ahrimaz said, feeling the cold and the damp that had been plaguing him drift out of his mouth on the fog of his every breath. "It seems to me that the way to actually address either Him, or Her, is to ask. We cannot know why the Gods do as they do. We cannot know how much our requests would interfere with our own or someone else's free will. But it is given to us to say 'Would this help?' or 'May I do this?' He coughed as he choked down tears suddenly threatening to burst out of his eyes and stop his throat.

I tried to force you to love me. Yolend, Pel, the babies even. And the only way I knew how to touch them was by controlling them, hurting them, terrorizing them. The country. My soldiers. No wonder they love my fetch self. He learned how to ask. Ahrimaz cringed inside at what this priest or the watching raconteur or the healer must be thinking, and let the tears flow. He couldn't help remembering the horrific, satisfying smash of his fist into his Yolend's face. He could make her cry. He could make her react to him. And Pelahir... *I could make him beg for me to hurt him. The way Father hooked pain to sex with me. I... don't think I ever want to have sex with anyone ever again.*

As he thought this he felt the Goddess withdraw from him, Her disapproval icy and suddenly he shivered again, the raw winter catching his skin and his throat.

Lyrian, I'll try. I'll try. Truly. I mean... how? And how may I ask you for help? I don't know. I don't know anything. The deadly cold clutching his heart faded.

"Asking the Gods anything is like letting snowflakes land on your hands and not melt," he said. He could hear the priest take a breath as if he were about to ask a question. "You have a lover, Charles? *Yes, that was his name.* A Hunter's Partner?" The boy nodded.

"So think of your partner and making love to them," Ahrimaz said. "Think of the heat that rises between you. Offer yourself to the God like that. Only war cats can get away with shoving their faces in to demand caresses." Another chuckle from the boy and a catch in his breath. "Think of how it feels to turn your cheek and anticipate being caught up by the God's love. The moment when the Divine breath warms your face, the first touch of God."

He could feel the young man's opening, following his words. He could feel the heat rising from his heartbeat and his blood and his sex. His heart rate sped up and suddenly all around the barge the copper wire under his hands began to warm up, then glow. One breath. Two breaths.

He's doing it. He's opening himself to the Fire of Heaven. Aeono, thank you. Lyrian? May I do this? May I try to rescue my friends in this world? Their **Rummummalos** *names are...*" and he dropped to the range of voice that so few people could hear. The rumble spread out from him, to the riverbank and washed back to reverberate in the water. The Horse Guard moved to be with their mounts as sailors shouted and the barge master went from indolent to active. Whistles, shouts, stragglers scrambling up the gangway one last girl clinging to it even as it came up and inboard with a crack.

The Hunter priest's altar showed a blazing fire now, though there was no fuel to burn, and the barge dropped a handspan as it melted free of the ice, that then broke into man-sized pieces. Teel scribbled madly in his book, Limyé nodding and looking thoughtful.

The wave came from nowhere, and everywhere, somehow a wave rolled down the river and the new ice shattered and broke into chunks.

Ahrimaz made the Ambassador's true names a prayer, his eyes closed, his hands loose, water pooling in his palms, pouring down his knees. He was lost remembering how it felt to be loved without reservation. Didara had shown him that. Love, not sex. Compassion. A creature so enormous, so strong, so careful that she didn't hurt him, even as she was dying and in fever and pain.

He didn't notice as the sailors sprang to untie them, and ride this miraculous wave downriver.

58 Throat-Sing and Lyrian, Destroyer

IT WAS SHELTER. It was safe from the storm that was now muffled as the snow built up on the half dome. But it kept getting smellier all the time with the deer and the horses and the elephants and the people, though there was a stone lined trench for a latrine that lead outside under the hoop wall. The problem was the sheer quantity that both Didara and Jagunjagun produced, even if it was herbivore dung and there was only so much liquid water to help the feces flow away especially once the weight of snow pinned the flap down and blocked anything from flowing anywhere.

Ologbon and the Cylak spent some time shovelling from inside and then threw ashes over the worst of it.

"If we had enough meltwater we could just spray it away," Jagunjagun said in the Innéan tongue, practicing. His trunk was curled tight into his muff where he had a dried apple studded with cloves to smell.

Didara, ears folded back tight with her hat flaps tied firmly under her chin, rocked back and forth the mirrors on her hat and the gems in her tusks glittering in the lantern light as she moved, eyes closed, distracted. "Hmm? What? Jagunjagun please leave me alone, I'm right in the middle of the precis and I'm trying to express it correctly!" She thrummed crossly and all across the shelter a dozen people turned to look at her.

Ologbon gazed around at them. "Look at that!" he said. "So many foreign iti-igi can hear you when you speak properly! Women and men both!"

The Cylak captain pulled a blanket up over her shoulders and edged between two of her riding deer and past the knot of warriors. "You sing?" she asked Ologbon.

"Sing? No… it is speaking for my partners."

"Perhaps we should sing for you." She turned to her group and with much laughter they arranged themselves in a semi-circle in front of the two elephants. "We call this throat-sing. Pass some more time before we sleep."

*   *   *   *   *

The black haired girl child is sitting next to the young priest and I. But her hair isn't black any longer. It is the colour of icicles in the night and her eyes are white and her skin. There are shards of ice in her hair and her eyelashes, clinging to the hair on her skin so she has razor chips glittering at the corners of her mouth and on the tips of her ears. Her bare hands are bone white and her long, long nails are black and colder than the ice and snow that make her flesh. I can feel the radiant freeze and when she smiles at me the inside of her mouth is black and her sharp teeth glitter like new fallen snow against that darkness.

I fear her. I love her. I know Her.

"So you can only welcome me as Lover when I am Destruction? How cold!" She laughs and her laughter falls from the sky whipped by the howling wind and runs before us.

"Lady…" I try to swallow and it feels as though the saliva in my throat is freezing as it goes down. "I know You."

"Not really. You know the Fire of Destruction. My Husband is the One who can engulf worlds in his Fires of Rage. He breaks all of Creation down and when all the fire is leached out it comes to me. I am the Darkness between Stars and Aeono sheets his Flames through me and yet does not touch the heart of my coldness."

"I have seen you in my mother's eyes."

"Rutaçyen in your world, not Wenhiffar. She will die of Me, soon and welcome her death. Her life in your world has been torture."

"Can't the other one save her?"

"He will. He will let her die, as you could not. And I will cool and soothe the burns your father scorched into her soul."

I can feel the tears freezing on my cheeks and the water that flowed from my hands become thick slush and then columns of ice flowing from my fingers over the floorboards. I cannot let Her freeze us all. "Lyrian Destroyer, thank you."

"What, for letting another part of Me help you? Because you asked properly?"

"Yes."

She stares at me, then flings her deadly laughter in my face and I can feel it sting as my tears crack. "Good. You needn't fear my husband's heat any longer, child. See?"

She draws a clear mirror in front of me and in it I can see the young priest's fires dancing, glittering and frozen. My scars don't ache, seeing them, even the brand on my chest. Her cheeks flush a faint pink and suddenly I'm hard. I want Her. "If my sex offends I'm sorry," I say, terrified. "But You are beautiful."

59   Thank the Greater Sky

TEEL TUCKED HIS NOTEBOOK AWAY AND SAT DOWN ON A BALE OF HAY, just watching Ahrimaz on the bow of the barge.

The Hunter priest came out of his prayers, when he hit the end of them. They were timed so that a priest didn't burn himself out getting lost in the Divine. He rose, and stretched, the fire on the altar burning itself out. Then he looked at Ahrimaz, apparently lost in speaking to the Goddess, ice riming the edge of every hair, every hem. He sat in a pool of water that ran over the boards and into the gunwales then on into the river.

"We need to break him out of that, or She'll kill him with kindness," Pelahir said and took off his massive fur mittens.

"Kindness? I've never found Our Lady to be very kind, in this mood, at this time of year," Teel said.

"Oh, you people!" Limyé pushed between them, horse blanket in his hands.

"Wait, wait! You'll just get it all wet. Let me help!" Pelahir strode over to Ahrimaz, knelt next to him and put his hands up before his face as though blowing feathers off his palms, whistling a little heat into the moisture.

The Hunter priest nodded and held his hands up so that Pel could blow across them, too, a tiny flame, like a match glowing on his fingertips. "Be careful," Limyé said. "You're already tired."

"Yes, Healer but it's not a lot of heat that he needs. Just a little."

The water pouring off Ahrimaz suddenly billowed up into a gust of steam, a swirl of snow and blew away as his cheeks suddenly went from pallid to rosy. Limyé flung the blanket around him and both he and Pelahir wrapped their arms tightly around him as he began to struggle. "No, no,

She's willing to let me die now, for all that I've done. The other Ahrimaz has saved the Empire and I've done enough of what She wants. She's willing to freeze my heart. No, don't warm me up!"

"Shut up, Shit Head," Pel said firmly. "We still need you and you were desperate to save your friend from that world in this one, weren't you? Didara? Is that her name?"

The setting sun broke through the clouds and the light sparkled on Ahrimaz's eyelashes and face as the ice sublimated and blew away as vapour and his eyes opened. He stared into Limyé's eyes for a long moment, reading the resolve there to not let him die. Then he twisted in the blanket to look into Pel's face. "Why are you doing this? You don't even like me. You can't like me. If I die I'm becoming convinced that She will bring your lover back to you. She's not as cruel as people are."

He buried his face down into the blanket and between Limyé and Pelahir they lifted him up and took him back to the cabin, feet staggering, slipping.

Teel shook his head and looked over at the Captain, who shrugged. "Goddesses and Gods are not my purview. But he just doesn't seem to understand that he's just done a miracle to get us moving again, taught a young priest something about how to pray, and connected to Herself, all at once; and now he's despairing and wanting to die?" She shook her head. "I read a story or two of our own Ahrimaz who had a tendency to demand too much of himself, because we demanded too much of him."

He shrugged back at her. "That Ahrimaz is just learning how hard it is to be a good man and he's punishing himself for having been a monster." He pulled out his notebook and scribbled down the Title 'Paying for it: Having Been A Monster'.

Charles, the Hunter Priest, took off his stole. "He's a good teacher," he said quietly. "I hope he teaches himself a thing or two."

Teel couldn't help but laugh. "Like most good teachers he's finding out that some students are pretty scorching stubborn about not hearing."

* * * * *

Jagunjagun sent out a happy thrum that resonated well below the iti-igi 'throat-singing' but found that it was a harmonic for that. Didara flapped her ears and added another level. The human's eyes grew round as their sound was reinforced and the ground began trembling slightly in time with their song.

"It's good," Olugbon said quietly to one of the lesser Stag people who wasn't singing, just sitting and clapping along. "It will take their minds off being shut in."

"It's good," the man agreed. "Storm should break up tomorrow."
"Oh, thank the Greater Sky!"

60

Much Hurried

On A Mission to Greet Ambassadors

—By Teel James, Raconteur for the Coalition News, Chronicles of Inné and Innéthel and their environs, Late Winter

Your intrepid raconteur is currently mailing his stories from White, a town that most Innéans living in the Thel only see in the summer, more rarely in spring after break-up, or fall before freeze up.

The river, our Lady's gift, has frozen hard behind our barges as we have been incredibly lucky. I am currently with the Lyrian Carbine Horse Guard and the Cylak King Stag and his *coronshion,* under the direction of Ahrimaz. We have trusted information that the Ambassadors from Rummummalos, very large and very lavishly ornamented courtiers, are under a dreadful threat to their lives and are tasked with intercepting them and escorting them safely to Innéthel. Our informant tells us that the Riga Cities did not give the Ambassadors sufficient escort. In this world this might be different but Inné cannot afford to risk this.

Rummummalos are willing to trade their tooth-ivory in exchange for made goods and they also have amazing makers, specializing in jewelry. Their gem stones are very rarely seen on this continent, another trade commodity. They are fantastic creatures that dwarf the Cylak great stags and might be willing to exchange apprentices for their lapidary industry and for our great works projects. As I recounted in one of my earlier stories, we were nearly frozen in at the military dock and were prayed free by our Hunter Priest, with assistance from Ahrimaz. Yes, the *other* Ahrimaz, who apparently has as strong a connection to our most precious and terrifying Goddess Lyrian as *our* Ahrimaz.

It is on the Hand's recognizance that Ahrimaz Kenaçyen is here, and in charge of the Horse Guard. The family, though cognizant of all the startling differences between the differently raised men, are acknowledging him as their own, as I have also said before.

Apparently these Ambassadors were also present in the world of the Empire and were attacked and injured for their jewels. One, a 'Curious', or inventor/researcher by the name of Didara, died and the survivor went home in grief, vowing to cut off any travel between their country and ours. In this world, Ahrimaz insists there is a chance to save the Ambassador Didara and to save the connection, the friendly and potentially lucrative exchange of ideas and goods with the Rummummalos.

White, in the winter, is very representative of its name. The marble it is known for and built from is white, the roof tiles are white and just after snowfall it all but vanishes. The Horse Guard, with silver shining armour high-blue greatcoats and gold braid, multi-coloured horses, and their silken banners blazoned with the flowering apple tree are a wild splash of colour, while the stags of the Stag, Cylak King Pelahir, throw up sprays of snow beside the road, the fields safely frozen under their shaggy feet, their antler bells ringing as they outrun the horses.

We have seven days to meet the Ambassadors in the hope of rescuing them from this prophesied attack. Seven days in the depth of winter, with the road-clearing crews much bogged down, we will be moving a military force across the country to the edges of the Grim Quagmire, in all its frozen leagues.

The Horse Guard laugh and say I should keep my carbine dry, since the Captain has decided that I should not only have my sword to defend myself but that I shall train with firearms, along with the rest of her Guard, firing at smaller and smaller targets in the snow when we stop for the nights.

I am sending the story back to White with my Broadsheet courier and the next the 'Sheet will hear is whether we have succeeded or not, as we tear through snow and cold and ice and slush, to the edge of the biggest patch of muck in all the known lands.

The call comes for me to be quick, to mount up. I pull my mitten back on with my teeth and hand off my missive to the courier waiting on her shaggy, rough pony.

I am, your much-hurried raconteur, Teel James.

61   This Scorching Antique!

TEEL CLUTCHED HIS MUG OF STEAMING HOT TEA AND SQUINTED AT THESE horribly active young men and women as they broke camp, but left their bags piled on the ground sheets for a short round of target practice.

Once the Horse Guard stopped for the night it was too dark for any such thing and they did their training in momentary increments in the morning, around breakfast and breaking camp.

Teel's own kit was already to be strapped behind his saddle but the Captain was beckoning him up to the line scratched in the snow.

"You have a musketoon, M'ser?" *How polite.*

"My uncle's, M'ser."

"Would you be willing to lend it to His Honour Ahrimaz?"

Ahrimaz looked startled at that. Of course, as Emperor he'd never had to think of *buying* or *inheriting* a weapon.

"Certainly, Captain." He drew it and offered Ahrimaz both it and the powder-horn.

"Thank you, M'ser," he said, not at all absently, and took it. "What do you want me to shoot," he asked the Captain.

A man-sized paper was being tacked to a tree close by and the Cylak, all with their bows, leaned back against their packed bags and just watched. The Captain waved a fur mitten at it. "That."

Ahrimaz expertly rammed a charge home, raised an eyebrow at being offered a ball as ammunition and set the round home, raised the short barrelled carbine across his forearm to brace it. The flint rasped and the gun boomed, the hole in the target in the left abdomen.

It is astonishing that he hit anything with a strange weapon, especially a muskatoon. The Captain hid her astonishment well and then clamped her jaw tight as Ahrimaz thrust the empty weapon back in Teel's direction and snarled at her. "So you've hazed me and found I can fire an antique like that. Give me something that my grandfather wouldn't recognize!"

"M'ser," Teel said mildly. "That is the finest weapon out of the gun shops of Innéthel and I'll thank you not to impugn my family's bequest to me!" The finely carved walnut stock and the tooled brass bit into his hand, even through the palm of his mitten as his hand clenched.

Ahrimaz stared at Teel and then at the Captain who nodded at her soldiers—who presented arms with a 'crack'. He stared at the snap locks and flintlocks and matchlocks, flared muzzles and 'tulip-stem' barrels... stared at them all. "You don't have smokeless powder? What the scorch are you doing? You distill mineral spirits don't you?"

"Smokeless powder? What are you talking about?"

Teel ran the cleaning cloth into the barrel of his weapon, quite glad that his own marksmanship wasn't being called into question. "I believe that there might be some difference between the worlds when it comes to military invention, Captain."

Everyone looked at Teel, who shrugged. "It makes sense. Empire. Wars... lots of military spending. Here our last war was nearly fifteen years ago."

The Captain shook her head. "Scorch my precious pink ass. Gunsmith!" The man presented himself with a snap of his boot heels. "We're setting out now, you lot," she snapped. "Ahrno, you ride next to this Ahrimaz of ours and ask him everything he knows about carbines and musketoons in his world. *Scorching antiques?* All day if you have to. All tomorrow or as long as he knows ANYTHING you don't, clear?"

"As ice on the river, Cap."

"Good. We don't really have time for this nonsense."

Ahrimaz bowed to the Captain and to James, both. "Teel, I did not mean to insult you or your family."

"No insult taken." He coughed and holstered his carbine in its saddle holster, swung up on the borrowed horse. "If you need, this *antique* is at your service, M'ser!" He resolved to ride just behind Ahrimaz and the gunsmith in the hopes of hearing their conversation.

"Teel..." Ahrimaz stared at him and Pel clapped him on the shoulder to encourage him to move. "Later. We have leagues to go today."

"And several days thereafter, M'ser. Look, Ahrimaz, just keep telling us about this stuff from your world, all right? You don't need to take it personally that we haven't developed the same things at the same rate."

"Blast. You're right."

The *coronshion* thundered ahead into scouting position and everyone was now mounted. A whistle and they moved. "Urgent," Ahrimaz said in an almost dazed voice. "This is *urgent* and it's why we're freezing our nethers off in this snow!"

"Introduce me when we meet them, hmmm?"

"Ass."

"Thank you."

62

Gun Lint

AHRIMAZ ACTUALLY HUNCHED IN THE SADDLE IN A WAY THAT WOULD have had the Old Monster clouting him off the horse. He folded the collar of his great coat up over his neck and the back of his head, buttoning it one handed. "I don't know," he snapped at the gunsmith. *Ahrno. That's his name.* "Look, Ahrno, you've asked me half a dozen times and I don't know any more precisely than that. I mostly used the stuff. You soak cotton lint, the fluff before it's woven, in sulphuric acid and nitric acid. You keep it cold while its soaking or it'll go bad. You keep it cold and you'll get the same reaction every time. Let it dry in the sun. You'll get something that you daren't put in these old muzzle loaders without blowing them to scorching flinders and taking someone's hand or head off."

"But..."

"Five grains of treated cotton will give you an explosion that puts thirty grains of black gunpowder to shame, however innocent it looks. Thirty grains of gunpowder will crack a granite rock. Five grains of gun cotton will blow it to gravel."

Ahrno went pale as far as Ahrimaz could see since he had a knitted muffler up over his face. "It would be best to invoke the God like that in the depth of winter where the Goddess controls the burn."

"That's a good way of putting it." *Perhaps that's one reason the Old Monster line suppressed Lyrian's worship. She controls the God and they couldn't stand that thought, even though it seems that He controls her in turn. They are equals in this world.*

The bicoloured mare's astonishing gait was as easy to ride as a hobby horse and they were all gaited like her, except the stags... Pel had laughed and laughed and told him the 'stags' were actually does since they kept their antlers longer, all the way to late winter. The does ploughed through the drifts like automata, but they devoured the bales of lichen everybody carried like snow melting in sunshine. The horses inhaled grain and sweet-feed as fast as the deer, who sneaked as much of the sweet-feed as they could. At least they could carry enough to take them through this cold quickly. Every other day they'd hit another village and slept warm. It made an immense difference.

In the Empire those villages had all been consolidated into more distant and larger towns and this kind of winter military action wouldn't have worked well at all.

The gunsmith urged his horse up to ride next to the Captain, riding rein-less to stab urgent fingers at his book and make wild waving gestures.

Ahrimaz grunted and sank deeper into his coat. He felt like he should be uncomfortable, the coat and the armour and the weapons *shouldn't* fit him perfectly even though he and the other Ahrimaz were nearly identical in so many ways. *I'm not him. He's a good man. I'm not. I was taught to be a monster. I don't deserve to be comfortable. I don't deserve the animals...* Heylia, on the back of his saddle bunted her head into the back of his and he could feel her purr as she clung to the leather pads on his shoulders.

The dogs ran at his horse's heels, all goofy lolling tongues and galumphing joy at going. It didn't seem to matter where as long as it was with him.

The great coat actually had a tuck-flap to cut the wind around his boots and he was warm enough from the exercise. Not a bad way to travel, if one must, in the winter.

The gunsmith was making more interesting waving motions with his arms as he babbled at the Captain who kept looking back at him. Gun-cotton. So simple. So innocent. So deadly.

Pel dropped back, his st—doe grumbling as she stepped onto the plowed road. "We'll make Champ de Navet while it's still light. If the weather holds we'll make it to the Mire in less than two days."

Ahrimaz nodded shortly. "Good. I have this horrid feeling we're cutting it too close as it is."

"We don't know that. We'll do our best. And we are going to save your friend. You are going to save your friend."

"Won't I be flouting the will of the Gods if I do? I mean in the other world this happened more than a year ago and I couldn't save her then."

"Perhaps that's one of the reasons you got swapped when you did."

Ahrimaz nearly stopped the mare in the road, staring at Pelahir. "You really think so?"

"I have no clue. It's a guess. What with free will and so forth how can anyone guess the minds of the Gods?"

Ahrimaz found himself looking up at the clouds that had relentlessly covered the sky like a threatening dark grey blanket for days and sniffed at the sudden wind. Pel turned his face up too. "Stag Lord's left nut. It's going to snow, or..." He put his hand on his doe's shoulder. "Rain. Frost rain it smells like."

"Scorch. Scorching anus of God."

63

Another Word for Hardened Water

"WE SHOULD HAVE STAYED IN THAT LITTLE VILLAGE," Didara complained swaying back and forth, her trunk curling up and down. Her be-jewelled tusks were now wound with bright yarn, which she thought was a bad compromise but she didn't want her carved tusks to crack in the wildly swinging temperatures.

Jagunjagun leaned up against her and swayed with her, Ologbon lying on her back and neck with a feather quilt over him, looking like a blue and white checked bump on her boiled woollen coat.

"This weather is making me vastly less curious! I'm almost not interested in yet another type of water in a hardened state!"

"It will be all right, Didara!" We'll get to this Innéth place and the stag people say they have big indoor spaces for their horses that are heated!"

"And their horses won't go crazy when they see us? It took days of training before these animals stopped jittering and they aren't even really horses. Deer and a couple of horses and mules and the mules are suspicious."

Jagunjagun pressed harder against her as she complained. There wasn't much wind and the shelter seemed safe enough but the ribs creaked and complained as the ice… another word for hard water – built up on the outside.

It was another Cylak shelter spot, opened up out of season as the rain began, a short day away from that village they called Mud. The land had flattened out and there were no nice hollows or old quarries to be half the shelter and have chimneys and latrines. Though this one was normally a rounded bump on flat land they'd not sealed it down tight like the first.

Jagunjagun could see out through the bare trees and in the setting sun the branches were black. It was just rain falling but when it landed it hardened and hardened enough to become instantly slick and tremendously dangerous for both the elephants and for everyone else too. They'd opened the shelter with the rain falling and the ice growing and Didara had nearly fallen, straining her forefeet.

The pattering sound was soothing though and it was warmer in the covered space. But her feet hurt and the ice just kept getting thicker and they weren't going anywhere anytime soon. They'd hoped to find the military road that led to White because the path they were on was become a muddy little track that had washes of freezing muck overflowing it here and there.

Jagunjagun didn't flinch when an explosive 'bang' echoed. They'd gotten used to the bursting tree limbs over the past few hours.

"Everything's grey and dirty and cold and sometimes freezing and cutting my feet and it's all black and nothing pretty, nothing to rest my eyes on," she complained, lifting first one forefoot, then the other.

"Little mother," Ologbon said from his nest on her neck. **"What if you raise your feet and rest them one at a time, let me rub some warming cream into them and wrap them up in wool?"**

"You have something?" Her trunk curled up and patted him. **"Bless you, iti-igi, bless you."**

"It's a rug from the city Queen. I'll get it mucky but I'm sure it will be washable."

"Tuck my coat under my belly and I'll lie down," Jagunjagun said. **"It will warm me up, while you do that."**

"All right. Why don't you move around so that you don't lie down in that stream of water?"

The floor of the shelter was hardly a dry space. Everyone was muddied, the deer and the horses to their bellies, even after grooming.

"I don't know why I'm so cranky," Didara said. **"This place makes me afraid and unhappy for some reason."**

"It's probably the weather."

*   *   *   *   *

"Hey, boss, we can't get to them while she rain like this." The bandits were wrapped up tight like balls of wool, hunkered together with a slicker blanket thrown over them all, the weight of the ice building up. Occasionally they'd stretch and groan and shuffle around so that the outside got to the warmer middle and the ice would crack and slide off.

"They can't move neither. Not to worry none, Saikrie. Nobody knows we here t'all out of the swamp."

"I wonder if them monsters is as good eatin' as deer?" His question had them suddenly hungry, drooling at the thought of fresh venison rather than more gator, or another frog stew.

"Donno, Saik. Guess we's about to find out, after we strip off them shinies. When we kin move again." The way the rain'd settled in it could be a couple of days.

"Yes, boss."

64

Big Sister

"WE'LL HAVE THE BOOTS ON THE HORSES IN LESS THAN BREAKFAST TIME," the Captain said to Ahrimaz who walked jittery fingers over the map, away from Champ de Navet to the muddy track that led all along the edge of the Mire to Riga. His fingers kept stopping and tapping at two fords. In this world they were named by the locals, Up Ford and Down Ford, though there was no evidence of any kind of village at either place. It was a choke spot for the Cylak herds both north and south and every year, joking, they swore that their aurochs trampled it wider.

"Boots. On horses and deer."

"Ankle wraps on the deer so the ice doesn't cut them up when they break through the crust on the road verge. Ice crampons laced to the horse's shoes."

Ahrimaz just shook his head. "Let's go then."

The Captain nodded and then left him sitting, the map spread on a box in a barn that was three quarters full of turnips, his coat puddled around him. Fingers walking up and back between the two fords. Up and back. "We'll get there," he muttered to himself. Limyé sat nearby, rolling bandages with Etienne. He looked up at Ahrimaz, then back down at his hands. Clearly listening.

"It's too scorching drowning close!" Ahrimaz snapped, then froze as Pel carried in an arms box and set it on the rammed earth floor next to him. An arms box branded with the Hand of the People symbol in it; so close to the burn on his own chest, but with no sign of the Flamon anywhere, only the raised Hand in the square wreath. "No, no, dear Gods and Scorching demons, Pel! You can't trust me with my own weapons!" He swallowed, raised his hands. "You saw how I was with that charming antique Teel lent me! No!"

"You are going to need more than just armour and a piss-load of soldiers to save your friends. I don't want you to go anywhere near a fight unarmed. You'd do something stupid like rushing in bare hands!"

"No. No. That's why I brought all you lot along. I'm not a proper warrior any longer. I don't revel in bathing in the blood of my enemies!"

"This is a good sign," Limyé said, from where he sat. "At one point you needed blood or pain or both to feel real. Now you are rejecting them."

Ahrimaz nodded abruptly. "Pel…" he slapped a hand on the empty scabbard at his belt. "I'm certain I won't do anything stupid."

Pelahir stared at him for a long, long moment before he nodded abruptly, pulled out his pocket watch and checked it before tucking it back into his vest pocket. "You do that. I'm going to be at your back, you realize. And you won't want a diplomatic incident like involving me in a fight that will get my Doe angry now, would you?"

Ahrimaz snorted. "Don't you try and make me laugh, you dirty Cylak bastard. In this world your Doe could probably stomp me into red slush!"

"Yes, she's my mate and she and her doe scare me! They would probably resurrect you and do it a second time, too."

"Spare me."

The squire whistled from the door and half a dozen men pushed it open against the crust of ice trying to lock it shut. Teel snapped his book shut where he sat, tucked it away in his own great coat and helped the healers close up their portable hospital, snapping the locks down with hard 'cracks'. "You've overdone the bandages, M'ser Limyé," he said and Physician Etienne, the younger of the two, smothered a laugh.

"You've not been in a battle before, Raconteur?"

"No, how did you know?"

"There's never such a thing as too many bandages."

*   *   *   *   *

The bandits slid down the hill on the slick leather of their coats, digging their heels in, carefully climbing to their feet. The wind blew into their faces oddly enough. Not typical for the land by the Mire. It was growing colder and the mud had frozen hard enough that their boots couldn't cut heel holes in them with stomping.

"We kin slide fer a ways, boss, but nohow we're going to get to Downford in less n' two days."

"An' we kin settle in at Upford and jus wait fer 'em to come tah us then."

"Ay."

"Upford it is then. Set to, boys and gals!"

* * * * *

Jagunjagun stomped his new mukluks, felt the chainmail on the soles cut through the ice and give him grip. "I approve!" he rumbled and Didara, looking almost dainty, minced out onto the road after him.

The Cylak were all on their deer and laughing as they took in the hugely modified deer boots that they'd made into elephant boots. Didara threw her head up, in the rain, and trumpeted. "I'm funny!!!!! Look at me dance!!!"

Their escort threw their hands over their ears and their deer shied as Jagunjagun joined her and they raised their forefeet before smashing them down through the ice.

One of the Cylak calmed his deer and actually rumbled disapproval at them. "Danger, here, not dance, not sing."

The two elephants calmed and swung to look at him. "Apologize to you, we do." They cast an amused look at each other and up at Ologbon on Jagunjagun's neck as their escort began a careful march. "I want to get to this Innéthel and rest for a while!"

"Then let us go, my big sister," he said and they swung out on the ice, carefully behind the track left by the deer.

65 A Crackle of Muskatoon Fire

THE WEATHER AFTER THE ICE STORM HAD CLEARED and the temperature had plummeted. The sun shone in an icy blue sky hard as stone. Every single horse soldier had tinted glass goggles to save their eyes and the riding animals had mesh over their faces it was so blinding. In the absolute stillness echoing cracks of trees exploding travelled for thousands of paces and often they groaned before they broke.

The war cats curled into their baskets, the dogs ran with their feet covered in boots, hoods tied over their heads and the short-haired breeds had coats even over their winter fur. The light struck as though it were cold manifest, chewing on anything that breathed or produced heat. Every crystal of snow, every fragment of crust reflected the light, breaking it into dozens of blinding glances.

The whole troop stood under one of the last stands of trees, the land falling away from them, down toward the Great Mire, a flat, ice covered expanse full of what looked like dead trees, all with no branches, mounds of scrub weighted down by ice here and there.

Ahrimaz tried to breathe slowly through his face covering, one hand on the mare. All of the animals had to rest, especially in this tearing, biting cold. He could feel the edges of everything he wore freezing as it got further away from the warmth of his body, and the warmth of his breath. "Of course this had to be in the middle of winter," he growled. "It's one reason no one was out, when the bandit—" his complaint was cut off by a whistle, a shriek from one of the Cylak scouts, trotting back slowly with his falcon huddled on his saddle-block, tearing at a bit of jerky.

"'Efants," he said slowly, as fast as he could without sucking icy air into his lungs. "North of Down Ford, nearly to Up Ford." Ahrimaz was about to cheer but he went on. "Ambush. UpFord, our side. Fording I'slow 'em down."

"Mount 'em!" the Captain's voice was thin in the cold but everyone jumped. "We'll see 'em safe!"

Ahrimaz had already swung up on the mare who had caught his urgency and threw her head up, stepping out as fast as she could in her best ground eating pace. It was too cold to try and gallop so far and no matter how badly he wanted to he could not make her kill herself for no reason.

He was just behind the scouts as they burst out of the scrubby trees on the edge of the cliff, the road beginning the long sweeping switchbacks to take them safely down to the lower ground and the edge of the swamp.

He could see the moving dots of the elephants even without an eyeglass, but it would be insane to make the horse cut across country, even if they could trust the snow crust. His head turned as they ran away, then back and away again, as the slowly, gently moving mountains, brightly coated and standing out as sharply in the white and grey and black landscape as the pain of a freshly smashed thumb.

Ahrimaz could see the blinding twinkle of hundreds of what looked like chips of light on the coat and head covering of one. "Didara," he said, and his hands tightened again and the mare shook her head in protest.

"Someone get me a drum!" Ahrimaz bellowed as his friends paced gently on toward the ambush, unknowing, even though there were surely Cylak scouting for them. Surely. He had to warn them, somehow.

It was a nightmare of plowing along over too slick footing, shards of broken ice that slashed through boots and wrappings, back and forth down the cliff face never seeming to get any closer.

Something was happening. Jagunjagun stopped and tapped Didara on her shoulder as she stepped around him. She stopped too.

They were too far away to hear anything. Even the deep rumbles they spoke with would carry differently through different ground, but someone thrust a drum into his hand and he didn't take it out of its case, afraid the hide would just freeze. He pounded on the case of it as he rode, eyes locked on the elephants, reins loose over his arm, the muffled thump seeming futile as their plunge down the cliff.

Danger danger ambush ambush danger ambush. Over and over again with the tiny drum in the hope that they would hear, or feel it through their feet.

Even as Jagunjagun's head swung up, muffled ears spread wide, just on the edge of the ford, a rank of men stood up and there was a tiny, fading crackle of muskatoon fire and a billow of black powder smoke. "NOOOOOO!" Ahrimaz dropped the drum and they cleared the last switchback, a clear run toward the ford. He lashed the mare trying to make her run and she bashed his face with her poll as she flung her head up, still moving quickly but refusing to run with ice under her feet.

66

I Am Not Voice. Voice Is Sanity.

IT WAS A NIGHTMARE BUILT OF ICE AND SILENCE, a peculiar ringing silence in his ears as he strained toward the ford.

The one bandit whose gun blew up instead of firing, leaving him writhing in scarlet splotch in the middle of the field of white, much darker than the wool fringes on the elephant's jackets, squalling in the centre of the red mark. The dark clot of bandits whose guns had fired or misfired, he couldn't count them at this distance, setting plug bayonets even as the Cylak bore down on them, the deer only slipping a little on the ice at the ford. It was frozen solid enough to carry them, perhaps all the way to the bottom.

Some bandits fled as their ambush failed and it turned into a stand-up fight. Ahrimaz could see the tiny figure on Didara's back apparently kneeling but he hurled his ammunition in a sling whipping around his head. *The iti-igi, always good at hurling rocks,* ran through Ahrimaz's head. That had happened in the other world, according to both elephants, before Didara had died.

Nightmare pounding, the Cylak he'd brought, Pel pulling his carbine in the brutal spray of ice shards his doe kicked up as they poured past him. Yustiç—the mare—The horses could only go so fast on ice... *no no no, Gods do you punish me to see Didara take her fatal wound? Instead of saving her? No, no no* It was a thunder of no and his blood pounding in his head and then, Ologbon... it must be him if it was Didara... running out of rocks, dumping the basket next to him, full of glittering shards, making her even harder to see as she trumpeted and spun.

Bandit after bandit was hurled into the frozen ground as the elephants joined the fray. Each step killed another man, their leggings soaked dark.

Yustiç stopped, plunging and rearing, refusing to go any further, Ahrimaz jammed his boot heels viciously into her sides and she went down and rolled. He managed to fling himself clear and the other horses of the Guard all around, bucked and balked and some threw their riders and ran back down the road. Elephants. These horses had never seen elephants before.

His slick-soled boots skidded on the icy road and his greatcoat billowed around him and he saw… he saw in the middle of the battle… a bandit roll out from under an elephant foot about to smash him into slush, rose to one knee, jabbed up under Jagunjagun's armpit with the broken bayonet. "NO!"

Jagunjagun spun, the man flew against Didara and she snatched him up with her trunk and flung him into a boulder at the edge of the ford.

The hideous, glorious, longed-for sounds of fighting and men dying. Screams and gunshots and deer bellowing suddenly rushed into Ahrimaz's head as he finally, finally got to the fight. To find it over. His head was full of the taste of blood and he grinned from ear to ear.

"**Welcome, Rummmummmalos,**" he could feel his words rumbling through his feet as the last of the Cylak escort came back from trying to chase stragglers, giving up as a deer went through the ice, and into mud below. "You do your Queen proud."

"**Thank you. Who are you who know us?**" Didara spoke, swaying and distressed.

"**Ah-rummmm-aaaaz.**" He gave his name the best roll he could. All around he could hear the Captain, and Pel, cleaning up the blood and shit stinking mess. "**Are you injured? Do you need assistance? We should get our injured back to shelter. There is a village not far.**"

"**I…am Didara the curious and this is Jagunjagun and our iti-igi Ologbon. I am uninjured—**"

"**I am hurt, I think,**" Jagunjagun said. 'that iti-igi hurt me."

"Ahrimaz, we've mostly got things together, we can take the injured back to Champ," Pel stood next to Ahrimaz gazing up at the bloody, distressed, now quiet elephants above, like mountains rocking. "We need to get out of this cold."

Ahrimaz nodded. "Pel, yes, I…" He reached out a hand, almost blindly to snatch at Etienne's sleeve and drag him toward Jagunjagun. "Surgeon. He is injured. See to him first." Then all his words stopped. He shuddered at the taste of blood in his mouth, frozen on the edges of his scarf where the mare had slammed her head into his face. His mind splintered into a thousand pieces, like the chips of glass and he watched through the thousand faceted eyes of a fly as he caught and calmed Yustiç, petted Heylia and Teh and Sure who all three helped round up the Horse Guard's fleeing mounts.

I cannot speak. I must not speak. If I speak this shattering will carry through my whole body and I will fall apart like an ice statue. I hear them… Ologbon can speak our tongue. I am swimming in all the blood I ever spilled, rubbed my face into, bathed in, washing my pain away with other people's screams. I am not whole and I was shattered by what the Monster my Father made me do, over and over and over again until I needed pain to function. I am blood. I AM shit. I AM the battlefield. I am not Voice. Voice is sanity.

67

Ambassadors of Rummummalos: Mountains That Think

—By Teel James, Raconteur for the Coalition News,
Chronicles of Inné and Innéthel and their environs,
Late Winter

The two Ambassadors, Didara, the Curious and Jagunjagun, the Fierce have been met by the joined forces of Cylak and Inné, with assistance from Riga. On their journey to Innéthel the sister and brother were attacked by bandits and with their escort successfully fought off the miscreants.

First let me describe the ambassadors. They stand on four limbs, like a dog or a horse, though their feet are round and thick enough that I cannot span their girth with my two hands. Their skin is grey and they have ears the size of bed-sheets on either side of their heads. In the centre of their faces is a limb that might be called a nose but it reaches to the ground and is prehensile with two fingers at the tip. This is strong enough to pick a man off the ground and hurl him five hundred paces away. I pause at this point to reassure my faithful reader that I, personally, witnessed this action, though the Horse Guard were more than a thousand paces away. I swear on my liquid self to Lyrian that this is true and factual to the absolute best of my powers of description.

To continue. The ambassadors have a family member with them who is a human, though their relationship is difficult to describe. The so-called 'iti-igi', which is also one of their names for their nose-tentacle, is raised with the young elephants and this gentleman, by the name of Ologbon, is of the height of a rather typical ten year old Innéan, only coming to my waist. He speaks excellent Rigan and Cylak and passable Innéan which is improving rapidly.

To return to the ambassadors. They both have two enormous tusks protruding from their mouths on either side of their noses, that have been elaborately decorated. More so in the case of Didara than her little brother Jagunjagun.

We are currently taking refuge in the village of Champ de Navet, in their largest turnip barn, since that is the only enclosed space large enough to house the ambassadors out of the cold. Jagunjagun is in his second surgery, with his sister the only one able to restrain him, since none of our healers know how to anaesthetize a creature so large and the **Rummummalos** themselves have never considered such an idea.

Jagunjagun was struck by several musketoon rounds during the battle and despite their robust skin and the boiled wool of their winter coats, was injured, with at least three balls penetrating his skin. There is an Imaryan healer and the chirurgeon of the Horse Guard and the House of the Hand both working on the ambassador. We shall be resting here until the younger ambassador is well enough to travel.

I am, Teel James, your most faithful raconteur of the latest news of Inné.

The Alien Emperor In Crisis

—By Teel James, Raconteur for the Coalition News,
Chronicles of Inné and Innéthel and their environs,
Late Winter

Ahrimaz, who was given lead of this rescue operation of the Ambassadors of **Rummummalos**, on his most urgent request, most successfully guided the Horse Guard and His Belling Lordliness, Pelahir, Stag Lord, to Up Ford, on the edge of the Grim Mire, where the **Rummummalos** had just successfully fought off a bandit ambush with their escort. (see other story "Mountains that Think").

In the process of attempted assistance, Ahrimaz was minorly injured (merely a bloody nose) and in the course of the clearing up of the battle, ceased to speak. At least he ceased to speak Innéan.

In the turnip barn where the ambassadors currently reside, he sits as close to one or the other elephant as he can, but when they move away, he does not follow, but sits, staring into the middle distance. He does not resist if someone leads him to the necessary, or places a bowl of stew in his hands, though he must be urged to eat. He—

Teel dropped his pen and threw both of his hands over his ears in a futile attempt to block the sound as Jagunjagun moaned. It wasn't as bad as him screaming but still shook everyone in the building. He was refusing to scream but had failed several times. In the ring of heat the young priest was praying for, the elephant lay on his side, with both Etienne and Limyé at his elbow, though the young chirurgeon was wearily climbing to his feet as Limyé finished tying off the bandage.

"He should be all right, Ahrimaz," Etienne said, going over to where he sat, staring, Pel with bowl and spoon urging him to eat.

He put a hand on Ahrimaz's shoulder and the man flung himself out from under it, Pel snatching the bowl out of the way, Ahrimaz lying prostrate on the ground arms wrapped around his head as Jagunjagun moaned once more, the broken form of the young man somehow echoing the broken form of the young elephant.

68
What a Story-Theory Song!

I AM EVIL INCARNATE. I'm bad, I'm wrong. I'm the cause of all the pain. I'm the cause of my own pain. I belong to Father, he says I'm making him do these things to me. My fault. If I make someone else hurt then I'm safe.

The taste of blood, screaming hundreds, they're hurting not me. I am a good warrior. I slaughter with the best. Blow holes in them with carbine, thrust holes in them with sword. Make the horse stamp someone to death. That is what I'm best at.

Flogging and beating makes people obey. They are safe. But Kinourae said he loved me still. He isn't in this world, or he's off doing some other job. He's not my body servant. Even if I hurt him, he said he understood that it is by Father's will.

The monster broke me and made me into another monster. Kill or maim all around you. Assault your younger brothers. Don't touch the girls, they're going to some other man, or Father will teach them properly.

Only Arnziel is left alive in my world, that world. He hates me. He blames me for what Father made me, made us do.

I hear the **Rummummalos** *tongue rumbling through my body. Didara is curious, always. Fascinated that I knew her from another world. Appalled that she is dead there. I didn't tell anyone in this world, other than her and Jagunjagun, that she died in that world. Limyé suspects this is the truth and he's right. I can hear them talking. Ologbon's Innéan is improving as fast as it did in the real world. My world.*

"Real world?" The voice I know. She is everywhere wound through my life. I am terrified of her. I must be a witch and someone will throw test powder on me, douse me with a bucket of water and watch me go up in flames. Maybe I'm ready for that.

It will hurt once more and then never again. I find that attractive.

"No, child. You will be able to serve as a healer for two worlds yet."

"Lyrian."

"Yes?"

"I heard what you said, oh Goddess, but it makes no sense."

*"Just as you are one of the only people on this continent, in fact on both continents who can hear and speak to the **Rummummalos**, you are the trigger for all of Inné in both worlds. Heal yourself and then we will speak again."*

"Goddess! I'm so crazy I can't!" I float in a sea of my screaming and I am scooped up out of it, floating as though I am held cupped in two hands.

"To me, child, you are already a flickering cloud of thought held to a particular body that enables you to perceive me and that is all right." The hands shake and I, the cloud of mirror particles shuffle and float and then settle again, edges closer. "See? That is how you change. Gather up the bits and put them back together for me."

How do shattered bits of glass reflect anything but ruin? But I answer Her obediently. "Yes, oh Lady of the Depths and Snow."

I can feel her smile. The black-haired girl who changes before me, grows rosy cheeked and ruddy, glowing with… heat? I don't understand. But I am finally warm, even the cold dead pieces of me that sat with my dead mother. That part of me might live again if I let it. I see a few green shoots growing out of the dead pieces.

How do green growing things and glass and volcanic heat have anything to do with one another? I see all three in Her eyes. She looks at me and I am not judged and found wanting. "Your poor Monster could never hear me," She says. "And ultimately you burned him to ashes, though his spirit is now far away from you."

"I hurt, Mama."

"I know. It will ease. Heal yourself. I will help you."

Ahrimaz could feel the stretch of his lungs in his body, became aware of his heartbeat, his clenched hands, the discomfort of his clothes knotted under his body. He could feel the worn wooden floor with waves of knots rising out of the smooth-worn surface like a benign ocean under the sun. The circle of heat around Jagunjagun was a blessing here at the empty end of the barn where the snow blasted through the walls when the wind howled.

Limyé's hand was on one of his shoulders and Didara's trunk fingers curled around his other shoulder as he lay, her bulk, in her mirrored wool coat was the other source of heat, shielding him from winter's teeth.

It was the Imaryan speaking. "Jagunjagun will be all right, Ahrimaz. You saved him, not by force of arms, or by slaughtering everyone who threatened them. You saved your friend by bringing Etienne and I to him when he needed us."

He could hear Jagunjagun snoring, comfortable enough to sleep, though not comfortable enough to sleep on his side. He stood in the dim light surrounded by bales of hay to lean against should he wish.

"The ammunition the bandits used had been smeared with filth and Didara assured me that we caught the blood-sepsis in time. Etienne is chagrined that he missed a ball the first time, but it's all right now."

Ahrimaz's eyes opened and found himself staring into Teh's eyes lying concerned just past his hands. When he looked at her she wiggled forward on her belly and he found himself somehow clutching the big white dog.

He coughed and turned toward Didara, who hadn't let go of him. "Did they tell you I'm not from this world? That I knew you in another place, another time?"

The rumble she made he recognized as laughter. "Fascinating idea. Such a story-Theory Song it will make!"

69   They Keep Him From Killing Himself

THE MARCH BACK TO WHITE WAS MUCH MUCH SLOWER than the breakneck pace they'd set out with, since they were moving at the recovering ambassador's pace.

Teel's wrists and arms and his legs and his back all hurt and he welcomed the switch from riding to walking, sliding down to lead his horse in place, rather than fighting the animal from its back. None of the Innéan horses were used to the elephants yet and tended to start and then bolt at the slightest excuse.

Pelahir rode up beside him, between the elephants and the horses, slid down and walked beside Teel. He didn't need to lead his doe, who was indifferent to the ambassadors once introduced. She followed along the cleared road at his shoulder and occasionally rubbed her eye shield against him, making him stagger. He just chuckled and scratched underneath.

"How is your horse coming on then, M'ser Raconteur?" His smile was obvious even behind his own goggles and the face mask drawn with wolverine fangs.

Teel pulled his own wool scarf down and rubbed a mittened hand over his dry lips, carefully. "Well enough. The whole lot of them seem like elephants make them crazy."

"Indeed." Just behind them, and beyond Jagunjagun's careful hobble so as not to overstretch the stitches on that side, they could hear Didara rumble singing in the white cold. Up on the doe's back Ologbon stirred where he'd been curled up against Pel's back in one of the Cylak feather bags, modified so he could put his hands out if he chose.

"She sing him song theory of 'Being Awake'," he said.

"Still?" Teel said. "Again? Didn't she sing him that yesterday?"

"Oh, no, that just beginning. Theory that people are awake even when sleeping or hurt. People BE. Song-theory is five days long."

"Five days," Teel said faintly. "So... Didara is equivalent to our scientists?"

"Yes/no, no/yes, maybe?"

Pel snorted laughter. "That clears it right up! From what Jagunjagun tells me it's a bit like our shamans and your priests AND inventors."

Jagunjagun, who listened, ear muffs flapping as he stepped gingerly on, in his fur mukluk boots and wool coat, nodded. He was learning Innéan with astonishing speed. "Your Ahrimmmmmaz has a people's ear," he said. "He can hear our language even below what our beloved iti-igi here can!"

"I refuse to be offended," Ologbon said in the snottiest Innéan accent and that made both Pel and Teel wheeze with laughter, pressing face masks tight to keep from sucking in too much cold air.

Ahrimaz lay on Didara's back and neck and head, covered by another feather bag as she strode slowly before her brother, making sure the footing was good enough for him, though they had assured her that the Innéan high road was much much better than the muddy and fading little Rigan/Cylak track.

Pel nodded and pointed at Jagunjagun's ears. They had just swivelled forward in what clearly was shock. "Ologbon what was just said? Did you hear?"

"Um... your Ahrimaz just added two whole sound cycles to Didara's theory. She's thinking about it. He's... odd, your Ahrimmmmmmaz."

"He is that," Pel said quietly. The whistle came back down the line for everyone to mount up and they were within resting distance of the next village, La Jolie Cuervos.

The groans of complaint were pretty evenly distributed between mounts and men as they mounted once more, but they knew that the military barracks at Cuervos would hold them all warm, even the ambassadors. The Cylak had sent ahead with one of their messenger raptors and a hay barn had been hurriedly modified.

"Pelahir?"

"Yes, raconteur?"

"Teel, please."

"Yes, Teel?"

"What does Limyé say about Ahrimaz and those... those olephants?"

"They are good for him. They might keep him from killing himself."

"Oh, that's good then." Ologbon sat up, looking between Pel and Teel, then rumbled something that had Jagunjagun flapping his ears and making the horses fidget.

70

Like a Man On Fire, Chivvied Into the Water

"HE WON'T GO INTO THE BARRACKS AND LIE DOWN IN A BED, WILL HE?" Pelahir asked Limyé quietly. The two men stood looking over the dimness that was the hay barn, barely large enough for the two elephants.

"No. I am amazed that he made himself step out of the cell, the stage of healing he was at," Limyé said. Pelahir's smile flickered across his face and then fell away. The elephants were dozing, with Jagunjagun lying down and Didara sleeping standing. Ahrimaz lay coiled in his feather bag tucked next to Jagunjagun and Ologbon. Sure and Teh and Heylia lay snuggled around the two men and even the mare stood with her ears pinned back flat, head down just inside the door, as close as she could get without getting too close to the grey, snoring mountains that upset her.

"I don't understand about the animals," Pel said. "They adored our Ahrimaz but this man has not loved animals, but rather tortured them."

"Been forced to torture them." Pelahir nodded acknowledgement of the Imaryan's point. "The moment he was out of that world, that whole world, he began changing."

"To fit this one?"

"Possibly. I don't have enough information to do more than guess." Limyé shrugged. "He's becoming more and more like our Ahrimaz every day. I am assuming our Ahrimaz is being similarly driven in the world of the Empire."

"He'd hate it. It would drive him crazy to…" Pel stopped. "Ah. So… perhaps… can our world heal their Ahrimaz and can our Ahrimaz heal that world before both men go completely berserk?"

Limyé made another note in his book. "It is entirely possible. I am starting to wonder if I should be consulting more closely with the Priestesses about this."

"There's a Shaman who has settled here. She works well with the young priestess in this village."

"I shall have time to consult, I believe," Limyé said, making another notation in his book. "I heard the plowmen talking to you when they came in."

"It is snowing again and the plows are behind. We'll be here for most of a week, it looks like." Pelahir shrugged again. "So once you've spent some more time with our broken Ahrimaz, come join Teel and I at the barracks. We have a very nice tea for you."

"I shall bring along a small bottle of medicinal brandy that I have in my possession."

"Excellent!"

*   *   *   *   *

I write from hell, albeit a hell that I now realize I have some control of, a hell that was forced onto and into my young mind and body by the monster. The Scorching Demon herself. In my father's mind. He took his own hell and poured it down my throat.

I… may be able to one day look at my actions without wanting to howl, to scream, to gnaw on my own limbs. The scars on my forearms are both raw and I haven't had an orgasm in days. I'm not sleeping well, though my dreams— when I do not have foaming nightmares—are gentle. Limyé gives me remedies that edge the whole world in gold or pink and blunt all the edges of my agony so that I have a chance of sleeping peacefully.

I imagine their Ahrimaz in my world. Soft, emotional, decent, horrified by ruthless dispatch, disgusted by the violence expected of him… If Mother and Uncle and perhaps Arnziel… no, he's too much a fool, they'd never talk to him if they discovered something so profoundly and potentially coercive. They would gleefully wring that Ahrimaz out and use him up to put themselves in power. Uncle's cadre are all military and when I was there, I would send them all out away from me in the hopes they'd get themselves killed. He'd never managed that so he's as dangerous as my brothers. He wants to be Emperor, I know. I wonder how this-Ahrimaz is handling that-Inné?

Did they find him out? Did they expose him and let the nobles kill him and begin trying to put their own on the throne? I don't feel he's dead. And these people who say that he's such a gentle person also say that they could see his violence and craziness merely exaggerated in me. Does this mean I have the same capacity to love as he does?

I look at this battered, water damaged, ink-spattered little volume of my introspections and wonder if Teel would be interested, since his ripping me open exposé has neither brought howling mobs to rip me limb from limb, nor secret cadres of would-be rulers wanting me to figurehead an Empire here. It did not even damage me, much.

Such an Imaryan idea. Living an open, whole-hearted life? The idea terrifies me, so of course I'm certain that is the way I shall be driven, like a man on fire, blind to his own salvation, being chivvied into the water.

And like such a victim I am fighting them blindly burning them as they struggle to fling blankets about my flaming soul. I wish I could see my direction so that I could fling myself into my own salvation, but until then my eyes are firmly clenched shut to save them from melting down my face.

I shall have to share this gruesome image with Limyé. He will make copious notes in his book and hear it all calmly, as he does everything.

It would be nice to not be running around with my symbolic hair on fire though, however metaphoric.

71

The Imaryans Never Learned to Hate

I AM SOAKED WITH BLOOD. I can smell it and taste it in the rancid air of their burning city. Shit too. Even the ones so scared they shit themselves before they died, did that. Even them. I HATE THEM. All the buildings around me are burning. My soldiers are hurling bodies into the flames not taking any care to see if they're already dead. I have a babe, or rather half a babe in one hand and the Flamen in the other. The sword is blazing, dripping red as the core of me. I am on fire, screaming as I hurl the dead child into the kneeling mother's face.

She catches the body and crouches lower, her hand raises in that strange 'patting motion' Imaryans use as a blessing and I swing the sword roaring in fear and rage. I hate them. I fear them. I HATE THEM. They must die. I'm screaming inside. Every death I feel like the whip on my skin. How dare they not fear me? How dare they bless me?

I woke up screaming again. My feather bag is soaked with sweat and Didara and Jagunjagun are both shaking me. "Sorry," I husk and roll over, out of the bag, stagger to the human sized door, rip it open to let the snow billow in and stagger out far enough to close it behind me before I vomit blood into the snow.

"I want to die. I killed them and tortured them and mocked them, trying to get them to hate and fear me and all they did was bless me and die! I'm never going to be able to pay for this!" I thrust my face into the clean snow. It's falling heavily enough that the scarlet splash of my spew is already dulled and disappearing in the gaslamp by the barn. No fire in the barn, but light outside, safely behind glass.

I don't feel the cold as I kneel here. It's nice. It's calm and quiet. "I'm a monster. Can I just fall asleep out here and remove me from this? And you needn't tell me that I'm not a monster in this world. In this world the city of

Imaryu is not burned, the people are not all slaughtered. I destroyed Yhom as well. I decimated the Cylak herds to break them and make them bow to the Empire."

"I certainly will not tell you that you are not a monster," Limyé says as he wraps a horse blanket over my snowy self, urges me to my feet and back into the barn, into the tiny leather and hay smelling equipment and tack room. He pushes me down to sit on the hay before settling across from me. "You horribly slaughtered thousands of people. If you succeed in killing yourself you can really only atone for one life. You want to atone for what you did? Stay alive and work for the great good of humanity."

I stare at him, my mouth full of the taste of blood and bile, the snow now melted and I'm sodden and shaking so hard I can hardly hold the blanket around me. Then I start laughing. It is a screaming kind of laugh. It is instead of screaming I understand and he lets me go on until I cannot draw breath any more. Then he shakes me silent and holds a cup to my lips. "It is just water," he says. "Let me dry you off."

The water on my face is snow I tell myself. And it is, mostly. He rubs my head dry with a towel that looks like it came out of one of the Horse Guard's saddlebags, or barracks, harsh and rough and efficient. The roughness helps, even though his touch is too gentle. The water has the weird metallic taste that it always has when one has vomited.

He hands me a shirt and a pair of breeches and I realize with a start that I was naked, had run out naked into the snow. I pull on the warm clothing and as I yank the shirt over my head I close my eyes and see flames again but I recognize them as funeral pyre flames, not the random burning of cities. I feel grief and rage that is not mine but is perfectly mine. I sit, stunned. I stare past Limyé, as though I've taken a sword through the guts.

"The other Ahrimaz... he's killed the mother in that world. Rutaçyen forced to pretend to be her twin. He's killed her."

"How do you know?"

"I feel it. I just saw her funeral pyre." I shake my head and finish the water, holding it out to him. "He's becoming more like me," I said. "He's killed her for betraying him, I imagine." I am glad that neither my hand nor my voice shake.

Limyé takes the cup and sets it down, looking away. Then he holds out his arms to invite an embrace. I shake my head. "No, Limyé, no. The demoness applies the whip and hook to the soul of those deserving." I shake my head again. "That was something you Imaryans just couldn't seem to learn. I deserve every pain, until I atone for theirs."

"One man cannot atone for the agony of thousands. We will talk about that more, later. Right now, as far as you know, you can only grieve that in your world both women who were your mother are dead."

He is too gentle to the pieces of me, all of me, the shattered bits of mirror that are being shuffled back together again, for some reason, by some Being or Beings… or just by the madness of Imaryu that thinks all humans can be healed.

How did I move to be enfolded in his arms? Where did the blasted cat come from? I know that I must have moved because he will only offer, I am required to take responsibility. He will not force comfort on me. I must take it up myself.

Heylia doesn't care for such niceties of consent for healing and has plastered herself along my back. This place. This place. This world. Mother is dead. Mama was dead years ago. But… Mother is dead. I cannot let myself weep, but neither can I pull myself from the comforting embrace of a blasted, scorching, be-damned Imaryan healer. Damn his eyes. Damn him. Scorch him. I am weeping. Silently. Mother is dead and burned. I am truly orphaned three times over. Mother is dead.

72 I Suppose He's Feeling Better

Pelahir settled on the brushed-off bench at the turn-off to the hay barn. In this village it belonged to the Elector, who was mostly off in Innéthel, to be in her seat when the Hand called for discussion. As such it was called 'Elector's Lane' and touched the White Road just outside the village. It was the furthest out the gas lamps came, the last one along the road and two just outside the barn doors.

The road lay, still half plowed and Teel sat on the bench already, his notebook open, breath steaming as he sat, warming his pen inside his mittened hand so that the ink not freeze and crack the reservoir.

Just visible down the hill was the local Goddess grove, neatly laid out stones all shovelled clear, ringed by gas lamps at all the cardinal points. Invisible, behind the central stone, Teel had seen Ahrimaz sit with the young priestess.

"We're just going to let a dangerous maniac sit alone with one of our holy people?" Teel asked Pel as he sat down.

"She's holy enough to defend herself, if she needs to, and he's broken enough to not attack other people at this point, Limyé says." Pel folded himself into his furs, beat the snow off his fur boots and tucked them up, cross-legged, under his gakti, they Cylak name for their heavy fur coat. "She's trying to point out to him that him killing himself pays for nothing. Especially not in this world where he hasn't sinned."

"The priestess's name is Mara? Named for her grandmother, the old priestess I understand?" Teel licked the point of his pen.

"Yes. Mara the Elder is apparently a priestess at the Veil now."

"Hmmm. I should get one of my colleagues to go talk to the lot of them at the Veil."

"You should. According to Mara—" Pel shrugged when Teel looked at him. "I talked to her last night to tell her our shaman wouldn't be able to make it from Riga... something otherworldly going on." The clouds were finally beginning to break up and the snow kicked up by the light breeze began to glitter all around as the sun came out. "According to Mara, there's a lot fewer people trying to end their lives at the Veil and at other Goddess shrines all over the country."

"Really?"

"Finding out that there is another world seems to have jolted a lot of people out of their death spirals," Pel said. "Buron, my shaman, sent a letter along and he mentioned that the spirit world is much troubled of late and there is upheaval everywhere. There's been a Fire Tiger seen and more people brought from that other world, apparently by the will of Aeono."

"I... see..." Teel's pen scribbled across the page. "I'm going to have to hire people all over the world to keep up with these stories!"

"But more people are buying your broadsheet because you're the ones telling everyone what's really going on, instead of making up fantasy stories."

"Hmm." He added three or four notes. "These other people—"

"Two men," Pel interrupted him. "Couriers, I believe, from that other world, but that's all I know. Outside of Riga States... in the middle of our herd-track."

"Thank you for telling me," Teel said. He looked up and around. "Where did the Ambassadors go? I saw them leave just a while ago."

"Didara is fascinated by the ink works here. And the paperworks. She's still being mobbed by children wherever she goes so that has to be settled first and then she's going to look at what she can see of the factories."

"And Jagunjagun? I hope he's still being careful, with his rec—"

Pel interrupted him with an upraised hand. Teel could see his grin even through his scarf. There was a rumble, a thunder building. He turned to look down the road to see an enormous bow-wave of snow curling up and billowing off to either side of the road. "What?"

"He was thinking about the snow-plows we use and saying that oxen are terribly slow," Pel said and started chuckling. "Ologbon modified a plow and..."

Teel and Pel both ducked, Teel tucking his book fast under his coat as the vertical wall of fluffy snow billowed over both of them, curling up and away from the road and from the trotting elephant. Ologbon, heavily covered in snow spray, sat on the elephant's neck chanting to him as he pushed the modified snowplow along the smooth military road. Ologbon waved merrily as they roared by, Jagunjagun's bright red earmuffs flapping, his tail sticking straight up out of his coat.

The rumble of their passage had faded by the time the snow wave settled enough for Teel to dig himself out of the wall of snow. Shovel crews recruited from the Horse Guard came rattling behind and began digging openings in the laneways.

"Heya, Staglord!"

"Hoya, Albin!"

The shovellers quickly had the bench dug out and left half a dozen people to dig out Elector's lane.

Teel stood on the newly plowed road, marvelling it had happened so quickly. "I suppose that Ambassador Jagunjagun is feeling much better."

"I think that too. I would not want to be the person trying to stop him in what he wishes to do." Pel was still grinning and beating snow out of his furs.

"No. Considering the weight of that plough he was pushing, and the weight of the snow… at speed."

"It is impressive."

"Indeed. I wouldn't want to go to war with their country, ever."

73   The Nature of the Divine

JAGUNJAGUN'S MODIFIED PLOW WAS FOUND TO BE USEABLE by a team of horses and on light snow they could plow the road almost as fast as an elephant showing off. They had passed through White and headed north, catching up to the regular plowing crews and having to stop and have people look and take notes and ask about getting their old plows re-done, or getting a break in taxes.

Ahrimaz lay on Didara's back, wrapped up warm, and could see over the heads of their escort to where the new plow was getting almost as much attention as the elephants. "Do you mind the crowds?" He asked, in Innéan, since she had expressed her intent to become fluent in the language and asked him to.

"Oh, no," she answered, swinging along in her slowest pace so as not to run over the horses and deer in front of her. By now they had grown accustomed to the elephants and no longer tried to bolt for the horizon. Yustiç paced just ahead of Didara, tacked up should Ahrimaz wish to ride her. She seemed very miffed that he chose the elephant's company over hers. "My little brother says I am an attention... sucker? Seeker. Yes. Seeker."

"I don't think so. You sometimes seem to endure the mob. Like me."

People, drawn by the elephants, would sometimes stop and cast their eyes over Ahrimaz, but not approach. He still felt as though their gazes were rasping his skin off, but he found that complaining to Limyé and writing in his book were making them almost bearable. "Did you want to continue our discussion about other worlds?" Didara rumbled.

Ahrimaz pulled the hood of the feather bag up over his head, cutting out the bright winter day. It eased his eyes and his head. Even with snow goggles, the light was almost a pressure and day after day it grew hard to bear. *Lyrian, this is how you relate to Aeono, isn't it? Unending, blinding light. From water.*

There was no answer to his stray thought and he shrugged. "You were postulating… theorizing… that my and my doppelganger's apparent exchange was not only solid evidence for more than one perceived existence but two, and it could therefore be argued that there is no upper limit presented for the number of possible worlds," he said.

"The word you used, when you described the vision you had," she answered. "Was infinite. In fact you said infinite in all directions and times."

In the dimness and warmth of the bag, with blinding flashes of light and cold just leaking in as Didara walked, Ahrimaz could almost remember that instant of transcendence. He took a deep breath, as everyone here was always telling him to do. "Yes. It… yes."

"I find it interesting that those two worlds were so close that for an instant one overlaid the other and you two hommes? Men… yes… slid into each other's places. Infinite monsters, infinite good men, and everything in between."

"Priests and healers are telling me that it might be the Goddess's will, as far as they can see, but… the Gods…"

"Your Gods, Male and Female, I theorize are the collective imaginings of your people, with enough faith and will to make them real."

"Didara… in this context what is 'real'?"

She was silent for long enough that he was almost beginning to doze. Finally she cleared her throat, and he could hear her footsteps change as she carefully stepped over one of the hundreds of bridges along White Road to Innéthel. "I can honestly say 'I don't know'," she said. "I don't even have a theory. All I can say is that I have not seen a country before where the Deities are so…" She paused, clearly trying to find a word that was neutral enough.

"Present?" He offered. "Dreams and Nightmares made manifest in this world? Interfering Busy Bodies with nothing better to do than mess with us poor creatures? Children playing with the ant farm?"

She had started to shake her head yes but froze and when he finished his outrageous litany she blasted a laugh that made Yustiç jump, hunch her back, flick both ears back at them, outraged.

"Present will do," Didara said. "In our country, the Divinity IS the land, so I suppose I should be used to it, but the Land works on such a big, slow scale we live too fast to notice, or be noticed. Especially not as individuals."

Ahrimaz stopped a moment and considered. "I find that concept of the

Land being the Divine terrifying."

"I can see that. But when we speak through our feet, our prayers go rumbling down and across and become part of the Land you see."

"That makes sense."

Her footsteps changed again. "We seem to be coming up on another village, Ahrimmmmaz. Your Captain is calling for a rest."

"Good. As much as I'd like to get you to Innéthel and into a warm place—the Cylak had sent a courier ahead, days ago, with instructions as to what would be necessary for the Ambassadors—I don't want to lame you or the other animals getting you there!"

"Thank you, my strange iti-igi," She said. He froze, hands clenched on his feather bag, grateful no one could see his face. It put him on the same footing in her family as Ologbon. For her to call him that, she must have spoken to Jagunjagun, who was getting stronger every day.

"Thank you, Didara," he said softly. "That means a lot to me."

She rumbled, wordlessly.

74

Home Again Home Again

THE WEATHER HAD HELD ALMOST. It was the very last day of travel, home to Innéthel and the roads had been very clear. Now the snow fell thick and fast so it was hard to see the horse in front of you. Even the elephants were disappearing into the dense white wall.

Ahrimaz rode next to Teel, buried up to his nose in his great coat, mildly confused where they were. In the Empire they would already have been at the outer city wall. This undefended city messed with his head.

He could smell the tanneries, faintly since they were downwind but there wasn't a breeze to really blow the stink anywhere, so it sat in damp puddles of air gradually spreading. They were in the similar place in Innéthel in his world. About a good two hours ride. On a good day.

Today they'd be lucky to get inside at the House of the Hand before dark. He rumbled that information to the two Ambassadors and got relieved thunder back that he and Yustiç could feel up through her hooves.

She was used to it now and only tossed her head a bit. "I am so glad we're home," Ahrimaz said to Teel who nodded.

"It feels like home to you now?" He said and Ahrimaz shrugged against Heylia's weight on his shoulders.

"Enough. More than anywhere else in this world."

"You required the Stag Lord and the bulk of his men go ahead last night."

"I did. They could travel faster."

"Do you mind me asking, as a friend, why you're avoiding him?"

Ahrimaz pulled the scarf down from his face and glared at Teel who gazed back, calmly. "It's that obvious?"

"It is."

"Well, I'm attracted to him. This trip has thrown us together hard and… and… I can understand why Ahrimaz loves him. I dare not fall in love with the man. If I am ever sent back, he will be my torture victim, not my lover."

"And if you are not?"

They rode in silence for a while and out of the white there came a faint creaking of mill wheels, still working even in the dead of winter, the sluices kept clear by the grace of Aeono.

"Then it would still be best if I treated him and Yolend and the rest of the family like an old uncle with a sketchy past, who needs healing. Not loving."

Teel didn't push him on it and Limyé, riding just behind, nodded.

*   *   *   *   *

"If that's Cooper's Quarter and the Glassworks over there we're nearly there," Ahrimaz said as the snow began to ease up, letting buildings and fires and gas lanterns actually drive the dimness back.

"Indeed. I hope the Ambassador's Quarters will be to their taste," Teel said, throwing a look back at their dim, hulking shapes in the snow, their coats heaped with white flakes, enough to completely bury Ologbon on Jagunjagun, turning their already mythical shapes into something surreal, unimagined by any human being.

"I think they'll be glad to rest," Ahrimaz said. "After all the obligatory cheering crowds and short parades."

They turned carefully along the narrow street that led up to the horse barn and Ahrimaz felt a huge knot loosen in his guts as he recognized the portico and the enormous sliding door. It was closed but people leaped to open it as the Captain hailed them. The gas lamps turned the snowflakes gold as they swirled in the gust of air from inside and they melted.

The door didn't open straight into the ring any longer, but was a long corridor that let the horses be led off to the stables on the left and the big slider groan shut behind them. The moment it was closed the temperature hit Ahrimaz between the eyes and Heylia melted off the back of Yustiç, purring. He and everyone else were shedding their coats and sodden hats and the elephants had space to shake themselves.

Once he could open his eyes again against the spray of water and melting snow, Ahrimaz grinned. "This is more like the temperature we need!"

The corridor wall slid open into two enormous doors and the warmth and light poured over them. There was no bare wall showing, no bare sand. The riding ring had been transformed into a hothouse garden with plants and flowers and grass and small trees in raised pots all around the edges.

One of the Lyrian priestesses had clearly begged the Goddess for warm water for a pool bubbled in the centre of what had been sand.

Ahrimiar and Wenhiffar stood beside the Hand, who came forward, holding out both hands. "Ambassadors Didara and Jagunjagun, please be welcome as long as you will, to Innéthel, and this will be your Embassy should you like it."

Ahrimaz stepped back to pick up his coat and found it already hung on a hook. Ologbon had slid down and begun unlacing elephant boots. Despite the fur lined boots both Didara and Jagunjagun had suffered from cold feet. Ahrimaz went to Didara and she ruffled his wet hair with her trunk, even as she addressed Ahriminash in her best Innéan. "We are astonished and pleased to be so welcomed, Hand," she said. "I shall have to make a story song about your garden in the snow!"

She stepped out of her booties into the warm sand and rumbled a groan of relief that Ahrimaz was certain only he heard.

"Please rest and refresh yourselves," Ahriminash said. "Formalities can wait until tomorrow."

"Of course, Hand."

Ahrimaz straightened to find himself enveloped in a double hug from Ahrimiar and Wenhiffar and managed not to strike out at them, only stiffening in their welcome. "We missed you, stepson," Wenhiffar said. "Welcome home, son," Ahrimiar chimed in. "You succeeded in saving your friends! We're very proud and want to hear the whole thing from yourself, rather than the stiff little bits and pieces we've been reading from M'ser James' Broadsheet stories."

"Am I dreaming this?" Ahrimaz asked faintly, letting his other parent's fuss over him as if he truly were a beloved son. "No." He checked the scabs on his forearms and they ached with cold, though that was going away. "It's real." He shut his eyes a moment. "I'm glad to be back," he said. "Let me help Didara get her coat off!"

Thankfully they let him go and he helped the grooms wrestle Didara's sodden wool coat off and over a wooden stand that held it off the sand to drip.

75

Home Again?

I AM HOME ON THE PRESENTATION BALCONY, watching the funeral pyre lit. The House of Gold is here all around me. Kinourae is at my back, holding the ermine and gold train that I wear when sitting in Judgment, when the Law is being upheld.

I look down at my right hand on the red and gold marble railing, the gold and white lace falling over my fingers and almost to my knees as I stand, the tall ebony walking stick in my left hand.

The funeral pyre has been stacked over the heading block where 'mother' and 'uncle' have both just been beheaded, hiding their bodies clothed in penitent whites and expiation scarlet as their heads came off.

The High Priest of Aeono and all his Temple Priests fling their books onto the pile whereupon every book bursts into white flame, showing that my judgment was correct and just, the flames roaring up to over top the walls, showing the gathered crowd that the traitors were dead.

Choirs roar, praising me for my Justice, I'm swaying. Kinourae surreptitiously props me up with one gentle old hand. "Don't touch me, I'm become a monster," I/he say.

"Sen-Lumes' Chasseur and Iraton and Houneau and Sen-Glor Moritaux are all watching to see if you've gotten as weak as they suspected."

I snarl at him. "I'll show them weak!" There are a couple of snapping noises from the middle of the hellish flames in the courtyard, the popping of a couple of skulls. I accept a glass of wine from one of my pages, kneeling nearby. "Good boy. Go off with you now." He scampers away from us and the Sen-Lumes and Sen-Glors and their retinues narrow their eyes at him as he goes, wondering if he is my new favourite. I drain the glass and turn on my high, red heels.

"We've seen justice done, M'sers and Mesdames," I snap. "Off with the lot of you." I pause before smiling into each Lord's face. "Go before I decide that my mother and my uncle

did not act against me alone. Go before I question you before God." The red column of an Apphoreitos stands right by the door, just to my hand should I wish it and the court frantically bows and curtseys casting their eyes down and away from me. They recognize a 'dangerous' mood and evaporate out of my sight like piss on hot stone.

"Kinourae." I say as the door closes behind us. Giving me privacy at last. "Kinourae. I cannot do this. I'm a monster. I cannot… I just… I just killed Rutacyen masquerading as Wenhiffar along with their brother. My family. I only have my brother Arnziel left and he's very sensibly run away from me." I crumple to my knees. KILL ME!" It's not a scream but a hiss so that no one outside can hear. Even as he/ I falls apart he/ we keeps quiet.

"Kill me, kill me… just let me die! I should have died, should have let them kill me…" I watch my hands pound upon the expensive rug and the stone floor, the skin of my hands breaking, the lace besmirched with my blood.

Oh, this is the other Ahrimaz, trying to be me. Poor soul. "It's all right." I say to him rather than out his mouth but he cannot hear me in the frenzy of his agony. "You can heal even from this."

"Kinourae, tell him!" He cannot hear me either, but he goes to interpose his own hands between the flailing fists of the Emperor writhing on the floor and the now damp carpet. The Emperor freezes rather than hurt the old man.

"Let me run your bath, son." My soul has tears though I have no body or mouth to express them, but those of the man playing Emperor and his tears are frozen as mine used to be, his mouth locked tight on… ah… on his forearm. His scars there are new. He was fortunate that I was ashamed of them and always wore wrist bands and gold cuffs to hide them. He would not have had them at the beginning.

Kinourae gets him up. Old man. I loved you. I hurt you. You were the only family I ever had that never betrayed me even after all we, I, did to you.

Now, when I am not here, I feel betrayed because you are showing love to this man, who I might have been. He has your heart. I see it in your eyes. You used to love me like that.

I watch as careful old hands strip away the elaborate lace and cloth of gold, the silks and the satins, the fire-gems, the expensive cotton underthings and ease this body into the hot, steaming bath that was my only place of safety as Emperor. Should I feel betrayed? Should I feel betrayed? Or thankful?

* * * * *

Ahrimaz woke in the velvet dark of the Elephant Hall, with Jagunjagun's snores and Didara's whistles marking where they stood in their new sanctuary.

He pulled his nightshirt up over his head and staggered over to the warm pool to plunge into the sandy, heated water, gasping as he rose just enough to float his head onto the pillowed edge.

I was there. I saw and felt how he was disintegrating. How much longer can he bear playing the monster before he becomes one?

I do believe I shall be thankful. It hurts less.

76

What Good?

THERE WERE WARM HANDS ON EITHER SIDE OF HIS HEAD as he dozed in the water. Before he opened his eyes he could hear Kinourae say, "What good does your suffering do? How does it atone for anything?"

His eyes opened slowly and he looked up into Limyé's face. "You might think about that while I get you out of there and dry," he said.

Ahrimaz blinked and he said "What? I didn't hear you."

"I asked you how does your suffering, your agony, atone for any of the evil you have done," Limyé said, and urged Ahrimaz out of the elephant's pool. "Especially in this world where you have done no evil?"

"But..."

"You feel bad and feel that it is just that you feel so wretched." Limyé wrapped him in a blanket towel and walked him toward the door to the House of the Hand. "Let me put you to bed. Not in the cell any longer." Heylia slid ahead and Yustiç neighed from her stall, more disgusted that she couldn't come along.

"But..."

"You said that already. There is a bedroom that was once yours... ah, his... as a boy, tidied up. No more cells. There are a number of people writing to the House protesting your treatment."

"But..."

"Brace yourself across the breezeway," Limyé said briskly. "The temperature dropped again last night and there's a crust on all that snow. The Ambassadors have said they wish another day of privacy before they greet us all."

"Didara wants to get her tusks shined and polished up," Ahrimaz said.

"And Jagunjagun will want to outline his scars with paint." The wind droned through the pillars but Limyé rushed him across so only his hair had time to freeze and tap against the blanket only once before falling limp in the warmth of the House. "Limyé, it's not right I shouldn't be…"

"…so comfortable?" The healer tipped his head to one side as he fended off the two dogs who were Ahrimaz's constant shadows now. "I repeat. What does your suffering pay for?"

Ahrimaz let himself be led up the stairs and down a hallway lined with honeywood paneling and bright green tile on the floor. To a door he almost knew. Children's rooms. He started to shake, then took a deep breath. "My room. In infinite worlds… very similar… My room."

"Yes. So let us set you up in bed and let you sleep more. You had very little sleep on the road, Teel and Pel tell me and the Captain corroborated them with her report. You needn't worry. There is nothing you need do for the next few days. No Ambassadors to save. You can train all day tomorrow if you like, Rutaçyen says. She has a whole new wave of classes just beginning and says 'we need more alternative world warriors to be a draw to the war school!'

"But…"

"Lie down, Ahrimaz."

"But…"

"Just sleep. And think on what I asked you."

"What good does my suffering do?"

Limyé pushed him over with one finger in the centre of his chest. "Sleep."

"But…"

He was asleep even as his head hit the feather pillow, felt the feather quilt pulled up to his chin, still trying to argue. "But…"

77

What Good, Indeed?

AHRIMAZ IS DEAD, Ahrimaz never born, Ahrimaz commits suicide age four, Ahrimaz killed by his brother Ahriminash, Ahrimaz Beloved Emperor, Ahrimaz reviled Hand of the People, Ahrimaz the Damaged, Ahrimaz the Brilliant, Ahrimaz killed by Pelahir, Ahrimaz killed by Cylak King, Ahrimaz kills the Cylak King and becomes Stag King, Ahrimaz is flung off the High City of Yhomdon, Ahrimaz killed by Yolend Heir of Yhom.

The images of who he was and could be and might be and all the worlds where humans never evolved, where the **Rummummalos** *lived and died in peace and eventually spread over their world, and traded with the* **Pfisirimmmm** *who swam in the sea.*

Ahrimaz opened his eyes to darkness, warm in a bed his mind didn't remember, but somehow his body did, even if he'd never slept in such a mean little cot as a child. It wasn't mean actually. It was a wooden bedstead and a strap support for a pair of feather mattresses. The quilt was feathers as well and four enormous pillows, warm enough that he had the window flung wide, even though the winter wind thrust icy fingers into his hair and under every edge not carefully tucked in.

"Ahrimaz, could you please close the window?" It was Wenhiffar tapping on his door. "The cold is howling along the floor out here, moaning under your door again."

"Sorry."

He reached out an arm and found he could just catch the braided wool cord... when had he tied it there?... to pull the pebbled glass pane shut, and clambered out from under the suddenly too hot bedding to lie on it, panting.

The room was green. Paintings of trees and vines were hung from waist high, to the ceiling and the ceiling was childishly painted with vines. Somehow he knew that the other Ahrimaz had painted them as a young boy. *It would have been gauche for me to paint my own rooms. Father would have had a fit and hired the best artist in the land to do it to his specifications. Not to mine, of course. Children are not allowed to know what they want.*

He buried his face in the pillows and just breathed in the scent of fresh laundry and a hint of sweat from his cooling skin. Naked. How is it that life just is like this? *I lie and breathe and do not hurt. No one requires anything from me. Nothing, either possible or impossible. How… strange.*

And those words echo in my head around and around and around. He reached to the side table and there was a chill, fresh cup of water and he could just drink. Pour another if he wished from the hand-made green jug next to it. Scorch, he could wander down to the water rooms and pour himself a bucket to pour over his head should he so desire, or sink himself into the hot water or… not.

For once the dogs were on the rug next the bed, driven off by his restless tossing, Heylia lay draped over the back of a worn brocade sofa, paws dangling as she purred in her sleep.

"What good does my suffering do anyone?" He said out loud and Sure started up to see if he were calling her, let her nose settle back down on top of Teh when he didn't look at her or address her further.

What good does my agony do? How does it help anyone? How does it help me? It rather causes people around me difficulty. It makes trouble for others. It makes Limyé dance attendance upon me, and the family. It causes problems for everyone around me.

What good does my suffering do?

What good?

What good does my suffering do for anyone?

78

Will We Do?

"AHRIMAZ." It was Limyé calling, tapping on the door.

"Would you come out please? Didara and Jagunjagun and Ologbon hope you would accompany them when the present themselves to your brother and your country."

"It's not my country and he's not my brother," Ahrimaz snarled into his pillows. He pulled another over his head trying not to hear the healer.

"Of course," Limyé said. "But they are your friends."

"Scorching flaming arseholes of God!" Ahrimaz flung the bedding onto the floor, onto the dogs, staggering over them as they lunged up to their feet, tangling everything into a floundering mass of feather bed and canine distress. He managed to lunge over them, palms slapping the wall by the door to save his balance and he yanked the door open. "If I do this will you just drowning, ash eating leave me alone you icicle-dicked HEALER!"

The Imaryan was perfectly turned out, as always, braid neat, robe freshly washed and pressed, smelling faintly of laundry soap and the iron, and Ahrimaz felt like a great, hairy, stinking and unkempt barbarian in front of him, hair needing a wash and plastered across his face, his beard uncombed and getting long enough that he could see the edges of it without straining hard. Unlaced sleep shirt stained with sweat and... nothing on his nethers, the shirt barely keeping him decent and covered, even as cold air swirled up underneath.

The dogs managed to get themselves untangled and barrelled out of the room, thinking that it was feeding time, bounding away down the hall. Heylia had sauntered out of the animal door in the wall an hour ago.

"Until you wish to speak to me again, certainly. However, I find you using the curse words and insulting names more associated with the Innéan Goddess quite encouraging."

Ahrimaz turned his back on the man, pulling the nightshirt tight around himself. "I'll get dressed… something from HIS closet I presume?"

"He wouldn't grudge you it, I assure you," Limyé said quietly.

"WELL I DO!" He was shaking. "I'll wear something and come out to the hall."

"There will be something to eat, Ahrimaz. And a cup of malak to warm you."

"I don't want food. Or malak."

"What good does your—"

"DON'T YOU SCORCHING SAY IT!"

They stood in silence for a time and in the distance a training shout and a ragged volley of fire from what, in Ahrimaz's world, had been the walled gun range. Knowing these people it was probably open and everybody and their pets could just wander into danger. He shook his head.

"I'll eat."

"I'll let you put yourself together. Didara said that she'll be wearing gold nails if that's important to you."

He could hear and feel her happy rumbles through his feet though he wasn't sure that Limyé could. He was astonished that he could, two floors up, and realized that their conversation had actually coloured his dreams. He nodded, head down, and waited until Limyé closed the door gently.

* * * * *

He turned around, trying to move normally rather than like a broken toy and suddenly found his eyes full of tears. He wanted Kinouraé. He wanted the old man there like he wanted his next breath. "Kin…" he savagely scrubbed his hands over his eyes, flung the night shirt onto the rug. So what if he'd have to tidy up after himself like a peasant. At least he wouldn't be crawling around a dungeon floor cleaning up the mess with his tongue.

He drew in a deep breath and managed to open the wardrobe door without ripping it off its hinges or cracking the wood. Then he stood and stared at his counterpart's wardrobe. What there was of it.

A dozen knitted sweaters. He recognized some of them that he'd already been given, downstairs. Only three pairs of stockings? What, one to wear, one to wash and one for emergencies like runs or stains? Of course. A weeks worth of small clothes. Four shirts, two cotton, one silk, one linen.

Likewise four breeches. Two black, one buff, one blue. Two brocade coats, one gold with red lining, one blue with silver lining. "Knowing him they're probably reversible," he muttered to himself. "For economy. Scorching bastard." And there were a dozen vests, some that he vaguely remembered from his first morning here, each one more wildly embroidered than the next. Eye-scorching combinations of reds and blues and greens and some even with gold thread. Apparently vests were an indulgence of his.

There were the filthy things in the saddle-bags, sitting at the end of the bed, but those were rough woven wool for winter work. The boots, sitting forlorn at the door were stained with mud and water and road salt. At least they salted the roads somewhat after plowing. They needed cleaning badly.

He bent to look down at the bottom of the wardrobe and found slippers, a pair of buckled shoes that were black with red heels, and another pair of boots, though they were not riding boots and of sueded leather. A shallow box under the shoes was labelled 'Summer Things'. And the last drawer had a small jewel box with a scattering of small gold rings, earrings that he could not wear because his ears were not pierced, and a heavy chain in silver and green and blue enamel. Not an Aeono confirmation chain in solid gold with rubies and diamonds, but one that had silver ice tigers and albino lions with sapphire blue eyes. "Lyrian."

He swallowed hard, grabbed the silk shirt, the velvet black breeches, a vest that was more red than anything else, smalls, stockings and he seized the red and gold coat and soft boots before padding downstairs to try and get clean fast.

"**Commmmminnnnnng**," he rumbled as he cleared the stairs, hoping that Didara could hear him, even as her calling him came through the stone more clearly downstairs.

Nothing to shave with. He raked his wet hair back, tried to tug his familiar/ unfamiliar clothing straight over damp skin and managed to stamp into the boots and out to the hall. It was still cold enough that his hair froze in the dash across to the hall and he said 'I'm here" as he closed the sliding door behind himself.

He slipped into the hall itself and stopped. "My gods, Didara! Jagunjagun! You're astonishingly beautiful!"

Didara crossed her front legs coquettishly, curled her trunk up and trumpeted, just a little. Her tusks were uncovered and polished, glittering in rainbow gems that were rivalled in brightness by a gold chain and mirror crown, the gold bells rippling down her gently flapping ears chiming sweetly. Her neck band was white lace with rose cut diamonds blazing along the flaring ends. Even the tuft of her tail had ribbons with mirrors on and her nails were painted gold.

Jagunjagun was painted with black streaks and lightning bolts, his scars…
not just the recent wounds in his armpit, but older badges of honour on his
trunk and chest… painted gold. He carried a carved ivory tusk/staff at the
ready. Ologbon in black silk, quilted jacket and turban with a scarlet feather
rising from a gold gemstone, also carried an ivory tusk. Jagunjagun laughed
and it came out as a trumpet, echoing Didara.

"Well, brother iti-igi, will we do as ambassadors to your little brother
and his people?"

AHRIMAZ WALKED UP TO DIDARA AND BURIED HIS HEAD IN HER SIDE, standing with his hands flat on her belly. **Joyandfierceness** "What was that?"

Didara rumbled, turned her head and ran her trunk down his back. "What? I like the coat on you. All that gold matches my toes." She raised one massive foot. "We should go and let your family greet us and then let everyone get comfortable again. Jagunjagun and I think we should host a party in our new Ambassadorial Hall with its glorious hot pool and all your iti can come in if they want."

"Our iti?"

"Dogs, cats, horses… even those birds and the deer the Cylak have. All iti-igi. She waved her trunk, pinching its fingers illustratively, like a man might wave a hand. "Come on. My crown is getting heavy."

"It's a weight of feather on you…" but Ahrimaz nodded at Ologbon and turned to face the hall door that was just being opened. "This isn't my world I don't know where we're going."

"Just follow the deer, dear." The deer that were Pel's *coronshion* were all there, harnessed up with every one of their bells, but no riders. Most of them had, by now, lost their antlers but their harnesses jingled brightly.

"Maybe a thumb length of leather not covered in bells?" Ahrimaz muttered nastily to himself. "You're not trying hard enough, Cylak."

"What was that?"

"I was snarling about how much the Cylak love bells, Didi," he answered, surprising himself that he just answered honestly, no dancing around for greatest advantage. "I was being a prick."

"What is that word?" Jagunjagun asked, pacing along behind them as they stepped out into the blinding sunlight of late winter sun on snow. "PRYK?"

Ahrimaz laughed. "Prick is a slang term for the male of our species' penis, mildly obscene and has overtones of 'something that pokes'." His voice faded as they walked down the street that was plowed down to the stones.

There was no way to go from stables to greeting place... he assumed the front portico of this little palace... without going out into the city. The streets and courtyards were mostly too narrow to take any kind of short route, so they marched out to the widest streets of Innéthel, where two carts could normally pass each other, and the people had decorated as best they could. Minor priests of both God and Goddess had apparently worked together because every lamp post, every overhanging beam that in the summer obviously held flower pots, had enormous decorative ice crystals hanging everywhere and in the centre of each fantastic creation a light shone.

"My little scorching Goddess," Ahrimaz whispered to himself and Didara began rumbling a descriptive story song, pieces, snatches of sound, as she began composing her view of Innéthel, the City of Crystals, she seemed to be calling it. **Joyandfierceness**

"You said that before," Ahrimaz said. And then the wave of sound from the crowds lining the decorated streets hit them. It was almost a physical sensation, people had never seen anything like the elephants before and cheered themselves hoarse. Ahrimaz resolutely kept his eyes ahead, looking at the back end of a bunch of deer rather than consider that all these people might want to see him.

It was actually a short walk around to the portico and Ahrimaz gasped when they turned the corner. He recognized it as the doors of his own House of Gold. The doors towered two storeys tall against the brightly painted wood and plaster House of the Hand. They were wooden in this world but gilded and painted to look like gold. The cleared pavement before them was bright yellow sandstone, with red grout between the blocks of stone, just as in the empire, with one enormous path leading to the doors, one leading off to the right to the temple of Aeono and a small path leading up the hill to the left and he knew, to join with the path to the Veil.

He stumbled as he realized that a tiny, dim version of his own world lay before him and Jagunjagun held him up with his trunk, poking him upright with his staff from behind. "But... this is my empire's doorway," he said faintly. "It's just the rest of the palace doesn't match."

There were flame torches all along the temple path, burning columns of flame ten feet high and fountains, still and filled with snow this time of year heading off to the hills.

The doors stood open and their deer escort opened up and took station on either side. The crowd noise was making Ahrimaz's ears ache and he thought he was used to being cheered.

Didara walked up the dozen steps in four strides as if climbing rough ground and stopped right at the threshold. Ahriminash, and Ahrimiar and Arnziel and the girls… all the girls… Ahrimaz couldn't see for tears standing in his eyes. Yolend and the baby next to Ahriminash, dressed in the flowing blue of the Yhom, her drummer and her piper attending her. "Oh, you and your sound. You loved the Cylak bells when we brought them," Ahrimaz muttered. Didara flipped a belled ear at him and he was silent.

Joyandfierceness vibrated under his hand and Ahrimaz turned slowly to stare up at Didara horrified, ecstatic fascination dawning. "You didn't tell me you were pregnant!" he snapped.

"You never asked," she said. "Hush and pay attention."

80   Didara's Welcome Song At A Distance

AHRIMAZ'S SIGHT WENT GREY AROUND THE EDGES AND HE SWAYED, but his hand on Didara's side and Jagunjagun's staff and trunk behind him helped him stay upright. Then Rutaçyen was at his side and had him companionably by the elbow as the procession stepped into the Great Hall. It wasn't galleries for fawning courtiers, he reminded himself. The galleries were filled with representatives from all over Inné.

And they weren't just voted in. They also had to pass the rigorous government tests. In the Empire there were just the clerk's tests that would let only the most intelligent, the most competent, into the House of Gold. No doubt here they had to be the most empathetic and sympathetic as well. These people. They were so far from his own. But they weren't. All at the same time.

Joyandfierceness trembled through his hand, the future baby elephant, just beginning to speak on the lowest frequencies. Though baby talk, high and sweet. His knees weakened and he felt choked as he realized what the jewelled construction in the centre of Didara's skeleton in the Empire's Hall… very near here in fact… was. It wasn't her heart, as he'd thought.

He wrenched his thoughts back to here. Here the Hall was open and empty, space for everyone in government to crowd around in a disorganized mob. There was no order, no precedence, everyone jostled up with everyone else.

Ahrimaz pressed his hand against his mouth, trying to keep his gorge and his fear down. All around him, thank the Gods for Rutaçyen keeping people off and Didara on the other side. They all wanted to touch her. Of course he understood that but touch him? He swallowed, swallowed again as Didara raised one foot, trumpeted loudly enough to blast everyone to silence and stillness.

She opened her mouth and sang her formal welcome, the subsonics rumbling through the crowd and a whole wave of people just suddenly sat down, hands pressed against the floor. She hesitated a moment as she realized how many people could hear her without Ologbon's translation.

"People of Inné, thank you for your tropical welcome. I am Didara, a Dreamer of the Queen..."

Ologbon, sitting on Jagunjagun's neck raised his sceptre high and his voice translating was a high counterpoint to Didara's, her formal phrases rolling around the hall, making people sway with it.

Jagunjagun said, quietly in Ahrimaz's ear, "oh wonderful you people can hear her and she has so many theories to sing! I'll have to go home without her in a year or two!"

"What she won't be finished by then? Are you being sarcastic?"

"What is he saying?" Rutaçyen asked. "I can just barely hear him, but he's speaking in Innéan!"

"He's being a little brother," Ahrimaz answered. Part of him wanted to laugh at how silly the young elephant was being, part of him was still nauseated and overwhelmed, part of him was sitting frozen and one part just screamed endlessly. *There is one part of me that is always screaming. No wonder I'm tired.*

"Jagunjagun, I placed Didara's staff into my brother's hand. I am here, my brother has Didara's attention and he can stand and listen for hours. I need... I can't..."

"Go, my friend. You stepped the threshold with us. Iti-igi Ahrimmmmmaz... go rest."

"She's pregnant."

"Yes, I know."

"You've gotten very good at Innéan."

He nodded, making it look like he was counterpointing something Didara had just sung. "I know. You've helped. Go rest, iti."

Ahrimaz was so close to tearing his way through the crowd with his bare hands and teeth he barely nodded and found that Rutaçyen had somehow opened a narrow way through the mob. He was still being touched but he found that she led him to a narrow doorway under a gallery and suddenly there was silence, except for the elephants deepest rumbles. He leaned against the solid door, nearly faint with relief.

"Back to bed with you. You don't do well in crowds," Rutaçyen said quietly. "Ah. Here they are." The dogs came cavorting down the hall. "Sure and Teh can bring you back to your room. You don't need to go outside again."

"I should stay. I shouldn't run. This is an important meeting." *I'm whining.*

"And you don't want to ruin their welcome song by vomiting at their feet, or killing some commoner who touched you wrong, now, do you?"

"No."

"To bed with you."

"Yes, mama," he said, smiling to make it a joke. It was like a knife in his gut as he said it.

She pretended to swat him. "When you've rested, come to the salle. You need a work-out."

81

Like a Bad Tooth

THE GREEN ROOM WAS ALREADY COMING TO SEEM LIKE A SAFE PLACE. No one had invaded to even pick up the night-shirt, though there was a knock on the door almost the moment he closed it behind him.

"Who is it?" He called, listlessly, struggling to not just fall onto the bed, fully clothed.

"Limyé."

"Scorch you," Ahrimaz said, but it was without heat and he opened the door without looking and stepped over to sink onto the couch. From there he leaned forward and clamped his hands over his face and sat, still, as Limyé came in.

He closed the door, softly, and picked up the night shirt off the floor, dropping it into a slot in the wall... ah, obviously, the laundry for smalls. Ahrimaz was aware of every move he made, however quiet, however soft, as he pulled the bed straight, shaking the feathers out. The animals scrambled in through their door, at least the dogs did, several times, in and out, panting joyously in his ear though he normally would have knocked any hound on the head with his fist for that sloppy tongue and informality. He just sat still and tolerated the touch. Heylia ghosted up and draped herself over the back of the couch. Apparently it was her place.

He shook. He couldn't stop it. He sat and shook and then froze when he realized he'd lost track of Limyé. He hadn't lost track of another person in the room in years. Then he relaxed. A footstep. Too close but he knew where he was. "Ahrimaz. Shall I take the coat and vest and boots?"

"You're not Kinouraé, you're not a body servant, you're not MY body servant I won't let you that close I won't trust you why don't you people stop TOUCHING ME!"

He was on his feet, fists clenched, but the dogs lying sprawled on the rug hadn't moved and neither had the blasted cat. He knew he was glaring, close enough to Limyé's face to feel his warm breath. Scorching, blasting, drowning hells he was close enough almost to touch noses. "Don't. Just don't touch me. Don't tend me." *Where in all the flaming, drowning, freezing hells is Kinouraé in this world? Is he even a valet? Is there such a thing?*

Without taking his eyes off Limyé, Ahrimaz deliberately wiggled out of the coat, working his arms free slowly. He flung it over his own arm and then worked the buttons of the vest open as well before he sidled toward the wardrobe. "I can do it myself."

"I know. I'm not saying anything about your competence and I'm not trying to take anyone's place."

"Good."

That was enough to let him break his gaze on the Imaryan and hang the coat and vest up himself, peasant work though that was. The elegant little boot-jack flipped out of the floor… exactly like the one at home and that was enough to send him back down on the floor, hands over his face again.

"I can't stand it." He managed to rasp. "I keep getting my balance and then something hits me, something throws me off. Everyone's here but Kinouraé or any of the servants. The war master is my aunt who in my world was forced to pretend to be my mother. I found out that the thing I took for a jewelled heart in my friend's memorial isn't… it's a jewelled unborn… and I never knew. She never told me. Perhaps she didn't know? Why? Why? And… I've dreamed of my mother's death and my aunt's death and my uncle… Did you know that your beloved Ahrimaz has, probably, in my world executed Rutaçyen and their brother? Probably for treason of some kind, maybe finding out that he is not me. Maybe trying to force him into their control."

He fell silent. Limyé settled on the rug across from him, shoving dog paws out of the way. Listening. But he couldn't force out another word.

"And now the driving force that drove you out of the cell, into this world, is finished for now? You're suddenly without direction and overwhelmed with all of us, hmmm?"

His nod was almost convulsive.

"We will pick up where we left off, then. You may treat this room the same as if it were the cell downstairs. I and the others will speak with you, if you permit. You need only go down to the water rooms at your body's urging, and to the salle and the arena where your friends are. The horses who grew used to them are the horses in that barn. You have only changed the basement room to this one. After your precipitous run to help your friends, it looks like they will safely be here at least a year now, given that Didara is not going to want to go away from a safe place, in a strange country and continent."

Again he managed a convulsive nod. "I... don't have to speak to anyone... all those people... all those crowds..."

"No. You are as safe here as you were in the cell. Should you wish I can ask that the family put a lock on the door."

"No. It's... it's all right. I... don't want to make one of the children crawl through a dog door to unlock it, should I have an emergency where I cannot."

"Very sensible of you, Ahrimaz. Shall I come back with tea?"

"Yes." The second word came as if wrenched out of his mouth with armoured fingers, like a bad tooth. "Please."

News at the House of the Hand

—By Teel James

Coalition News, for Hand Press, Innéthel Printers, Spring, Year Two of Ahrimiar Kenaçyen's Sitting

First this author must comment upon the recent explosion at the House. The Innovators of the House had taken Ahrimaz's comments concerning the so-called 'gun cotton' quite seriously, but apparently not seriously enough.

The research facility had made tiny amounts, based on the ideas that came out of the journey to greet the **Rummummalos** Ambassadors and had proposed to make a rather larger quantity.

The Innovators, led by M'ser had planned for their demonstration to be in the open courtyard before the Great Hall until a late season ice storm had them move into the Hall itself. The Emperor of Strange Inné, Ahrimaz, gracing the gathering after his regular morning training with Sword-master Rutaçyen, was just straightening his cuffs when he entered and saw the quantity of gun cotton they were about to light.

His bellow of "NO! Out out, everyone out NOW!"

He undoubtedly saved a number of lives, since most witnesses had been in the military and reacted to the command with alacrity. Ahrimaz leaped into the centre of the Hall where M'ser Lachemi was just lighting the fuse, grabbed him and his assistant by the collar and bodily dragged them through the partially open doors and outside into the freezing rain, even as the flame reached the small pile of gun cotton and it exploded.

Of the hundred or so people, already fleeing the hall when the gun cotton went off, forty-one were trapped in the rubble of the galleries crumbling. Four elderly people who either did not hear, or react in time, were killed outright in the blast.

Ahrimaz and the Innovators were all three injured slightly by the doors of the Hall as they were blown off their hinges and splintered. Everyone had their hearing damaged to some degree, the Lyrian priesthood and the Imaryan healers report, but it should come back in a few days.

This reporter heard, with his own somewhat damaged ears, Ahrimaz say to the dazed Innovator, M'ser Lachemi, "Didn't I tell you? What did I tell you?" All three lay on the ice covered cobbles, half buried in enormous gilded splinters that could have, with a bit more energy behind them, become lethal weapons.

"M'ser... I should have attended more carefully. Emilié, take a note."

"What? Oh, yes M'ser."

We encourage the researchers and Innovators to not disregard the information supplied to them, especially in regards to the safety of Innéan citizens.

We also thank the **Rummummalos** Ambassadors for their invaluable assistance in freeing our citizens from the mostly ruined centre block of our Governmental House.

The committee for Maintenance and Repair are already discussing the logistics of rebuilding the public venue.

Healing of the Emperor: Continues

—By Teel James

Coalition News, for Hand Press, Innéthel Printers,
Spring, Year Two of Ahrimiar Kenaçyen's Sitting

The spectacle yesterday, of Didara the Curious, carrying a screaming, cursing flailing Ahrimaz, through the town hoisted up to near second story height, by one ankle, is easily explained.

The House healer Limyé explained that the Emperor made an abortive attempt at self-harm while in the Ambassador's presence and when prevented, proceeded to argue with Didara. Unfortunately things escalated until the Ambassador acted, with both dispatch and alacrity.

This reporter was first made aware of the incident when the howling Emperor was carried, swinging, past the Broadsheet's windows. His coat hung inside out over his head and muffled the worst of his invective and impecunious language. This reporter rushed outside and proceeded to follow the Ambassador as she carried Ahrimaz down to the river - to the Puddle - and proceeded to dunk him in the icy water to, as I later ascertained, "Cool his head."

She then placed him, dripping and mortified, upon her back and calmly walked back to the Ambassadorial Hall and the hot pool in their reception theatre, where this reporter was barred from immediate entry.

Ahrimaz declined to explain, when interrogated later, turning an intriguing shade of embarrassment red. This reporter intends to continue following the healing of Ahrimaz, and continue training with the man.

The High Priestess of the Veil, the honourable Mara d'Rom, has accepted Ahrimaz into the ranks of her priesthood, his investiture to proceed later in the spring when the weather turns.

"We don't want to give our new priestesses and priests lung thick by having them go into the Veil when it is freezing," she said. "However much we pride ourselves in controlling the water temperature around us, acolytes and students and new clergy often have difficulties there, so of course we take that into consideration. Ahrimaz will be re-invested, since he, in his other incarnation, was invested as a priest of Lyrian then."

83   I Am So Humiliated

I SWEAR THESE PEOPLE WILL BE THE DEATH OF ME. The humiliation I feel burns and I cannot lash out in rage. Truly they are ALL like this… Even the scorching shit elephants and the ice-assed High Priestesses.

They nearly blow themselves up because gun cotton looks 'so innocent'. One idiot, one fool, one moron with ice and shit for brains offered to *sit on* the box containing the explosive. I heard afterwards, when they were picking the shards off us and the elephants were lifting wooden beams off people, that this self-copulating, hydrocephalic fool fainted dead away, confusing people who were trying to help victims of the explosion.

These people. *It looks so innocent?* Freeze and scorch me I might just keel over in a dead faint myself should anyone show some useful cynicism! I should never have said anything. And M'ser Lachemi has the insufferable gall, the inexpressible, unutterable and ineffable elephant balls to ask me about MORE things that the empire has come up with.

Fountain pens, enclosed air stoves, and high explosives aren't ENOUGH? I reeled off float glass, moveable type, which my friend M'ser James says they have but made of hand-carved ironwood rather than poured metal, and lift locks on the river to make the navigation head somewhat higher into Innéan country than here and the man is gibbering. He's taking EVERYTHING I say now entirely seriously and it makes me want to start throwing fantasies at him. Like the fool who showed me a children's toy fire-balloon and tried to convince me that it could be up-scaled to a military observation platform. Silk gas-bags driven by leg-rowed spinning propellers!

Or the asinine idea of using water wheels to draw wire! Wire rope! A fat-based paint that stops rust on military gear. Can I throw all these wild theories at them to overwhelm them and make them leave me alone? Hmmm. Perhaps I will just throw everything at these Innovators. At least they will then shut up and go away, leave me mostly alone. I have a plan. It will take them years to sort out which ideas are viable and which are merely chaff that I may hide behind.

And… and… I continue to avoid both Pel and Yolend and his children. It hurts too much. This makes the High Priestess's offer to invest me as a priest up at the Veil much more appealing. I just… can't keep it together around people. I want to learn to love them. Too much. Too much. They… are lovable and I just do NOT know how to love without tying it to injury and torture.

I pull out the ink stick and the paper and begin to try and calm my mind. Grind the ink. Mix the ink. Wet the brush. Breathe. Try to draw a line. Try to draw a circle. Try to draw the image of Lyrian's Peace which has all the ink strokes in it. Crumple them all and jam them into the closed stove in my room… the newly installed closed stove. Ashes. I have not one single clean line. My mind is chattering and flailing and the ink shows it. My hands are covered in ink spots and ashes.

Rutaçyen's hands are always clean. Her lines are clean. I have managed ONE clean line and that was when I was so shaking exhausted I couldn't see straight.

Didara can draw a better line than I. Jagunjagun loves the idea of the ink sword and draws every day. Innéans come to speak to him, to see him draw, to spirit away his ink marked pieces of paper. I sit and am nothing but an embarrassment.

An embarrassment that needs to be dangled by one ankle and dunked in ice water until I obey. I hate them all. I hate them all. Of course I hate them. They humiliate me. I hate them. I want to love them so badly. But that's hard. It is easier to hate them. I have never done 'easy', though.

84

Sacred Suicide

AHRIMAZ PULLED HIMSELF OUT OF THE MUD NEXT TO ONE OF THE VEIL platforms, where he'd actually fallen, face first. Rutaçyen sat, cross-legged, next to the High Priestess. They looked almost like bookends, though Rutaçyen had the Kenaçyen blond hair, cut short and sharp now, and High Priestess Mara had long dark brown hair that coiled all around her as she sat.

"Go get cleaned up, Ahrimaz," Rutaçyen said. "The water is warm enough now."

"Maybe to an ice-tits like you."

"Give me fifty push ups," she said without heat. "Then go get clean. I have clean clothes for you when you have the mud off."

Ahrimaz glared at her, hands convulsively opening and closing. The weather had finally shifted and the snow had melted in the warm rain that came day after day. Today the sun was making a rare appearance and the water surging around his ankles was actually swimmable. He was aware of Pelahir meditating on another platform down the Veil, far enough that the rushing sound of the water would give everyone privacy.

Yolend sat with him and the child... now running like a mad thing... made a beeline right to him. "...shups?" he inquired in his piping voice. He insisted on trying to do what Ahrimaz was doing, especially if it was training of any kind and would cry if Ahrimaz tried to tell him he wasn't 'daddy' but 'uncle'.

"Daaaaah? ...shups?"

"Yes, pushups," Ahrimaz snarled, splashed down and began. The baby did too, his bum in the air as he wobbled through four press-ups before sitting down and beginning to throw mud as Ahrimaz finished his fast fifty. "You stay with the war master while I swim!" Ahrimaz snapped, scooped him up and dumped the messy toddler on Rutaçyen's lap, mud and all, with an evil grin.

She grinned back and encircled the toddler, heedless of the dirt and the water. "If you have trouble getting into the water I'll call Didara." The elephant had found the Veil waterfall or waterfalls... the whole amazing length of them, to be her favourite place outside and was currently up-vale standing under one of the more energetic showers.

"No," Ahrimaz snapped, and yanked his shirt up over his head, flinging it into the dirt, with his trousers, turned and walked into the nearest pool.

Rutaçyen handed the toddler to an acolyte who carted the child back to Yolend who took him and offered him her breast. He began nursing and was asleep in moments, arms and legs relaxing over his mother's knee.

"So you think he's ready for this?" Rutaçyen asked quietly and the High Priestess shrugged.

"Soon if not now..." There was an unaccustomed shout from higher up the valley. "See? Even if he doesn't realize it, he's ready to do the work." The shout was from one of the priestesses who came running down the hill, leaving her basket behind her, spilling early bulbs all down the hill. She was chanting something under her breath as she plunged into the water near the main waterfall, the Goddess's Hair.

Ahrimaz had stood up from where he'd been scrubbing mud and sweat out of his hair, before the woman had called, his head turning toward the falls. "He knows, even if he doesn't yet understand."

The priestess dove under the thundering waterfall and a moment later came up with a young man, hauling him out by the hair. They couldn't hear what was being said but she shifted her grip the moment his face broke into air and he tried to fight her, to drive himself under again. "They feel so much pain," the High Priestess said. "This year it's worse than it has been in the past three years."

"Is it in part the knowledge that there are other worlds?" Rutaçyen folded her hands and looked over at Ahrimaz, watching another priest wade over to the would-be suicide, one of the youngsters pelting up the path to fetch Limyé or another Imaryan healer from Innéthel.

"I think so. Some people just give up and think "in another world I didn't do this. Let that 'me' go on. This life hurts too much."

Mara nodded. "But She lets us know if it is not their time. Some years She allows the self murder and calls home but we know, then."

"And Ahrimaz, our stranger, can tell."

"He's already a priest. He already knows. He's just fighting it because it seems too good to be true for him. He still thinks it necessary to be in pain, to pay for the evil he did in that other world."

"I see." Rutaçyen smiled brightly as Ahrimaz sloshed out of the water, clean. His face was troubled.

"That boy..." he said. "How did I know it wasn't his time? How did I hear him howling about how he had to die?"

The High Priestess handed him a clean robe and a towel. "Probably because you have had the same urge. It will make you sensitive to it."

"Oh." He dropped the robe over his head, then looked up in shock. "This is a priest's robe!"

"Yes. That's all the investiture you're getting," the High Priestess said. "You are now welcome onto the private meditation platforms. Please don't set them on fire if you get upset." She smiled at him and nodded to Rutaçyen. "I'll be over with Yo and Pel. Limyé will, no doubt, report to me once he's calmed that young man down."

"Ahrimaz, you need to rest. You pushed yourself to half-crazy today and are still shaking with fatigue." He was watching the boy being led out of the water, escorted by the two priests and the healer who had just arrived, running.

"Hmmm?" He took a deep breath, sank down to the platform. "Yes, teacher."

85

She is Yes

"WHY ARE YOU SO ANGRY?" The voice out of the darkness was feminine, though not overtly female, Ahrimaz thought. What? How can a voice be feminine and not female?

"Ummmm." I sound like an elephant calf. "Because I'm frightened. Rage and despite and anger all keep me safe."

"Do they keep you safe, in a world where only one person has ever truly attacked you, and he's dead?"

"You mean the Cylak King who Pel replaced." Even here he would not say the man's name.

"Yes."

"In my world he was an ineffectual, foolish man who insisted that the world was by right his. I disabused him of that thought."

"You also disassociated him from his head as I recall."

"Yes." For a moment Ahrimaz had the flash of memory in his hand as the Flamen burned through the man's neck. At full gallop, he didn't have time to see him fall off his deer. One more opponent lost on the battlefield. One more killing he could use to try and assuage his rage and his pain. He didn't see him fall, but he knew the man's clothing and body would be on fire. The Flamen did that to people. And things.

"Who are you?" He asked though he knew icy well. Scorching well. He knew.

"Lyrian is what you call me in this tiny portion of understanding."

"Goddess. Demon. Divinity."

"Some of what I am. I just am."

"And You're just talking to me."

"Why not?"

"Because You are those things? Because I killed Your followers? Because I raped and beat my wife to control her, and beat my daughter because she was defiant? I am a monster,

not a... a... priest."

"*Don't you already long to correct those things? To recompense the innocent, somehow? That is part of the pain you feel. Your inability to fix what you did. I am speaking only to you. You are broken enough to hear Me.*"

"I'm certainly broken." Below... Ahrimaz suddenly realized he could see the salt pan below him again, and he could see a man struggling across the waste that was salt and brine and reflection of sky and sun and nothing else.

"Who is that?"

"*You know.*"

Ahrimaz watched his brother stop at an enormous canyon broken into the land, where fire rose from below. There was a bridge across it but it was made up of weapons. Sharp weapons. On this side of the bridge there were the stinking corpses of the Kenaçyen family shambling around, slashing each other with words and with whips, bleeding on each other and the land.

Across the bridge a little girl sat on a white tiger, green plants growing up out of every one of the great cat's footprints.

"Go! Arnziel you can get out! Don't be afraid!" For an instant he was the older brother, hiding his little brother under his bed and stepping in to take the beating his father wished to lay on someone's hide. It didn't matter if you had done wrong. The old monster just had to make one, or all of them, hurt.

The image faded as Arnziel stepped out, barefoot on the bridge of swords.

"It's not really swords he's walking on," Ahrimaz said. "It's his fear that makes them edged weapons. He's doing that to himself."

"He'll learn that," Lyrian said. "But it will take his own time to do so. Just as you will."

"Are we all different in all the worlds we exist in?"

"*Yes.*"

"How do You stand it? It would be a cacophony of prayers."

"*It is.*" He could sense her smile. "*You might be able to understand it if you consider it a choir or a garden. A tapestry. An opera. A story. A vast chord that encompasses everything. I am a music lover.*"

"And You like apples."

"And songbirds."

"And cats that kill songbirds."

"*Yes.*"

Ahrimaz glared around himself looking in the dark, in the light, in the rainbow of colours in the vastness that had no edges, no limits, no time forward or backward, struggling to glare the Goddess in the face. "EVERYTHING IS A YES TO YOU ISN'T IT!?"

His rage fell into the enormity and was less than a dust speck's dust speck. He felt another scar of his rip open, with the rush of pain and joy and relief. "It's not about me, is it?"

He could hear her smile. "Not really. Though I could say yes."

He had no air to laugh with, but laughter bubbled through him and around him, the only response other than a shattering madness.

"Yes," She said.

86 Pain Has Always Been an Old Friend

I SIT IN THE MIDDLE OF THIS ROOM, this green room, painted by my younger, other self, and rock. I feel safe here. That raises my anxiety for some reason. Growing up there never was a place that was safe. The old monster could burst in at any time, send a servant, send a guard, send the mother to fetch us, drag us out of safety.

Here no one ever does. They knock. The only creatures who have free access to me are the animals, and now, the baby who doesn't know any better. I know he's here because he's climbed onto my shoulders and is bouncing. What sane person would leave a baby with me?

I unfold and he slides down into my arms and my lap. If I were on the bed or sitting properly on a chair or the couch he wouldn't be so forward, I think, but then laugh at myself. I'm joking. This child would thrust himself into the mouth of the tiger if he wanted to pet the big kitty.

I examine him again, as though I've never seen him before, as he examines me, his fists knotted in my beard. It is getting long and I'm actually considering shaving it off. They know I'm not *him*. It's just a matter of convincing me that I am not becoming *him*.

The baby pushes against my chest and I run a finger over his misty, nearly non-existent eyebrows, and then over my own and he giggles. I touch his nose and find my mouth falling open in a grin. You would think I was happy. He copies me and then shrieks.

A knock came at my door and Yolend called, "Ahrimaz is he in there with you again?"

"Yes, and his puppy has piddled on the floor again." These people give their children dogs young.

She laughed. "I have a page to clean it up."

He rose and stepped over the mess, scooped up the little vermin and manage to open the door without dropping either baby or puppy.

She knew dogs. The page rushed in with a couple of lidded buckets and a rag, swished up the puddle off the stone floor, dampen the rag with the hot water and soap in the other and gave the stone a scrub and a wipe. All while he stood there, looking into her eyes. *She is not my wife. I miss her. I miss the woman I'm allowed to love. I miss her. I owe her.* He loaded the boy and the dog into her arms and as the page skittered out with the messy pails, touched her arm. "Wait, please."

She paused and he didn't know what to say... at last he managed to open his mouth to talk to the ice bitch Goddess's priestess wife... um to Yolend... "Next time... next time we spar would you obliged me by trying to land a bruise here?" He touched his left cheek. She smiled at him which made him want to slap the expression off her face because he already knew how she would answer.

"Sorry, Ahrimaz, but no. That would violate the salle rules and Rutaçyen would have me do several hundred pull ups if I actually tried to injure you. And you would be doing the same for not blocking and inviting the injury." She blocked the baby from snatching at her head band and with the child's fist safely in her hand looked at him intently. "I do not owe you bruises or scars. SHE does."

He nodded and stepped back, so enraged he could almost not see her even as he closed the door softly. He waited till he heard her walk away, before sinking down on the floor and rocking again. He could feel the hardness and slight dampness of the floor under me, the verdant breeze from the window. He felt the press of forearm scars around raised knees.

I will not bite. I do not deserve pain. She is right. What am I afraid of?

I don't know. I don't know I don't... I'm afraid that I'm not hurting enough. That someone is going to show up and make me hurt as much as I'm supposed to.

I and pain are such old friends I don't want to let it go. It's too easy to just let it go, let it be. It's too soft. It's not right that life should just be easy. Pain... where are you? Why are you leaving me too?

Ah. There. Pain has always been there. Now I am feeling bereft of one more thing. But... what good does my pain do? It has always been there... almost. There was a time before pain but my life was arranged so that the only constant, the only unfailing rock under everything in my life, was Pain.

They want Pain to leave me too.

87

Peace is No Longer an Assault

AHRIMAZ GAZED AROUND THE BEDROOM, his bedroom, and realized he hadn't been outside the building in several days. They were finally leaving him alone with his thoughts more and more, since Limyé had noted his forearm scars were finally healed up enough to be heavy callus rather than weeping sores with bite-mark edges. Every bath now they where easing, flaking off, being rubbed away with soap and hot water and a scrubbing cloth.

He was no longer attacking himself, at least physically, and so the watch on him was less. The weather was full-on spring and he found he could bear all this verdancy. In fact he quite liked it. He needed to go out, to where he'd found some kind of solace from the old monster, even if it was supposed to be hunting ground. The old man had wanted blood spilled in the Vale, to 'keep the witches out', had torn down the ribbons that kept appearing on the massive old tree at the entrance.

The Emperor had, a generation ago, cut that apple tree down. An oak on the other side of the path, he'd left and it had grown huge. And the apple had come back from the roots, as if it were recovering from a natural disaster instead of from deliberate attack.

In this world an ice storm had shattered the apple tree and it had also come back, nearly identical to the one in his own world.

His hand hovered over the priest's robe for a moment, then he grabbed the plain cotton training clothes, soft from all the washing. Barefoot, he walked out past the massive building project at the front, rebuilding the polity's hall. It would look even more like the entrance to the House of Gold in his world when it was finished, but he said nothing about it.

The other enormous building project they were taking on was installing the first massive sheets of float-glass windows, both in the entrance and all along the Elephant Ambassadors hall, showing the lush and luxuriant garden within, and letting in much more light to the great good benefit of both the plants and the ambassadors.

Jagunjagun was paying for these extravagant windows by travelling all around central Inné doing song instructions describing his home. He had found himself uncomfortable doing this at first, but Didara only did the ones in Innéthel itself, as her pregnancy progressed, and her exercise became a series of specific walk arounds to not overtax herself. Ahrimaz had insisted and Jagunjagun had supported him, much to her disgruntlement.

The glue and the stench of metal-work stung his nose, the thock of mallets on wood, and the harsher ring of hammer on metal and anvil tumbled through his ears but somehow didn't manage to exacerbate the howling under his skin. People's shouting direction to one another had nothing to do with him, nothing he was responsible for, however much he'd given them ideas dragged out of another world. It was similar enough an existence that any other Innéan could have thought the same things.

The yellow brick was warm under his feet and he felt curiously isolated, safely insulated somehow, from the business all around him. The family were all busy, every one, and he could finally draw breath without someone else standing close enough to inhale what he exhaled.

He turned away from the plaza and went up the hill, the wide brick path shrinking as he distanced himself from the noise and mess of other people's lives, realizing that he carried the noise and mess of his own life contained in himself. The roaring in his head, the shrieking in his veins, the readiness to fight or flee or endure all ticking and pulsing and quivering just under his skin.

It was surprising how much he'd controlled it, really. It was still consuming him but not as much as it used to. Limyé had pointed out how much the Empire constrained him in the shape he'd been hammered into. Another reason he hurt. It was like unclenching a tight-held fist.

The trees at the entrance to the Vale were in full leaf and the apple was in full flower, the lower branches festooned with ribbons drifting in the wind and empty wicker cages, the birds released to Her glory cheeping and singing and screeching and chattering all the way to the waterfalls.

Ahrimaz nodded at the priest scattering cracked corn for the ground feeders and to the priestess raking the path. A young acolyte, high in the tree, tiny to not disturb the fragile old branches, removed the oldest cages so they not foul the trees growth. They all smiled at him and he found his own mouth stretching in that strangest of grimaces, an open smile at another person.

He didn't have to fear them. He didn't have to make them obey him. He didn't have to hurt them.

He found that his father had taught him to try and force people to fill the aching void in his chest. It was possible to fill himself up with passion, and pain, but simple connection was somehow far more satisfying. Where before he'd thought it insipid, too weak, too superficial, it now felt far deeper than any connection he'd ever had before.

He was mourning the loss of pain, he knew; mourning the loss of all the strong and violent emotions in his life, he'd been taught were the only constant companions. Limyé and he had talked about it, for far longer than he wished to remember, thinking that the time was being wasted. That pain and violence and anger and fear were all like separate relationships and he would have to let all of them go.

"Break up with them, as it were," Limyé had said. "Not necessarily a widower to them because they are not dead to you. If you need them, as a warrior, they will always be there. But you will need to conscript them."

"For a pacifist you talk quite a bit about war."

"I've studied the trauma of warriors all my career as a healer. Why do you think I was Ahrimaz's personal physician?"

"I see."

Didara sounded a lot like Limyé and Ahrimaz had no wish to inflict and project his healing flames to her new baby, so rather than sit in her armpit and talk, he came up here more.

The platform near the highest Veil waterfall was empty, the pool below a froth of white and green. He settled to his knees and lost himself in the roar of the water, the touch of the wind, the occasional spray upon his face, even the odd green or fishy smell kicked up by the falling water. When he'd first sat here the peace had both reminded him of when he was a child, hiding from hell, and later like an assault on his bulwark of horror.

Now it just was. And he was able to be in it, without quivering or running or shouting at it. People moved along the paths and drifted in and out of his perception as he knelt.

Then, sharp as knife in the guts, came a silent wail of despair that Ahrimaz knew all too well, for having lived it this past year. He shot to his feet, the sharp whistle of alarm bursting past his fingers that would call the healers and other priestesses and priests. His hand rose to join the other and Ahrimaz, the Emperor, dove into the foam of the Veil, hands sweeping for the body he knew had to be there.

The attempted sacred suicides had dropped off once the weather had changed but people still despaired of their lives.

The water smashed Ahrimaz down to the bottom and there, clinging to the smooth stones, was the one trying to inhale the Goddess's essence and drown. His fingers clenched in hair and clothing, he planted his feet on the stones, shoving them both to the surface, away from the hammer of falling water.

Ahrimaz looked down into the clenched shut eyes of the young woman he'd hauled out, weeping invisible in the water pouring off her face, hair tangled across, clenched in his fist as he kept her in the air. He shook her slightly. "Breathe, woman. You are still needed in this life, in this place. The Goddess Lyrian says so." He knew it, in his bones. There was no uncertainty in him. This young woman's time to die was not now.

And then the others were there, splashing out to take this troublesome, hurting child out of his hands. He wasn't sure what he would be able to do if someone didn't come and take them away. He wasn't a healer.

He sloshed over to boulders at the edge and sat down to catch his own breath. A towel appeared for him… a dry robe. He managed at nod at the priest who brought them silently. It was understood that if you hauled someone away from death you would be the first to speak afterwards.

It was a slightly muddy scramble back up to the platform, since the stone steps were wet and his feet were still covered in algae and muck. He pulled off his wet clothing and began rubbing his hair dry, sitting naked in the sun.

The High priestess Mara nodded at him, from her own mediation spot and he began laughing as he took up the priest's robe. "Even if I don't start by wearing this, You'll have me in them by the end of the day, somehow, hmmm, Lyrian?"

88
Willing to Uncover His Face

THE RUMBLE OF THE WORK ON THE HOUSE OF THE HAND REACHED EVEN down into the water rooms. All of Inné was taken with the novelty of gun cotton and in the old quarry, it was suddenly creating all kinds of stone for building use, and just north of the city someone had discovered a whole new seam of hard coal that the gun cotton just opened up to everyone's use. People were starting to call it Ahrimaz's Fire or Aeono's Fluff.

Ahrimaz sat in the hottest pool in the water rooms up to his chin, beard soaking in the steaming water, watching the occasional ripples jiggle through what would normally have been a still pool, and flinched, imagining the explosion so far away.

Didara said she and Jagunjagun heard it as a basso chirrup and then a roll as if the earth were drumming. Mostly pleasant.

Sure put her muzzle on top of his head and hung her paws in the water on either side treating him as though his head were a harder bolster on the edge of a pond. She licked her dewlaps and Ahrimaz snorted at the sensation and noise and went under.

The dog managed not to fall on him but looked very affronted when he re-surfaced, spitting sulphury water at her.

Ahrimaz was clean but he knew that if he got out of the water all the feelings, the pressure, the tears he could feel like a band around his head and chewing all along the backs of his cheekbones, would come pouring out. He had no energy to bear that. He sank down again, holding his breath, watching the water grow still, releasing a bubble or two to fly up and become part of his underwater sky.

His lungs were screaming at him by now and he ignored that pain. It was tiny compared to what he was used to. But he knew, just as he'd known for the girl, that it was not his time to drown, so he pushed up, bursting out of the water, startling the dogs and landed sitting on the edge.

"I was starting to wonder if I should interrupt," Pelahir's voice went from muffled to clear as the water ran out of Ahrimaz's ears. "So, Shit-Head," he asked. "How are you doing?"

Ahrimaz shrugged, tilting his head away from the Cylak man as he settled next to him, naked. *He's beautiful and my scorching dick is noticing.* "Aside from wanting to have sex with you," Ahrimaz said, "I'm fine."

"Ah." Pel slid into the water and then burst out, back up onto the edge almost in one motion. He'd washed clean before coming to soak and water glistened on ever hair. He smiled. "I'm a little bristly and I don't think I'm up for the kind of sex you want. Sorry."

Ahrimaz nodded abruptly. He still couldn't manage to come without some pain being involved. Either his or someone else's. His hand scratched idly at his chin, tangled in the hair, then knotted in it. He turned to Pel. "I'd like to borrow your razor."

"I can get you a new one. Mine's due for replacing. You keep pulling on it like that and you'll likely pull your face off." He paused a moment. "As long as you're only planning to cut hair with it."

"Only hair. I swear…" he stopped, feeling the shape of his face under the full beard. "You've been keeping mirrors away from me, on Limyé's orders haven't you?"

"Yes, we have. You might have noticed the space in your room where it used to stand."

"I… I'm not sure I'd be safe with my own hand on a razor and seeing this face." He waved a hand in front of it.

Pel didn't answer but just sat silent for a while. "A barber?"

"No."

More watery, echoing silence. "Would you trust my hand? Or Yolend? Or Limyé?" Pel was apparently as interested in having sex as Ahrimaz was, by the way his penis stood hard in the nest of his pubic hair. Ahrimaz tore his eyes away, turning away from Pel. His skin felt too hot, too inflamed. As if Aeono would burst through if Ahrimaz lost control of anything. He held his breath.

Pel waited until Ahrimaz gasped, then held out a glass of water, with cold beads running down it in this steamy atmosphere.

He took it, managed a sip, then a gulp, before draining the glass – not precisely dry – but empty, at the least. "Ru… Rutaçyen, I think," he managed to stammer. "Ink sword hand, sword hand… good with a razor."

"Good choice. I'm glad to see you willing to uncover your face, come out of hiding." He grinned. "I actually have a freshly sharpened razor for you." He threw a towel around his loins, to Ahrimaz's exhaled relief, and threw a cheerful, "I'll be right back," over his shoulder.

89

Shave

IN THE WATER ROOMS, THERE WERE BARBER CHAIRS. Both for having someone shave you and shaving one's self. Those were kneeling chairs with horrible little mirrors, though recently someone had replaced them with the new, smoothly silvered and coppered ones that were being made out of float glass.

Ahrimaz dried himself off completely, tying his damp hair back, avoided those chairs. He stood in the alcove with the other kind of chair, dithering whether he could make himself sit down. *My hair is long enough to choke me, my beard I can grab with both hands and have it come through my fingers. I don't like the weeds on my face. I don't like the scraggly hair-ends.*

Once the old man's funeral was finished and the handfuls of hair he'd flung onto the pyre had grown back, he'd decreed that mourning wigs were no longer fashionable. A generation ago Great Grandfather had lost all his hair and powdered wigs had been fashionable. As far as Ahrimaz was concerned, they itched. They were also home to lice and other bugs, stank no matter how much perfume you used and were utterly useless under a helmet, in fact they were downright dangerous on the battlefield.

Everyone knew the story of how Sen-Grand Guyard de Haute's peruke had slid down between his gorget and his breastplate, gotten hung up there and as he fought he'd inhaled enough hair that he choked upon it. It was a funny children's story now because he'd won the battle but didn't live to accept his opponent's surrender.

"You can sit, Ahrimaz," Rutagyon said. She and Pel were both there and, as usual, managed to walk in without him hearing them. *You would think I'd be able to anticipate this, by now,* he chided himself.

He sat down and leaned back in the chair, carefully tipping his head back. "You want me to trim it? Or take it down to the skin?" She asked, cheerfully washing her hands. She had obviously just dismissed a sword class because she was still armed.

"Why don't you use that," he nodded at her belt. "To give me a trim… oh about here?" He indicated shoulder height and she snorted.

"I could but I don't generally help my students kill themselves."

"You keep saying that and then steal our breath every class." He smiled, safely hidden behind the beard, still.

"You only feel like you're dying," she teased. "Not for real." Pel had a carved brain-wood shaving case just open, pulled out a beautiful horn-handled razor. The soap cup and the lotion bottle were both Yhom blue crystalware, the brush was boar's hair with a polished white-nut handle.

"Don't tell me that was *his*…" Ahrimaz made to sit up but found himself held down with a light touch on his shoulder from Rutaçyen.

"No," Pel said. "This was made just for you."

"What? I have no… I mean… why?"

"Because I thought you might want it soon."

"But…"

"Shush now," Rutaçyen said, unfolding one of the hot towels she'd just fetched from the shelf, wrapping it around his face, giving him more darkness to hide behind. He tensed up until he realized she was careful and left him sufficient and comfortable breathing room. *Of course she would. She's as good as my personal barber, in that world.* His heart hammered in his chest as someone took up the length of his hair and began combing it out.

She changed the towels three times and his hair was now being brushed, by Pel, with a luxurious bristle brush that soothed his cramped scalp. "You needn't say anything else, but you never said, short or shave, just one word to answer the question."

"Sh…sh…shave," he managed to say as the cooler air hit his tingling skin. He couldn't focus on one thing, hair or face and behind closed eyes he was almost forced to relax.

The clink of soap being foamed up in the bowl, the oiled hands massaging his face with long, slow circles, through the beard, gentle over the cheekbones and eyes and up into his hair, strong kneading fingers on his scalp. He was suddenly limp and his mouth opened slightly. Relaxed.

Clipping noises, more hair brushing. Then smooth, gentle tugging as the long hair on his chin was trimmed down to where it could be shaved. The scent of vanilla. Then lemon, from the elephant's orangery, as the warm foam swirled into his cheeks in even circles, lathered onto his face and neck. It was nearly impossible to be afraid, even with his neck exposed to the gentle, firm gliding pull that he knew had to be the razor.

90

Relax

HE FLOATED ON A SEA OF SENSATION, where none of it was discomfort. It was gentle and soothing. Like Limyé's best trauma soothing, happiness building, astonishingly powerful remedies.

Rutaçyen set the razor down with a click. "There we are," she said softly, gently stroking the last of the foam and hair stubble off his cheeks, smoothing a double handful of lotion across his cheeks and chin and neck. "I'm all done with the facial hair." He heard her steps as she left and he knew it must be Pelahir with his hands buried in his hair, easing his scalp, rubbing in long, slow circles. When... when had another pair of hands begun work, massaging his feet? Oh, Gods, massaging his feet. He cracked open his eyes just a bit and then closed them again, practically melting in the chair as Yolend's astonishingly strong hands chased tension and soreness out of his soles... and his toes. He nearly groaned.

He found himself remembering the dark and hideous dungeon when, in his world, he had Pelahir at his mercy, a man who hated him with all his soul, who he'd broken and made his slave. He did groan, his guts suddenly a jumble of remembered lust and pain and desire and the darkling ecstasy of perfect control of another human being.

He clenched his teeth, hardening under the towel thrown over his mid-section, tensing all over. "Shh. Now..." Pelahir's voice and Yolend's together as they dug into suddenly painful spots on his head and feet. He struggled to fight all four hands on his body, confused and trying to tense, partially still relaxed and couldn't fight them. Relaxation flowed up from his feet and down from his head, his neck and jaw loosening, his knees relaxing, hips... oh. He could feel every strand of the soft towel across his middle, the bathrobe fallen away, unbelted...

One of Pelahir's hands cupped the back of his head and gently pulled. "...mmm not gon' get taller," Ahrimaz mumbled, smiling slightly, trying desperately to distract from how hard his penis had gotten and how hot under the terry cloth.

"I know," Pel said and his hands began rubbing his ears. Ears? Oh… then down his neck, still sore from the sudden tension, soothing… Yolend had… when had she lathered up more soap? Both her hands were full of lather, working up from his ankles toward his knees.

Both of them had their hands full of lather, the citrus-scented soap, thick and creamy and their hands were hot and moving languorously in circles on his skin. His hands clenched on the arms of the chair as he felt himself beginning to thrust up into the towel and he quivered all over as he suppressed all the sexual feelings he could.

One hand… Pelahir's hand… left off rubbing foam over his skin and Ahrimaz's eyes snapped open just in time to see him lift the razor up in front of his face. "Relax, you," Pel said softly and slowly lowered the gleaming blade to his chest. Ahrimaz froze, terrified, quivering with need and yes, he wanted to see that thin line of blood on his chest.

But the Cylak didn't cut him, just shaved a single swipe, a scant palm width, bare pink skin cleaned of foam and lotion and hair, just above the nubbly skin around a nipple. Then he lifted it clear, wiped it clean, held it over Ahrimaz where he could see it clearly.

Ahrimaz began to curse him, "You…" and froze again, silenced, mouth open, with the flat of the razor pressed lightly across his lips. He could feel the dangerously beautiful edge as his lips quivered and at that moment Yolend's hands finally worked their slow and careful circles past his knees, and stopped, warm on his inner thighs. He couldn't swallow, staring up into Pelahir's cool and interested eyes.

"You'll relax," the Cylak said softly. He lifted the razor, that deadly edge, patted a newly smoothed cheek with the blade. "And let us do as we will."

91

Quivering on the Edge

AHRIMAZ COULDN'T MAKE HIMSELF MOVE. His eyes followed the razor, then blinked shut as Yolend's hands began kneading the insides of his thighs. He was so hard he ached. He felt the edge of the razor and the sliding, almost melting sensation as Pelahir drew it gently over his chest. He couldn't look, desperately wanting the stinging of hair-fine cuts.

Then there was a burning smack across his chest, across one of his nipples and he caught his breath. *Had Pel actually cut him?* He couldn't look. He had to look... no, just smacked him with the flat or the back of the blade. He clenched his eyes shut again.

He sank into the sensation and Yolend ran her lotion covered hands over his whole groin, her touch hot as fire and he could feel Aeono's spark roaring up in him, and with it... with it... behind it, under it... Her flood.

He caught his lip in his teeth and clamped down on his feelings. He could come... he needed to. He had to. He couldn't.

As he tightened up, quivering, another slashing near-pain and he yelped and relaxed. Pel had swiped the back of the razor hard over one of his nipples. "Let us do as we will, you," Pel said again and Yolend started humming.

The damned Yhom were always singing, humming, whistling, clicking their fingers or lips or teeth. Something. It seemed as though they were never, ever still. But this hum was so deep he could feel it in her fingers, her palms her fingertips... like the sound the elephants made.

He couldn't help it, he relaxed a little more, the sound shaking him loose from his clinging. His whole chest was shaved and Pel gently set the razor into the foam on his abdomen, the line of hair he had, like a fawn, down his centre.

"P...p....p... oh Gods! Please!" He nearly screamed the word, hating himself for begging, his plea an echo of what he did in hatred to the man in the other world. As Pelahir slowly, carefully began shaving down toward his navel he felt the hot tracks of tears on his face and it just added to his confusion. Was this enough pain? Would they allow him to come? No, they would insist on it.

He was so confused.

She had his penis in her hands, the razor threat on his skin, like a predator's teeth lightly scratching. He moaned when she began to suck on him and then the flash of cold air when she let him go, lotion, hot hands RazorlotionmouthohG..g...gods...

Pel kissed him, holding the blade against the pulse of his neck as Yolend... my Gods had she filled her mouth with fire? ...pulled him deep into her mouth and...

His confusion tumbled him into Aeono's Fire and Lyrian's Flood, full, free, as he and Pel clicked teeth and he tore his face away, screaming and it went on, and on. There was no more pain in it. It just was. It burned through the rotten chains his father had scorched into his soul and the skin of his back burned as if he were being flogged.

His screams became tears and sobbing. "I've always loved you," he stammered. "I've always loved you both. I'm sorry I'm sorry I loved you, I hurt you... I hated you... I'm sorry, I'm sorry."

Ahrimaz kept repeating those words even as they devolved into an incoherent mumble and the Cylak and the Yhom woman wiped him clean with warm towels and bundled him up and took him up to the humble bed he'd first woken up in, wrapped in their arms.

Out of the Darkness

"You are hiding in my dark, my son."

I am.

I am? But I just barely know you, and I am healing and I'm allowing them to look after me.

"You are lying in the childhood bed with soft bands upon your arms to stop you tearing at yourself with your teeth because you are screaming that all you deserve is pain. This is part of your healing."

I am?

I don't deserve pain. I don't think I do. I don't believe I do.

"Then you need to come back to your body that is thrashing and writhing and attempting to do itself an injury."

My conscience. But I'm just making it worse, being so awful. Someone has to care for me and I have to add that guilt onto my former guilt and it becomes a never ending spiral until I manage to die.

"To stop that, you have to reach into yourself, my son, and forgive yourself. The others have already forgiven you, for all that you cannot see or bear it. This is your worst crisis. You must forgive yourself."

I.

The silence here is wilder than any roaring, raging star. Where Aeono burns and flings Himself into the dark, She is a vaster deep than even He can fill. They can fill? My Gods what an idea. What if our Goddess is One and the Gods many?

I am distracting myself from the main point. The point is. The point is. The point is…

Do I have the strength, the mercy, the capacity to forgive myself?

I see the little boy playing with his toys, the carved and painted soldiers and dragons and horses, singing to himself. I see the old Monster watching. Then I see him deliberately and viciously smashing the child's toys, paying particular attention to the ones he loved most. I see him punching a much younger Kinourae because the little boy loved him. I am angry for the child. I wish to protect him but I am helpless.

"You at not helpless. You are that child. Forgive him for raging at his father until the old man knocks him unconscious. The old man set up the whole scene to lead to that beating. You love yourself, your younger self. You no longer have to hate him for being a victim."

Every abused child begins to hate themselves because they come to believe they are somehow responsible for their pain. Every abused child begins to hate others for not saving them. Do I need to hate other people any longer? Do I need to hate myself?

I was innocent. I made myself culpable. No. He made me culpable in my own destruction. I... I want to go back to being innocent of hurting people.

"You may. Listen to the elephant singing to her child. Let her joy rumble through your soul. Let Limyé's medications heal the scars in your mind as well as in your brain. Let the lovers of a great soul show you how to be like him. Let them love you. I cannot say it will not hurt but I know you. In all your incarnations in all the worlds. You are capable of this."

Am I? I am, am I? Goddess I'm tired.

"I understand. If you choose to rest, you may. If you choose to go on, you may do that also. I cherish either decision, for you reflect your world to me in your own unique way. There is no other soul like you, however similar all the other Ahrimaz's, all the other hateful Emperors, are. You can be the one who healed."

I can hear Didara rumbling to her calf... and her calf to her. It's like floating on sound. I can hear Pelahir and Yolend holding me. I can hear his father and his mother holding me. It no longer hurts.

I can be the one who heals? Or one of the ones who heals? But it is up to me. I must choose.

I choose. I choose.

Yes.

* * * * *

Ahrimaz opened his eyes to a blazing mid-day, sun pouring into the green child's room. He looked down at the bloodstained bandages restraining his arms and felt the cotton in his mouth.

He felt terrible. His whole body hurt.

He felt wonderful. He didn't have to do this any longer.

Yolend sat up from where she'd laid down on the sofa and looked at him.

She was beautiful, even as tired as she was. Her soul shone almost brighter than he could stand. The wash stand and basin next to her was somehow just as bright and just as shining. It was glorious. It was real. It wasn't a dream. It was the dream of the divine, who could not interact with their own worlds, without help. Everything shone.

Even with the bite-gag in his mouth, he smiled.

Limyé got up from the chair by the door and came over to check him, fingers on his neck. "Is your paroxysm over?" He asked, softly.

Ahrimaz managed a sore-muscled nod and when Limyé removed the gag and he could feel the rawness inside his own mouth and the taste of blood on his tongue he just started to laugh because it was so wonderful that he could. "It's so real. It's so solid."

His voice and his laughter was a rasping whisper but Limyé smiled back and gave him water, and that was in itself miraculous.

93

After the Last Relapse

AFTER THE HARSHEST RE-LAPSE WHEN THEY HAD TO TIE ME TO THE BED, things began to finally, finally shift.

I was apparently a whole moon a ravening maniac again, but with no words. I do not remember, but Limyé treated me and kept me from tearing at myself too badly.

It was the monster's last gasp and I was sick as a dog for several weeks after that, with colds and grips and my stomach in rebellion, trying to leave the empire of my body in both directions.

My loves... they were with me the whole time. I love them. How on the drowning green earth and in all the waterless cosmos did that happen?

This morning. This morning I woke drowning in bodies, in love and heat. Yolend lay on my right shoulder, Pel on my left. Sure, silly dog, lay grunting and unfortunately farting across my legs.

I was sweaty and immobilized and I gently managed to pull my hair out from under Yolend's cheek without waking her, though she did murmur and roll over to put her hand on the baby who snored in his bed/crib attached to her side. He was snoring the tiniest, highest baby snore that whistled like a bird and I nearly laughed.

Laughed instead of clawing my way out of all this touch and comfort and love. I may not deserve it but it is freely offered and I can accept it without agony. I am still not perfectly comfortable with it. I still hate getting sweated on. It makes my skin itch sometimes. But I can now mostly bear it. Enjoy it. Mostly it is good.

I know I am not him. I keep telling them and they just laugh and call me Shit Head. The baby is starting to call me 'itead' instead of 'Uncle' as I tried to teach him.

I cannot initiate contact, afraid that it is the rapist and monster in me, but I can accept. And they shower me with their free touch. My mother in this world... I can accept and return her hugs and they no longer reduce me to tears. I can sit with my father in this life, though I cannot touch him, and we talk late into the night about politics and economics and elephants.

Pel blinked his eyes open and smiles at me, runs a finger down my nose. I pretend to bite him but I'm smiling and he kisses my ear. "No extra fun for me today," he whispers in my ear. "The *corashion* is going—"

"—down to meet the herds coming home... yes." It hurt to say but I made myself say it. "I'll miss you."

"It will only be for a few days," he said and slid quietly out of bed, padded around to kiss Yolend and the baby... my son in all but world. When did my heart get so full? In the dim light of dawn just shining in the rippled glass windows I wish I could paint to capture that picture. One of the most beautiful men I've ever seen bending over one of the most beautiful women, and the peacefully snoring babe.

"Travel safe," I whisper and ease out of the bed after him, grabbing up a towel and a robe even as he picks up his pack by the door.

"You aren't coming down to see me off?" he teases. I manage a grin at him and throw the robe around my nakedness.

"Of course, you Shit-Head Lover!"

The *corashion* was mostly saddled up just outside the Ambassador's Hall and I watched him check his girth and the tender velvetted antlers of his doe before handing his pack to his human fawn, to be lashed behind the saddle.

The warriors tease him and he grins at me before seizing me up in a huge hug and a smacking kiss. I startle but relax in time not to smash my teeth into his, and I enjoy myself before he sets me down to all the whistling and smacking of lips from his herd. I will not be embarrassed I will not be embarrassed...

He, and they, swung into their saddles in that flashy way of theirs and dashed off in a thunder of hooves into a bright, cold morning.

I pulled my robe shut over gooseflesh skin and slipped into the Ambassador's Hall where it is luxuriously warm and found Didara awake and alone, Jagunjagun not yet returned from his latest expedition.

"How are you feeling?"

"Excellent!" She rumbled happily. "You'll need to come sleep here with me if you want to be part of the birth celebration of my elephant child!"

"You're in..." I froze, staring up at her. "What do you need? What can I do? I'll call Limyé... wait the staff need to know... is there something you need for a ceremony? What does Ologbon need to help you... is it warm enough? Is there enough light—" I cut off as she gently wrapped her trunk around me and lifted me up to her eye level.

"Calm please, iti-igi," she said. "If you want you can bring me a new pretty for my right tooth. But what we need most is calm. Jagunjagun is going to be here by this evening—I can hear him through my feet—so." She set me down firmly. "I am not yet in labour. Not yet. A day or two." She patted me on the head with her trunk. "You don't handle change well, iti, so I thought I'd warn you."

"Oh... Lyrian... drown me." I sank down on the edge of the pool. "Um. Calm. You need calm. Thank you."

94 — Like That Cloud

AHRIMAZ FOUND HIMSELF TOO JITTERY TO SETTLE IN THE Ambassador's Hall immediately and ran down to the river to swim hard in the 'Puddle', the eddy built above the harbour, so that people could swim and not be swept away. There was enough of a current for him to thrash his nervousness out against the water and when he got out, hair down to his shoulders dripping, he found he had to turn and bow, genuflecting to the image of Lyrian set in the rocks above the Puddle.

"You can do that without feeling any irony?" Limyé had come while Ahrimaz was swimming. He held up a hand quietly as Ahrimaz drew breath. "I've already checked Didara as best I can and consulted with Ologbon. She is comfortable. It is interesting that apparently elephants tell their mothers when they are about to be born."

"Really? That's astonishing. Yolend would have loved to know and perhaps..." Ahrimaz fell silent. The elephants had shown him that their rumbles were akin to human throat singing and the Yhom, if nothing else, knew how to sing through everything life could throw at them. "Perhaps she did know, though I've never heard anyone say anything about that ability in iti people."

Since the Ambassadors had come people had picked up their name for human people ('trunk-hands' people) because it was a handy differentiation between dogs and cats and horses and deer. Mostly because it didn't have the weight to assumption behind it, that 'human' meant something different than 'animal'. People were people whether they had skin, fur, feathers, or hide.

"I am finding that I need to pray more often. To Her. It eases me."

"I'm glad to hear that."

"I'm going to be going up to see Mara at the Veil after the elephant's child is born."

"Good. I'm nearly finished my book about you and your other self."

Ahrimaz took a deep breath. "And may I ask your conclusions?"

Limyé smile was bright against his dark face. A cloud passed over, throwing them both into shadow for a moment. He gestured up at the sky. "Like that cloud," he said. "Against the Earth, it is a shadow that cools, or drops devastation upon that which is below, but it is temporary. Fleeting. The sky, the Eye of God, even the cloud are fundamentally the same, just as you and your doppelgänger are. The catastrophe of your male parent, like an eruption, or an earth shake, or avalanche, can be both borne and healed from."

"My father was more like a flaming ball of fire falling from the sky than a mere cloud," Ahrimaz said, surprised to find that he could just say it, without feeling a corresponding welling of burning emotion. "Though it appears that the destruction in my soul has finally stopped."

Limyé nodded. "The fact that you can see it and not let it destroy you further is what I'm actually looking for."

They turned away from the river's edge and walked slowly back up toward the House of the Hand. People working, walking in the street, waved or nodded at them as they passed. Limyé didn't say anything about the fact that Ahrimaz acknowledged the greetings without much reaction. "People don't bother you as much as they did."

"No, it just seems like..." Ahrimaz pulled the towel off his shoulders and rubbed at his hair. From somewhere, Sure appeared at his heel and he petted her absently. Teh was more often with the baby now, leaving the younger dog to dog his heels. "It seems like the whole city is a rumble that I can feel in my feet. Their lives... I mean the Goddess showed me them all as light. And I'm starting to dream about people as light or dark."

"That's interesting," Limyé said. "Let me see your arms, please."

It was cool enough that gooseflesh stood up along Ahrimaz's bare arms and he shivered as Limyé ran careful fingers over the scars on his forearms. "They've healed up well."

"Since I'm getting..." he paused, struggling for words. "um... bedded... laid... I don't like those words any longer..."

"Loved?" Limyé suggested. Ahrimaz thought about it for a moment and nodded and shrugged.

"It will do." He hung his robe and his towel on the hook by the Ambassador's inner door and settled the towel kilt around his hips. "Since

I'm not savaging myself any more I've realized that I did that to fix me in the present. I used to feel entirely adrift in the world, rejecting my past out of sheer horror and cringing away from, driven toward a future I didn't want and didn't think I could bear."

"And now?"

Ahrimaz smiled. "There is too much happening in the present for me to worry about future and I think my past, though it still hurts me, has healed over enough for me to not need to tend it constantly."

"May I finish my book with this exchange?"

Limyé sat down beside Ahrimaz in the sand, Didara a vague shape in the stand of bamboo at the end of the hall.

"You may." Ahrimaz looked down at his hands. "I'm feeling... dismay. It seems that you are wishing me farewell as a patient."

"But not farewell as a friend."

"I see." They sat, side by side, in the humid, heated space feeling Didara rumble/sing to her daughter to be.

95

Birthing

IT WAS THE MIDDLE OF THE NIGHT, in the luminous time when the full moon outshone all the gas lanterns and turned the twisting streets and buildings strange and ghostly; when people and dogs and cats who couldn't sleep became creatures of legend walking, turned silver and black.

That was when Didara let out a rumble so long and deep that at first Ahrimaz snapped awake thinking that the earth was dancing. Yolend opened the door. "She's starting," she whispered and wearing only her robe, bare feet sinking into the sands around the hot pool, walked over to Ahrimaz and held out her hand. "Come on. Let us sing our new friend into our world."

He took her hand without thinking and she swung him up out of his blanket and as they turned toward the stand of young bamboo, Jagunjagun, still showing his harness marks from his trip, pushed out of the greenery and held it aside for Didara to sway out into the open.

The bamboo hissed as it closed behind her and her next rumble shook Ologbon on her back so that he seemed to bounce in place like a ball on a jet of water. Jagunjagun ran his trunk along her bare back. She was as naked as she ever got and her tusks glittered wildly in the moonlight through the new windows.

Yolend stepped forward and held out her hands to the elephant, singing the high, sweet Yhom birthing song and rested her forehead against Didara's trunk. Ahrimaz didn't know where it came from, but the low rumble rising out of his own chest matched Yolend's somehow and he stopped up under Didara's ear. Ologbon slid down and took up position on the other side, just under her cheek and as she rocked from side to side, the three iti rocked with her and sang chorus to her.

To her and the baby, whose chirping and jittering, tiny and new and excited, had slowed as the calf seemed to reach for her mother's song, stretching into silence and the important business of being born.

In between rolling waves of sound, Ahrimaz whispered to Yolend, "I thought I'd be disgusted at all this female... muck and blood and..."

"Shush," Yolend grinned at him. "You've made more muck on a battlefield." Then she raised her voice and turned her attention back to Didara who was beginning to make squealing, trumpeting sounds as her rocking and stamping crested and a burst of mucus gushed down her back legs.

"Doesn't she need to... Don't you need to lie down?" Ahrimaz said plaintively.

"No no." Ologbon said. "Is good. First birth very fast."

"MY FACE IS ITCHY," Didara said. "MY WHOLE SKIN IS ITCHY. Kidogo, kidogo, yenye thamani. Ndege ya Maneno, njoo nje. LITTLE LIGHT, MWANGA KIDOGO, YENYE THAMANI. PLEASE. I ITCH!" she complained and moaned.

"I called Limyé when I came down. He should be here soon," Yolend said digging her fingers into Didara's skin to scratch. Ologbon had his ceremonial stick with the hook that dug perfectly into the worst of the itchy spots apparently.

Didara grumbled and walked away from the muddy spot in the sand, walking, with Jagunjagun at her side to help her, hold her, touch her.

Ologbon scooped up the mess with a shovel and one of the Innéan grooms filled her cart with it and trundled it out, quietly. "There's more mess to come," Yolend said.

"What did he mean 'First Birth?!'" Ahrimaz's voice had risen and she shushed him.

"It's her first child. Let's go walk with her. The ground rings differently here and she's being petulant that she can't reach her own herd other than Jagunjagun."

"That's thousands of leagues away!" Ahrimaz gaped at the dimly seen shapes of the elephants.

"She knows she won't reach them."

"Didara," Jagunjagun rumbled. "Don't be a brat. I'm here. I'll sing her song with you to the home herd when we get there... if we decide to all go home. We might stay. It's a good place."

"I'M TIRED OF BEING NICE AND CALM AND NOT FRETFUL! I'LL FRET IF I WANT... MWANGA KIDOGO YENYE... OH STOP TOUCHING

ME! I'm going for a swim."

"Ah. That's a good sign," Yolend said. "I don't think the baby will be born in the water though. It's the wrong shaped pool for her..."

Didara wheeled suddenly and splashed into the hot pool throwing water all over everyone. "i'm tired of being pregnant and i'm done done done!i±

It was another hour or two, and Ahrimaz was very glad he didn't have his pocket watch with him to check. It would have been irreparably damaged by water and sand, and even dirt from a ripped up plant or two that Didara flung at people as she laboured.

Yolend laughed at his expression. "Not so peaceful and calm?" Her robe was soaked and had a crust of sand and earth all the way to her shoulders and she pulled it off to stand naked next to Didara, singing suddenly through her hands, her whole body shaking.

Ahrimaz scowled at her but matched her song, ignoring his own body reaction as Didara stopped, spraddled her back legs and began a rhythmic grunt. Jagunjagun picked up the instrument he'd journeyed down river to fetch, an enormous trunk trumpet that he put against the ground and the beat of Didara's labour was echoed by him till the whole building shook.

She took a deep breath and squatted slightly, all four legs and the babies head domed behind and below her. No sound from the calf at all and Ahrimaz's heart clenched. He found that Yolend had reached out and curled her arm around him so they supported each other against Didara's cheek and thrummed and sang, higher, lower, louder. "COME OUT."

Didara trumpeted and with a rush of fluids and blood the baby elephant eased and then tumbled and then thumped down to the sand.

For a moment everything and everyone was still, then Didara began to turn just as the smallest thrum carried through their feet, even as the calf drew her first breath. "I HERE.i±

"MMMMMMWWWWWWWWAAAAANNNNNGGGGGAAAAAAAA!" Didara trumpeted and then rumbled a soft hello to her newborn.

Ologbon began to help her clean the baby and Yolend took up a soft brush. "Me too!" Ahrimaz snapped, but found a brush thrust into his hand.

"Be nice now." Yolend sang. "The Little Light of Didara's Knowledge is listening!"

"Sorry." He found himself on his knees, brushing, helping Mwanga to her feet and her trunk waved in the air and smacked him in the head, knocked Ologbon right over.

"My child..." Didara's voice descended to where only Jagunjagun could hear, though they could feel the tremble sometimes through the floor. And Mwanga staggered to begin nursing for the first time. Ologbon had his arms around Didara's hind leg and he looked over just to give a tired wave before sliding down to nap.

Ahrimaz set the brush down, peeled his crusty shirt off over his head, looking at Didara with her trunk wrapped around Jagunjagun, Mwanga making grunting, sucking noises. "I... think I could have a bath, myself."

He looked and Yolend smiled at him. "I'll join you, shall I?" she said.

"Yes." Pause. "Please."

She turned to him, put her hands on either side of his face and kissed him so hard his knees went weak. "That was for the 'please'," she said.

Why is my healing always about beds, sex and hot baths?

96

Priest

I AM SEEING EVERYONE AND EVERYTHING OUTLINED IN THIS... GLOW...
this... shine... I finally asked my priestly brother and he sat and gazed at me
and past me, closed his eyes and prayed hard enough that flickers of fire
danced before his brow, breathing deep and slow and then smiling just as
slowly.

I forced myself to sit and watch and not shove him into a carpet and roll
him about the floor beating on him to put out the flames. He laughed out
loud when I said that to him. "What *doesn't* glow for you?" he asked.

The questions. Goddess they never ask the easy ones. Once I should have
wanted to shake the sacred out of him... shake the fool who would be so in
tune with his God that he... he would have let me shake him. It wouldn't have
touched him no matter how loud I raved or foamed into his face. That's what
I am feeling.

Even as I stand aghast and in awe of the whole world... don't get me
started on babies, kittens, puppies... young things... I am bursting into smiles
and tears just looking at them. Mwanga glows like a bonfire even as she knocks
me over trying to sit on my lap.

*   *   *   *   *

Ahrimaz closed the book and scratched behind Mwanga's ears with his
bare toes. *This is unreal how much I have changed. The monster is still
there, inside me, sleeping now that I have managed to ease the pressure of
fear and pain. He is still there, poised to come roaring up out of his pit
should I be threatened or injured. I will have to be careful while training. I
am a better warrior when I am not a monster.*

He squirmed out from under the giggling elephant calf and ran a light hand along Didara's trunk where it rested half on him and half on Mwanga.

"I'm going up to talk to Mara," he said.

"Good," she rumbled. **"You need more time up there."**

"And you want more time alone with the baby-girl here."

Mwanga didn't say anything at first, but hoisted herself up with her mother's trunk, humming to herself. **"Bye!"** She said when she'd gained her feet. **"Mama mama mama happy happy mama!"**

Didara patted him absently again as she turned back to singing Mwanga another of the learning songs.

In the green bedroom Ahrimaz tucked his much-battered journal into the desk drawer, pulled the early winter priest robe over his head, took up the Lyrian chain from its box. He didn't bother pulling on any of the shoes but went barefoot up to the Vale.

He found Mara deep in conversation with an older couple who looked quite distressed. Rather than interrupt he joined a couple of priests who were building a new meditation platform down the Vale, almost outside of the dip in the landscape, with a glorious view through the trees. The trees up this high were already mostly bare except for the evergreen oaks, but below the fiery colours of fall still painted the country with reds and hot yellows. The priests, Hollis and Lar, smiled at him as he brought a jug of beer up with him and girded up his robe for work. They didn't need to talk much and after they'd finished their beers pointed him over to the pile of flat stones.

"Base is finished, we just need to make the top now, Ahri," Hollis said.

He nodded. "You place, I'll haul." Lar began shovelling fine sand into place as he lifted the first stone.

*   *   *   *   *

"I hope you helped those people, Mara," he said later that afternoon.

"I did. It wasn't so hard once they gave up their suffering and actually focused on what they needed to do."

Ahrimaz wasn't sure what she meant exactly but nodded anyway. "I guess I'll understand you someday," he said.

She poured tea for him and they sat, Ahrimaz's muscles pleasantly sore from the work. "So, are you ready to come to the Vale?"

Ahrimaz finished his tea and pulled out the flat box. "You said that the robe was all the investiture I was getting, so I should give this to the Vale's keeping. It's his, not mine."

The High Priestess opened the box and set it down. "Hmm. Let us see."

The chain, in her hand, glittered silver, green and blue in the warm light of late afternoon. "Come along."

She led him out of her favourite patch of roses and down to the pool. "Go on in and pray for a sign."

Ahrimaz looked at her, then at the chain, shrugged and dove into the pool. He stood up under the waterfall, unable to see anything but the flow of water from above, and raised his hands.

The water was still summer warm and thundered down on him, rinsing the sweat off his skin, the worries from his soul, the ache of his scarred emotions, easing him. "Lyrian, Mara asked me to pray for a sign. A sign for what I have no idea. Please?"

He caught a wild splash directly in the face as he put up his hands to make a breathing space and staggered out from under the cascade, coughing. Mara was laughing as he sat down abruptly on one of the rocks set for the purpose and he shook the water out of his face, confused. "There. I asked."

He was certain that this was just a way for Mara to take the priest's chain gracefully. After all, what kind of sign did he deserve? And for what, actually? That he was a priest? No matter how much they said so, he was certain…

The warm afternoon light went strange and electric as though a thunderstorm loomed and Ahrimaz found himself holding his breath.

To my beloved son, I give a sign.

A white tiger cub, with shining blue eyes, pounced out of the waterfall, scattering diamond drops all around, splashed him hard and romped all around until Ahrimaz, dizzy trying to watch fell over, off his rock, into the water. The cub, though it was small, pounced again and somehow lifted him, fished him out of the water bodily, flew straight up to Mara and dropped him at her feet before diving up into the sky and dissolving into a tiny snow flurry.

Ahrimaz, gazing up at Mara and behind her into the sky where the ice tiger had vanished, started laughing when she placed the chain around his neck. "No, She thinks this is yours," she said. "You keep it. I'll see you tomorrow. I have a couple of children who need guidance that you can help."

He couldn't get up, even after she smiled at him and went back to her roses, but lay laughing like a maniac. "Ask for a sign, says she," he gasped. "A sign. Oh, drown and freeze me. I got my sign that I'm a Lyrian priest and even I can't dismiss this one."

97

I Write My Gratitude

I WRITE. Thoughts wish to pour out of me but I find it hard to express what I am seeing and feeling. Emotions of fear and anger and hatred are so much easier to spew. Very much like mental and verbal cholera.

I am using this enormous baby's back as a desk and Mwanga insists on rumbling laughter at me—in her baby pitch—every time she catches me indulging, watching her sacredness! The elephants hear this lightness, this brightness I see, as sound. Fascinating.

Having witnessed her birth, I am no longer terrified of female things, of birthing blood. The blood and the fluids no longer disgust me, no longer make me think of my own mother's dissolving body on the floor of a dungeon. My mother loved me and loves me and is either with the Gods, both male and female, or is off to another life, another creation. There is more to the world than I can imagine, and I have a very fertile imagination, especially now.

How do I deserve this? I am writing in the Elephant's Orangery which is what this Ambassador's Hall, once riding hall, is now being called. There are more animals and children playing around me than I had ever thought to allow, ever in my life. The cat. The dogs. The horse who is currently slobbering in my hair. The elephants who are not animals but people, or they are as much people as I am an animal. I finally understand that.

Limyé, my constant presence, is writing his own book, as I write mine. The family are off working… Pelahir—this spring… like clockwork the herds come and go. He's taken his does and his stags and has gone off to meet the migration as it comes around the continent. He doesn't like being sedentary, but he likes being part of the family, so he splits his time. I wonder how he does, how he is, in my world. Has our paladin Ahrimaz saved him? Held himself together to unravel the evil I did? I hope so.

Teel shall be coming to question me about his next story idea. I fear they have mined out all my odd ideas and innovations from my Empire, at least I cannot seem to come up with anything much new lately, as I watch people's souls glow through their skins. Last fall Arnziel fell off his chair when I answered him his question. "I even see rocks glowing, step-brother." Rocks. I think the only thing I can look at without seeing its life, its blessedness, is clear air and I'm starting to wonder about that.

I live here in the House of the Hand, still but go up to the Vale every day. The winter and the spring have both been very warm. Aeono the God has a fever and the world sweats.

My daughter is home from her studies, a graduate. I am astonished at her skill with people. She does not use truth-telling as a bludgeon, but a scalpel. She smiles at me quite a bit.

I find that I don't mind my brother sitting as Hand of the People. He knows this world far better than I ever could and I'm burnt hollow when it comes to politics. It still hurts thinking of when I was Emperor.

I… am concerned about being a Lyrian priest full time even without the evidence of ice tiger cubs pushing me into the water if I get too full of myself.

I do not think I have the balance yet. I have achieved a point where I will not punish my poor, suffering body for its existence and for its emotions. But I don't know how long that peace will last. Who knows when the wheel of my thoughts will spin and I fall into hell once more? Mara says that hell gets less hellish every time around. I shall have to believe her.

I put on the robe every day and go barefoot to Lyrian's Vale and do the chores and listen to the supplicants who find me. Feed the birds. Rake the paths.

Thank you. My gratitude for such peace is much bigger than my heart can hold. Thank you.

98

As You Will

THE SNOW WAS COMPLETELY GONE, except for one or two grubby patches in the shadows of cliffs and under coniferous trees.

The water of the Veil ran freely again, though icy and only the dedicate priestesses and priests meditated on the stones or platforms scattered throughout the whole Vale. Only those driven to come for help braved the chill air.

The elephants were beginning to trek up from their Orangery and little Mwanga wasn't so small any longer though she still pretended to try and sit in Ahrimaz's lap.

Didara and Jagunjagun were beginning to talk of going home and sending other ambassadors. Innéans were talking about visiting them. They would have a faster way to sail home, it seemed, if they took ship all the way down the Innéthel to the sea, though it angled away from their continent. Overland to that side of the continent was still slower. Perhaps when Mwanga was a full year old they would begin.

Ahrimaz came up the path, scrubbing his hair dry, tying it back with a lace after working with Rutaçyen all morning, since before sun-up. He wore the priest's robe comfortably now and paused at the Goddess tree to scatter a handful of seed for the birds and clear away an empty cage or two. New ribbons fluttered from the branches and he smiled as he imagined people setting their prayers here, on the wind.

Most of his prayers went either to Lyrian herself, or in support of his doppelgänger, lost in the Empire of another world. Who knew if they helped? Or hindered? Only She knew. For now it was enough to continue healing his own damaged soul.

His towel went onto the peg in the shed, hidden just off the path, where the empty bird cages were kept and cleaned before going down to the city to be refilled with birds so that people could release them. Some birds had been captured and released so many times they hopped into the cages in the square voluntarily.

He smiled again and picked up one of the rakes and a basket of wood chips. The meltwater made it all muddy in spots and he cheerfully went to make up the path.

Once he would have thought that he would be screamingly bored if forced into the life of a priest but he found that once chosen, it was amazingly peaceful. Sure, who had been clinging close to him for some reason these past days, lay in a patch of sunlight, panting, as he emptied his basket and raked. Limyé would be up later to have luncheon with him at the waterfall and they would talk about how his book "Nature or Nurture: The Monster Within" was being received.

A class of children giggled by and he nodded at their greetings. It is possible we need to set a brick or two here. It is always treacherous here whenever it gets too wet.

Several priestesses, staffs and rakes in hand passed him the other way, going out to begin building the new rock garden outside the Vale and he didn't address them but everyone bowed. It was very quiet.

The birds went still and Ahrimaz dropped his rake where he stood. Someone is trying to die.

He spun on his heel and ran, Sure on his heels, whistling for healers and assistance. It was cold still and very practically, few people tried to give themselves to the Goddess this early in the spring. Ever practical the Innéans, they didn't want to be uncomfortable as they died. He smirked to himself and ran faster. She didn't want this one dead, he could feel it. This supplicant truly didn't wish to die either. It was the sense of 'people will be better without me' cry.

Ahrimaz dove into the pool in a flat, seeking dive, aware that the Vale behind him was suddenly full of urgency, his hands swept through the roiled up foam. Nothing. He burst to the surface, gasping with the shock of cold. Sure had plunged into the water after him. "Get away, dog!"

He went under again and kicked, the pain as Sure set her teeth in his ankle even as he jarred a finger upon a stone, felt the pounding of the water on his back, on his head, he was dizzy, spinning, light-headed… there! His hands locked in cloth and he dragged the would-be suicide to the surface.

He caught sight of priests and priestess coming running down the valley as he looked down into his own face. His fingers were locked in the neck-cloth of gold. Hair draggled across his own face. Him. Dressed as an Emperor, distraught, grieving, fighting to go under again. Ahrimaz shook himself once, twice, until his eyes opened and locked, disbelieving, on his own face. The other Ahrimaz. Himself.

"Whatever you have done," Ahrimaz said to himself, "is forgivable."

Disorientation like a whirl of foam, a thundercrack of light and dark and he found himself standing all but alone in the water, a white dog biting on his booted ankle. His priestly robes were gone. In their place were the bedraggled and hampering court clothes of an Emperor. His neck was sore, his lungs sore where he'd apparently managed to inhale some water. Sure surged to the surface, coughing, barking and he gave her a boost toward the rocks behind the waterfall. His ankle, where she had bitten him to come with him, hurt.

The Vale was changed. There was only one meditation platform. The rest was wild, as it had been when he was a boy. There were no healers running to save him. No mind priests or Imaryans. He was alone, save for the dog who had followed him. He was home.

He threw back his head and looked up the waterfall, splashing on his face like tears and would have howled but he knew... he knew that it would not help. *Goddess... ow. Scorch me. Scorch me. It will hurt no less.*

Yolend, the Empress, screaming imprecations at him, came sliding down the muddy, untended path to splash her gaudy robes into the water, slosh up to him and begin slapping his face.

He flinched but let her hit him. This Yolend was trained enough to hurt him but her strikes were open handed.

"Excuse me, lady, I did not mean to flinch away." He turned his head back toward her. "Please, strike again for I surely deserve it."

She froze. "Ahrimaz?"

"Yes."

Sure scrambled out and around barking at the man coming down the hill after her who was dressed in a way the Empire hadn't seen in a dozen decades. He bore the chain of a Senator-Immaculate, the singular position under the Emperor, the Regent should the Emperor die.

"Ahrimaz, come out. We can fix this. You needn't..." His voice faded as he took in how Yolend was looking at him, the white dog guarding.

"Sure. Down, dog," Ahrimaz said mildly and offered Yolend his hand. She grasped it as though picking up a venomous serpent and they waded out to the shore. He handed her up to the stocky man now standing on the edge. When she was safely clear he followed her, looking down at ruined boots and silks and brocades on his body, loathing every stitch, mourning his homecoming. Sure pressed against him, whining.

He took a deep breath and went to his knees before the Sen-Immac and the Empress who both gazed at him, dumb.

"I am Ahrimaz Kenaçyen, once Emperor. I..." He fumbled with his coat and cravat, pulled open his sodden shirt to expose the brand on his chest, with the Flamen in the centre. He could feel his tears begin and could not stop them.

"... I was away for a time. You are obviously an exceptional man or Ahrimaz, from the other world, would not have appointed you. Knowing the nature of this cruel world my family made it is very likely that you shall have to execute me to let the good the other Ahrimaz has done continue. So be it." He drew a sobbing breath and kowtowed to them, putting his forehead on the stone.

"Do with me as you will."

15497168R00183

Made in the USA
San Bernardino, CA
17 December 2018